LEGION III:
KINGS OF
OBLIVION

VAN ALLEN PLEXICO

WHITE ROCKET BOOKS

This book is for John Ringer.
In the grim darkness of the far future,
there is only War. (Eagle.)

This book is also available as a limited edition hardcover from White Rocket Books.

This is a work of fiction. All the characters and events portrayed in this book are either products of the author's imagination or are used fictitiously.

LEGION III: KINGS OF OBLIVION (THE SHATTERING)
Copyright 2014 by Van Allen Plexico
Cover art by Mark Williams
Cover design by Van Allen Plexico

A White Rocket Book
www.whiterocketbooks.com
ISBN-13: 978-0692021453
ISBN-10: 0692021450

First hardcover printing: Apriil 2014
First paperback printing: April 2014

0 9 8 7 6 5 4 3 2 1

AFTER THE GODS, BEFORE THE SHATTERING...

It is the dawn of the 17th Millennium, and the galaxy stands on the brink of annihilation.

Hordes of horrific aliens from beyond the galaxy now relentlessly advance upon the Inner Worlds, their ultimate goal clear: Sacred Terra, the mother world of humanity. Meanwhile, the Empire finds itself divided by a bloody civil war.

The defeat of the rebel Governor Rameses came too late to prevent a further erosion of support for General Marcus Ezekial Tamerlane and his regime. General Ioan Iapetus has declared himself Regent of the Empire. He controls the lone surviving member of the old royal family, Princess Marens, along with the fabled Sword of Baranak, the most valuable object in the galaxy. His forces are fresh and largely intact, while the other two legions have suffered tremendous losses and find themselves in a position of severe disadvantage.

To make matters worse, General Agrippa and his finest soldiers have, at the behest of the goddess Aurore, departed the mortal plane on a quest to prevent the supposed "shattering" of the galaxy. Following the goddess into a strange, fog-enshrouded level of the Above, they have been abandoned and wander the barren wilderness, possibly lost forever.

But humans no longer face the alien onslaught alone. Other races from across the galaxy have been dragged into the conflict, and some of them—some much more ancient and powerful than Mankind—are considering the most radical of solutions to the crisis that confronts us all...

"Those who have lost everything no longer have anything to fear."
—Don Juan Matus

"No doubt the nearness of death and the brotherhood of men-at-wars, at whatever time and in whatever country, always produce an atmosphere favorable to the extraordinary, to all that rises above the human condition."
—Octavio Paz

"If you want to see new vistas of Truth, go question the man who wants to kill you."
—Masato Igarashi Storm

DRAMATIS PERSONAE

Legion I: Lords of Fire
Colors: Red and gold
General Marcus Ezekial Tamerlane, "The Relentless."
Acting supreme commander of the loyalist forces.
Colonel Niobe Arani, former commander, *Nizam* Legion.
Major Titus Elaro, former infiltration officer, II Legion.
Captain Harras Dequoi, commanding officer of the I Legion
flagship *Ascanius*.
Commander Ehrens, executive officer of the *Ascanius*.
Major Talin Trekiyak, commander of marine special ops
team, *Ascanius*.
Captain Darius Pettway, special ops marine, *Ascanius*.

Legion II: Sons of Terra
Colors: Blue and silver; later black and gold
General Ioan Iapetus, "The Unyielding." Self-proclaimed
Taiko and Regent.
Colonel Berens Barbarossa, "The Daring." Second-in-
command of II Legion.
Colonel Piryu, officer aboard the II Legion flagship *Atlantia*.

Legion III: The Golden Phalanx (Kings of Oblivion)
Colors: Green, white and gold
General Arnem Agrippa, "The Golden." Staunch ally of Tamerlane and I Legion.
Colonel Yevgeni Vostok, "The Cold."
Colonel Selim Iksander, "The Lightning."
Major Darius Torgon, Colossus and hovertank commander.
Captain Felix Dakkan, hovertank commander.
Holland, Faraday, Harker and Obomanu, members of Agrippa's Bravo Squad.

The Dyonari
Glossis, tank commander.
Siklar, Commander.
Merrin, Commander.
Ralin, Commander.
Madalena, Co-Commander, covert squad.
Mirana, Co-Commander, covert squad.
Vinizan, warrior, covert squad.

The Old Gods (selected)
Aurore, goddess of distraction and deception.
Goraddon, god of persuasion and disciple of Vorthan.
Lohandar, portfolio unrevealed.
Lucian, god of evil and mischief who once rebelled against the other gods.
Moranna, goddess of vanity.
Solonis, the seer.
Vorthan, god of toil; later labeled a death god.

Others of Note

The Princess Marens, sole surviving heir to the Imperial throne.

Sister Leisle Delain, Inquisitor and aide to the Grand Inquisitor.

Amon Rameses, former Planetary Governor of Ahknaton.

Iyesu Tokugawa, Planetary Governor of Edo.

Suleyman Mehemet, Planetary Governor of Bursa.

Twice!

Twice now I have been countered in my attempts to place a Demon Prince upon the throne of humankind.

Inconceivable. How could these mere mortals hinder me?

Tamerlane with his dogged persistence. Agrippa with his arrogance and annoying charisma. And Iapetus—Iapetus with his seeming invulnerability to my persuasion. Even now, as Iapetus has ascended to the heights of power as Regent of the Empire, still he manages to avoid me and my influence. It is maddening. And thus twice have they foiled my most carefully laid schemes.

There will not be a third occasion for them to try.

I have decided to wipe the board clean and begin anew. I have commanded all of my extra-galactic forces—the bloodthirsty, insectoid Skrazzi and their psychic masters, the Phaedrons—to sweep across this galaxy en masse, to bathe it in blood, and to leave no survivors in their wake. Their comets already descend like a cleansing rain over the worlds of Man. But not just Man—no, all the dominant life forms of the mortal realm will be destroyed. The human worlds lie mostly in ruin, yes, but the process has begun elsewhere, as well.

And once they have all been eliminated—all the humans and their allies and foes combined—and once my soldiers stand triumphant upon the homeworld of humanity, then I can begin again. I can begin the long, slow process of bringing Hell to that world called Earth—and to this galaxy.

Now watch, as everything burns...

—Unattributed fragment from the archives of the data storehouses of Ahknaton

PROLOGUE:

The ghost of a god stood on a dead world and screamed his frustration at the shattered stars.

It had happened. Despite all his hopes, all his efforts, all his travels and his labors, it had happened. The galaxy had been torn asunder—broken to pieces by cosmic forces too vast and powerful to contemplate.

He gazed out at the ruins of the old empires and the wreckage of starships beyond counting—to say nothing of the dead, in their incomprehensible numbers. He could feel the vibration in the very fabric of reality; he could sense the shockwave that had traveled here and now, from the dim past, to wreak this disaster.

Futility. All of his feelings as he confronted this cataclysm could be summed up in that single word: Futility.

It could have been different. But for a tiny happenstance here and there, it *would* have been different. It all would have been avoided, and the galaxy would have continued on as it had before—as it deserved to.

But no. For all his knowledge and experience and power, he had been unable to shift the course of galactic history by even the tiniest bit.

Time now to give up, then? Time to declare his labors a failure? Time to accept the course of history as it seemed to be irrevocably written? In a galaxy where so many untold trillions had died—where even the gods themselves could die—was it time at last for him, too, to lie down and die?

The temptation was great. His energy was ebbing; his corporeal form could not long endure. So easy to just give up, to let it all go. To let the galaxy die.

But no. No, he could not accept that. Not so long as life and energy remained to him. Not so long as some measure of the Power yet resonated throughout the cosmos.

No, he would try again. He would pick himself up and go back again and this time—*this time*—he would succeed. This time he would correct all those little things that had caused his failure. This time he would get it all right.

He moved then, a ghost drifting over a graveyard—but a ghost with purpose. Perhaps the most ironic purpose of all, for one of his sort: the purpose of preserving life.

He would need a way to get back—back to the critical moment. Back to the great cosmic splash whose ripples had led him this far into the future, and to their ultimate result— a shattered galaxy. He would need a conveyance back through time.

He could build such a device. He knew he could; somehow he knew he had done so before. The components could be found easily enough, amidst the wreckage of so many great star empires. It would not be easy—but then, nothing about his mission would be easy. He would construct a sort of temporal vault; a *time tomb*, to carry his body back to the proper time and place.

His body. He looked down and recalled that he truly was a ghost now. His ephemeral self could not travel within such a machine.

Fine, he told himself. First things first.

To begin, he would need a new body...

BOOK NINE

THE GOD
IN THE TOMB

1

Gritting his teeth, the golden eye emblem on his chest tarnished but still gleaming, General Ioan Iapetus gripped a matte-black blast pistol in either hand and fired a continuous barrage at the oncoming enemy forces. As he did, he called over the partially jammed and heavily distorted Aether link, "That's it—fall back! You men upstairs—get the Princess to the shuttle! *Now!*"

To his left, Colonel Berens Barbarossa glanced over at him and frowned, even as he, too, kept up an onslaught of blaster fire. "The shuttle? We are retreating, General? Abandoning the Imperial capital world?"

Iapetus offered the colonel a withering look. "I have no interest in holding this world purely for sentimental reasons, Colonel," Iapetus replied. "Our positions here are compromised and soon even our routes of withdrawal to orbit will be cut off." The black-clad general fired another barrage down the hallway, taking out a pair of insectoid alien Skrazzi that had been charging. The remaining enemy fighters dropped back into cover momentarily, giving the humans their first respite since their shuttles had landed.

"We are therefore leaving," Iapetus said, "the moment we have the Princess in our custody."

"I—yes, sir," Barbarossa said. His expression clearly betrayed his uneasiness at that decision, but he wasn't about to question Iapetus—at least, not publicly. In any case, it wouldn't have mattered; the general wasn't paying him any attention. He was engaged in a terse conversation with another unit of II Legion, elsewhere in the palace.

Iapetus looked at him as soon as that exchange had ended. "The extraction team upstairs is cut off. They're trapped." He was already moving in the direction of the central foyer—and the grand staircase it contained—as he called back, "Let's go!"

With a grunt of frustration, Barbarossa abandoned the barricade his soldiers had hastily erected only a short while earlier and hurried after Iapetus.

They dashed along the main central hallway of the Royal Palace, ignoring the fires burning in places where the opening salvos of the attackers had smashed through the ceiling and walls. Rubble lay everywhere, partially blocking the way and causing them to have to weave back and forth to avoid the larger piles of debris. Smoke was beginning to clog the air, and some of the soldiers ahead of Barbarossa were coughing as they ran.

At the head of their little formation, the general was in no mood to waste time now and Barbarossa had to sprint to avoid falling farther behind. He caught Iapetus and the others as they reached the end of the long central corridor and emerged into the vast open space of the grand foyer. Gold and silver and jewels beyond counting decorated nearly every surface, and the floor was of veined black and white marble. The main staircase—a broad, purple-carpeted affair that led up to the royal residence halls—lay just across from them. Before they could start toward it, however, a deafening cacophony of sound washed from the hallway opposite, and out stormed a horde of Skrazzi, their black carapaces gleaming in the dim light. Some leapt to the attack, stabbing and slicing with their deadly curved blade-arms. Others held back and aimed their disintegrator-cannon arms at his soldiers from afar, willing to take out their own comrades in order to score a few hits against the enemy.

The Sons of Terra had to dive for whatever cover was available to avoid being shredded by the multiple beams that knifed out from the techno-organic weapon-limbs of the horrific aliens. Some of the legionaries didn't make it in time and could only scream in agony as the disintegrator waves tore through armor, smartcloth and flesh.

The low hum of multiple disintegrators had alerted Barbarossa to dive for cover just in the nick of time. An instant after he did, a massive tapestry hanging on the far wall disappeared in a puff of threads and dust. He cringed at the thought; that could have been him.

"General," he called over the Aether link. "We have to get out of here *now*. They're using their disintegrators."

Silence for a moment, and Barbarossa waited, continuing to fire at the alien creatures as they emerged into the open on the attack. His pistol was hot now; the grip was almost impossible to continue to hold. Then Iapetus came back, "We have to get the Princess out. We are not leaving without her."

Barbarossa stifled another curse and started to respond with a reasoned but passionate argument for doing just that, when he was interrupted by the sounds of a small crowd of men and women just behind him crying out. As he whirled about, he expected to see the Skrazzi at their throats, but this was not the case. Instead, about a dozen of his fellow legionaries that had accompanied them from their previous position were now climbing over rubble and charging directly at the stairs.

Barbarossa bared his teeth as the low hum began again, and from multiple sources. The disintegrators were firing.

The Skrazzi were aiming their deadly distance-weapon limbs directly at the soldiers who were running for the stairs.

The suicide squad—for that, in truth, was what they had become—made it very close to the stairway before the first of them screamed in agony and fell to the floor. Blood was spraying out from multiple spots on his body, from head to toe, where the disintegrator waves had struck. His uniform was simply gone in places, as was the flesh beneath it. Bare bone shone through in numerous spots. He rolled about on the floor, screaming, until a Skrazzi leapt upon him and, in an almost merciful action, drove its curved blade-arm down into his chest.

The others of the squad continued on, and one after another of them dropped before reaching the stairs. Two more made it to the bottom flight and started up, only to be shot in the back and then pounced upon by the Skrazzi. Smoke was filling the corridor, its smell mingled with the coppery tang of blood. At that point Iapetus intervened and ordered the assault abandoned.

The surviving legionaries managed to regroup in secure positions just in time to unleash their own barrage on the first group of Skrazzi to attempt to go for the stairs themselves. The Sons of Terra punched gaping holes in the black bug-creatures with their blast-rifles and pistols, driving the survivors back into cover.

"A standoff," Barbarossa noted, staring across what had been an elegant foyer but was now no-man's-land. "We can't go for the Princess, but neither can they."

Now Iapetus was truly angry. He accessed the Aether and mentally "spoke" with the detachment upstairs, ordering them to stay where they were—their escape route was now cut off. He took a quick look around, assessing the situation. Then, after a string of profanities, he barked at Barbarossa, "If I had expected an invasion force to land and attack the palace so soon after our arrival, I would have brought down a much bigger force."

Barbarossa started to ask if they could simply call down reinforcements from the *Atlantia*, high up in orbit above them, but then he realized how useless that would be. The aliens were here, now, on the attack. By the time an assault team from the flagship could be scrambled and loaded onto a shuttle, not to mention flown all the way down to them and unloaded again, they would all have been dead for quite a while.

"Times like these are when I most regret allowing Teluria to escape me," he growled, eyeing Barbarossa. "It was inexcusably stupid." He shook his head. "She could've simply opened a portal and we could have walked right out of here."

Barbarossa had worked with the general far too long to think it wise to say anything back to that.

"Ah, well," he said. "No sense in worrying about it now. She will be back under our control soon enough." He issued another set of orders, this time telling the upstairs contingent to keep the Princess safe and otherwise block off the stairs. Next he designated half a dozen of his troops there around him to stay in position and defeat any attempts by the aliens to try again for the stairs. Finally he turned to Barbarossa and motioned in the direction they had just come. "Back this way, Colonel," he said. "The rest of you, too. Let's go."

"This way, sir?"

"Back to the shuttle," Iapetus called back, already hurrying along the grand hallway.

Barbarossa was shocked. They were leaving? Without the Princess?

"General," he shouted, very concerned now, "I don't believe our troops back there can hold out for long."

"Then you'd better run faster, eh, Colonel?"

Barbarossa reddened but picked up his pace, trailing along behind Iapetus and five other soldiers in black.

They had to fight their way back out of the palace but, after that, fortune was with them: their main shuttle was still intact on the broad concrete parking lot. The boarding ramp lowered as they approached and they all hurried aboard. Before the last soldier had even seated herself in the passenger compartment, Iapetus had already moved to the cockpit and yanked the pilot out of his seat. The pilot dropped into a spare co-pilot's spot and looked on in wide-eyed wonder as the supreme commander of II Legion began to operate the controls of the vehicle like a seasoned pro, lifting the little ship off the ground in seconds.

"Where is she?" Iapetus called over the Aether. "Where is the Princess? Is she still safe?"

"We have her, General, and she's fine," came a response from one of the II Legion units in the royal suites. "We have been cut off, and are preparing to fight our way out."

"No," Iapetus almost shouted aloud. "No—do not endanger her. Stay there. *We* will come to *you*."

"Come to *us*?"

Iapetus ignored the question and devoted his attention to the controls, pivoting the shuttle around to face the palace. At that moment a horde of Skrazzi emerged from the same doorway the legionaries had just used. They waved their blade-arms and emitted blood-curdling roars. In response Iapetus remotely accessed the anti-personnel guns along the bottom of the shuttle and opened fire; the Skrazzi disintegrated in puffs of black dust and blood as energy pulses tore through them.

The Aether was now abuzz with calls from both the troops at the bottom of the stairs and the ones guarding the Princess. It seemed the enemy was in the process of launching a major assault.

The general absorbed this information but had nothing to say about it. Instead, "Get the Princess back from the windows," he called to them over the Aether. "Everyone in the royal quarters—get away from the windows and the outer wall! As far back as you can safely go!"

He allowed seven seconds—seconds during which he had to open up again with the anti-personnel weapons on a new group of Skrazzi—and then dropped the shuttle's nose and stomped on the accelerator.

The dull gray, boxy shuttle shot forward and smashed into the side of the palace, shattering windows and cracking the wall before bouncing partway back and hovering there. Inside, some of the troops in the passenger cabin—the ones who hadn't bothered yet to fasten their crash webbing in place—tumbled from their seats. The wall, meanwhile, held. Iapetus cursed, gritted his teeth, and slammed the shuttle into the palace again. This time the tough metal hull ripped through the masonry entirely and exposed the sumptuous private suites within to open air.

"Open the hatch and pull those people in here," the general shouted to his still-reeling legionaries in the back. "Let's go! Hurry!"

Astonished, the Sons of Terra dropped the ramp open and leapt out into the now half-demolished bedroom of the Princess. The soldiers who were with her had just figured out what was happening and were bringing her forward to meet them. Together they climbed into the shuttle and barely had time to close the ramp again before Iapetus had wheeled the craft around and aimed upward. A horde of Skrazzi emerged into the bedroom, blades and gun-arms waving, arriving in time to watch as the shuttle rocketed up into the sky.

Once they had achieved orbit and the *Atlantia* was in sight, Iapetus stood and handed the controls back over to the pilot, who looked at him with newfound respect—and no small amount of fear. "That was a remarkable bit of flying, General," the pilot said.

Iapetus nodded once to him and moved into the cabin, quickly locating the little princess in her white dress.

Barbarossa was standing at attention next to her, and a handful of older men and women waited behind her—household retainers and servants, no doubt.

The blonde girl, about ten years of age, dusted herself off and looked up at the two men. "My thanks," she told them, very formally, though in the voice of the little girl she still was. She clearly had been trained from infancy in the royal manner. "Are we abandoning the palace to the enemy?" she asked, focusing on Iapetus.

"Indeed we are, Your Majesty," the general replied. "And the planet with it, I'm afraid."

"The planet?" She appeared shocked. For an instant it looked as if she were about to burst into tears—and to reveal that she was, after all, a little girl. "That—that is unacceptable!"

Iapetus spread his hands. "I'm sorry, Majesty," he said, "but there is nothing to be done. The enemy has overrun the entire planet—the entire sector. The Empire is being rolled back, on a direct line for Earth. All we can do is retreat and dig in—defend the homeworld to the end."

"And so we abandon the throne world entirely?"

"I've already issued orders to that effect," Iapetus replied. He shook his head. "It is no longer defensible. We must withdraw behind secure boundaries."

The little girl looked at him, raising one eyebrow. "Is *anywhere* secure now, General? Even Earth?"

Iapetus didn't miss a beat. "Yes," he replied. "Sacred Terra is inviolate—and will remain so." He attempted to grace her with a smile, but such a thing appeared entirely unnatural on his rugged features. "We will have you at the Old Palace in a matter of hours, Majesty. In the halls where your illustrious predecessors—"

"Spare me, General," the girl said, cutting him off. "I know you care nothing for me. You have gone to such great lengths on my behalf only because you need me." She turned quickly and glanced back at one of her servants, as if seeking approval for these words. The older men and women made a show of looking elsewhere and in no way seeming to support the young girl's statement.

But then the older woman directly behind the Princess appeared to make up her mind about something—or to change it. She looked directly at Iapetus and stated sharply, "You need Her Majesty to validate your own position, as she requires you to defend her realm. Consequently we have advised the Princess to go along with your wishes. But do not mistake that for approval."

Iapetus regarded the older woman with contempt for a moment, then stared down at the little girl. Any semblance of deference had vanished. "You are useful, yes," he growled. "But if something... *unfortunate*... were to happen to you, I would simply find some long-lost relative of yours that no one had ever heard of before, and *they* would confirm my appointment as Regent of the Empire."

The Princess appeared ready to argue that point, but the older woman behind her tapped her once on the shoulder and she held her tongue.

Before anyone else could speak, the cabin rocked violently.

"We're taking fire from enemy units on the ground and in orbit, General," one of the pilots called back.

Iapetus gave the Princess and her advisor one last long, sharp look, then turned away. "Have the *Atlantia* come down to meet us—to cut us an avenue for escape," he shouted toward the cockpit. "And try to keep us in one piece, if you will, gentlemen," he added, "until she gets here."

Barbarossa moved forward to join him, and as the colonel leaned down he could see the massive silver bulk of the *Atlantia*—flagship of II Legion—moving their way, blasting enemy fighters to bits as it approached. The sight warmed his heart. Maybe, he thought, we will survive this business after all.

A few moments later the shuttle reached the big ship and passed through the opening of Bay Four, coming to a halt on the broad, gray metal deck. The passengers and crew had to wait another couple of minutes while the other shuttles arrived, and then the bay was sealed against the outside vacuum and repressurized. At that point they were able to disembark. Iapetus ordered for an honor guard of six officers to escort the Princess to the finest cabin available. Then he turned to Barbarossa.

"Top speed for Earth," he ordered tersely.

Barbarossa nodded once to acknowledge the order. "So—we are taking up permanent position there, General?" he asked.

The general shook his head. "We are depositing our royal cargo and then leaving."

Barbarossa was surprised by this. He had assumed Iapetus intended to withdraw all their forces—especially including the *Atlantia*—back to Earth to make one last stand.

In response to Barbarossa's tactfully-phrased question to this effect, Iapetus replied, "I must grudgingly admit that General Tamerlane was right about one thing during his confrontation with our wayward Governor Rameses, and I have learned from it."

Barbarossa was surprised again. "Oh, sir?"

"When facing an overwhelming external threat, you must first eliminate all *internal* threats."

Barbarossa took this in and nodded slowly; meanwhile, knowing his commander as well as he did, he moved his right hand down so that his fingers brushed against the grip of his blast pistol in its holster. "Ah," he said. "So—you do intend that we should make a stand defending Sacred Terra, eventually."

"Of course," the general in black replied. "We have no other options now." He paused, looking Barbarossa straight in the eye. "But when we do, I intend that we should have no opposition present in our ranks." He smiled now. "If we

24

must all die, I guarantee you Ezekial Tamerlane and his traitors will die before we do."

Barbarossa swallowed at this but gathered himself and, moving his hand away from his gun, he saluted. "Yes, General." He turned away and began issuing orders over the Aether link.

The *Atlantia* wheeled about and leapt into hyperspace.

.

Z

Two tall, slender, and entirely alien forms strode along winding corridors lit only by the pale glow of flickering soul-fires. They wore loose-fitting robes of deep blue and green, gemstones woven into the material sparkling as they moved. The illuminating globes that lit their way were spaced out every half-dozen meters or so, casting the swooping, gothic architecture in a dappled, jarring interplay of light and shadow.

The two figures were slightly bent as by great age and physical infirmity, yet they hurried along as if in the prime of their lives—or as if pursued by some horrific nightmare. As they traveled they spoke to one another in sharp whispers.

"The end times draw near," said one. "The Adversary has unleashed the fullness of his fury upon the galaxy. For now the humans bear the brunt of his wrath. Soon enough, however, his gaze will turn upon us—upon the Star-Cities—and eventually upon even fair Dalen-Shala."

"Yes," the other agreed, struggling to keep pace with the first. "But what possible mitigation might we offer? What resistance?"

"None whatsoever." The first figure slowed and turned his aged, narrow features toward the other. "There is no hope remaining. All is done."

The second being frowned at this. "Surely not," he whispered. "For all of our knowledge, our power—for the greatness that was once ours—surely there must be some way to blunt his attack. If not to defeat it, then perhaps to redirect it…?"

The other pursed his wrinkled lips and narrowed his eyes, as if giving this suggestion serious consideration. A second later, he shook his head and turned away, hurrying off once more. "There can be no dissuading the Adversary. You know this. All the efforts the humans have hurled at him have served only to strengthen his resolve. He has set his mind and his efforts to eradicating all life in this galaxy—and replacing it with his own twisted servants, the Phaedrons and the Skrazzi."

"But—we cannot allow this to happen," the other said.

"No," the first agreed. "We cannot."

They came to the end of the winding corridor and to a tall, narrow door. Two guards in transparent, rainbow-colored, glass-like armor stood at attention before it. At the sight of the two, they stepped smartly aside and the door slid open.

"We are not to be disturbed," the first figure said to the nearer of the two guards.

"It shall be as you say, First Seer," the guard replied with a respectful nod.

The two elderly figures passed through the doorway and it closed behind them. They stood now in a broad, domed room some twenty meters in diameter. Smoke curled here and there from open braziers. The smell of exotic spices and incense filled the air. Pale light shone down from soul-fires high overhead.

The one that had been addressed as First Seer took a seat on a low, cushioned platform and hunched forward. Despite his associate and himself being the only living beings within the room, he continued to speak in hushed tones, perhaps out of habit—or caution.

"You are quite correct in that we must act," he told the other. "As First and Second Seers of Dalen-Shala, the duty and the responsibility—dare I say the *honor*—fall to us."

"But—you said there was nothing we could do," the Second Seer replied, puzzled.

"No—I said there was no resistance we could offer; no way to defeat or save the Star-Cities."

"Then what—?"

"But we might yet deny the Adversary his victory—and spare the galaxy the nightmare of destruction or enslavement at his hands."

The Second Seer stared back at his counterpart, puzzled.

"We cannot win," the First Seer elaborated, "but we can take his victory from him. Take away the spoils of his war—and a great many of his forces, in the bargain."

The Second Seer blinked, looking down, thinking. As grim realization came to him, he looked up at his colleague, his dark eyes widening. "You—you cannot mean—"

The First Seer merely gazed impassively back at him. For several long moments, neither of them spoke. The Second Seer reached out with seemingly insensate hands and, finding a cushion, lowered himself into a seated position as well. Together they sat there, the one struggling to comprehend what the other had suggested.

Finally, the Second Seer looked up and shook his head slowly. "How?" he whispered, his brows furrowed. "How would we be able to do such a thing?"

"Easily," the other said. "As a mercy."

"No—no," the Second Seer blurted quickly. "I mean—by what mechanism or artifice might such an endeavor be brought to fruition?"

"Ah." The First Seer gazed up into the thin clouds of smoke that floated about and above them. He gestured and the image of a planet—all browns and yellows—appeared, floating there, as if by holographic projection. "It can be done," he said, "though the task will not be easy, and we will require assistance from a number of our warriors." He motioned again and the planet vanished, replaced by a rapidly-changing series of images.

The Second Seer watched as his colleague laid out the steps necessary. When the last image faded into the clouds and vanished, he turned back to the First. "By the stars and the Star-Cities," he breathed. "It—it *can* be done."

"As I said." The other spread his spindly hands. "This stratagem was developed by one of our earliest seers, ages ago. It has been handed down only to First Seers. Eventually I would have shared it with you, whether we intended to enact it or not. But, now..." His voice trailed off and he raised his arms in a kind of shrug.

The Second Seer appeared stunned and uncertain of himself. "We will require assistance both physical and metaphysical. Who would help us—who would perform the necessary steps?" He shook his head nervously. "If word of this got out to our warriors, some might agree that it is necessary, but many more might resist—or outright refuse. They might attempt to thwart it." He met the other's gaze evenly. "Or even rally the others against us."

"A valid concern," the First Seer replied.

"What can we do, then, if their thoughts run in that direction?"

The First Seer stroked his narrow chin. "We must not allow that scenario to become a possibility. If their thinking does sway toward rejection of our plans, then we will have no choice. We will have to *alter* their thinking."

"Alter?" The Second Seer stared back at his counterpart for several long seconds, speechless.

"How now?" asked the First, leaning forward, his black eyes peering up through heavy lids. "Does my proposal disturb you so? Cause you to lose so much complexion?"

"I—" The Second Seer opened and closed his mouth several times, but said nothing.

The First Seer smiled flatly. "You seem far more troubled by the thought of deceiving our warriors than by the other—"

"No, no," the Second Seer replied hastily. "I was merely...*surprised*. But I agree—that is the only option." He nodded his head once. "I consent to your suggestion."

"It was no *suggestion*," the First Seer snapped. Then he softened his tone and added, "But I welcome your agreement and your cooperation."

Somewhat mollified, the Second Seer nodded again. He looked away, thinking. "And what of us? Will we—?"

"We will move on," the First Seer stated firmly. "We will transcend. We will *ascend*. To the Above." He met the other's eyes. "It is only fitting. There should be witnesses. Someone to remember what was. To preserve the memories..."

Eyes wide now, the Second Seer could only agree.

"But we shall take our leave of the mortal plane only at the last moment," the First added. "We will remain here as long as possible, to make certain all goes as it should. And then, as the critical moment arrives," he said, "we shall..." He trailed off and then gazed upward, into the smoke and light above their heads.

"I...understand," the Second Seer said quickly.

The First Seer steepled his slender fingers beneath his pointed chin. "I will choose the warriors best suited to our needs, and have them brought here for programming. Then we will be ready for when the Adversary strikes. When the need becomes absolute for us to act."

The Second Seer winced at the other's use of the term "programming," but reluctantly he nodded.

LEGION III: KINGS OF OBLIVION

"Excellent," said the First Seer—and a smile spread across his face; the other found it highly disturbing, if not downright chilling. "Then let us begin," he said.

3

Days later, and a universe away:

General Arnem rippa and his men had nearly given up hope when at last they stumbled across the tomb.

It was not, at first glance, at all evident that it was a tomb. It stood some two meters above the barren ground, wreathed in nearly impenetrable fog that swirled about its base and about their legs. Its surface was smooth and unmarred by any cracks or indicators—natural or artificial—of what it might be, or how long it had rested there. It might have been metal or stone or something else; that, too, was not at all clear.

Agrippa approached it almost gleefully. For hours he had led his Bravo Squad—finest soldiers of the Imperial III Legion, officially called the "Golden Phalanx" but more widely known as the "Kings of Oblivion"—through an unending ocean of nothingness. All along he had exhorted the troops to keep going; to not give in or give up hope, because he knew precisely where he was going. Of course, he knew no such thing at all. But he'd had to tell them so. It was that, or lie down and give up.

As a feeling of despair had begun to descend upon his soul, one of the forward lookouts had called, "Something up here, General!"

Agrippa had hurried forward with a renewed strength he'd scarcely guessed he still possessed. And now, as he reached it, he found himself quite startled.

"What—what is it?" Torgon asked, frowning at it. "Is it—?"

Agrippa raised one white-gauntleted hand to halt the speculative conversation before it could start. He stepped toward the object and studied it carefully, but from a respectful distance. *It* being the first solid object they had encountered in all the hours since the alleged goddess, Aurore, had seemingly disintegrated before their very eyes and abandoned them here in this strange limbo realm, he intended to do nothing to disturb it. At least, not quite yet.

"Readings?" he demanded of the officer who carried a small broad-spectrum scanning unit built into one sleeve of his armor. "Anything coming in or going out?"

"No, General," the trooper replied, tapping a few spots on the sleeve unit. "It's not active, as far as I can tell."

Agrippa nodded and moved right up next to the object. He paused for a few seconds, thinking, then began to remove his right gauntlet, exposing his hand. As the others looked on, some of them holding their breath, he ran his fingertips lightly over the surface.

"It's cold," he said. "Smooth and cold."

"It's a tomb," Obomanu whispered, finally vocalizing what all of them had been thinking all along.

"Maybe so," Agrippa said with a shrug. "Maybe not."

"General," the scan man interjected, his voice suddenly urgent. "I'm picking up something now. Okay, wow," he added. "The readings are going crazy."

The others stepped back from the tomb.

"What does that mean, precisely?" Agrippa asked, keeping his voice casual. "Crazy how?"

The scan man shook his head; his helmet was off and hanging from a tether at his side, just as Agrippa's was. The fog swirled up and around his features, making him somewhat difficult to see. "I'm not sure, sir," he replied. "It's not just one thing. It's all the readings. Electromagnetic activity; radio waves; heat; temporal—"

Agrippa stopped him there with a quickly raised hand. He frowned deeply. "Temporal? What—?"

"Temporal readings are all over the place," the man replied, still staring at the readout on his armor's sleeve. "I've never seen anything like it."

Agrippa felt his patience slipping away. "Start over," he said, his voice calm but rock-solid and powerful. "What do you mean by temporal readings being all over the place? How can that be possible?"

"I—I don't know, General," the scan man said, his voice strained. "If I understood it myself, sir, I would try to explain it clearly—but I don't. I have no idea."

Agrippa bit back a sharp retort and instead merely nodded. Maintaining the morale of the men was critical right now, and reprimanding one of them wouldn't serve that cause at all. He cursed the fact for the thousandth time in his adult life that being a leader meant more than just being the bravest fighter in combat; one had to carefully manage the spirits of the troops and keep them at just the right balance of caution and aggressiveness. And never, ever allow them to give up hope. "Well, figure it out as quickly as you can," he said, scowling.

"Yes, sir."

"Contact!" cried another soldier, one of the few females that made up the company, off to the right on the perimeter.

Agrippa looked up, his quad-rifle in hand, ready now for anything in this bizarre nowhere realm. "What is it?"

The woman—a Lieutenant Holland, Agrippa recalled—paused before responding. "Intruders approaching. Five of them. Six. Now seven."

"Humans?" Agrippa asked, even as his troops around him brought up their pistols, rifles and swords.

"...Negative," the perimeter guard replied. She must have been struggling to get a clear reading in the strange atmospheric conditions that surrounded them. Finally she said, "Definitely alien, General, but I can't tell exactly what they are."

"Ready all weapons," Agrippa said, though everyone had already done so and was moving into defensive positions. He turned back to the tomb, studying it anew. Was there something intrinsically valuable about it? Was this new group—aliens, apparently—looking for it? Would they want to fight for it? Was it valuable enough or useful enough to Agrippa and his team that it was *worth* fighting for—or should he simply order his forces to move aside and let them have possession of it? Thinking through all of this, he cursed his lack of answers. He needed more information. The goddess Aurore had led them here, to this barren level of the Above, with the understanding that they were desperately needed to prevent some vast, galactic catastrophe that the seer-god Solonis had foreseen. But then, once they had arrived, she had seemingly disintegrated, abandoning them with no way back home, no goal in sight, no understanding of the mission beyond those basics, and no way forward other than to simply slog through the fog. It was all very frustrating and infuriating, and Agrippa was struggling to hold his team together in the face of it all.

"Intruders have halted," the perimeter guard said, bringing him back to the moment. She, like the others, was having to rely on actual voice communication, their usual mental link via the Aether connection not working terribly well in this strange environment.

"How many now, Lieutenant?" he asked, actually finding himself pleased to have a presumably real-world opponent to concern himself with. Fighting aliens was something he knew how to do, and knew how to do very effectively.

"Seven, sir."

Agrippa nodded, his mind working, trying to figure out how to proceed. Probably the other party was now aware of them, too, and their leader was thinking much the same thing.

"General," the scan man called in a low voice, as though that wouldn't prevent Agrippa from keeping up with what was happening around them. "The readings are even crazier now. The temporal numbers are off the charts."

Agrippa came very close to smacking the guy. His patience was exhausted. "Tell me what that means, in real terms," he ordered in a tone that was low but very sharp. "If you can't give me concrete facts to go by, Corporal, I'd as soon you kept your mouth shut."

Rebuked, the scan man opened and closed his mouth a couple of times before saying, "I—I think, General, that it means that this tomb—or whatever is inside it—is actively traveling in time."

This brought Agrippa's head around to stare at the man with wide eyes. "Traveling," he said, "in time."

"I—um, yes, sir. Yes, just so. Traveling in time."

"Intruders are on the move again, sir," came the voice of Holland, the perimeter guard.

"Where?" Agrippa demanded, growing annoyed with having to bounce back and forth between the two separate conversations. He was also growing frustrated with the inactivity. He was not alone in that, he knew. Around him, the other troopers of his Bravo Squad stood about uneasily. Certainly they all gave the visible impression to anyone who might have been looking at them that they were overwhelmingly confident and sure of themselves, and there was no doubt that they constituted a remarkably formidable force, for one composed of so few individuals. But Agrippa knew them better than that, and could read the smallest signs in their voices, their posture, their movements. They were nervous and jittery, and this inactivity only amplified that condition. At least when they had been marching they had been doing something, if only trudging through a foggy wasteland. Now, they had nothing to do save peer into that very fog and wait for an attack that might never come—or might come in another second.

Holland had pulled back closer to the main body of the Bravo Squad so that the others could see her, and now she was gesturing in a broad arc. "All across there, that way, sir," she said to Agrippa. "They're approaching—slowly— and they're fanning out."

Agrippa nodded. He turned back to the corporal with the scanner. "Anything more of note besides that this box is somehow traveling in time?" he asked, his feelings about that report quite clearly conveyed in his tone.

The corporal seemed reluctant to add anything, but at last he noted in a low tone, "Just that each of the effects I reported earlier is now amplified, and growing greater by the moment." He hesitated, then added, "It's as if this box— this tomb—was far away from us when we found it, but now it's getting closer and closer to us."

Agrippa pursed his lips, wondering if he should have the medic check the man for head injury. "Corporal," he said, "you do understand that this tomb has been sitting right here the entire time. It's not 'getting closer' to anything. You, however, are getting closer to testing the limits of my patience."

"In time, I mean," the man said quickly. "It's as if it is approaching us in time, not in space."

Agrippa stared at him blankly.

The corporal blanched. "I'm sorry, General," he said quickly. "I apologize for doing a poor job of describing—of explaining—what I'm sensing here. It's just—" He stared down at his readouts again for a long second, then looked back up at the big blond man. "It's just that I haven't encountered anything like this before, and I don't know quite how to put it into words."

Agrippa nodded. "That's fine. Just keep an eye on things and let me know if it's about to explode or change into a killer robot or something."

The man clearly didn't see any humor in Agrippa's order. He merely nodded, his expression serious as ever, and returned his attention to the small display panels on his sleeve.

The tomb, meanwhile, began to glow a soft white—just barely visible enough for Agrippa to notice.

"Humans," came a voice suddenly in all of their heads. "Please move away from the Temporal Vault."

Agrippa reacted more quickly than anyone else and, given the makeup of his team—all highly trained and skilled soldiers of the III Legion—that was saying something. He raised his massive quad-rifle and leveled it, aiming out into the fog before him. "Who goes there?" he shouted. "Identify yourselves."

For a moment there was only silence around them. Then shapes began to move within the fog; to move, and to emerge. They were tall and almost impossibly thin, and they carried extremely dangerous-looking pistols in one hand and curved, transparent swords in the other.

"Move away," the telepathic voice repeated, "or we will be forced to engage in extreme violence."

4

Tall, slender, vaguely humanoid shapes moved within the fog, as the men and women of the Kings of Oblivion Legion's Bravo Squad looked on. As the beings emerged, the weapons they carried became extremely obvious.

"We are the Dalen-Shala Kazi Vor Tarr," the voice in their heads announced, its tone smooth and musical and not at all unpleasant. "In your words, the First Company of the Star-City of Dalen-Shala."

The voice, or at least its tones, sounded very familiar to Agrippa. He began to suspect with whom he was dealing. Indeed, a moment later a particularly tall, slender form emerged fully from the fog and into the open. Colorful, glasslike armor gleamed on its body.

"You know our people," the mental voice said, "as the Dyonari." A pause, then, "My name is Merrin. It is my honor to command this team."

Agrippa brightened. Of all the aliens he could have encountered at this moment, given what had transpired for him and his company over the past couple of days, the

Dyonari seemed to him undoubtedly to provide the least cause for concern. That, he reflected, was probably not something he would have ever thought prior to his recent combat duty on Eingrad-6. But now he felt his opinion of them had changed somewhat. When his team had been battling a rival human empire in a bloody conflict on that planet, he had encountered a Dyonari combat squad of roughly the same size and makeup as his own, and they had ended up becoming allies, at least temporarily. Of course, he remembered, given the horrific nature of their mutual foe, it was difficult to imagine any other outcome between them at that moment in time. In short, he reminded himself, striking up a working friendship with one Dyonari tank commander did not necessarily put him on good terms with any of the others in the galaxy. And the tall, spindly aliens had always been preceded across most of the Milky Way by reputations as cruel and selfish as any beings humanity had yet to meet. Maybe Glossis, the tank commander, had simply been "one of the good ones," he considered. Maybe even that had been a trick of some sort, though Agrippa found that last bit a little hard to swallow. Glossis had been genuinely friendly, in his alien way. That, for Agrippa, earned this new bunch some measure of the benefit of the doubt. Within reason, of course.

"Yes, I do think I know you," Agrippa called to the Dyonari officer who was standing just visible beyond the edge of the fog. "Or at least I know your people—and know them better than I did only a short while ago." He paused, then, "I am General Arnem Agrippa of the III Legion. Perhaps you know of me, Commander Merrin? Perhaps you have heard a report about me and my men from a commander of yours called Glossis?" Quickly Agrippa offered a summary of his team's interaction with that other squad.

"I know that Glossis is one of the commanders from the Resig-Tal Star-City," the alien replied, his voice echoing

40

within Agrippa's head. "Beyond that, I am not familiar with him," Merrin continued. "And I must confess that I have not heard of you. But I extend greetings in the name of the high seat of Dalen-Shala. All who show kindness to our people will be accorded all possible respect and appreciation."

Agrippa nodded formally at this. "Likewise."

"I must confess I am surprised to find humans here, in the Vel Shah—the Low Above," Merrin said.

"We had...business...here," Agrippa replied, leaving it at that for now.

"I see." The alien studied the human commander and the others visible around him. "Is your business concluded?"

"I am...not at liberty to say," Agrippa replied.

"Does it involve the Temporal Vault?"

Agrippa looked down at the strange gray tomb. It had to be what the guy was referring to. "I am, again, not at liberty to say."

The alien took this in and had no reply, at least for the moment.

Agrippa's mind was working. He needed the help of these beings, but didn't want to reveal just how helpless he and his troops were in the process. Not unless there was no other choice. And he certainly didn't want to hand over to them anything particularly valuable—or potentially dangerous.

"It would be unfortunate if your business here did involve the Vault," Merrin said after a brief period of silence. "For my orders are very specific and very clear."

Agrippa nodded once at this, still thinking. What he needed was leverage of some sort. He tried to remember the words the alien had used to describe the tomb, and found them. "So—you are here for the Temporal Vault, then?" he asked, keeping his tone even and reasonable. "May I ask— what is your interest in it?"

"That is our concern, General," Merrin replied, speaking out loud now, his tone testy. "But we have laid claim to it, and would ask again that you and your soldiers move away from it."

Agrippa frowned at this. "You have laid claim to it?" He looked down at the plain gray tomb, then rapped on the surface with his knuckles. "I'm not certain what that means in real terms. You intend to try to move it? To take it with you? Why? *How*?"

"That is, again, our concern," Merrin said. He moved fully into the open now, flanked by two more of his men, each wielding one of the famed and deadly Dyonari curved swords. "Do not mistake my willingness to converse with you for weakness on our part."

Agrippa considered this. On the one hand, he never responded well to threats, even when they came couched in civil behavior. On the other, this…Temporal Vault, whatever it was, didn't belong to him. He had no idea what it was, or what he would do with it if he managed to successfully defend it from the Dyonari. All he knew as that it represented the only solid object—other than these aliens—he had encountered here in this barren wilderness. And it also represented the only leverage over them he could think of.

On top of that, he felt a strong but indefinable feeling that it wouldn't be good to let the aliens have possession of the thing. Why that should be, he had no idea.

Nothing to do but play the gambit out, he thought to himself. He set his quad-rifle down against the side of the tomb, fitted a smile upon his face, and started forward in the direction of the aliens.

The two guards flanking Merrin raised their swords, preparing to defend against any attack, but Agrippa only allowed his smile to widen and raised his empty hands. "I believe I may have an equitable solution for both of us," he called to the other commander. He stopped halfway and waited.

Merrin said nothing for a few seconds, then gave a quick, sharp order to his guards. Reluctantly, it seemed, they lowered their swords, and then Merrin walked slowly forward, out into the open. He advanced until he was only a few paces away from Agrippa. His long, narrow head cocked slightly to one side, as if to say, "I'm listening."

"I believe we can help one another," Agrippa began.

"We do not need your help," Merrin countered. "We merely require the Temporal Vault."

"Wouldn't you prefer to take possession of it without first suffering horrific casualties to your forces?" Agrippa asked, still smiling, his tone incongruously friendly. "Assuming, of course, that your side wins such a conflict at all?"

"You would fight over it?" Merrin asked. "You desire it, too?"

Agrippa shrugged. "Perhaps."

The alien studied him for a long second. "You are not at all familiar with the Temporal Vault, are you?" A pause. "Perhaps you have only just encountered it for the first time, and have gotten to it before us purely by chance."

"Perhaps," Agrippa repeated.

The alien stood in silent contemplation for a few seconds more. "If you do not know what it is, or what to do with it," Merrin asked at length, "why would you fight to the death to keep it from us?"

Agrippa chuckled. He knew his gambit had reached the end of its thread. Now only honesty remained. Now there would be cooperation, or there would be violence. "Because, truth be told," he said, "it's all we have as a bargaining chip with you."

The alien appeared to be surprised by this. "A bargaining chip?"

"Leverage. To persuade you to help us."

Merrin tilted his head slightly. "If you needed our help, why did you not simply ask?"

Agrippa laughed again, harder. "Because I didn't want to reveal our weakness to you—at least not too quickly. I couldn't know how you would respond."

"Such thinking has inevitably led to great catastrophe for our people in days gone by."

Agrippa nodded. "Very true—for our people, too."

"What help do you require?"

Agrippa allowed himself to feel a bit of encouragement at those words. Perhaps, he thought, I have been too cautious—too paranoid. But then, *Nonsense*, he told himself quickly. *Your troops are under your protection and are your responsibility and you had to do whatever was necessary to keep them safe and to return them to the Empire alive and well.*

He returned Merrin's gaze levelly. "From our dealings with Glossis," he said, "we know that your people possess the means to travel in and out of the lower levels of the Above. Your presence here, now, attests to that."

The alien nodded once in acknowledgement.

"We were led here by an individual—a being—that has since abandoned us, for reasons not yet clear. We need a way back home."

"Ah," the Dyonari said. "A *lien-dahl*. A doorway. Of course." He emitted a sound that might have been laughter. "I had begun to suspect that your presence here indicated that your people, too, now possessed a means of entering this level of the Above."

"We might," Agrippa said, "but that was not the manner of our arrival here."

Merrin nodded. "Very well. If you will assemble your warriors and have them move away from the Temporal Vault, I will order a portal to be opened that will take you back to your realm."

"Thank you," Agrippa said, but his tone changed before the words were entirely out of his mouth. Something was bothering him, but he couldn't quite put his finger on it. *Something…*

"General!" came the call from one of his soldiers behind him. And even as the man spoke, Agrippa realized what was bugging him: Aurore had brought him and his Bravo Squad here to stop a galactic catastrophe she claimed was coming—and the instigators of that catastrophe, according to her, were… *Dyonari*. And who were the first beings they had encountered here?

It all seemed too convenient somehow.

Merrin was turning away and likely issuing mental orders to his own forces, who were still positioned off in the fog. Agrippa hurried back to where his squad were scattered, on the other side of the tomb. The corporal with the scanning equipment build into the sleeve of his armor had his helmet off and his expression was one of shock and astonishment.

"What is it now?" Agrippa demanded.

"The temporal waves coming from the tomb have ceased," the man reported, his voice strained. "But everything else—electromagnetic, heat, all of it—has increased."

"What does that mean in basic terms? What do I need to know?"

The corporal frowned for a moment, then met the general's eyes. "Remember that I said before it seemed as if whatever was inside this tomb was far away in time, but coming closer and closer?"

Agrippa nodded, not fully understanding.

"Well, General," the corporal said, looking from his commanding officer to the strange gray box and back, "whatever it is—it's here. It has arrived."

5

omething has arrived? Where?" demanded Agrippa. "Inside the tomb? And better yet— *what?*"

The corporal looked back down at his indicators and shook his head. "I have no way of knowing precisely, General," he said. "But if we wait just a minute, we may find out." *Whether we like it or not*, he almost added.

Agrippa gazed back out across the open area in which he had been parleying with the Dyonari commander. He was uncertain as to how to proceed, and he didn't like that fact. For a while during their discussion he'd attempted to keep as much secret as possible, for the protection of his squad and to provide as much leverage over the aliens as possible. Eventually, though, he'd had to admit that they needed a way out of this bizarre, barren dimension into which they'd been led. He was experiencing second thoughts now as to whether he should have shared that fact with a potential foe. It did, after all, reveal much about the depths of their plight as well as their powerlessness, and thus handed an advantage to the Dyonari. *I've always been a soldier first and a diplomat a very distant second*, he fretted. *This sort of thing is not at all what I'm cut out for. Give me a quad-rifle and a gladius and I'll carve my way into the enemy with glee. But force me to play a verbal chess match with a bunch of telepathic aliens, and...*

No, he told himself firmly. *That's no way to think. You did as good a job as you could, and the Bravo Squad of III Legion is still intact. Don't lose your nerve now. Just take the aliens up on their offer. Let them open a way to get out of here. What matter that they end up in control of the tomb thing? It's just a big gray box. Maybe just a solid sculpture—a marker of some kind. What harm in them "claiming" it?*

Even so, that little voice continued to nag at the back of his mind. It wouldn't stop. Scowling, he turned and motioned sharply for Major Torgon, the next-highest-ranking officer in the company. As Torgon nodded and hurried his way, the white and green Deising-Arry Mark V plate armor's internal servos whining as he came, Agrippa wished for the dozenth time that Colonel Iksander was with him. Iksander was a shrewd man, gifted with insights that Agrippa could usually only see after the fact. Unfortunately, "the Lightning," as he was called, was back on Eingrad-6, presumably mopping up the last of the enemy forces there in Agrippa's absence.

"Yes, General?" Torgon asked, saluting, his helmet off and dangling from its strap at his side.

Agrippa led him off to one side and spoke in a low voice, carefully laying out his nagging worries about the Dyonari, the tomb, and the words of Aurore before she had disintegrated and abandoned them. When he was done, the major frowned and ran a hand through his dark hair. "I think I understand your concerns, sir, but we have no way of knowing if these Dyonari are the ones she wanted us to stop. If we start some sort of conflict with them for no real reason…" He trailed off for a second, then, "Even if we won the fight, we'd have no way back home."

Agrippa nodded. "Absolutely right, Torgon," he said. "And yet, I simply can't shake the feeling that—"

"General! You need to see this!"

Agrippa and Torgon looked up from where they'd been huddling. What they saw caused both men to gasp involuntarily.

The top portion of the gray tomb was moving slowly down, like the lid of a box sliding open. Like a sarcophagus opening itself from the inside.

Agrippa suppressed a shudder and moved quickly to the side of the tomb. The other members of the squad gathered around, looking on in puzzlement.

"General," came the voice of the Dyonari across the clearing—too far away and at the wrong angle to see the lid moving. "Is something the matter? Your men seem… agitated."

"No, no," Agrippa called back over his shoulder, his eyes not moving from the strange sight. "Just one moment, if you don't mind."

The tomb—the Temporal Vault, as the Dyonari would have it—continued to open, but slowly. Oh so slowly.

"There's someone inside," exclaimed one of the men in a relatively loud voice, earning a reproving glance from the general.

Indeed, as the lid slid down it revealed a humanoid shape lying inside. The inside of the box was very dark; as of yet, no details could be determined.

From across the clearing came the sounds of the Dyonari, curious as to what the humans were doing with the Temporal Vault, slowly moving closer.

Agrippa ignored them. He was almost in a daze. It was all very surreal to him. He nearly laughed as he visualized the old tomb raiders of ancient times, opening up Egyptian pyramids and burial sites. It was absurd, of course; this wasn't Egypt and he was no archaeologist. And yet here he was, about to be face-to-face with—a mummy?

The lid had nearly moved halfway down now, and the body inside was revealed to be entirely human. Human, and not decomposed at all. The skin was dark, the hair black and long. The eyes were closed, but as he gazed upon the face— a relatively youthful face—he was taken with the sense that those eyes could open at any moment.

And then they did.

Half the men and women of the III Legion Bravo Squad nearly jumped right out of their combat armor.

Agrippa fought to control his suddenly flaring emotions. A part of him found that puzzling; certainly this was disturbing and unexpected in a way, but he had always prided himself on his resolute determination in the face of the strangest things the galaxy had to throw at him. To be so spooked by a body in a tomb—albeit one that had just, apparently, come back to life—was on many levels embarrassing to him.

"What is happening?" came the voice of Merrin, the Dyonari commander, both telepathically and aloud. It was very near; the aliens had crossed the clearing and were almost on top of them now.

Agrippa prepared to make another denial but then saw that it was too late. The Dyonari commander was right behind him and could see exactly what was happening.

"You have opened it," the alien nearly gasped. "Why have you done this?"

"We didn't do anything," Agrippa snapped back. "It happened by itself."

"By itself?" Merrin appeared wrong-footed by that bit of information. He recovered quickly. "But that can only mean…"

"What?" Agrippa demanded, turning to look at the tall alien. "It's time for answers, Commander. What exactly is this thing—and who is that?" He pointed at the seemingly human body that lay inside, unmoving, eyes now wide open but staring unseeingly straight up. "And what did you want with him? Because, I would point out now, the fact that the person inside this thing is a *human* gives me a bit more legal jurisdiction over this tomb, and him, than I had a few seconds ago.

The alien commander said nothing for several seconds. His eyes darted from those of the general to Torgon's and back again. At last he moved his head from side to side in what was possibly the Dyonari equivalent of a shrug. "You have been honest with me—somewhat—General," Merrin said. "I am now obligated to return the favor." He nodded toward the tomb and its strange, apparently comatose inhabitant. "This Temporal Vault, and the being inside of it, were spoken of to my people by our greatest seers. The Vault and its inhabitant are supposed to represent the best hope of saving the entire galaxy from an approaching threat of incalculable magnitude."

Agrippa listened to this, the wheels in his head turning. "So," he said at length, "you and yours are here to try to save the galaxy, just as we were brought here to do."

"That is so," Merrin replied.

"Then we should work together."

"Agreed," Merrin said, nodding. "That would seem best."

Satisfied at least for the moment, Agrippa turned back to the tomb and the figure within it. He leaned over the edge and gazed down. The man was relatively young in appearance; somewhere in his thirties, probably. His eyes were dark and his lips were full and he was very clearly breathing, if very shallowly.

"Faraday," Agrippa called, motioning for his medic to approach. "Take a look at this…person…and see if you can determine what's wrong with him and—"

At that moment the man in the tomb gasped loudly and sat straight up.

Agrippa involuntarily moved back a half-step, then gave the medic a quick glance. "Never mind," he said.

The dark man in the tomb looked around almost frantically, taking in the faces of the armored men and women who were staring down at him.

"Where—*when*—am I?" he asked, clearly very confused.

"Tough one to answer," Agrippa said as he reached out and steadied the man with one gloved hand. "We're not entirely sure ourselves."

Hearing that, the man's expression grew even more frantic. "Why was I awakened here and now, then?" he asked, glaring at the general. "Why have you brought me here?"

"Brought you here? We did no such thing. In case you don't know it, you're inside a casket of some kind. That's not our doing. You were here when we arrived."

"Actually, General," the scanner corporal interjected at that point, "he may be telling the truth. When we came here, I would've sworn to you this casket was empty. And I definitely saw readings that indicated something was approaching... approaching from the *inside* of the box."

Agrippa glared at the corporal. "So you're saying he wasn't here before, and something we did caused him to *come* here—both in space and in time?"

The corporal appeared to consider how ridiculous that sounded. Then he shrugged and nodded. "I believe so, General."

Agrippa made a sour expression before turning back to the man who sat in the big gray casket. "Does any of this make sense to you?" he asked. "Did you travel here from elsewhere—or from some other moment in time?"

The man nodded slowly. "I believe so..." He brought a hand up and rubbed at his eyes. "It is...difficult to think..."

Agrippa's piercing blue eyes regarded the dark-haired man carefully, taking his measure. "You're saying you're a time traveler, then?" He gestured broadly toward the gray box, made of some strange substance that seemed neither stone nor metal yet smooth like both. Within it the man now sat in a shallow recess, very much like a mummy's sarcophagus. "This—this thing is a time machine?"

The man rubbed at his eyes and then returned Agrippa's gaze. "In a manner of speaking, yes," he said. "I ask again—why am I here, and why now?"

"And I say again, I do not know," Agrippa answered. "We did nothing, to my knowledge, to wake you—or to bring you here."

The man pulled himself up higher so that he could better see over the edge and out. Beyond the Kings of Oblivion soldiers that stood in a long arc around that side of the tomb, he could see only the barren ground stretching a short distance away before disappearing beneath the waves of fog. He stared for a moment and then gasped. "The Desolate Stretches," he said. "The lower Above. So." He looked up at Agrippa with eyes now wide, perhaps in surprise. "It returns to me. I have come to the place I saw before." He brightened. "All is as it should be. The time has come at last."

Agrippa frowned at this. "I'm sorry," he said, "but I don't understand—"

The man had started to turn the other way. As he did, he saw Commander Merrin and his alien troops approaching, and his scream cut Agrippa off in mid-sentence. Frantically he began to scramble to pull himself out of the tomb.

"No—no," Agrippa attempted to reassure him. "They are friends. They are—"

"They are Dyonari," the man growled, eyes fierce now.

"Yes, but—"

"Kill them," he shouted. "For the sake of all existence— kill them all! *Kill them all!*"

5

grippa, to his credit as a wise leader and for many reasons, did not immediately follow the strange man's counsel and order the Kings of Oblivion to open fire on the Dyonari. But he did take note of the sharp rise in tensions among his troops as they heard the man's strident cries. At the same time he saw the Dyonari halt and gaze warily at the man. Instinctively Agrippa knew that they all teetered on the edge of a disaster. He also understood that the game had just changed again, and again he cursed the fact that he was the senior officer present, charged with making sense of it all and handling it. Quickly he raised both hands and gestured for all present to calm down.

"Torgon," he said to the major to his left, "help this man out of there."

As Torgon and one of his other troopers moved forward and assisted the man in climbing up and out of the gray tomb, Agrippa glanced in the direction of the Dyonari. Commander Merrin and his officers were standing only a short distance away, unmoving, taking no actions provocative or otherwise. It was likely they were conversing mentally among themselves. He waited a moment, then called aloud, "Commander. Would you object to me taking a few moments to converse with this man and attempt to come to some greater understanding of our situation?" He nodded toward the open tomb. "We will not tamper with this..." He searched for the perfect word and couldn't find it, so he said, "...This sarcophagus."

The Dyonari leader appeared to consider this for a moment, then nodded once. Within Agrippa's mind, he heard the words, "That is acceptable. But please hurry. Our mission presses upon us."

"Thank you." Agrippa nodded back to the alien, then moved closer to the strange man. The man had removed some sort of cloak from the tomb and now had it draped over his shoulders, covering all but his head and neck. "Let's start with this," Agrippa said in a quiet tone. "Who are you?"

The man still appeared agitated; he kept glancing over at the Dyonari as if deeply suspicious of them. "I will tell you," he said at last, "though you will not believe me."

"Let me decide that."

The dark-skinned man chuckled at that. "I am Solonis," he said.

Agrippa blinked, processing what the man had said. He started to reply, then hesitated. Next to him, Torgon simply laughed. Agrippa shot the major a look that shut him up quickly.

"You did say I wouldn't believe you," Agrippa pointed out. He was peering at the man closely.

"Yes." The man looked back at him, dark eyes meeting blue ones, both sets unflinching. "And yet, you do."

Agrippa's frown deepened. "I do?" He snorted; it could've been a derisive snort, but it also could have been an ironic laugh.

"Yes. I sense it. I see it, plainly. You are not so much the simple warrior as you would have others believe."

Agrippa smiled flatly at that. "I would scarcely be General of the III Legion if I was."

"Yes." The man now scrutinized Agrippa carefully. "It is possible," he said, "that you are part of the vision—part of what I have witnessed." He brought one dark hand up to his forehead and closed his eyes, as if in pain. "It is so unclear now. It was all perfectly obvious to me when I departed to come here."

"Departed? Departed where?"

"Where? Here, of course."

Agrippa scowled. "You departed *here*...to come *here*?"

The man laughed. "The question is *when*, not where."

Agrippa pursed his lips, then looked back at the gray box. "Temporal Vault. Ah."

The man raised his dark eyebrows at that, then shrugged. "As good a name as any, for what is essentially a time machine."

"That's what they called it," the general said, nodding toward the aliens.

Looking over at them, the man bristled again. "Dyonari," he muttered. "Here. Now. It cannot be an accident."

"What is your issue with them?"

"I have seen what they will do," he snapped. "I remember it clearly. I—" He halted in mid-sentence and frowned. "I—I did remember it. But now, it seems to be slipping away." He shook his head angrily. "I must not forget. I must not! Everything—everything—depends upon stopping... stopping..." He looked at the Dyonari again. "Stopping them! From..."

"From what?"

A long silence, and then the man met Agrippa's eyes. "From some great evil. It will come to me…"

The general pointed toward Merrin and his warriors, who stood huddled together about thirty meters away. "But you're certain they are the ones who—"

"Not that group specifically," the man said quickly. "But it is most assuredly Dyonari, and that group is here, now. And so..."

Agrippa exhaled slowly. He thought of what the goddess Aurore had said earlier, when they'd set out on this insane mission: that the Dyonari were about to...what was the word she had used? To *shatter* the galaxy. He started to mention that, but then decided to withhold it for now—at least until he had a clearer understanding of this strange man, and how he fit into the larger situation.

"I can't stop these Dyonari here from doing something terrible if I don't know what that thing is. And if I don't know if these particular Dyonari are the ones who did it. Or are going to do it." Frustratedly he ran a hand through his short blond hair. "I take it, from what you have said, that you believe you have come to us from the future."

"I have," the man replied. He hesitated, then added, "Though I died far back in the past."

Agrippa gave him a look that spoke volumes. "I have no idea what to do with that," he said, "so let us set it aside, at least for now, and stick to pertinent matters."

The man nodded.

"You would have us believe that you are the god Solonis, the seer. And that you have traveled back to this moment from some future point in time."

"That is correct."

"To prevent a tragedy of galactic proportions."

"Yes."

Agrippa nodded at this. "I have no reason to believe anything you say. But then again, I have no reason to doubt you, either. And so here we are."

The man nodded. "Indeed."

Agrippa regarded the man for a moment, pursed his lips, and looked away. A second later he said, "We spoke of Solonis recently, ourselves, as a matter of fact."

The man appeared interested to hear that. "Oh? With whom, may I ask?"

"With a young woman who claimed to be the goddess Aurore."

The man smiled at this. "Ah. Yes. Aurore." He chuckled. "So—it worked." He looked Agrippa and his men over now as if seeing them all for the first time. "She chose you, then?"

Agrippa shrugged. "In a manner of speaking. We struck a deal with her. My team and I were to help her to avert some great catastrophe. But then, after we arrived here..." He shrugged again. "She disappeared. Right before our eyes."

The man who called himself Solonis laughed again. "She performed as I required," he said. "Excellent." He gave Agrippa a sidelong look. "And you believed she was who she claimed to be?"

"She possessed the power to lead us here," Agrippa said by way of answer.

The man nodded thoughtfully. "She performed a miracle, and so she must have been divine. Yes." He chuckled softly. "And yet, I must tell you that she was not in truth the goddess she claimed to be, or believed herself to be."

"What do you mean? How would you know that?"

"Because Aurore died long ago, as did I. The woman you encountered was a kind of ghost—a representation of everything that Aurore was—kept intact by an infusion of the Power, the cosmic energy that makes the gods what they are."

"She was a ghost," Agrippa repeated dubiously. He raised one eyebrow at the man. "And you know this how?"

"Because I created her ghost. I bound it together with the Power. Just as I created this form for myself, so to speak."

Agrippa just looked at him.

"I did tell you, after all," the man said, "that I died long ago."

Agrippa growled in the back of his throat. "I intended that this conversation should make things clearer," he grumbled, "but I fear it is having the opposite effect."

The other man shrugged. "Time travel will do that," he said. "But perhaps—"

What he was about to say would never be known, for at that moment the perimeter scout to Agrippa's left called out, "Contact!"

7

eneral Agrippa grasped the barrel of his quad-rifle and hoisted it up. "What is it?"

"Some sort of vehicle, sir," the scout called from a short distance away. "Very small."

Agrippa leapt atop the gray sarcophagus and peered into the ever-present fog, his cyber-optics working to compensate for the terribly low visibility. He could just make out the shapes of three more Dyonari approaching aboard a transparent, levitating platform that skimmed a few centimeters above the ground. As he looked on, the vehicle came to a halt and the alien in the middle of the trio hopped down on long, slender legs. He wore a slightly more elaborate suit of shimmering, glasslike armor and seemed to be exchanging harsh words—though likely silently, via telepathy, since his mouth didn't move but his posture reflected an aggressive stance—with Merrin, the commander. After a couple of seconds of this, both the newcomer and Merrin turned and began gesturing toward the gray tomb—and toward the humans.

"I don't like this a bit," Agrippa muttered. He hopped down from the tomb and began to stroll in what he hoped was a leisurely manner toward the huddle of aliens. He raised his right hand in what he hoped would be interpreted as a friendly gesture as he approached.

"Hello," he called, smiling. He quickly sized up the new figure and assessed that he was now the ranking Dyonari officer present. "I am Arnem Agrippa," he said, nodding toward that one. "General of the III Legion of the Empire. And you are..?"

The new officer seemed to regard Agrippa as if he were a somewhat annoying insect. "You will move away from the Temporal Vault," came a voice within Agrippa's head—forceful verging on aggressive.

The general's eyebrows knitted together. He raised both hands now, gesturing for this new Dyonari to calm himself. "Hold on, now," he said. "I've reached an agreement with Commander Merrin here, and—"

"Any agreements you struck with the Commander are null and void," the voice shot back.

"But we negotiated in good faith, and came to an equitable—"

"There will be no negotiations, human. Your forces must move away from the Vault immediately."

Agrippa felt himself growing angry. Clearly this new Dyonari—who hadn't even seen fit to introduce himself—was the highest ranking member of the group, and wasn't willing to concede anything. This was the type of Dyonari Agrippa had encountered in the past, before the incident on Eingrad-6: arrogant, enigmatic, and hostile. In a way, it felt reassuring to him; reassuring to know that he hadn't entirely misjudged them up until then.

"All we seek is a way out of here," Agrippa said—but as soon as the words escaped his lips, he realized that they were no longer true. He had come here with his squad on a mission, albeit an ill-defined one. He felt a responsibility to see it through, if possible—particularly if he'd been told the truth: that the safety of the entire galaxy was at stake. He only wished he understood the particulars better. Or at all.

"Your desires are of no interest to me," the new leader snapped, still speaking telepathically. "This is your final warning. Order your warriors away from the Temporal Vault."

"The Vault doesn't belong to me, nor to you," Agrippa replied. "I assume it belongs to the man who came out of it just now."

The leader reacted visibly to this. He turned and stared silently at Merrin; surely a spirited telepathic conversation was underway between the two of them. After a few seconds the leader turned back to Agrippa. "If the being that dwelt inside the Vault has now emerged, he must be handed over to us, as well."

"What? Why?"

The leader ignored Agrippa's questions and strode imperiously away. Merrin remained nearby and his embarrassment was obvious even upon his slender Dyonari features. After a moment he sent to Agrippa a telepathic message: "Our seers informed us that we would likely meet resistance from an alien army while carrying out this mission. And also that we would encounter a being hurled from the time stream. He was to be very important—vital—to our mission, and we were to secure him and preserve him at all costs."

Agrippa glanced back at the dark-complexioned man who had climbed out of the tomb, then nodded to Merrin. "I believe I understand, but—"

"Merrin!" shouted the leader, using not telepathy but actual voice, and proving quite adept at it. "Come!"

Commander Merrin gave Agrippa one last look, disappointment and regret clear on his alien features, before hurrying along after the others. Now standing alone in the center of the space that lay between the two small armies,

Agrippa began to withdraw back to his own side. Even as he moved, he kept his eyes on the Dyonari warriors, watching as at some unspoken order they lined up in what was clearly an attack formation, swords and pistols drawn and ready.

"Major Torgon," Agrippa called as he reached the tomb and leapt up upon it, "ready the men to defend this position."

"Sir." Torgon saluted, now all formality, and barked orders to the troops. Instantly the dozen men and women of the III Legion—the Kings of Oblivion—moved into strategic spots around and atop the tomb.

"Not to question your thinking, of course, General," Torgon whispered to Agrippa as the last of the Kings moved into position, "but are we certain this—whatever it is—" He nodded down at the gray Temporal Vault they stood upon. "—is worth fighting for?"

"I wish I knew the answer to that, Major," Agrippa replied quietly, so that no one else could hear.

"Is there no chance we could persuade this new leader of theirs to simply open a way for us and let us leave?"

Agrippa seemed to consider this for a few quiet seconds. Then, "Perhaps. But circumstances have now changed." He faced Torgon directly, keeping his voice very soft. "I don't fully grasp all of this, no. But what I do know is that we agreed to come here to stop a group of Dyonari from doing something that would potentially destroy the galaxy. This man—" He nodded his head toward the one who called himself Solonis. "—claims he sent the goddess, or whatever she was, who delivered that message. And he claims he came here from the future to help prevent the catastrophe."

"I—think I followed all of that, sir."

Agrippa chuckled. "And so here we are, standing atop the only solid object we have encountered anywhere in this dimension that we were brought to. And right over there—" He gestured toward the aliens across the way. "—are a

62

group of Dyonari. And they want this object, and the man that came from it."

"It does all seem rather connected, doesn't it, sir?"

Agrippa nodded once. "Until I know otherwise—until I get answers that are clear and logical— my priority is to deny those creatures over there anything and everything."

Torgon nodded. "I understand, sir."

Agrippa clapped the major on the back. "What of the others?" he asked a second later. "Should I attempt to explain—"

Torgon was shaking his head and Agrippa trailed off. "No need, sir," the major replied firmly. "They are Bravo Squad. They will do whatever you require of them. Explaining is not necessary."

Agrippa allowed himself a slight smile. "Very well."

There was movement within the fog directly across the open space. "Here they come!" shouted the scout off to their right.

Gleaming glass swords raised high and pistols firing, a wave of Dyonari warriors charged at Agrippa's line.

8

grippa opened up with his quad-rifle, the twin energy-weapon barrels on either side firing an unceasing barrage of blinding and deadly streaks of coherent light and heat into the center of the Dyonari ranks. To his surprise, the aliens didn't immediately go down. When he'd unleashed such firepower upon human enemies, there were rarely more than a couple of seconds to pass before smartcloth outfits melted and even heavy-duty deflector suits gave way. These aliens, though, in their shiny armor made from what looked to the humans like stained glass, absorbed the strikes and kept coming.

For the III Legion's part, he saw to his immense relief, the same was true. The Dyonari pistols fired shimmering violet beams of hard-light, but the Kings of Oblivion in their bulky white and green Deising-Arry combat armor weren't taking massive damage when the blasts struck home. It appeared that in the eternal duel of offensive vs defensive weaponry, they operated this day within a time when defenses were ahead.

That, Agrippa knew, only meant the fighting would soon turn to that oldest, most reliable, and most viscerally brutal of all methods of killing an enemy: hand-to-hand combat, the way humans had done it for so many millennia, back to the Stone Age.

Of course, he also knew, those Stone Age fighters hadn't worn heavy combat armor or carried transparent swords that could slice through almost anything.

As the Dyonari reached the far side of the tomb, the Kings of Oblivion rushed out and crashed into them, surging in a broad wave across the clearing. In engagement after engagement, long, curved sword dueled with short, thick gladius. Shiny, transparent armor crashed against heavy metal and ceramics. The shouts, cries and grunts of humans and aliens locked in mortal combat echoed up from the flat, otherwise lifeless plain.

Snarling at the sight he beheld before him, infuriated at the Dyonari for causing the situation to come to this, he glanced once at Major Torgon—the major's eyes glinted with combat fury—and then crouched, preparing to launch himself off the gray edifice and down into the fray.

Before he could, a voice pierced the foggy air, high and shrill and most definitely not belonging to any of the combatants on either side: "Stop this! Stop this now!"

Agrippa sought out the source of the call; it had come from only a short distance to his left. There, at the far end of the tomb, stood the man claiming to be the god Solonis, the seer. He stood with both hands raised, his dark skin covered only by a sort of brown loincloth lashed about his waist. His fingers were splayed wide in the air and blue lightning danced across them, lighting up the area and driving back the fog.

"You know me! You know who I am, and why I am here! You will cease this madness and take heed!"

As one, the two sides in the battle halted their fighting and stood staring up at him. To his surprise, Agrippa found that he was doing that, as well.

"I have come here, to this time and place, to save the galaxy from utter annihilation," the man said. "If you would help me, help me. And if not..." Blue lightning flashed, blindingly bright now. "If not, I will kill every single one of you and then do it myself."

olonis's display had served two very necessary purposes. It had caused the humans and the Dyonari to stop fighting one another before the situation could progress to the point that only one side's victory and the other's death would settle affairs. It had also persuaded both sides that this man who stood before them was, indeed, the seer-god, Solonis. His wielding of the blue lightning, drawing it from that universal source of cosmic energy called the Power and calling it down to strike between the two blurring lines at the critical moment, had left no room for doubt.

As both sides had stepped back and paid heed to him at last, he had stood atop the Temporal Vault—the tomb-like machine that existed in many places and times at once and that had carried his current body back in time from the far future—and he had told them the story of how he came to this time, this place, and this form.

"I understand now that both of your teams have come here for the same reason I have," Solonis said, his gaze sweeping from the humans who stood to the left of him in front of the tomb to the Dyonari who stood to his right. "We must work together. That must begin with everyone here understanding the full situation... as best it can be understood. We must share our knowledge across both groups."

At the forefront of his group, General Agrippa raised his hand and Solonis nodded toward him.

"Then let us get this out of the way first and foremost, since you would now have us trust and work with the Dyonari," the blond general stated in his booming voice. He looked across the open space to the ranks of alien warriors in their glass-like armor. "When you first awakened and saw them present here, you demanded that my troops kill them."

The Dyonari reacted visibly at this, but none of them moved to start up the violence again. Yet.

Solonis nodded. "I reacted out of instinctive fear," he said, his voice smooth and calm. "I recalled that the Dyonari played some part in the crisis I had come to prevent, but could no longer recall precisely what that part was. At some basic level I feared they were the cause of it. I realize now that I was mistaken—at least with regard to this group."

"You have remembered more than you had earlier, then?" Agrippa asked.

"I have," Solonis replied.

Agrippa met his eyes and could tell instantly that he was not speaking the truth in that regard. He slowly moved his right hand down to the grip of his gladius; Solonis's lie had only served to heighten his sense of being prepared for any eventuality that could occur in the next few moments.

"You now believe you, the humans and we all share a common cause, then?" the unnamed Dyonari leader asked.

"I do. We all seek the preservation of the galaxy." He focused his gaze directly upon the leader. "That is, after all, your goal, is it not?"

The alien did not flinch. "It is," he said.

Solonis smiled back at him; the alien appeared utterly uninterested.

"You said to us that Aurore—the goddess who convinced us to come and who brought us here—was a ghost," Agrippa went on. "And that you were one, as well."

"In a manner of speaking," Solonis said. He paused, touching his dark finger to his lips, then continued, "The goddess Aurore, she of beauty and wisdom and above all stealth, was slain during the Vorthan incident, thousands of years ago. But, like all the gods, some measure of her spirit lingered on. I took a portion of the Power—that cosmic energy that issues from the Fountain of the Golden City and sustains us across the planes of reality—and used it to bring her back, in a manner of speaking. I blew upon the last glowing embers and summoned forth a flame—albeit a tiny one, and one that would burn for only a short time. Then I sent her to you, or rather to whomever she could find at the appointed time and place, to bring back those capable of helping me to fulfill my task. Once that was done, and the last of her reserve of the Power gone, she vanished."

"Indeed she did," Agrippa said, nodding. "Right in front of us." He glanced over at Torgon, who appeared mystified by it all. "Well. A ghost." Agrippa shook his head. "Alright. Then how are *you* a ghost?"

"I, too, died many centuries ago. But one of my godly abilities had always been to detach my spirit from my physical body—to separate what one might call my astral form from my physical form— and send it into the future. This is why I was called the seer-god. I had not only seen the future—I had visited it, repeatedly, in spiritual form, and returned with newfound knowledge of it."

"You sent your soul forward in time?"

"That is one way of putting it, yes." Solonis hesitated, seeming to consider his next words. "During the period when the gods were being murdered, I sought to discover who was doing the killing. I concluded that if I traveled far enough into the future, at some point there would be only one other god left alive in the universe, and he or she would likely be the guilty party. Not an entirely foolproof plan, I concede, but you must understand that things had grown quite desperate—and frantic—at that time. Something had shut off the Fountain in the City and thus the Power had been denied to us for centuries, and around me my fellow gods and goddesses were disappearing; I later learned the reason for that, but it is of no matter to the point I am making now. In any case, at long last the Power returned and I took that opportunity to dispatch my astral form far into the future."

"You left your body behind in your original time, but your spirit traveled forward, yes?" Agrippa asked, clarifying his understanding.

"Indeed," Solonis said. "And, as I moved forward in time, I began to notice something extremely curious and disturbing. There were..." He paused, looking down, seemingly struggling to find the right words to express the concepts in his mind. "There were waves radiating backward in time from some future point. Shockwaves. Cracks, if you will, in the fabric of spacetime and reality. Spiraling outward from some future event, traveling back even as I traveled forward. I realized then that those waves had been there all along, for all the time that I had been moving. In other words, they continued back in time to before the moment that I had left my body behind. To what point in history before that they were proceeding, I did not know, and still do not. Perhaps they reach back to the origins of the universe; I cannot say. In any case, I kept going forward, into the future, now following them like lines on a map, seeking the point of their origin, leaping greater and greater distances in time. They were always there, coming back to me and continuing on behind me, moving into the past as I moved into the future. It was most peculiar; like traveling upstream against a flowing river."

"Cracks in the fabric of time and space," Agrippa grumbled. He looked over at the aliens standing a short distance away. "That doesn't sound to me like something even the Dyonari could have caused."

"No," said Commander Merrin.

Agrippa looked back at Solonis. "Continue," he said.

The dark-skinned, young-seeming god-man appeared momentarily angered by the general's brusque order, but set it aside and spoke again. "My leaps carried me farther even than I anticipated; they carried me onward, beyond this time where we currently exist. But then, after I passed this current time and continued forward, I discovered something unexpected: the shockwaves in spacetime were now moving *forward*, alongside me, into the future."

Agrippa blinked his eyes, processing this point. "*Forward* now?"

"Yes. So I continued to move into the future. The waves continued to move along with me. It was like hearing the echoes from an explosion that had never actually happened; or as if I had been tracing ripples in a pond radiating one way, and now I was finding them radiating in the other direction—but with no pebble striking the water in between. All spiraling ripples, no splash."

"I...think I follow," Agrippa said. "The point in time where you should have found your metaphorical 'splash' was..."

"It was now," the Dyonari commander interjected. "Whatever caused the shockwaves in both directions, the epicenter of it was our time, right here, right now."

Solonis nodded. "And that is why I came back, using this body and the Temporal Vault, to this time. To find that splash, that explosion—which must be here and now, somewhere and somehow, but hidden—and to prevent it."

"Why prevent it?" Agrippa asked. "It sounds as if, strange as it is, it has done no actual harm."

Solonis made a sound that Agrippa realized was a humorless laugh. "Oh, it did harm," he said. "Or rather, it will. In the future. For I have yet to tell you what I found at the farthest reaches of my journey forward."

Agrippa felt his stomach sinking. He remembered what the Aurore-ghost had told him. "A shattering," he said.

Solonis looked at him, then nodded once. "Just so. A shattering." He gazed out at the two audiences and seeing that both sets of soldiers were listening now with rapt attention. "At the extremity of my leaps into the future, I discovered something of utterly profound importance. Not the identity of the murderer of the gods, as I had originally hoped to find, but something infinitely worse: that the entire galaxy had been obliterated."

At that, Solonis stopped speaking and the silence hung there; both groups of soldiers, human and alien, moved about uncomfortably and glanced at one another.

"Obliterated," Agrippa repeated.

"Almost completely destroyed," Solonis said. "Stars blown out; solar systems engulfed by novas; arms of the galactic spiral cataclysmically disrupted. Of the empires of Man or any other race, no traces remained. Only a very few huddled survivors on the remains of their shattered worlds."

"And you believe it resulted from this 'shockwave' in spacetime? Then what caused the wave?" Agrippa demanded.

"And how can we prevent it?" the Dyonari commander added.

Solonis's gaze moved from the alien ranks to the humans. He shook his head. "The cause? That is something I have been attempting to understand all along, with no success," he said. "And the prevention? That," he concluded sadly, "I have never, ever known."

10

A goddess opened the way for them, and they emerged into a scene straight out of Hell.

As the lady Teluria ripped the fabric of spacetime asunder and ushered a unit of I Legion soldiers through, their commander, General Marcus Ezekial Tamerlane, blazed the trail—literally.

Summoning the cosmic flame that was his to command, Tamerlane gestured with one hand and then the other, directing the flow, unleashing waves of fire at the enemy.

And what an enemy they faced in these ravenous, slavering hordes of alien creatures from beyond the Milky Way galaxy. Vicious, chitin-covered Skrazzi in numbers beyond counting, each of them brandishing its razor-sharp cutting claw and its genetically engineered disintegrator-gun arm. Horrific, nightmare-inducing Phaedrons that somehow seemed to command the Skrazzi as foot soldiers while projecting waves of psychic fear ahead of them. Both working together in the service of some higher—or *lower*— power, with the clear objective of scouring all native sentient life from the galaxy.

Their unholy mission had brought them here, to Tolkar, an industrial world renowned throughout the Empire for its tremendous production capabilities. The factories and foundries of Tolkar supplied weapons, ammunition, armor and equipment for all of the legions and planetary defense forces. Cyclopean cranes, lifters and smokestacks towered over a bare, concrete-and-steel landscape as smoke belched from uncountable blast furnaces.

But the orbital defenses had been breached, and the planetary defense forces were falling back in disarray. The world was gripped by chaos. As the blood-red comets of the enemy rained down upon the surface, breaking open to disgorge vicious enemy troops by the thousands, the people of Tolkar ran from their factories, abandoned their posts, and fled in terror.

Into that situation stepped the men and women of the I Legion—the Lords of Fire—horribly outnumbered but determined not to give in. Determined to resist the enemy to the bitter end. They emerged from the cosmic portal and onto a broad gray concrete plain, weapons at the ready, and opened fire immediately. Finding something to shoot at was not a problem. It was easy—all too easy. The enemy was everywhere.

As the I Legion troopers followed Colonel Niobe Arani and Major Titus Elaro, fanning out and opening fire, Teluria kept close to Tamerlane. She allowed the portal she had brought them all through to close, but both she and Tamerlane knew she could open it again—and reestablish the pathway back to the *Ascanius*, the Legion's flagship—at a moment's notice.

"Why do you persist in these futile efforts?" she asked Tamerlane as she stood just behind him, gazing out at the hordes of alien creatures. "You know by now that your cause is hopeless. Your empire cannot be saved. Nor any of the worlds beyond it. Why not simply flee? Take all that you have and quit this galaxy? Why have me bring you and your soldiers directly into the midst of these—these *monsters*?"

"We have to try," Tamerlane shouted over the insane din of noise from the battle. "We can't just give up, give in, and welcome death."

Teluria scowled at this. "I will continue to assist you for a short while longer, General," she said. "But my time in this realm is drawing to a close, and the Golden City, for all its flaws, seems far more appealing now."

"Leave whenever you please," Tamerlane replied, not looking back at her. He was far too busy sending columns of flame into the ranks of attacking Skrazzi. "I have never attempted to compel you to help us." Now he did look back, for an instant. "Not like Iapetus," he added.

"Iapetus." She spat the name. "He is one of the reasons I continue to help you. For all the contempt I feel for your little empire, it is as nothing compared to the loathing I carry for that man. To think of him somehow winning this war and emerging at the top afterward..." She grunted. "No. That must not happen."

"I see now how foolish I was," Tamerlane told her as he shifted to the right and blasted a formation of attackers. Around him, the armored soldiers of the unit were firing away with their energy rifles and pistols. A couple even carried the An-Ro quad-rifles so favored by General Agrippa and his III Legion.

"What do you mean?" Teluria asked.

"I wasted all that time, while Nakamura was ill, doing virtually nothing. Just hoping that he would recover. And practically begging Iapetus to get more involved—to get involved at all!—in the war against our neighboring empires. He never did, of course, and meanwhile I and III Legions were ground down to almost nothing." He issued a quick order via the Aether link and then shifted position again, flinging fireballs, helping to soften up the Skrazzi positions. "So now the bloody-handed Sons of Terra control the

Princess, the homeworld and the core Inner Worlds, while my legion and Agrippa's are reduced to raids like this one, nibbling at the edges of the enemy's advance."

"Yes," Teluria said. "You fight and die, and he sits back on Earth and reaps the benefits of your great labors and sacrifices, and does nothing."

Tamerlane gritted his teeth at that. "I can at least take solace in the fact that he will soon have much to do. We cannot hold out for long—the hordes of the enemy will overrun the Inner Worlds within weeks, if not days."

A trio of slavering Skrazzi emerged from the smoke behind Tamerlane and raced at his back, their deadly dagger-arms raised to impale him. Seeing them, Teluria summoned up a ball of lightning and flung it at the center of their formation. The explosion got Tamerlane's attention better than any shouted alarm would have, and by the time he whirled about to face the attackers he saw that they were writhing on the ground, tendrils of electricity playing over them. He nodded his thanks to the goddess, and she actually gave him a half-smile in return. Then he incinerated them.

"You see?" he asked, looking back at her briefly. "You're a better person than you believe. You enjoy fighting alongside my legion, helping us."

Teluria snorted. "Hardly." As she flung another ball of lightning, she looked at him sidelong. "I will admit I somewhat misjudged you before," she said. "I thought you a typically weak, sniveling human. But now I can see that you are more than that. You have a certain nobility, General— not to mention your command of the flame. You might have made a decent god. Perhaps you are someone's secret bastard offspring? Vashtaar, perhaps? He was quite handy with fire."

Tamerlane ignored this and kept blasting with his flames.

"Of course, I merely obeyed Goraddon in those days. I did not think for myself nearly as much as I should have."

Her voice dropped from its usual imperial haughtiness and she added, "I regret that now."

Tamerlane glanced over at her, surprised to hear her admit such things.

"What?" she demanded, as though offended by his look.

He laughed. "In the weeks you've worked with us, I've never heard you say such things."

"Oh?" She shrugged offhandedly. "Perhaps I am grown melancholy, here at the death of your galaxy."

"It's your galaxy, too—isn't it?"

She seemed to consider this. "Perhaps it is. If only for a little while longer." She hurled more bolts of lightning and then actually punched a Skrazzi that was attempting to fire its disintegrator-arm at her. The blow, striking as it did the hard insectoid shell of the creature, didn't appear to hurt her hand in the slightest. As it stumbled back, she zapped it with lightning and it fell, dead before it hit the ground.

"Do any of your kind know where you came from?" Tamerlane asked.

"The City," she said, as if it were the silliest question ever asked.

"Yes—but before that. You seem human in appearance. All of you. Could you once have been... *us*?"

Teluria pursed her lips as a lull appeared in the fighting. The Lords of Fire drew back, reloading their weapons and wiping sweat and soot and blood and alien gore from their faces and hands. "I understand that the origin of my kind is a question your kind has asked itself for millennia," she said at length. "But for my part—for *our* part—we care nothing for the answer." She stopped and looked directly at him. "We are, General. *We are*. And that is enough."

Tamerlane nodded at this. What else could he do?

"General!"

The cry from Colonel Arani, standing off to his left, brought him back to the current predicament. He took in the situation instantly: the Skrazzi were rallying and charging.

Titus Elaro carried an An-Ro quad-rifle with his right arm, the weight and recoil of the thing savage but the damage it wrought upon the enemy extremely satisfying. For the life of him, though, he couldn't imagine how General Agrippa lugged one of the things around with him everywhere he went.

"Over there," shouted Colonel Arani. She pointed toward a cluster of Skrazzi rushing at them.

Elaro swung the big weapon around and opened fire with the particle-beam cannon. The blast of coherent light sliced out, cutting the insect-like aliens down where they stood. The few survivors from that group charged, this time brandishing the disintegrator guns built into their arms. Elaro noted that the Skrazzi probably would enjoy much greater success in their conflicts with Man if they relied more on those disintegrators and less on their stabbing blade arms. The horrific creatures, however, seemed predisposed to leading with their blade-arms. They relished close-quarters combat and had recourse to their distance weapon arms only, it appeared, as a last resort. That was something Elaro was quite pleased about.

"I'm glad you found one of those in the *Ascanius's* arsenal," Arani said as they turned to face the next charge. "It's making a difference."

"I was surprised the Kings of Oblivion hadn't acquired all of them," Elaro replied. As he opened fire again, this time with the energy-blast barrel—he was keeping the projectiles in reserve, since they were in relatively short supply—he glanced at Arani out of the corner of his eye. "Are we okay?" he asked.

"Okay?" Arani shot him a look of incredulity. "We're facing an army of giant bug-aliens with ray guns built into their arms. How is any of this okay?"

"I mean *us*. You and me."

She did a double-take at him. "You're asking me about that *now*?"

Elaro shrugged. "Hey—as you said, we're facing a giant army of bug creatures. I might not get another chance to ask—I might be dead in five minutes."

Arani gave him a sour look. "Oh, please." She carried a blast pistol in each hand and now she opened up with both of them, driving an attacking Skrazzi back. "Let's focus on what matters, huh?"

"That *does* matter," Elaro said, his voice low enough that only she could hear him. "I know you still think I'm some kind of double-agent, working an angle on behalf of Iapetus and the Sons, but—"

"Yes?" she said, cutting him off. "You're going to tell me that isn't true?"

"It isn't any longer," he said. He pointed down to the new, dark red uniform he wore. "I was a member of II Legion from the time I enlisted in the Imperial military academy, but that wasn't my choice. They chose me. I'm a member of the Lords of Fire now. General Tamerlane gave me the opportunity to pick where I wanted to place my loyalties, and I respect and admire that about him. So I've changed sides—permanently."

"Mmm hmm," she said, still firing both pistols into the enemy formations.

"You don't believe in redemption?" he asked.

She shot him a look. "I believe in actions," she said. "Everything else is just talk."

He considered this and then nodded. "Okay. I understand. I have to show you, and so I will."

"You can—" she started to say, but then a Skrazzi leapt in, flying over the top of the one that had stood in front of it. Before she could fire, the creature lashed out with its stabbing arm, the needle-tipped point driving toward her chest.

And then she was being flung out of the way.

Rolling to a stop, she popped onto her feet and looked back toward Alaro. He was engaged in a sort of wrestling match with the big bug. It had its gun-arm off to one side, holding down his quad-rifle, while its stabbing arm raised high and aimed for his heart.

The shots took the Skrazzi's head off cleanly at the shoulders. The body kept fighting for another long second and then slumped to the ground even as Elaro struggled to get clear of it. He gasped for breath and looked up, seeing Arani standing there, her two pistols smoking. He blinked, then grinned at her. "Thanks for that," he said.

She shrugged. "I'd hate for one of those things to kill you," she said.

"There's that, anyway."

She gave him a half-smile. "That's *my* job."

Elaro frowned at this, not sure how to take it. Before he could speak, however, a sheet of ice formed beneath his feet and he nearly fell.

Ice. He looked down at it, then up at a now wide-eyed Arani. They both turned to Tamerlane where he and the goddess stood, a short distance away, battling the aliens. They said the name at the same time:

"Phaedrons."

11

The Phadrons—three of them, their bizarre beetle-forms swathed in fluttering black rags and their silver skull-faces leering—advanced from the rear ranks of the enemy army.

No one had yet discovered precisely what manner of beings the Phaedrons were. None of their bodies had been recovered from any battle; either they had yet to be killed in a conflict, or else they recovered their fallen comrades' corpses very efficiently during and after a conflict. Or perhaps they simply dissolved to nothingness. In any case, the only information anyone in the Empire had on them was what little could be observed visually during the briefest of moments between a human spotting one and then turning and fleeing in terror.

For ahead of the Phaedrons, always, spread wave upon wave of raw fear.

It was utterly irrational, of course; the Phaedrons had yet to demonstrate any actions in battle to justify the terror they engendered. It was purely a telepathic effect, mentally projected by them as their primary weapon. And it was devastatingly effective.

"General," Titus Elaro called to Tamerlane, "I'm thinking we really need to be getting out of here."

Colonel Arani started to criticize Elaro for his sudden cowardice, but found she couldn't—for, to her, nothing now seemed more important than fleeing this battlefield, and with all possible haste. A part of her brain kept trying to tell the rest of it that this was not a rational set of thoughts—that the weird aliens were making her think this—but the rest of her brain was increasingly disinterested in that line of thinking. It simply screamed at her, "*Go!*"

Tamerlane meanwhile found himself giving ground, moving backwards, one step at a time. As he became aware of this, he frowned in confusion; he hadn't consciously made the decision to retreat, yet his body was doing exactly that. He looked to the others and saw many of them doing the same. Such was the telepathic power of the Phaedrons—and particularly an unholy *trinity* of them, such as they faced now.

"Teluria!" he called loudly, only to see that she was right behind him. He opened his mouth to speak to her, and found himself wrestling between two different things he wanted to say. His original thought had been to ask her if she had any way of combatting their psychic powers. When he started to speak the words, however, he found them coming out as, "Open a portal and get us out of here!"

Teluria raised her hand to begin the process, but Tamerlane stopped her. "Wait," he said, and she looked back at him, surprised and expectant. By sheer force of will he managed to convey his intended message, to which she shrugged and then shook her head.

Tamerlane cursed. His troops were in full retreat now, the broad arc of advance they had carved into the Skrazzi ranks collapsing, the objective they had been aiming for now utterly lost. The Phaedrons had turned the tide of the battle and it was pointless to deny it. He started to re-issue the order to open a portal and escape when he was abruptly knocked to the ground, his head smacking the concrete and sending stars and comets through his vision. He recovered his senses a second later, only to see Teluria lying nearby, also dazed, about to be attacked by a Skrazzi. He rolled over to her and shoved her out of the way, then raised his hand just as the insectoid attacker lunged. Flames leapt out and engulfed the creature—but it kept coming, now a moving, blazing apparition of death. He redoubled his efforts and sheathed the creature in blast-furnace fire; in nova-flame. It stumbled forward, crumbling to ashes as it moved. He leapt to his feet as the last charred remnants of it hit the ground directly in front of him.

Teluria was up as well, and was trying to say something to him, but he couldn't hear her over the din. Elaro and Arani reached them then, having fought their way across the short distance that had separated them. They formed a little triangle around Teluria and blasted away at the attacking horde, as Tamerlane issued the emergency retreat order via the Aether link.

For long moments they held out, the Skrazzi now all around them. A dozen more legionaries made it to their location and expanded the defensive formation, but Tamerlane was realizing now that he had lost a great many of his troops in only the last few seconds. He concluded that his desire to abandon this battlefield was not entirely an artificial idea placed in his head by the Phaedrons, but also a genuine tactical evaluation of their current situation. As soldiers on either side of him fired into the swarm, he took a moment to close his eyes and access the full Aether mental display. On it, glowing dots of color represented each of the troopers under his command in the local theater of action. Soldiers no longer among the living were marked by a gray X. He could see many gray Xs but only a few red dots, and all of the dots were clustered around his current position.

Everyone who was able to retreat, then, had retreated. Now all that remained was to escape.

"Teluria!" he shouted. "Time to go! Open a portal for us!"

Looking back at him wild-eyed, she shook her head. "I cannot! We are surrounded—there is nowhere for me to—"

"Alright," he barked back. He looked around at the others of I Legion, firing desperately into the rapidly-constricting ring of alien fighters about to engulf them. "Down," he shouted, while simultaneously sending the message across the Aether. "Everyone down!"

Puzzled, the soldiers all obeyed their general and crouched down low. They continued to fire as best they could.

"You too," he yelled at Teluria.

"What?"

He reached out, grasped her shoulder, and pushed her into a crouch, over her strenuous objections. Then he raised back up, now the only one standing in the circle, and lifted both arms out to his sides, perpendicular to his body.

The Skrazzi roared their fury and launched themselves at the circle of kneeling humans.

Tamerlane closed his eyes, turned slowly, and unleashed the full power of his flame blast.

Like the effects of a detonating warhead, the ring of fire ignited just beyond where his soldiers knelt and spread rapidly in every direction, washing over all of the Skrazzi.

Tamerlane gritted his teeth and poured it on, not letting up for an instant. He visualized a sea of charred and broken alien bodies and he opened his eyes and made that happen.

At last he ran out of energy and, with a gasp, he dropped to a knee himself.

Elaro and Arani were up then, supporting him on either side. Sweat dripped from his brow and he could barely see, his head swimming as though he'd just run three marathons. As he came back to himself and looked up, he beheld the exact sight he'd imagined: all around them lay the burned-out husks of the Skrazzi horde. Of the Phaedrons there was no sign whatsoever. He pulled away from the two officers and stood there, staring out at what he had wrought.

"That was amazing, General," Elaro told him, grinning. "You took them all out!"

Tamerlane attempted to reply but all he could manage was a series of painful coughs. He started to slump down again but Elaro caught him and lowered him gently to a clean portion of the concrete. He sat there, coughing for another minute, as the others fanned out, weapons at the ready in case any more enemy elements should appear.

"No sign of enemy activity, General," one of the legionaries reported in.

Tamerlane acknowledged this via the Aether, then used the same method to address the others. His throat felt too raw to speak. "Mark this facility as liberated, Colonel." He winced. "One down, a million to go."

"A victory is a victory, sir," Arani replied, before turning away to send word back to the *Ascanius*. With luck, a I Legion battle cruiser would be somewhere in the neighborhood and would now be able to secure the manufactures of Tolkar without massive loss of life and expenditure of munitions in the process.

"If you can do that a few dozen more times, General," Elaro was saying, "we have a real chance in this war."

Tamerlane shook his head. "I can't," he croaked. "I probably shouldn't have done it at all." Speaking was too painful; he switched back to the Aether. "I probably won't have the power back again for a day or more. And," he added, "let's be honest. It would be a few hundred more times. Or a few thousand."

Elaro appeared crestfallen. He nodded his acknowledgement of the general's more accurate estimate.

"Organize the troops, Colonel," Tamerlane sent to Arani. "Time to get out of here." He allowed Elaro to help him back to his feet, then turned to the lady Teluria. She appeared shaken—something extremely unusual for her.

"Very impressive, General," she said. "I doubt Vashtaar himself could have done better."

"I doubt he'd be this wiped out afterward," Tamerlane replied. He nodded to her. "Time to go."

Teluria raised her right hand and exerted her will and the fabric of reality obeyed. Spacetime parted and a portal ripped itself open, lights and fog swirling within.

"The *Ascanius* awaits," she said.

Tamerlane motioned for the others to pass into the portal first. When they were all safely through, he and Arani and Elaro stepped into it, followed by Teluria.

He took one last look back before Teluria allowed it to close. His expression was bitter.

"You should be happy," the goddess said to him. "You won a victory today—a victory over a relentless and implacable foe."

He looked at her, then shook his head. "No."

"No?"

"It's too little, too late. The Empire is almost in ruins. Liberating Tolkar will only allow us to resist a little longer."

The opposite end of the portal opened onto the strategium deck of the flagship. The troops emerged, Tamerlane and Teluria coming through last. The goddess gestured and the pathway through dimensions closed.

Arani and Elaro were engaged in an intense conversation and moved off to one side. Meanwhile support staff—who all appeared shocked at the much smaller number of soldiers coming back than had originally gone through—came forward to assist the wounded and help remove armor and weapons. The exhausted soldiers practically collapsed into their arms. The general himself dropped heavily into a dull gray metal chair, Teluria hovering nearby.

After issuing orders to go back and secure Tolkar and retrieve the bodies of the fallen, Tamerlane looked up at

Teluria and nodded toward his wrung-out troops. "You see? And these are the cream of the crop of I Legion." He motioned to her and she leaned in closer, so that he could whisper to her. "We control the manufacturies again," he said, "but what good are more guns and bullets and blasters when we are rapidly running out of soldiers to use them?"

Teluria frowned at this but had nothing to say in reply.

Tamerlane shook his head. "It's no good." He reached up and allowed one of the medics to help him to his feet. As he made his way toward the exit, he looked back at her and caught her eye. "We have to find a better way," he said, "and soon. Before there's no Empire left to save."

BOOK TEN

SNOWFLAKES FALLING

1

Days earlier...

Snowflakes the size of cities floated peacefully in the void. Comets the color of blood knifed toward them, filled with malice and malevolence.

Realization of their impending doom came slowly but with inexorable force to the poor, unfortunate Dyonari who stood on the curving glass bridges and walkways of the outermost snowflake city-ship. Waves of pure psychic force preceded the comets; waves powerful enough to bring the telepathically-sensitive inhabitants to their knees, clutching their heads in agony and numbing fear. Those who could manage to do so looked up despite the pain and stared in awe and in horror at the sight that greeted them. What they saw was, simply put, their doom.

The first of the comets struck the first of the Star-Cities dead-center, with the ballistic force of a Minie-ball impacting a watermelon. The city-ship shattered, flinging glasslike shards outward in a rapidly expanding sphere of debris. Mixed among the broken pieces of the ship hurtled the bodies of untold thousands of Dyonari, most of them never having the opportunity to know what was happening to them, nor even to cry out before the end.

Two more snowflake-cities exploded under the impact of the leading edge of the comets before the Dyonari even began to understand what was happening. Once realization came, however, they gathered their wits and their resources and fought back. A powerfully psychic race, the alien Dyonari quickly worked to combine their telepathic powers to form a wall of sheer force that surrounded the formation and deflected the next few comets away.

The sinister intelligence that drove the comets on was not about to allow itself to be denied a victory so easily, however. The creatures that dwelt deep within the comets gathered their own massive psychic powers together and pushed back, forming an invisible wedge, forcing the second wave of comets through the Dyonari barrier.

Slowed by their difficult passage through the barrier, this second wave crashed into the surviving snowflake city-ships like bowling balls, penetrating but not obliterating the fragile psychic atmospheric bubbles that surrounded them and held in their atmospheres. Still wreaking incalculable destruction as they struck, these comets tumbled across open spaces and gouged out jagged troughs in the outer surfaces before lodging themselves into buildings and walkways.

As the last of the comets came to a halt on the surfaces of the last few of the snowflake-cities, the terrified Dyonari inhabitants began to emerge from their homes and places of refuge to inspect the damage and to look upon these strange attackers. They allowed themselves to believe that perhaps they had won, or at least survived with the loss of only a handful of their majestic city-ships.

They were very wrong.

Even as they tentatively ventured out into the streets and began to congregate around the still-glowing red comets where they rested, half-buried in the glasslike material of the cities, fresh waves of fear emanated from the strange objects. Crying out, the Dyonari stumbled backward, each of them driven in an instant almost into a frenzy. Meanwhile layers of ice formed in expanding concentric rings all around the crash sites as the temperature plunged.

Dyonari soldiers—impossibly tall and slender warriors in translucent glass armor of many different colors—moved through the retreating crowds and forced themselves to advance on the glowing red objects. Their long, curved swords in hand, the soldiers peered at the comets in wonder. It appeared the objects were composed of ice, each of them some twenty to thirty meters in diameter and radiating a baleful red glow. The ice itself was dark and impossible to see very far into.

"Advance with caution," called the commander of the forces on the innermost Star-City, called by its inhabitants Dalen-Shala. "Be prepared for anything."

"They are merely projectiles, are they not, Commander Siklar?" asked the Dyonari soldier to the leader's right.

"Perhaps. But how would that account for the psychic power we yet feel emanating from them?"

The soldier considered this and said nothing.

Just ahead, the first two warriors reached the comet and began to prod it carefully with the tips of their curved swords.

"Where are the seers?" Commander Siklar demanded of anyone within hearing distance. "We must have more information before we can safely proceed." He became aware then of the warriors poking the comet with their swords and sent a powerful telepathic order for them to desist. Chagrined, the two backed away, still holding their weapons at the ready.

In truth, Siklar acknowledged internally, it was miraculous that his soldiers were holding up as well as they were. The level of pure psychic energy—most of it very negative, very malignant, very hateful—that radiated from this comet, and presumably from all the others, was almost enough to send him running away, gibbering mindlessly all the while. Only by sheerest force of will were any of them managing to behave in a reasonable, professional manner. That was a credit to his troops and to himself for having trained them in both physical and mental discipline.

A message brushed his mind, coming from behind him. He turned even as he heard the words within his mind: "The seers have arrived, Commander."

Siklar looked into the crowd of terrified citizens crowded just behind him. They were Dyonari whose curiosity about the strange attackers just barely managed to overcome their fear and caution, bringing them out here in the street to look. He wished they would leave—would go home and seek refuge until he had the situation better in hand—but for now he could only ignore them. He had other matters with which to attend besides crowd control at the moment.

As he looked on, the crowd parted and two elderly Dyonari moved into view. Each leaned heavily upon a long, slim staff and each walked very slowly and deliberately.

"Seers," he said, addressing them without preamble. "What do you sense?" he asked each immediately and in turn, ignoring the traditional protocol of working one's way slowly to the point of the conversation. There was simply no time.

The nearer of the two seers gave him a look of annoyance at the impertinence but the other, perhaps comprehending the urgency of the matter, caught the eye of the first and waved the slight away. "There is great and continuing danger here," the old Dyonari intoned. "There is an intelligence within each of these objects, and it lingers still."

"An intelligence?" Commander Siklar frowned at the elderly seer and then turned back to gaze at the rough, glowing sphere of ice. "I myself can sense...*something*...inside, but—"

"More than one," the other seer interjected sharply. "Several points of intelligence within each. Restless, furtive, and filled with hatred."

94

"This is so," the first seer agreed, nodding his long, slender head. "Five of our cities have been utterly destroyed in the time since the attack began, and all I can sense within this ball of ice is a desire—an overwhelming desire—to destroy still more."

"Hatred," the second seer said. "Pure hatred."

Siklar blinked and shook his head in incomprehension. "Who, or what, *are* they?" he asked. "Why do they hate us so?"

"I believe," the first seer said a few seconds later, "it is not specifically *us* they hate. It is all life in general."

"Nihilists?" Siklar instinctively gripped his sword more tightly.

"And they are not done with us yet," the second seer added, his eyes entirely white and glowing now as he reached out with his psychic power to touch the comet. "Not at all. They—" He gasped suddenly and fell backwards; one of the soldiers rushed forward and caught him, supporting him as he moaned softly.

The first seer looked at Siklar and now a sense of surprise and fear radiated from him. Siklar's mouth twisted in disgust at what he was seeing and sensing. He turned to his officers. "That's it," he called. "I want this...*thing*...and all the others like it off our city-ships now. Now!"

Uncertain but obedient, the soldiers acknowledged his order and started forward. Even as they moved, however, a new wave of fear washed out, striking like ripples in a pond caused by the impact of a very large rock at the center. Those waves struck the surrounding Dyonari with full force, driving the civilians back and causing even the advancing warriors to pause.

"It is opening," the first seer cried, pointing. "They are emerging!"

Siklar gaped as a crack formed down the side of the huge ball of ice, widening rapidly. "Weapons at the ready," he called, both mentally and verbally. He used his voice because of the enormous psychic feedback now washing over all of them; he doubted anyone had heard his telepathic order.

Baleful red light spilled out from the crack in the ice. Awful shapes drenched in shadow moved within it.

"Weapons!" he cried again, this time only with his physical voice. No one could have heard a mental order, he knew. He could scarcely hear himself think at the moment, so great was the psychic interference from the things inside the comet.

And then they emerged.

Siklar stumbled back a few steps in shock. He couldn't help it. None present could have stood resolute in the face of the menace revealing itself at that moment, and none did.

The first to emerge was a bizarre figure all of black, with an insect-like head and limbs, seemingly covered in a chitinous exoskeleton. It gazed out at the Dyonari with multiple glowing red eyes and it raised each of its two forelimbs in a threatening gesture; one was in the form of a long, curving, sharply pointed blade, while the other took the shape of a long, narrow cylinder. Siklar had little time to ponder the purpose of the second limb. As soon as the creature raised it and pointed it, a low hum filled the air and the Dyonari directly ahead of it began to cry out and stumble away. Siklar rushed to the warrior's aid, but it was already too late. The soldier's glass armor had shattered within the first two seconds and now fell away in shards, even as blood gouted from his mouth and eyes.

"Beware!" cried Siklar. "The round limb is a gun of some kind—a *disintegrator*."

Another Dyonari warrior leaped to the attack, his long sword swinging around in a confident arc. The blow was blocked however by a lightning-fast counter by the insectoid, moving its blade-limb up to parry. As the surprised Dyonari stood motionless for the merest instant, the creature lashed out with its cylinder-arm, using it as a club, knocking the warrior aside. As the Dyonari leapt to his feet once more, the insectoid's blade-limb stabbed out, skewering him, slicing upwards, eviscerating him in one smooth stroke.

The other Dyonari looked at one in horror and disbelief.

Siklar repressed the need to vomit. He drew his own pistol, aimed and fired. The shot did no apparent damage. "Fall back," he shouted to the others, firing again. "Fall back!"

Soldiers took the arms of the two seers and attempted to hustle them away from the area of danger, but the first seer resisted for a moment. He caught the commander's attention and said in barely above a whisper, "I can read their thoughts, rudimentary and primitive as they are. They are known as the Skrazzi. And they are not from our galaxy."

"Not from this galaxy?" Siklar blinked as he absorbed this information. "Why are they here?" he asked.

"As we first believed," the seer replied, his eyes wide and his expression one of horror verging on surrender. "To kill. Simply to kill."

Siklar shook his head slowly. "Why? Why *do* such a thing? What—?"

"What of it?" the elderly Dyonari asked by way of answer. "Is it not enough that they wish to slay us all—and that they have come here, now, to do so?"

Siklar started to reply but found that he had nothing to say. He turned back toward the big chunk of ice, surveying the scene. The soldiers ahead of him were crying out and backing away, some dragging the bodies of their fallen comrades along with them as they came. No one was firing back at the invader. The situation was getting very rapidly out of hand.

"Stand firm," he called out. "Defend the city!"

It was not immediately clear if anyone heard him, or cared.

Now more of the black insectoids were emerging from the ice. Three more joined the first, and together they advanced on the crowd and the soldiers, all of whom had already been psychically driven to near-hysteria by the combination of the waves radiating from the comet and from what they had just witnessed. The hum of the Skrazzi disintegrator-arms sounded in chorus, followed immediately by the cries of the victims—some of them soldiers, some the last of the civilians who had not yet fled.

"We may yet stop them if we rally and fight together as one!" Siklar shouted. Even as the words escaped his thin lips, however, he knew no one would take heed. Terror was upon them now, and they sought only to flee—even his finest soldiers. He understood. It was all he could do not to join them in headlong flight. All that kept him standing there, a rock in the stream of retreating Dyonari, was the fact that enough of his rational mind remained that he could form the thought, "Flee to *where*?"

Siklar turned back to the warriors who were serving as escorts to the seers. The first seer appeared shaken but resolute; the second seer yet remained in a semi-conscious state. "Get them out of here," he ordered. "Get them to safety. Somewhere."

"Safety?" one of the soldiers blurted, seemingly shocked by the very concept. He wilted under Siklar's reproving gaze and nodded once—"Yes, Commander!"—then moved to help the two elderly Dyonari retreat from what had become a battlefield. Or a killing ground.

Is it over already? Siklar wondered. *Have we fallen so easily? Are we finished as a people?* He gritted his teeth and fought to keep his wits about him. His eyes moved from the four black insect-creatures to the still-widening crack in the ice behind them. Something more was happening there. Something else was stirring. Dark shapes, hideous and horrific—somehow far worse even than the insectoid Skrazzi.

"You sense them, do you not?" came the mental words of the first seer, even as he and his still-silent counterpart were being led away by the guards. "You sense the masters, within the ice, only now making their presence known, now that victory is at hand."

Siklar nodded, pointlessly. "Yes." His mental voice was flat now, as flat and hopeless as his spirits. He knew that he was only a moment away from death. But he was determined to stand firm, and to die face to face and toe to toe with these insidious invaders. If nothing else, it would mean that at least one Dyonari died facing his enemy and not running away from it.

"They are the Phaedrons," the seer told him. "They are worse than anything we have ever encountered."

"You know this how?"

"They no longer guard their thoughts," the seer explained. "They sense inevitable victory."

"They are correct, are they not?"

A pause, and then the seer responded, "Yes."

Siklar nodded. It was over. All of it, over. He could see that clearly now. His people, his civilization, was one of the oldest and greatest in the galaxy; it had endured for millions of years and reached heights of success undreamed of by almost any other race. It traveled across the slowly-spinning swirl of the Milky Way in vast snowflake-like city-ships and observed all there was to see, learned all there was to know. And now, at the hands of a foe from beyond that galaxy, it had reached its end at last.

"Phaedrons," he repeated, tasting the name, sensing its inherent wrongness, feeling the malice that dwelt within the sound itself. "These Skrazzi are but footsoldiers for them, aren't they?"

"Yes," the first seer agreed. "The Phaedrons are a curse upon the universe. A virus. I fear there can be no stopping them. Ever."

"They hate our people so?"

"They hate all life. I sense it even now. A new wave of these comets, sweeping all across the galaxy. Our people will scarcely be the only ones to fall in the days to come."

Siklar absorbed this with grim resignation. "The only ones that matter," he said.

Ahead of him, the four Skrazzi insectoids had spread out, pushing forward, slaughtering the insensate Dyonari, most of whom had by now been rendered insane by the raw psychic energy that washed over them. Behind them, having fully emerged from the crack in the ice, shambled two massive figures apparently draped in black. It hurt to look upon them, but Siklar forced himself. Their faces were gleaming silver metal, formed in the shape of alien skulls. Glowing red eyes peered out and surveyed their handiwork. Slender claws twitched from under the black covering, grasping at nothing. Something within Siklar's deepest intellect snapped upon gazing at them and he began to lose his nerve at last. He backed away, his sword still raised, fear now overcoming him.

"Commander!" came a shout within his mind. "Listen to me!"

Siklar regained his senses and understood that he had given way to madness for a few seconds. His eyes had grown wild and his intellect had slipped beneath the surface. Only the telepathic cry—he realized immediately that it had been the mental voice of the *second* seer—had been able to snap him back to reality, if only for the moment. "Yes?" he responded, in some ways angry at being called back to rationality. "Yes, elder? You have come back to us?"

"I have recovered sufficiently to warn you. You must fall back. You must—"

"Why?" Siklar scowled at the oncoming Skrazzi. "Why not go down fighting—with honor?"

"Because there is something you must do," the second seer replied, urgency powerful within his telepathic "voice." "Something critically important."

"What?" Siklar meant only to humor the old Dyonari; to go along with his mad ravings until the alien attackers reached him and he was given one last opportunity to test his curving blade against their hard black shells. "What could possibly be so important now, here at the end of all things?"

"You must help me to save the galaxy."

Siklar had no idea what to say to that. He watched as the nearest Skrazzi struck down another Dyonari warrior and then took notice of him.

"Do you hear me, Commander?"

"Yes, I hear you, elder. But I do not understand."

"I have dared to read their thoughts—to venture inside the minds of the Phaedrons. I have learned great and terrible things. And I have seen the future they bring with them."

"You—you went inside their minds—?"

"I did, though it nearly destroyed me," the elder replied, and for the first time Siklar could sense just how weak and frail his mental voice had become. "For now, you must gather up what remains of your warriors and meet me at the starport deck."

"But—"

"You *must*," the first seer interjected. "He is sharing his vision with me now. I understand. All of existence is at stake."

Frustrated but ever the obedient soldier, Siklar agreed. Yet even as he broke the mental connection to the elders, the Skrazzi nearest him rushed forward, blade-limb up and swinging round. Siklar reacted with all the instinct, skill and ability afforded him by centuries of training. He brought his sword up, blocking the blow, then kicked out at the midsection of the invader. The kick did little or no damage but did send the Skrazzi stumbling back a step. Clearly infuriated by the resistance Siklar was offering, the Skrazzi chose to mindlessly charge forward again rather than to utilize its disintegrator weapon—and this time it ran itself directly onto Siklar's sword, impaling itself.

The Commander managed to pull his blade free by the hardest, only to see that the Skrazzi was not dead—not by any means. It lay on its side but was already struggling to rise. From beyond it, a fresh wave of fear emanated from the Phaedrons, threatening to hurl Siklar back into the depths of insanity. He resisted, turned tail, and sprinted away, shouting for any surviving warriors to join him.

Arriving some moments later at the relative safety of the starport deck, Siklar looked all around. He had gathered up some two dozen of the surviving Dyonari soldiers—clearly the most mentally resilient they had to offer, given that these had not yet yielded to the insanity pushed upon them by the Phaedron invaders—and brought them along with him. To his left, he spotted the elderly seers being all-but-carried along by two more troopers. One of the old Dyonari had been wounded, he saw; blood pooled around his left side, despite the field dressing his escorts had made for him.

"Quickly," the second seer said to them, now using his spoken voice. "We have little time, and I may well be dead soon." He ordered for the escorts to lay him down on the surface, and the others gathered in a circle around him. The blood continued to run. "I have much to share with you," he said, "so clear your thoughts—as difficult as that might be at this moment—and prepare yourselves."

The others moved in closer around the seer and he managed a slight smile as he gazed up at them. Then he sent forth a telepathic wave that nearly knocked them all off their feet.

Z

ou hear me, do you not, Commander?

"I—yes, I do," Siklar managed to answer. He understood instantly that he was speaking telepathically, and doing so with the seer. "You have information for us?"

For you, Commander. The others are receiving a general set of thoughts and images concerning our foes—as will you— but this conversation is for you alone. The others will not understand. They will have to be manipulated. *Are you up for that task?*

"Manipulated?" Siklar hesitated. "What do you mean?" And then, "Seer—do we have time for this? Shouldn't we be moving along?"

The entirety of this conversation is happening within the space between two heartbeats. We have more than enough time.

Siklar digested this. "Very well," he said. "What would you have of me?"

I would have you understand the full breadth of your mission. It is such that you may have to carry its secret

VAN ALLEN PLEXICO

alone, your fellow warriors kept from the full knowledge until the end.

"And what is the full breadth of my mission?"

See.

-FLASH-

Siklar staggered. Had he been interacting with the seer in the physical world instead of purely on the psychic plane, he likely would have fallen down. Instead he quickly sorted his thoughts and recovered. As he did so, the full magnitude of the seer's vision unfolded itself before his inner eyes.

"By the cities and the stars," Siklar whispered. And, "Must I do this?"

You must.

"But—"

There is no other choice. It is your duty, entrusted to you alone.

"I—" He started to object again, but found his resistance crumbling. Slowly but surely he found himself acquiescing to the seer's plan. "Very well," he said. "It will be done."

I would have your absolute dedication in the mission.

"You have it."

You understand what must be done?

Within his mind, Siklar felt repulsed, but he agreed. "Yes, I understand." He hesitated. "There is something more?"

The means. The manner in which you can carry out your mission.

"Yes?"

When the time comes to do what you must do, you will need sufficient power, and a way to channel it properly.

Siklar took this in. "Yes, I understand. But I cannot imagine where in all the galaxy such power could be found—"

It cannot be found in our galaxy.

"What? But then—?"

Not even in this universe.

Siklar thought about this for a moment and understanding dawned upon him. As it did so, he beheld within his mind's eye a towering geyser of sparkling energies.

"Ah," he said. "There."

Indeed.

"But—surely that cannot be possible. How could we ever—"

I will show you. There is a way.

Siklar was surprised to hear that. "Very well—but once those energies are released, how to harness them? How to channel them in the manner you desire? Not even the greatest engineering accomplishments of our people could—"

There is a way. There is a device, a machine, older even than our people. It links all the stars together—though for a different purpose than that which we intend.

Siklar absorbed this. A device older than the Dyonari themselves? It was hard for him to imagine—even with new images appearing in his mental vision, showing a great metal tower alone in a fog-enshrouded field. "Where do I find this ancient construct?"

It exists on many worlds, but I know of one in a remote sector that should be open to you and your warriors, and relatively simple to break into and bend to our needs.

Another compressed message entered Siklar's mind, coming from that of the seer, this time containing images and coordinates along with other details of this objective.

Siklar's head was spinning. "I—yes, I believe I understand now," he said to the voice of the seer.

Good. Any last questions?

Siklar considered. His head was pounding and he could feel a sickness in his stomach, despite the fact that all of this had transpired within less than two seconds of time in the real world.

"Seer, are you absolutely certain this is the only way? If I am to do this thing, I must believe it is the only viable option."

It is.

Mentally, Siklar nodded to the seer and to himself. "Very well," he said. "I will do what must be done. No matter the cost."

But, he thought to himself as the mental connection dissolved and reality returned around him, *such cost....*

3

Siklar recovered first. He helped the warrior next to him back onto his feet, then looked at the seer. The elder's eyes were closed and he did not appear to be breathing.

"Is he—?"

"He is dead," the first seer said. "But most of what he was, who he was, has passed to me." The old Dyonari tapped the side of his head. "He dwells here now, and I fully understand what he saw and what he requires of you and your forces. What we all require of you." He paused and then raised his right hand; it was very long and appeared very frail and delicate. "Understand," he whispered, and unlocked the message in all of their minds.

For several seconds no one spoke, as the enormity of the seer's telepathic words—a long message, compressed into a single second's transmission—unfolded and took hold in their consciousnesses. They all closed their eyes involuntarily and allowed it to spool out, in words and images.

Siklar had already seen it. He waited, gazing at the others, waiting. "You all received his message, yes?" he asked when they had all opened their eyes again. "You saw his vision?"

The others—twenty-six in all—answered in the affirmative. One of them across the circle added, "But I do not understand."

Others made sounds of agreement with this.

"Ours is not to understand implicitly," Siklar replied. "Ours is to obey. But," he added, "what I do understand, and understand quite clearly now, is the magnitude of the danger the galaxy faces." He nodded down at the seer. "He saw it very clearly—saw who these aliens are, and what they intend. He saw what will result if they are allowed to succeed. He saw all of it—past, present and future—and he has shared it with us. Who among us yet harbors doubts?"

No one spoke up. They all returned Siklar's gaze evenly, their expressions grim.

Siklar nodded. "Very well. Each of us knows what he or she must do, and where he or she must go. There is no alternative now but to succeed."

The others drew their swords simultaneously and held them high. One of their number led them in a sacred pledge. Then they sheathed their swords as Siklar looked upon them with appreciation and respect.

"There is nothing more for us here," he told them. He turned to two female officers who waited nearby, and they quickly stood at attention. "Mirana," he said to one. "Madalena," the other. "You will be co-commanders of one phase of our mission. Your orders have already been implanted. Take four warriors of your choosing and go."

The two saluted Siklar and chose the nearest four Dyonari, who then moved around behind them, at the ready.

"Now—let us take our leave, and quickly," Siklar said. He raised his right hand and concentrated, but nothing happened.

"Commander?" asked one of the warriors to his left. "What is the matter?"

108

"I—do not know," Siklar replied, strain evident in his voice. "I cannot open a way..."

"The Phaedrons are blocking the path," came the weak sound of the seer, lying at the center of their circle. His eyes were barely open—mere slits—and his color was pale. "They do not intend that any of us escape the scene of the slaughter."

"What can we do?" Siklar asked, reeling, sensing defeat closing in again. "Is there no way? No hope?"

"There is one," the seer responded. He started to pull himself up.

Siklar moved forward quickly. "Do not strain yourself, elder," he said. "Lie back."

"Now is not the time to lie back and wait to die, Commander," the elderly seer responded. "Now is the time for action!"

Siklar marveled at the old seer's resolve and inner strength. He reminded himself that the elder supposedly now carried another of equal power within himself, and for the briefest moment he wondered if that had been the first he had absorbed. Who knew how many ancient Dyonari had merged their essences with this one, over the years? Shaking his head at the thought—*I'm just a warrior, thank the stars*—he helped the seer to his feet and supported him. "You said there was one hope. What is it?"

"The Phaedrons believe they have cut us off from the rest of the multiverse. They think we are cornered and ripe for the slaughter. They are almost—*almost*—correct."

The old seer raised his staff high overhead and the upper end of it, decorated with swirls of iridescent color, shimmered and took on an otherworldly glow.

"But," he continued, "they did not count on one of our number being as strong as I am—nor on my willingness to give my all to break through their barrier."

Siklar blinked at this, understanding only too late. "Give your all? Wait—do you mean—?"

The seer raised the staff even higher and cried out, his voice strengthening just long enough to cause the sound to echo across the area. Then it trailed off and his body slumped to the deck. His staff, however, did not fall. It hung there, floating in midair, light now pouring from it, becoming almost blinding. A flash, and then the light disappeared.

In its place stood a swirling round rip in the fabric of reality. Bizarre colors and clouds of smoke and fog billowed within it.

Siklar hesitated for only an instant. Then he barked out sharply at the others, "Now! Through the portal! The elder gave the last of his life-force to provide us this escape, and we shall not squander it!" He all but shoved the nearest trooper toward it. "Go!"

The twenty-six warriors dashed through the gateway and vanished. A second later, only the commander and the elder remained behind. Siklar knelt down, checking the life signs of the seer. As he had suspected—as he had known—the elder was dead. A wave of sadness, magnified by the psychic attack of the enemy, washed over him, but by now he had grown quite accomplished at ignoring such things. It was why he was still alive, and why he was about to escape this slaughterhouse.

Nodding in respect and appreciation to the body of the seer, Siklar turned and ran through the portal. An instant later it snapped closed and vanished, leaving no traces behind of the warriors who had passed through it, or of where they had gone. All that remained was the lifeless body of the elder Dyonari, staring through sightless eyes up at the heavens.

For thousands of miles all around him, the comets rained down and the great snowflake-cities burned.

4

A short time after the portal had closed, the two seemingly dead Dyonari seers blinked their eyes and sat up. They looked at the devastation all around them, then at one another.

"Did it work?" the second seer asked. "Did they believe?"

"They are convinced we are dead," the first seer replied. "That we have given our lives in the cause we have dispatched them to fight for."

"Excellent," said the second seer. "Then all goes according to plan." He smiled. "I have always found that nothing motivates the young and already-dedicated like a little death thrown into the mix."

The first seer nodded. He rose and helped the other up.

"Now," the second seer said, "let us go and convince these invaders that they have succeeded in killing us all, that they might take their leave while we still have a Star-City upon which to dwell."

"We can only hope we are as persuasive with them as we were with our own warriors," the other added.

"We will be," said the second seer. "Their minds are as weak in their way as are those of our own warriors."

The first seer agreed, then added, "For all their weakness, we must hope our warriors succeed—or else that they die. For if they return, having failed, and find us *alive*…"

"They will not fail," the second seer stated with conviction.

"I agree," the first seer said. "But if they do…"

The second seer mentally shrugged. "Then they will not live long enough to challenge our plans."

5

With a swirl of color and light, the very substance of spacetime collapsed inward and formed a circular portal leading out of one layer of the Above and into another. Through that gate walked six tall, slender figures clad in what appeared to be armor made all of multicolored glass. They carried firearms as exotic as themselves, and behind them they pulled a floating palate loaded high with more strange equipment. They stopped just clear of the portal and looked around, taking in their surroundings, then continued on.

They were Dyonari warriors, and they had just emerged onto the Road.

Never had mortals of their own volition penetrated this far into the above. This little group of Dyonari knew this. They understood it implicitly. Longtime travelers in the pathways of the lower Above, the Dyonari in almost their entirety as a people knew their way around the dimensions immediately adjacent to their own. But none of them had ever come all the way to the far end of the Road.

"Keep moving," one of their co-leaders—the taller of the two, by a hair— sent via their telepathic link. "We cannot slow or stop now. The dangers are far too great, and our time is short. And the High Commander chose us for this portion of the mission because he had the utmost faith in us—and we will not disappoint him!"

"They understand that, Madalena," the other, slightly shorter co-leader stated, weariness plain in her telepathic voice. "There is no need to harass them."

"If I feel the need to urge them on, Mirana," the first leader replied, "I will not hesitate to do so."

Mirana groaned inwardly at this but made no retort that anyone could detect.

They marched along the Road, their equipment following along behind them. Their objective loomed in the distance, still more than a few kilometers away.

"It would have been much better if we could have emerged onto the Road closer to our goal," Mirana noted.

"Certainly it would have," Madalena replied. "It would also have been preferable for the High Commander to place me in sole command of this mission. Unfortunately, he did not; he saddled me with you. Similarly, your lamentation regarding our location is a waste of the mental effort it took to project it to the rest of us. For it is impossible to emerge into this region of the Above any closer to our objective. It is impossible even for the gods, much less for us."

"I am aware of that," Mirana grumbled. "My point, however, stands. It would have been preferable."

Madalena merely shot her an annoyed look, while resting her left arm on the white leather-looking satchel she wore over her shoulder. The others pointedly ignored their repartee, as they had done for the duration of the mission already.

How long that mission had gone on was a matter of some dispute.

LEGION III: KINGS OF OBLIVION

The entire team had set out together from the low Above under the orders of their High Commander what seemed like only a short time ago. But time flowed differently at every level of the Above and the Below, not to mention in the real world they had left behind even before that. They had no real way of knowing exactly how much time had passed for the rest of their little army, back where they had started out. In truth, it scarcely mattered. They had a job to do, and they intended to do it—regardless of how long they would ultimately be gone, or if they ever had the opportunity to return.

"How was the High Commander able to open a pathway for us all the way to the Road?" Mirana asked.

"Even if I knew," Madalena replied, "I might not tell you."

"Why not?" Mirana asked, her voice sounding almost hurt.

"Because such information is not relevant to our mission," the taller Dyonari said.

"That does not preclude me from seeking to obtain it," the shorter one replied.

Madalena did not answer that and the two continued on in silence for some time, the other four and the stack of equipment following along silently in their wake.

They passed into a forest of low, deciduous trees and the temperature dropped. A small creek ran just alongside the Road now. The path they walked was firm and smooth, as though worn down by many feet over many years. The sky, they noted just before the foliage blocked most of it out, was orange.

The warriors kept their guns at the ready and their eyes trained to either side, looking for trouble. For a long while, they didn't find any, and they grew slightly complacent.

"I believe we may have been quite lucky in drawing this detail," Mirana said after a long stretch of silence.

"Just so long as trouble doesn't find—"

A horn sounded in the distance, very faint.

The two Dyonari leaders exchanged nervous glances. They raised their energy rifles and also drew their favored weapons—their long, curved, gleaming swords, seemingly made of glass but much stronger. The four warriors behind them did likewise, and together the six of them formed a circle, facing outwards in a defensive formation, weapons at the ready. They waited like that for a very long minute, and had nearly concluded the horn sound had not represented a threat to them, when it came again—and much closer.

"There," Mirana cried, pointing toward an opening in the dense foliage a few meters further along the Road and to their left. "Something is coming!"

In a flash, it was out of the woods and almost upon them. The six Dyonari tensed, ready to fight for their mission and for their lives. Then they saw what had emerged and they merely stared, their dark eyes wide.

It appeared to be a human, a male, mounted upon a horse. He had long, straight, dark hair and wore what looked like scaled mail armor painted white. A hunting horn hung on a chain about his neck. The animal he rode was jet black, like a figure straight out of nightmare.

Mirana kept her eyes firmly upon the horse and rider as she whispered to her co-commander, "What in the name of the sun and the stars do you make of that?"

"I—I cannot say," Madalena replied. "But if he is a god, our mission may be over before it has scarcely begun."

The rider drew near, and the little group reformed so that all but one of them was facing toward him; the sixth Dyonari kept watch to their rear.

The man stared down at them, possibly even more startled to lay eyes on them than they were to see him. He spoke then, saying something in a language they didn't recognize.

"I will seek to acquire his language from him," Madalena whispered. She closed her eyes and reached out with her mind, attempting to carefully enter the horseman's mind.

The man recoiled, nearly falling from his horse. He flashed a look of extreme anger and barked something in his own language. Madalena, meanwhile, stumbled backwards and into the warrior who was standing rear guard. The two barely avoided crashing to the ground.

Mirana, fearing their operation was collapsing even as she watched, addressed the horseman. "Sir," she called, "do you come from the City?" She nodded toward the massive wall and the gleaming towers visible at the far end of the Road.

The man regarded her with what appeared to be scarcely-contained rage. Then—saying nothing all the while—he reared the horse back, wheeled it around, and spurred it forward. Horse and rider disappeared into the woods.

"What did you make of that?" Mirana said to no one in particular, once he was gone.

"I have no point of reference from which to draw a conclusion," Madalena said, dusting off her glass armor and silk-like cloth clothing. "But I did note that he did not ride toward the City."

"Then perhaps they do not know we are coming," Mirana said. "Perhaps we can continue the mission."

Madalena looked at her. "Mirana. If there is anyone in the City—even one single god—our mission will be over the moment we go inside. And we will likely spend the rest of our lives locked in the dungeons."

Mirana considered this, then nodded. "So," she said, turning toward the gleaming citadel in the distance, "onward, then!"

Madalena reacted with a touch of surprise at this. She inhaled deeply and exhaled, then nodded. "Yes. Onward!"

Together, the six Dyonari turned and continued to march toward the Golden City of the gods.

Behind them, a horn sounded again. And then another, from a slightly different direction. And then a third.

They glanced at one another, then walked faster.

Horsemen had emerged from the woods and harassed them on four occasions since they had first met the man in scaled white mail. Each had been different, with different armor and a different color of horse. Each time, they had managed to drive the horseman away. To their great disappointment, they had confirmed very quickly that their technology no longer worked; their energy rifles and other gadgets had become fancy paperweights. But they always had their swords, and the mastery of them that long hours of practice over centuries of life had provided. Against six long, curved, transparent, razor-sharp blades wielded by high-ranking Dyonari warriors, even a god would have reason to hesitate; whatever the horsemen were, they exhibited little interest in testing their armor or their skills in such a manner.

Thus eventually the six Dyonari arrived at the front entrance to the Golden City of the gods.

"Where is the knob?" Co-Commander Mirana asked as she stared at the massive, golden gates that barred their path.

"The knob?" her comrade, Co-Commander Madalena, asked.

"The knob. The latch. The lever. The button. The *something*, to activate it. To *open* it."

Madalena gazed at her shorter comrade and offered her a very thin smile. "There is no knob," she said. "No knob, no latch, no lever, no... What was the other thing?"

Mirana scrunched her eyebrows and looked away, thinking. "Button," she said at last.

Madalena brightened. "Button. Yes." She shook her head. "No button, either."

"But then—how will we enter?" Mirana stared at the tall gate and towering walls that curved around away from them. "Can we not fly over?"

Madalena half-bowed. "Be my guest."

Mirana eyed her co-commander suspiciously for a second, then dropped into a crouch and mentally activated the antigrav units in her glass-like boots.

Nothing happened.

Madalena, arms crossed and expression conveying the sense of great laughter being barely contained, asked, "Something wrong?"

Mirana reddened. She crouched and waited again. Still nothing happened.

"To answer your earlier question," Madalena said, "it would appear that, *no*, we *cannot* simply fly over."

"How can this be?" Mirana wondered aloud. "Faulty equipment? Sabotage?"

Madalena shook her head. "Ages ago, the gods willed that such technology would not work in their realm. And so it does not."

Mirana considered this, appearing extremely annoyed. Then she looked up again, eyes sparkling. "I know," she said. "We could pole-vault over."

Madalena took this suggestion in, eyes widening. She pondered it for a few seconds before turning back to her comrade. "If your goal is to place me in sole command of this mission," she said, "then by all means, pole-vault away."

Mirana blinked at this, then gazed back up at the wall, towering over them some unguessable height. "You're saying that won't work, either."

"I am."

"Then how did the gods open it?"

Madalena smiled again. She had accessed all the data files available on the subject while they had been en route. "As near as I can tell," she said, "they touched it. And wished."

"What?" Mirana looked at her in surprise and befuddlement.

Madalena merely shrugged.

Mirana walked up to the gate and raised her right hand before her. She pulled the thin glove off and brushed her incredibly long, thin fingers against the cold, gold surface. She closed her eyes.

"It will not work for you," Madalena said.

Mirana opened her eyes and looked up at the gate. It was still closed.

"It did not work for me," she said.

"Indeed."

Mirana consulted the same data file her comrade had. The other Dyonari continued to stand at attention, awaiting further orders.

"The gates will only open at the touch of a god," she said at length.

"Yes," her comrade agreed, exhibiting what she felt was enormous self-restraint. "I thought I had made that quite clear."

Mirana reluctantly nodded her head. "Are we defeated, then? Before we've even begun?"

"Not at all."

Mirana looked up at her. "No? Why not?"

"Because our High Commander anticipated that we would encounter this obstacle," Madalena said, "and took steps to help us overcome it."

"Oh? And that would be—what?"

Madalena removed the white satchel from her shoulder and opened it. A pale light emanated from within. A not-quite-audible ringing sound echoed from every nearby surface.

Puzzled and somewhat disconcerted, Mirana moved closer, trying to look inside.

Madalena reached into the satchel and grasped what it contained. She drew it forth.

Despite their great military discipline, all of the others gathered around and stared at the grisly object Co-Commander Madalena was holding aloft.

"Our great and wise leader knew that we might need a hand," she told the others, "and so he gave us one."

7

o-Commander Madalena stood before the gates of the Golden City of the gods and held aloft a hand. A severed hand. A severed human-looking hand.

The other Dyonari commandos gathered around her and gawked.

"What in the name of the seven realms and the seventeen pathways is THAT?" asked Co-Commander Mirana, eyes wide and nose wrinkled in disgust.

"It is our way inside," Madalena replied smugly.

"That?" Mirana simply shook her head. "How can that possibly be so?

Madalena smiled back at her co-commander. "Allow me to tell you the story," she said, "as it was passed along to me by the seers." And she began:

Thousands of years earlier:

LEGION III: KINGS OF OBLIVION

The battle—if such it could truly be called—was over, and the few remaining gods had been liberated from the threat of Vorthan.

Now, all that remained for the survivors was to gather up the bodies of their fallen brothers and sisters, and dispose of them.

They returned to the Golden City from all across the realms of the multiverse. Many of them had not set foot within its walls in centuries, if not millennia. Others had only recently fled, fearing they would be the next victim of the mysterious murderer of the gods. But now, heeding the call of Karilyne, among others—she of the silver and black, the sword and the axe, the grim demeanor and the well-earned respect of nearly all her fellow gods—they had come. If only to pay their respects to the last of the fallen, to see their remains properly tended to, and in some cases to make one last visit to the home of their kind, they had come.

"I never thought to gaze upon this realm again," said Lohandar—he of the red and gold, the dark hair and darker skin, the sparkling green eyes and, until recently, jovial demeanor. He gazed at the bodies, all still clad in the black outfits that had been forced upon them, laid out in a row along the near arc of the central plaza. The geyser-like eruption of the restored Fountain at the center of the square cast a pale light over everything. "Of course, I never dreamed so many of us had met the final end. It is almost inconceivable."

Beside him, Moranna of the white-blonde hair and pale blue eyes nodded slowly. Her diaphanous robes swirled about her, all pale green and aqua. "Scarcely two dozen of us remain, if Karilyne is to be believed," she said.

"And why should I not be believed?" the ice queen asked, her words carrying across the distance from the far side of the square, despite the roaring of the Fountain. "Do you dispute my account of what has befallen us?"

"No—certainly not," Moranna stammered, shocked that she had been overheard. "I simply—"

"What has befallen *us*?" Lohandar interrupted. "My dear Karilyne—nothing has befallen *us*. That is why we are able to be here at all, tending to the bodies of those who *did* have something *befall* them."

The woman in silver and black rose from where she had been inspecting the body of a slain god. Lines of anger marred her usually ultra-reserved features. She strode regally around the perimeter of the square, her dark eyes locked onto those of Lohandar. "We are *all* diminished by the loss of so many of our number," she asserted.

Lohandar made a show of shrugging. "I have lost nothing," he said, "and do not feel diminished in the least."

Karilyne looked to want to punch him. Or worse. Her fingers twitched on the hilt of her axe.

Moranna had quickly stepped out from between them the moment the goddess in silver had approached, but now she raised a hand and interjected, "Please! Both of you! Show some respect for those who have fallen."

"That is precisely what I am attempting to do," Karilyne hissed. She regarded Lohandar with contempt. "If only everyone here felt that way."

"Being *told* how to feel and how to react to events is precisely why I left the City in the first place," Lohandar said.

"And attitudes such as yours are why I never plan to return here," Karilyne retorted.

"That and the fact that Baranak no longer walks the halls of power."

Quick as a flash, Karilyne had her sword out and against the throat of Lohandar. "Think carefully on your next words," she growled, "lest you discover the joys of growing a new body for yourself, from the neck down."

Lohandar glared at her but kept his mouth shut; clearly Karilyne's reputation remained sterling with even the most obstinate of the gods.

After a few seconds Karilyne released him and he stumbled back, coughing and furious but still silent. She gave Moranna a quick glance and seemed to conclude that the slender blonde goddess represented neither threat nor insult. Turning, she stalked back in the direction from which she had come.

"Karilyne," Moranna called suddenly, impulsively. "One question."

Karilyne stopped in her tracks but didn't turn around. "What?" she asked over her shoulder. Her posture made clear the unspoken line, "And it had better be a good one."

"What of Lucian?"

Now Karilyne turned around and peered back at Moranna. "Lucian. *That's* who you're curious about?"

"I had assumed he would be thrown into the dungeon—or the Fountain—at the conclusion of events."

The lady in silver and black shrugged. "Circumstances merited a different outcome."

"So he has walked away free?"

Karilyne considered this question for a moment, then said, "In a manner of speaking. Not entirely."

"Was he not the architect of this catastrophe?"

She looked at Moranna quizzically. "You said *one* question."

"My apologies. Do you not wish to answer that one?"

"I will answer. He was not."

Moranna appeared to be considering this. "So he did nothing wrong, then, after all?"

Lohandar turned to her, hands on hips. "Did you not hear Karilyne's words?" he asked crossly, clearly trying now to curry favor with the ice queen. The mark on his throat still shone red. "She said Lucian is innocent."

"I have never described Lucian as *innocent* in any way," Karilyne said quickly. "He was not, however, responsible for this particular set of events." She looked away. "That does not, of course, mean that I approve of him, his past actions, or—most probably—anything he is likely to do in the future. And that is yet another reason why I am taking my leave of this place." She looked the two of them up and down, contempt clear upon her face. "Now—if you will allow me to get back to work. The sooner we are done here, the sooner I can take my leave."

As Karilyne stalked away, a frowning Moranna turned back to Lohandar. "I had another question," she said, clearly disappointed.

"What is it?" the other god asked, apparently still in a helpful mood after his brush with the ice queen.

She gestured toward the row of bodies. "Should we remove the black clothing from them? It seems rather disrespectful to send them to their eternal rest in...*these* outfits."

Lohandar shook his head.

"The Fountain will do it, now that they are dead and gone. Now that the crystal that held their lives is lost." He stepped forward, raised his right hand toward the towering column of raw energy and gestured very faintly. In response, a tentacle-like tendril separated from it and reached out, shimmering and churning, to brush against the nearest of the dead. A flash, and all the black uniforms that covered the dead gods of the nearest row vanished. Moranna looked and saw what the Power of the Fountain had wrought—the traditional clothing of the dead had been restored—and she was pleased.

But then she noticed something. A dull red metal chain circled the right wrist of the nearest god. It did not remotely match his outfit and other accessories. Curious, she looked from him to the goddess to his left. Same thing. Same chain, same color. Frowning now, she began to walk along the arc of the plaza, looking down at the right wrist of each god and goddess. They all wore it.

"What are you doing?" Lohandar asked, hurrying up behind her.

She pointed out to him what she had discovered.

He seemed to be thinking about it for a minute. Then, "Likely some additional form of control put in place by the evil one."

"I agree." She knelt beside the nearest goddess, grasped the chain and tugged at it. When it failed to slide off, and after further attempts that all proved fruitless, she looked back up at Lohandar, perplexed. "It won't come off," she said simply.

"We have to get them off," Lohandar said. "They are just as much the mark of the evil one as were the black uniforms."

"I agree. But what can we do? Ask Karilyne—or one of the others?"

"No, no," Lohandar said hurriedly, almost frantically. "I have had quite enough of prevailing upon and otherwise disturbing the ice queen today."

"Then how—?"

Lohandar ran a hand over his narrow chin and thought for a moment. Then he nodded off to his right, in the direction of a row of temples and other buildings, most of which Moranna had never entered and knew nothing about. "In the nearest one there," he said, "our late Vorthan kept certain elements of his work. Perhaps...?"

"Why not?"

Moranna gestured and the nearest body floated up from the smooth pavement of the plaza. She began to walk in the direction of the building Lohandar had indicated, and the body followed along obediently behind her.

"Do you want me to come along?" Lohandar asked.

"No—stay here. Look busy. If Karilyne sees both of us missing, she might come looking." Moranna grinned. "If I can find a way to remove these things before she even realizes they exist, perhaps we can impress her— get back in her good graces."

"We have never been in her good graces to begin with," Lohandar pointed out. But Moranna and already turned and was leading the floating body off towards the building. Shrugging, Lohandar also turned and strolled casually back to the rows of the dead.

8

Moranna entered Vorthan's little workshop carefully, timidly, filled with trepidation. She first stuck her head in partway, looking around. It was dark and dusty. She half-expected some leftover guardian conjured by the god of toil to pounce upon her. When, in fact, nothing happened, she was relieved but also quite surprised.

She walked the rest of the way in, her aqua dress muted by the almost oppressive darkness, then gestured to summon the floating body in behind her. The room contained three large work tables, two of which were covered with strange instruments that, upon the slightest inspection, chilled her blood. The third was clear, and she directed the body up onto it. Once that was done, she began to look around for tools that could be of some use.

One after another, she lifted the instruments, held them aloft, and tried to discern how to activate them—and what they were for. Fifteen or twenty minutes passed with no success, until at last she picked up a small cylinder, all of silver and gold, with a jewel fitted into one end. She held aloft and tapped a stud of green crystal on the side. Instantly a swirling disc of many-colored light, about ten inches in diameter, formed at the end that held the jewel.

Moranna didn't move it first. She knew the stories of the potency of Vorthan's instruments. Holding this tool very carefully in her right hand, she moved her eyes across the work surface before her and located a small gray box made of some sort of dull metal. She brought the instrument she was holding down and moved the swirling circle of light against the side of the box. There was a flash and she jumped back, shocked, then stared down in amazement: The box had been sheared completely in half.

"Ah, yes," she whispered, grinning down at the tool she held. She touched the stud again, deactivating the blade. Then she turned and walked back over to the body.

For the first time she actually looked at the face of the dead goddess, and realize with a start that she recognized her. This was Dorvala, she of the moon and the tides. With the black uniform having been removed, she now wore a blue-gray dress that had once washed all about her in slow rhythm but now hung limp and lifeless as its wearer.

Moranna felt a pang of grief for the goddess's fate, but she set it aside and got to work.

Leaning over the body, she reactivated the swirling light-blade and touched its edge ever so delicately to the iron chain. A second later, she moved it away.

Nothing had happened. The metal of the chain appeared absolutely unscathed.

Anger swelled within Moranna. She did not like to be denied anything, but in this case she honestly believed she had discovered something important—something that the others would be pleased with her for finding. Refusing to be denied her victory by this stubborn chain, she brought the light-blade down again, harder this time. As she did so, she lost her balance and fell forward, across Dorvala's body. The cylindrical metal instrument she held thacked against the tabletop, and there came a soft thud from below and to her left.

Climbing off the body and regaining her feet, Moranna gazed down at the object that had made the strange noise as it had hit the floor. It was Dorvala's hand. The blade had sheared it off at the wrist. There was no blood; the gods were driven forward by the Power of the Fountain, of course, not by primitive circulatory fluid. For some reason, the image passed through her mind of the hand beginning to crawl of its own accord across the floor. But it did not. It merely lay there, motionless, almost appearing to greet her.

For a few moments, Moranna merely gawked at what she had done, and panic swelled within her. Then her wits slowly returned. She thought quickly, frantically. Reaching down, she grasped the iron chain that still encircled Dorvala's wrist and tugged at it. It slipped easily off of the goddess's stump. She held it up, frowned at it, and stashed away in a pocket of her robes. She could worry about it later. Returning her gaze to the hand where it lay on the floor, a new idea began to form within her mind. The panic receded. Almost in spite of herself, she began to smile.

ou are certain the message was genuine?" asked High Seer Korvu. "It is possible that—"

"Of course I am certain," replied Second Seer Esron impatiently. "I would not have called you here if—

"Calm yourself, Esron," the High Seer snapped. "Do not address me with such impudence."

A pause. Then, "My apologies, High Seer. But I believe the message was both genuine and urgent."

"Very well." The High Seer raised both hands in the traditional method of those of his vocation. "We shall know soon enough, I suppose."

The two seers and four of their acolytes waited in the darkened temple, which in turn lay at the heart of a snowflake Star-City drifting through interstellar space. Together they represented the supreme spiritual leadership of this particular city. They waited and meditated and occasionally looked about and at one another, and then waited some more.

Time passed slowly, and the candles that had been arrayed about the chamber burned down to pools of molten wax. The air was mostly still, disturbed only by the faint flow of recirculated wind from hidden vents situated higher up on the rear wall. Only the faintest hum of the Star-City's great generators disturbed the otherwise pervasive silence.

"Esron," the High Seer said after a very long wait, "I'm afraid you have been deceived, and we are wasting our time."

The Second Seer frowned at this and shook his head. "No—not yet," he said. "I'm certain the message that came to me was genuine. I'm sure of it."

"And yet," said the other, "the goddess does not materialize. I can only conclude—"

"My children," said a disembodied voice that simultaneously filled the room and seemed to sound only in the ears of those who heard it, "it has been too long."

The High Seer gasped. He looked at the other momentarily, his brow furrowed, as if suspecting some trick were being perpetrated against him. Then he gasped again as a pale light shone down from overhead. He, the Second Seer, and the acolytes all looked up.

A few meters above their heads floated a circle of slowly spinning brightness. Its center billowed with clouds and a ring of fire raced around its outer edge. As they looked on, a female form swathed in slowly swirling green and aqua gauze descended through the clouds and out the bottom of the circle. A human-looking form, with blonde hair and pale skin. She remained floating there, gazing down at them with an angelic, benevolent expression, between the seers and the circle of fire.

"Great lady!" the High Seer blurted, astonished, recognizing her at once. "Lady Moranna! You return to us!"

The woman studied the High Seer's face for a moment. Her smile warmed. "Acolyte Korvu," she said softly. "You yet live."

"I am High Seer now," Korvu told her. He appeared filled with pride, with life, as though he were young again.

"Indeed?" She nodded respectfully to him, then gazed about at the others for a few seconds before continuing. "Your kind are my favorites—it is no secret," she said, her voice louder now, so that all in the temple could hear. "Your people were old when the humans were infants; your culture rich beyond measure."

"The humans are infants yet," the High Seer chuckled.

Moranna smiled at this as though she and the High Seer had shared some private joke. "Yes—and thus I extend my favor to the people of the Star-Cities—to *your* people."

"We treasure your favor, Lady," the High Seer intoned, "and would welcome it—and your presence—much more often."

Her complexion darkened slightly. "You are saying I have not visited often enough?"

The seer blanched. "I—I am—I—"

Moranna proffered him a sour look. "You will celebrate my visits when they occur," she said, "and treat them as the momentous events they are."

"Of course, Lady," the High Seer said quickly, attempting to cover his embarrassment. "Of course."

She hesitated, then, "We have had our troubles. The Golden City is not what it once was."

The seers and acolytes frowned at this and glanced at one another.

"But—such things are not your concern," she said. "At least—not at this time."

"No, lady," the High Seer replied—though his voice carried a hint of puzzlement.

The goddess rotated slowly in the air as she floated above them, curls of smoke wafting up from the dying candles and spiraling lazily around her. They stared up at her and waited, wondering, anticipating the purpose for this visit.

"To reaffirm my love for you," she said after a moment, "I bring you all a gift. May it serve as a symbol of my patronage of your kind—now, and in the centuries and millennia to come."

"A gift, lady?" The High Seer gazed up at her, wide-eyed, his many years of life seeming to fall away in her presence. "What—what might it be?" The others subconsciously moved in a bit closer around him, staring up at her, anxious to hear—to see what she had for them.

"I bring you a key," she said. "A key that opens the greatest doorway of all."

They merely waited, almost breathless.

Moranna reached into a sort of satchel that had been hidden, up until now, within her flowing robes. She drew something out and held it up. It was not what they had expected. It was something, in short, that was very strange.

The seers stared at it. They blinked. They looked at one another. They blinked again. They looked back at her.

"This is my gift to the Dyonari," said Moranna of Those Who Remain. "I grant you the key to my kingdom." She bent down and extended it out toward the High Seer, who was now standing.

With great hesitation and trepidation, he reached up and accepted it. He looked at it, holding it not so much with reverence as with extreme confusion and a hint of revulsion.

"My lady," the High Seer said to her, speaking slowly and carefully, as though she had somehow made a terrible mistake and had yet to realize it, "this is not a key. This is a *hand*. A severed hand."

"Indeed," she said with a semi-smile. "It is a hand. The hand of a god. It is therefore also a key."

At that the High Seer's eyes widened in surprise and he nearly dropped the object before clutching it tightly to his chest.

"It is the way inside the Golden City," Moranna intoned.

"You—you allow us a way inside?" the Second Seer gasped. "Inside the domain of the gods themselves?"

"I want you to have it," she said with a warm smile. "The City will be deserted and possibly forgotten soon. There are too few of us left. Someone must remember it and cherish it. I favor *you*—the Dyonari. You have my blessing."

The seers and acolytes all bowed low, and then she began to rise back up through the air, toward the slowly rotating circle of light.

"Guard it well," she called down to them. "Use it only when absolutely necessary. Keep it safe, against the day that it will be needed—the day your people's existence depends upon it."

The seers chanted her name twice, thrice—and then she was gone, the circle blipping out in the blink of an eye.

High Seer Korvu had been staring up at the goddess where she floated above them. Now he lowered his eyes to the strange object he had been given. It felt not cold and leathery but soft and almost alive. He frowned at it, then motioned for one of the acolytes to approach.

"See to this," he said. "Carefully."

The acolyte accepted the strange object and started to carry it away, but the Second Seer stopped him. He took it from the acolyte and held it up, inspecting it closely. Frowning, he looked at Korvu. "You believe it truly is what she claimed?" he asked. His expression was dubious.

"Why would the Lady Moranna lie to us?" Korvu asked. He made the Dyonari equivalent of a shrug. "In any case, we must treat it as if it were the most valuable object in the galaxy. For it might well be."

The Second Seer considered this and nodded. "Yes, High Seer." He looked at the object and then around at the otherwise empty room. "Um. Can I give you a hand with it?"

10

"Y ou invented that last part," Mirana declared, her cynicism plainly visible.

Madalena allowed the tiniest of smiles to drift across her face. "Perhaps," she said. "But it doesn't invalidate the larger story."

Madalena had finished recounting the tale of how the seers of her Star-City had come to possess the hand of a god. The others of her team were all staring back at her, wide-eyed.

"So she simply gave the seers a god's hand?" Mirana asked, incredulous.

Madalena nodded. "I presented it to you as the seers presented it to me." She paused, then added, "More or less."

Mirana regarded her with a look of disbelief. "And how did *you* acquire it?"

"The Seer that charged us with this mission gave it to me, along with the knowledge of its origin and purpose." Madalena smiled. "And now we have a way inside, where until now only the gods have traveled."

"Possibly," Mirana replied. "Although I somehow suspect our people might have found the cutting tool more useful, down through the centuries."

Madalena ignored this. She raised the hand to touch it to the gates, but Mirana grasped her wrist and stopped her before it made contact. "Wait," she said. "How do we know no other gods are present in the City? If even *one* is there, and discovers us—"

Madalena nodded at this. "Yes, but it is a chance we must take, in order to fulfill the mission." She looked at each of the members of the team in turn; they appeared resolute and determined. Then she turned back to Mirana. "All of the stories we have heard have claimed that no god resides here any longer. Lucian was the last, and..."

Mirana nodded. "Yes, yes, I know," she said. "But, still..."

"We have no choice," Madalena said. "We must complete our mission."

Reluctantly Mirana moved aside and Madalena raised the severed hand. She spoke a few words in a language none of the others had ever heard—words taught to her by the seer who had given her the hand. Then she brushed the fingers against the surface of the gate.

The others stood ready, gazing up at the towering doors set into the even-more-towering walls.

Nothing happened.

Frowning, Madalena lifted the hand again and this time pressed it hard against the gleaming surface.

Still nothing.

Madalena looked to Mirana, eyes wide. "It isn't working," she said, as much to herself as to anyone else.

"I cannot disagree with that assessment," Mirana said, growing more impatient by the moment. She turned and looked around, then looked straight up, as if certain a lightning bolt from the sky was about to strike them all down.

"The Lady Moranna assured the seers that this would work," Madalena said, frustration more than evident in her tone. She pressed the hand to the gold surface of the gate yet again.

One of the warriors under their command leaned in and whispered something to Mirana. The shorter commander listened for a moment, then moved back and looked at the warrior. "You are certain of this?"

The warrior shrugged, then offered a faint nod.

Madalena had missed the brief exchange entirely. She was still holding the hand up to the gate and repeating the phrase over and over, all the while growing more and more frustrated and agitated.

Mirana tapped her on the shoulder. Madalena nearly jumped a meter off the ground. She whirled on her co-commander. "*What?*"

Mirana stood her ground. She nodded toward the warrior. "He said you should *wish* for the doors to open."

Madalena regarded her with an expression that managed to convey both condescension and contempt. "He believes I do *not* wish that?"

Mirana shook her head. "No, no. You misunderstand. I believe he means you must *consciously*—perhaps *vocally*—request it. As you touch the hand to the surface."

Madalena appeared about to dismiss this suggestion, but then she shrugged. "Why not?" she asked, rhetorically. She kept the hand pressed to the gates and meanwhile closed her eyes and said aloud, "*I want in!*"

Still nothing happened.

"Gather around her," the warrior who had made the suggestion said. He motioned for the others to move in closer. "Now—hold hands. Concentrate on your desire to see the gates open."

"How do you know all this, Vinizan?" Madalena asked, scowling at him. "Are you just making it all up?"

"No," he said. He continued to maneuver the other warriors into a tight circle around the two commanders and himself. "I was pledged to become an acolyte to the current seers."

The two co-commanders looked at him in surprise. "An acolyte? You?"

"I would have been," the slender Dyonari replied. "I was still an apprentice. But I did not meet their high standards for certain abilities. Psychic abilities, in particular." He offered a half-shrug. "So I was kicked out of the guild and transferred to the military."

The co-commanders took this in. "But how—" Madalena began.

"I overheard a conversation once between the First Seer and two acolytes," he began. "They did not notice my presence, and I immediately took steps to conceal myself further."

"That is a serious violation," Madalena began.

"They have already dismissed me," Vinizan replied.

"True." Madelena noted. "And so what did you discover?"

"That they possessed a key of some sort to a great city—though I did not recognize which city—or which key—until we arrived here. And also the method by which the key was to be utilized."

"The wish," Madalena said, still skeptical.

"The wish, yes."

"So let us try it," Mirana impatiently interjected. She looked at Madalena. "Assuming you are now satisfied with the way in which the information was acquired."

Madalena didn't bother to respond. She simply nodded to the others. "Hold hands, then—and concentrate on the desire for the gates to open!"

They did so. For nearly two full minutes they did so. And, at last, as they were nearly giving up hope, the gold barrier before them split in half, each doorway swinging away and leaving a path in between.

"Go!" Madalena barked. "Before it closes! Go!"

The six Dyonari warriors rushed through the gateway. Once they were on the other side, it silently swung closed behind them.

They stood together in a little circle, just inside the walls, and gazed at their surroundings in awe. Towers and halls and parapets gleamed gold and silver, many encrusted in jewels. Small fountains stood at the intersections of walkways, water spouting from them before curving down into broad pools. Everything was clean and new and perfect. It took their breath away. They gawked.

"We did it," Mirana breathed. "We actually *did* it!"

Madalena nodded. "We did," she said. "We're in."

They had penetrated the realm of the gods. They were inside the Golden City.

11

The six members of the Dyonari infiltration team wandered as if in a daze along the thoroughfares of the Golden City. Try as they might to focus on the mission assigned to them, they were continuously being distracted by their surroundings. In terms of splendor, glory and grandeur, the City was everything one could imagine.

"Is it just me, or does this place seem increasingly similar to a Star-City?" Mirana asked as the six more or less forced themselves to come back together as a group and remember their orders.

Madalena looked around and shrugged. "Perhaps. Not overtly."

"It seems quite overt to me," Mirana stated. "Right down to some of the words inscribed on the faces of buildings being written in our own language."

Madalena looked around again and gasped. "You're right! I do see Dyonari writing now."

The warrior who had trained to be an acolyte spoke up again. "Yes. It is not just you, co-commander," he said. "It is how this place works."

"What do you mean?"

"The city of the gods reflects in its appearance—in what it looks like, and how spectacularly that is presented—the esteem its inhabitants hold for it."

"What?" Madalena asked, confused. She shook her head. "I didn't get a word of that."

"I understood it," Mirana said. "We hold it in high esteem, and so it appears glorious to us. And we are Dyonari, so parts of it have begun to take that form, as we look at it."

"Precisely," the warrior said, nodding.

"So—you're saying it doesn't *really* look this way?" Madalena asked. "This is just an illusion, for our benefit?"

"Not necessarily for our benefit," the warrior said. "But that is how I understand that it works. As to the other…" He shrugged. "I do not know."

"Fascinating," Madalena stated, gazing about one more time, "but not relevant to our purpose here. We have a job to do, and we will focus entirely on that job." She looked at the others sharply. "Am I understood?"

"Understood, co-commander," the others said quickly.

Moving to the front of the formation, Madalena urged them onward again.

"Where are we going?" Mirana asked after they had passed out of the square they'd occupied previously and were traveling along a narrow alley. They had now left behind the broad avenue that led away from the gates. She pointed to a plume of something that towered above the tops of the buildings off to their left. It flowed up and rained back down like water from a geyser, but didn't take the form of water. It was luminous; it glowed, spilling forth brightness. At more careful inspection, it was a column of light—of raw energy.

Of *the Power*.

"This is not the way," Mirana added, sounding puzzled.

"We are taking an indirect route," responded her co-commander. "To avoid any who might yet linger here."

"Ah. A good plan," Mirana commented.

They continued on in that manner until at last they arrived on the outer fringes of the central plaza. There they stopped and merely stood, staring, for at least a full minute.

Ahead of them, at the center of the square, the Fountain of the City roared up into the too-blue sky. Suns and stars and constellations danced about the great column of energy.

"That—" Mirana almost choked, cleared her throat, and tried again: "That—is the Fountain of the gods!"

"It is."

"I never dreamed I would see it," she said, her voice filled with wonder. "Not in the flesh." She gazed up at the luminous column of raw Power. Then she glanced over at her co-commander, frowned at what she saw, and turned fully to stare at her.

Madalena had stripped off her armor and the uniform underneath and stood there naked now, tearing at something in the inner lining of her uniform. She looked back at Mirana as if her behavior was the most natural thing one would have expected to see under these circumstances. "What?" she asked, still pulling at the lining.

"What in the name of the Lower Pathways are you doing?"

Before Madalena could answer, a part of the lining ripped and came loose. The co-commander grinned and pulled it free along its entire length, from ankle to wrist. She held the resulting long band of what appeared to be fabric out for Mirana to inspect. "There," she said with a look of great satisfaction. "You see? It worked."

Mirana's frown deepened. "First, put your uniform back on," she hissed. "Second—*what* worked?"

"Wha—? Oh…" Madalena seemed to realize for the first time that she was naked. She swiftly pulled her uniform back on. "As I was saying—"

"Keep going," Mirana insisted. "The rest of it."

Madalena gave her an ugly look but sat down on the smooth walkway that surrounded the central square of the City and began to pull her transparent armor back on, piece by piece. When she was finished, she again held up the strip she had pulled out of her uniform. "This," she said, as though the other should easily recognize it.

Mirana understood by now that her co-commander had not taken leave of her senses. Instead, most likely, she had been given something—or knowledge of something—that the others had not. And it involved whatever she had just ripped out of her clothing. She leaned in closer and peered at the ribbon of fabric. "What is it?" she asked.

"Tear yours out, too," she said by way of reply.

"Mine?" Mirana's eyebrows knitted together and she slowly stared down at herself. "I have a whatever-that-is in my clothing, too?"

"I certainly hope so," Madalena replied. She turned to the other four Dyonari there with them. "All of you—do as I just did. Tear out this strip. Now!"

At the sound of the barked order, the other Dyonari all quickly shed their reservations and inhibitions, followed quickly by their uniforms. A few moments later, they had undressed, found the ribbons, pulled them free, and re-dressed.

Madalena moved among them quickly, gathering the thin cloth strips. "This was deemed to be the safest way to transport them into the City," she said in answer to their questioning expressions.

"I ask again," Mirana said, shaking her head slowly, "what are they? What are they for?"

"All I know is what I was told to do," Madalena said. She tapped the side of her head as she gazed back at the others. "And what I was shown."

"Shown?" Mirana looked puzzled at first, but then realization dawned upon her. "Ah. The seer."

Madalena nodded. "The mission," she said.

145

The strips of cloth seemed to possess some sort of magnetic or adhesive quality, and Mirana watched as the other commander connected each together, nose to tail. Soon she held a single long piece about fifteen meters in length. Gathering it up in her long-fingered hands, she began to walk toward the Fountain.

The others watched her move for only a couple of seconds before they shot one another questioning looks, and then followed along after her.

No one spoke until they arrived at the edge of the broad, shallow basin that lay at the foot of the Fountain. What first looked like water but upon closer inspection revealed itself to be raw cosmic energy shimmered within the basin, sloshing about restlessly. Madalena paused for a few seconds, her eyes staring blankly ahead as she accessed information planted there by the seers. Then she blinked, looked down at the basin, and lowered one end of the ribbon into the gently churning pool. She trailed the rest of the ribbon out into the plaza, laying it on the ground in a straight line that pointed back in the direction of the City's gates.

Almost immediately tendrils of shimmering energy surged up out of the basin and wound their way along the ribbon, lacing and spiraling around it like fast-growing ivy. The coruscating threads of raw cosmic power reached the end and continued on for a short distance before curving back around in tight arcs and working their way back toward the basin.

"Quite lovely," Mirana observed. "But it doesn't seem terribly useful."

"It isn't finished," Madalena said. "If only I can remember the other part..."

"Remember?" Mirana turned to her, puzzled. "Oh," she said after a moment. "They did not see fit to give you conscious access to all the information up front. You can only unlock the steps one at a time."

Madalena's lack of response was all the confirmation Mirana needed.

"So," she went on after a brief reflection, "you don't even know the ultimate objective of our mission, do you?"

Madalena paused and glared at her. "I have no need to," she snapped. "Just as you have no need to ask about it."

Mirana appeared to sulk after that. Madalena, meanwhile, brightened, as though some good idea had just struck her. She sat down on the ground and once again removed her boots. This time she actually began to dismantle the heels.

"Ah," said Mirana, watching her. "I see you have remembered the next step. Either that, or you have lost your mind."

Madalena did not see fit to respond to this. Instead she continued to work with the components she had removed from the soles of her boots, rapidly assembling from the little devices a single, larger mechanism. At last she looked up at Mirana expectantly.

The co-commander required only a moment to understand what was being required of her. She in turn sat down and began to remove her own boots. "The others, too?" she asked as she did so.

"Not this time," Madalena said.

As the four warriors looked on silently, Mirana unfastened the hidden components from the soles of her boots—components that, until this moment, she'd had no idea were there—and handed them over. As she did so, she asked, "Why did they require these components to be hidden?"

"The seers did not know whom we might encounter on the way to the city, or after we arrived," Madalena replied. "They did not want us to be stopped by anyone who might recognize the equipment we brought with us in an assembled condition."

"I see."

Madalena added the new components to the device she was building. When she was finished, a few moments later, she held up a cube about six inches square, transparent, and with multicolored lights flashing inside it. Faint lines were traced along its surfaces, like printed circuits. As more memories were unlocked within her mind, she learned the next step. In retrospect, it appeared obvious. She stood and walked over to the ribbon she had laid out—upon closer inspection, it, too, was covered with faint circuit lines—and set the little cube down upon its end. The same invisible force that had fastened the individual strands of cloth together took hold again, attaching the ribbon firmly to the cube. The cosmic energies now flowed over, into, and through the cube, lighting it up with a million colors. And then, as the others looked on in surprise, the cube began to grow. In seconds it had expanded to nearly a meter per side, the lights within it growing even brighter.

The six of them stood there, staring in wonder at the strange object Madalena had constructed. Energy continued to flow along the ribbon and into the cube. The cube continued to glow. Seconds passed, then minutes. Nothing new happened.

"Is there anything more?" Mirana wondered aloud. "What is it doing? What is it *for*?"

Madalena closed her eyes and appeared to be concentrating. Then she opened them again and looked at Mirana. "I don't know," she said. "There doesn't seem to be anything else planted within my memories."

The two co-commanders looked at one another, growing more concerned by the second. Neither of them spoke, but it was obvious to the other four, as well as to each other, what they were thinking: *Have we come so far and done so much, only to fail in our mission here at the end, because we cannot remember the final steps that should have been implanted in our memories?*

And then one of the warriors stepped forward. "I have it," he said. "I remember. I know what to do."

The two co-commanders looked at him skeptically. "You?" demanded Madalena. "You were given the final steps, and not one of us?"

"I cannot imagine that's true," added Mirana. "Prove it."

At that, the warrior nodded respectfully to each of his two co-commanders—he seemed unfazed by their lack of confidence in his claims—and strode confidently toward the cube. Kneeling in front of it, he laid both hands upon it and closed his eyes. For several seconds, nothing happened. The two co-commanders looked at one another, looks of scorn and derision beginning to spring forth upon their faces.

And then the top of the cube began to change.

The top panel curved inwards, like a bowl. It spread out, much wider than the width of the cube from which it was extruding. In less than a minute it had formed a sort of dish shape, two meters in diameter. A protrusion in the form of an antenna emerged from the center of the dish and reached upward a few inches.

"What is that?" Madalena demanded, moving forward to study this new development. "Why did you make it do that?"

The warrior shook his head. "I know as little about it all as you two do. Probably less."

"The seers must not have wanted you to have all the fun, Madalena," Mirana said—to which the other commander shot her an ugly look.

"What now?" the two co-commanders said at precisely the same time. The four others did something then that Dyonari warriors rarely did: they laughed. The co-commanders ignored them.

The six of them stood there, waiting, uncertain of what to do.

"Our orders were to stay and guard whatever we constructed," Madalena said.

"Guard it from what? From whom?" Mirana gestured broadly at the plaza and the Golden City beyond. "It is obvious that this place is deserted, just as we suspected it would be. No one has lived here in a very long time. Nearly all the gods are dead now. Perhaps Moranna is the last one. Perhaps even she has been dead all these long centuries since she presented those early seers with the hand."

Madalena considered this. "Still," she said, "if *we* could find our way here, others could, too." She shrugged. "And, in any case, we have our orders. We are to remain here and guard this machine until further notice."

Mirana didn't appear entirely persuaded by that argument. She started to say something in objection—but no one present would ever learn what it was going to be. For at that moment the energy flowing from the Fountain into the cube spilled out into the parabolic dish at its top—and then blasted into the sky in a broad, blinding beam of raw, coruscating power. The column of elemental cosmic plasma ripped a hole in the sky and shot through it, disappearing beyond that point. The stream continued as the six looked on, as if it was steadily pumping the energies of the Fountain off to some other dimension, for some unimaginable purpose.

All talk of leaving now having evaporated, the six Dyonari sat down upon the smooth ground of the plaza, stared at the device they had built with undisguised awe, and pondered exactly what it was doing, and why.

And they waited.

BOOK ELEVEN

THE TOWER
BETWEEN
THE WORLDS

1

The Dyonari troops marched through the fog, their swords out and at the ready. Behind them followed the Bravo Squad troopers of the Imperial III Legion. Within an enclosed space between the two formations came General Arnem Agrippa, Major Darius Torgon, the two Dyonari commanders, and Solonis the seer-god.

Once it became clear that the two groups of soldiers, human and alien, were going to cooperate to attempt to stop the future destruction of the galaxy, the second Dyonari leader had at last identified himself and greeted Agrippa with something approaching respect. His name, as it turned out, was Ralin. Now he looked toward the blond human general and said, "The rest of our forces are only a short distance away."

"You're sure about that?" Agrippa asked, his mouth twisting in a half-smile. "In all this fog and distortion, we've found it difficult to gauge distances."

The Dyonari looked back at him for a moment but said nothing.

Beside them, Major Torgon had been glancing occasionally and curiously at Solonis. Finally the seer-god

153

looked back at him. "Yes, Major?" he asked. "You have a question for me?"

Torgon was taken aback but summoned up his courage and said, "There's something I don't quite understand."

Solonis appeared weary, but he spared this a laugh that was not unkind. "By all means, then—ask away."

"You said your..." Torgon sought the correct term, found it. "Your *astral* form could move forward and backward in time."

"Indeed."

"But this—" Torgon nodded toward Solonis. "This is a real body, yes? Not an astral form. And you needed that tomb thing to travel to our time here."

"The Temporal Vault, yes." Solonis smiled. "And you are quite correct: this is not my original body."

Now Agrippa was interested. "I had wondered," he rumbled. "In ancient times, your appearance was not described as anything like the way you now appear. That was part of why I was so dubious of your claims at first."

"It was a matter of necessity," Solonis said. "For, even as I was returning from the future, my physical body in the past was killed."

"Killed?" Torgon's eyes widened.

"Likely by Vorthan or one of his accomplices, during the war." He shook his head. "I will probably never learn the details."

"How do you know it was killed?" Agrippa asked.

The seer-god almost laughed at that. "How could I *not* know?" He grinned at Agrippa. "Believe me, General—one can tell."

Torgon gestured toward him. "You were killed. Yet...you're still here."

"Very observant, Major." Solonis grinned at him now. "Yes—but, as you have observed, in a new body." He shrugged. "I told you earlier that I am essentially a ghost." He hesitated a moment, growing wistful. "It was a very strange sensation, somewhat like having one's legs cut out from underneath. I felt...*untethered*. My connection to the past—to my own natural time—grew weaker, more tenuous." He spread his hands. "I had no choice. I inhabited—perhaps you would prefer the term 'possessed,' though I don't—this body, in order to sustain my existence while I continued my investigation." At Agrippa's frown, he quickly added, "The individual to whom this body originally belonged was already dead—the body was brain-dead, from some sort of accident or incident. My astral form animates it and it has served me well."

Agrippa continued to regard him with some degree of skepticism.

"But you couldn't travel back in time in your usual manner while inhabiting a physical body," Torgon said, looking up with excitement as if he'd unraveled some great mystery.

"Precisely, Major" Solonis said, nodding. "Yet if I hadn't assumed a physical form, I would've...drifted away, I suppose." He shook his head. "I am not certain exactly what would've happened, to be honest. But I didn't wish to find out. And so, inhabiting a real body again, I constructed—at great trouble and expense—a Temporal Vault, to carry both my spirit and this new body backwards in time. I set the controls to take me back, back, all the way to the moment when the shockwaves switched from moving forwards to moving backwards. Or rather," he added, "to a moment just days or hours prior to that."

"To just before the cosmic splash," Torgon said. "I see. Yes." He paused. "So—it hasn't happened yet, but we should have enough time to find the cause, and to stop it, then?"

Solonis gave him a quick, flat smile. "I fervently hope so, Major. I certainly hope so."

2

As vast as it was, the warfleet that dropped hyper just beyond the outermost inhabited world of the Stopholod system represented only a fraction of the former might of the I and III Legions. Many of those legions' ships had in recent weeks been destroyed in heavy fighting with the alien Rao and with other human empires, particularly the ever-hostile Riyahadi Caliphate. Many others remained in position along the frontiers, supporting planetary actions or escorting troop ships. The fleet that currently sailed along in the wake of the *Ascanius* represented what had survived and what could be spared—though in truth, given the state of those campaigns, *nothing* could be spared.

And so some fifteen mighty starships, a mixture of destroyers, heavy cruisers and carriers, sailed along the path being blazed by the flagship of I Legion, under the overall command of General Ezekial Tamerlane. Each ship was to some degree cylindrical, with a bulging spherical shape somewhere along its length, representing the containment section for the hyperdrive—the inconceivably powerful unit, energized by a tiny, magnetically/gravitically contained black hole, that could rip open a wound in spacetime and thrust the ship through and into the low Above. In that way, the ships were able to take shortcuts from point to point in the real universe, thus allowing for much faster transition times and giving the effect of faster than light travel.

On the triple-decked bridge level of the *Ascanius*, General Tamerlane stood facing the broad, curved viewport, his hands clasped behind his back and his demeanor grim. He watched as the normal universe rematerialized around his ship, the black of space and the sparkling stars replacing the hazy, gauzy dimness of the dimension through which they had been traveling.

"Well done, as always, Captain," he said over his shoulder to the aged master of the *Ascanius*, Harras Dequoi. Old Dequoi had served in the Imperial Navy for longer than Tamerlane had been alive, and knew his way around the Empire and associated territories instinctively. Tamerlane doubted a state-of-the-art navigational computer could have dropped the fleet more accurately or with the amazing rapidity that Dequoi had achieved. "Did all the other ships make it through?"

Dequoi appeared somewhat offended by the question; even the merest hint that he could have lost one of their fleet's ships in transit hurt his pride. He consulted one of the tactical officers for a moment and then addressed the general in curt tones: "All ships are accounted for, General," he said, not even looking Tamerlane's way.

Tamerlane couldn't help but smile at this. He admired the old captain and appreciated the man's pride in his abilities and accomplishments. And, truth be told, it was good to have something to smile about, after weeks of nearly continuous defeats in every theater.

"Captain," the general started to say, "I think—"

"Contact!" cried the nearest tactical officer, nearly jumping out of her seat. "Two ships. Three. Four."

"Where?" Dequoi demanded, already signaling for evasive maneuvers via the Aether link.

"Five," the tactical officer corrected. "Six. They're right on top of us, Captain. Seven. They are dropping hyper all around us. Eight. Nine."

Dequoi cursed. He spared Tamerlane a quick glance. "Excuse me, General, while I attempt to save all our lives."

Gripping the forward railing, Tamerlane gave Dequoi a quick nod. "That would be very much appreciated, Captain."

Dequoi didn't hear the reply. He was already fully immersed within the fleet's Aether network, mentally issuing commands and carrying out procedures more quickly than he could have ordered someone to do them.

"Fifteen," the tactical officer updated, and Tamerlane paled. "Seventeen. Twenty."

The tactical holographic cloud-image of their current situation filled the forward area of the bridge, its edge just brushing up against the crimson-uniformed Tamerlane. The general turned and attempted to take it all in visually. What he saw made him extremely uncomfortable. The *Ascanius* and its support fleet were being advanced upon by a larger force, with new ships dropping in every second or two. There could be no doubt to whom they belonged: They were Imperial ships, like the *Ascanius* and its fleet—but in the service of the wrong legion. These were II Legion vessels, operated by the fanatical and now rebellious Sons of Terra.

Technically, of course, it was Tamerlane and his I Legion—not to mention Agrippa and his III—that were the rebels. The II Legion commander, General Ioan Iapetus, had been named *Taiko*—military commander of the Empire—by the sole surviving heir of the royal Rahkmanov Dynasty, the child princess, Marens. But scratch a tiny bit deeper, and one would discover that the princess had essentially been kidnapped by Iapetus and taken into his custody, with the little girl forced at gunpoint to name Iapetus her commander-in-chief. Similarly, this explained why she had suddenly declared Tamerlane and Agrippa to be outlaws, stripped of their ranks and any titles and funds.

All that Tamerlane had left now were the remnants of I and III Legions and this fleet—this squadron of ships that answered directly to him. The men and women of these starships understood the situation, and they had chosen to stick with him. They knew who was legitimate and who was not. They also knew they might not last much longer, either way, in a galaxy overrun by hostile aliens as well as a hostile and largely intact II Legion.

The main doorway leading onto the bridge level hissed open behind Tamerlane. He glanced back and saw the lady Teluria striding out, her black hair uncovered and her dark red cloak held tightly about her. She started to ask something—likely wanting to know what was happening—but then, to her credit, she simply studied the tactical display and arrived at an understanding for herself.

"Here they come," Captain Dequoi growled.

The II Legion ships, most of them still painted navy blue and not yet converted to the black of Iapetus's preference, drove in hard against the edge of Tamerlane's fleet's formation. Great banks of guns along their sides took aim and fired, shearing away entire sections of the I Legion ships. Particle beams and high-mass/high-impact projectiles ripped holes in hulls and bulkheads, venting engine rooms, command decks, and living quarters to the vacuum of space.

Tamerlane's ships fought back, firing every weapon at their disposal, and the narrow void that separated the two groups of combatants became quickly filled with vivid, blinding beams and streaking slugs and warheads. Explosions blossomed silently; energy shields overloaded and evaporated while drive systems imploded, the no-longer-contained singularities within dragging other compartments of their ships down into nothingness.

"Status!" Tamerlane demanded, knowing the numbers he was seeing on the holographic display were already woefully outdated. "What have we lost?"

Dequoi was now plugged directly into the ship's strategic computer via the Aether link. He could almost feel each ship die as it was struck by enemy fire. He struggled to form words as his mind was bombarded by the carnage; at last he gasped, "Seven of our ships destroyed; three of theirs gone."

"Totals?" Tamerlane pressed.

"Eight remaining for us, twenty-four for them."

"Withdraw! Get us out of here as quickly as you can." Tamerlane cursed. This was what came from having the I and III Legions out actually battling on the frontiers for the past few months, while the Sons of Terra clung tightly to their defensive positions on and around the Inner Worlds. He had known at the time that it was a bad arrangement. He had tried to change it. He had failed.

"I have been attempting to execute a strategic withdrawal from the moment General Iapetus's ships appeared," Dequoi barked back at Tamerlane. "I assumed you did not seek a straight-up battle with him in our current state."

Tamerlane ignored the insubordination that filled the captain's remark. Frankly he didn't blame Dequoi. And in the face of Iapteus's treachery, a bit of impudence from old Harras Dequoi was practically endearing.

"What's holding us back from leaving?" Tamerlane asked, circling around the holographic display to study it from every angle. He watched as the blue ships of II Legion almost entirely encircled his own dwindling fleet. "Why can't we jump?"

Dequoi motioned and in response one of the blue enemy vessels in the display flashed orange on and off for a few seconds. "That big one there—it's got a mass-generator," he said. "They have us locked out of hyper. They're warping spacetime right around us so that we can't break through the barriers."

Being a general and not an admiral, Tamerlane understood only the rudiments of that explanation: The enemy was doing something with one of their ships that was preventing Tamerlane's own fleet from escaping. "All right, then," he said, "we need to kill that ship."

"Sage advice, General," Dequoi said mockingly. "And I've been attempting to do that from the start. They are screening it with smaller vessels and they have it well-shielded."

Tamerlane looked to Teluria, who now stood against the low railing to his right. "Is there anything you can do?" he asked her.

The woman in red frowned as she studied the tactical display. "Doubtful," she said after a moment. "But if the alternative is being captured by Iapetus again, I will try very hard to think of something."

"Good." Tamerlane turned back to the forward screen. He was about to ask the captain a question when alarms shrieked across the bridge.

"Contact!" shouted the sensor officer to Tamerlane's left. "Ships dropping hyper. No—wait. Not ships." She stared at the data flowing over her screens, puzzled.

"Not ships?" Tamerlane repeated, moving toward her. "What do you—?"

A second later, everything became apparent.

The space all around the two fleets warped and distorted as holes from the Above appeared, ripped open by the approaching objects. They flashed into normal space and immediately streaked toward the Imperial ships. Toward ships of *both* fleets.

"What in the name of the gods are those?" Captain Dequoi barked, standing from his center seat and moving forward, staring at the new objects as they emerged one by one out into the universe. "What are—oh..."

Dequoi's gasp was echoed by others around the bridge. Tamerlane meanwhile scowled and also stepped closer to the holographic cloud image, as if seeing the objects in greater detail might somehow reveal that they were in fact harmless travel pods or asteroids and not the dreaded vessels they appeared to be.

Alas, proximity changed nothing. They were what everyone on the bridge of the *Ascanius* feared they were: blood-red comets. Comets that had traveled through the hyperspace lanes of the Above. Comets that contained the horrific alien Phaedrons and perhaps their footsoldiers, the Skrazzi.

"Back us out, Captain!" Tamerlane shouted, but Dequoi was already doing just that. As orders disseminated to the other remaining ships of their combined fleet, commanding the ships to immediately disengage from the II Legion's vessels, the *Ascanius* herself began to pull away from the melee. The ships of the Sons of Terra, meanwhile, reacted more slowly, remaining in place as though their captains were confused by what was happening and uncertain of how to respond.

That hesitation was all it took.

The comets crashed into the edge of the II Legion fleet and instantly annihilated two of Iapetus's capital ships farthest from the *Atlantia*. More of the comets dropped from hyperspace every moment, and some actually came to a halt once they had entered realspace—meaning they carried some form of onboard propulsion. That, or else the raw psychic might of the Phaedrons inside them was able to move them and brake them using pure telekinetic force. Those that had stopped split open, disgorging smaller chunks of ice that flew about like fighter ships.

On the bridge of the *Ascanius*, Tamerlane watched in revulsion as a thin layer of ice began to form on the floor and the walls of the bridge. Residue of the massive wave of psychic energy being created and directed by the Phaedrons, it signaled their presence and their might. He turned and met Dequoi's eyes. "Fire everything we have at those comets, Captain!" he ordered. Then he faced the holographic tactical display and studied the rapidly changing layout of the battle.

"Everything? But—what of Iapetus's fleet?" Dequoi asked, frowning.

"Forget about them for now," Tamerlane responded. "These creatures represent a danger of a completely different magnitude."

Almost reluctantly, it seemed to the general, Dequoi began issuing orders vocally and via the Aether link, directing the *Ascanius's* firepower and that of the remaining support ships against the comets. The already brightly-lit space surrounding the three antagonists was now spotlighted by coruscating beams of coherent light and streaking missiles and projectiles that tore into the comets and the smaller fighter-pieces.

The bulk of the battle lasted less than five minutes. With all of the weapons on the ships of both human fleets firing at highest rate, the relatively small number of Phaedron comets couldn't long evade. One after another, they exploded as they were hit by particle beams and projectiles coming from the *Ascanius*, the *Atlantia*, or one of the increasingly few other ships. In the meantime, however, they succeeded in utterly vaporizing several more of the humans' ships and seizing control of quite a few others. More than once, seconds after a smaller chunk of ice had collided with a human ship, the ship had turned on its fellows and opened fire, its crew now mentally enthralled by the horrific Phaedrons. On at least three occasions, either the *Atlantia* or the *Ascanius* had to open fire on a fellow human ship and destroy it before the psychic control net could be spread any wider. While doing so did kill one of the Phaedrons, it also obviously reduced the number of ships available to Iapetus and Tamerlane with which to fight back. Consequently, the battle ran very close, and for a time it appeared the humans would simply run out of ships before the enemy ran out of comets.

Fortunately, the gunners and pilots of the Lords of Fire and the Sons of Terra proved up to the task—but just barely.

As what looked to be the final shard of ice was vaporized halfway between the two flagships, Tamerlane assessed the tactical situation and was shocked to see that only his flagship and that of Iapetus had survived. They were down to just a handful of fighter craft on each side, as well. All of the other capital ships had been destroyed.

Tamerlane cursed. "All gone," he snapped. "Everything we had left!" He wanted to weep, to rage, to gnash his teeth in fury at having lost so many fine soldiers and sailors. It infuriated him.

Dequoi merely appeared sick.

"It does put you on even standing with Iapetus, however," Teluria pointed out as she glided nearer. She nodded toward the magnified view of the *Atlantia* on one of the forward monitors, darker patches of scoring from weapons fire and collisions obvious against its blue and silver hull. "And his ship appears rather extensively damaged," she noted. "Perhaps if you were to press your advantage against him..."

Tamerlane pulled himself back from the abyss of despair. He looked at her and then out at the *Atlantia*. He said nothing for a few seconds, considering. Before he could reply, however, he felt a signal reaching him over the Aether link. He checked the mental display board and saw a black rectangle with a stylized golden eye at its center floating there, spinning slowly. He recognized it immediately, of course—*always watching*—and was not entirely surprised to see it, given the current state of affairs between them.

"He's hailing me now," he said to Teluria and the captain. "This should be interesting."

Neither of them appeared terribly excited by that news.

Tamerlane mentally "touched" the black icon and it opened out into a two-dimensional view of General Ioan Iapetus, commander of II Legion, standing on the bridge of the *Atlantia*. Behind him, officers and technicians swarmed, fighting fires and dealing with the damage wrought during the battle.

Iapetus looked up, flashed a tight and wholly unconvincing smile, and nodded his head ever so slightly. "Ezekial," he said. "Well. Our positions appear to have reversed. The slings and arrows of outrageous fortune, eh?"

Tamerlane didn't recognize the quote at first, but the Aether link instantly provided the source and context, and he could only laugh morbidly as he tossed out the next line: "'Or to take arms against a sea of troubles.'" He shook his head. "A vast understatement."

"Indeed." Iapetus said nothing more for several seconds, instead merely staring down at the floor, and Tamerlane began to wonder if he were simply stalling for time, perhaps preparing another attack or some other treacherous action. When he at last looked back up, his expression was unreadable—but not the usual grim arrogance that usually resided there. Clearly the man was uncomfortable; as uncomfortable as Tamerlane had ever seen him. He spoke at last: "I would like to meet with you in person, Ezekial."

"Why?"

"To discuss our current circumstances. It is obvious we will have to change our tactics, given the current strategic conditions. Even the Inner Worlds of the Empire are now besieged. We cannot afford any more of this costly internal strife."

"I couldn't agree more," Tamerlane said, keeping his eyes level and locked onto the other man's. "But a direct meeting is probably not going to happen," he went on, "because I'm not setting foot aboard your ship, and I doubt you'd be willing to come over here and—"

"I would be delighted to come aboard your flagship," Iapetus interrupted. He paused. "That is—assuming there was an invitation in there somewhere."

Tamerlane was taken aback. "Um—yes, yes. You can take that as an invitation. Provided you come alone."

"I will."

"And leave your weapons on your own ship."

A pause, then, "Yes. Yes, that is acceptable."

It is? Tamerlane thought to himself. He was shocked, but managed to hide his reaction. "Very well, then," he said, "you may take a shuttle over. No fighter escort."

"Understood." Iapetus started to turn away, then stopped and looked back at Tamerlane. "And since you have the Lady Teluria present, you can be sure I will remain on my best behavior." He cocked his head to one side. "She is there with you, is she not?"

"She is indeed," Tamerlane replied. "And you may rest assured that she will be keeping at least one eye on you at all times."

"Excellent," Iapetus said. This time he actually smiled, though Tamerlane wasn't entirely sure why. "Very good," he went on. "We of the Sons of Terra are, after all, *always watching*. It will be refreshing to have someone else performing the surveillance for a change."

And with that, Iapetus closed the connection.

Tamerlane mentally stepped out of the Aether link and his consciousness returned to the bridge of the *Ascanius*. He looked to Dequoi. "They're sending a shuttle over. Keep a gun on it at all times, and scan it from stem to stern for anything out of the ordinary."

"I'll keep a whole battery on it, if it's coming from Iapetus's ship," Dequoi replied testily.

"I trusted that you would," Tamerlane said with a smile.

"He is coming here?" Teluria asked, frowning.

"He is indeed."

She looked as if she'd bitten into something extremely sour. "I would advise that you send out a couple of torpedoes to greet his shuttle," she said.

He laughed at this, ever so slightly, but quickly came to understand that she was deadly serious.

"I can't do that," he told her. "He's at a position of disadvantage now. I have to see what concessions I can extract from him. If he could be brought back over to our side—convinced to fight the enemy and not fight my government—he would be a formidable addition to our ranks."

Teluria simply shook her head at him. "How did you rise so far, so young, when you are so naive?" she wondered aloud.

Dequoi and some of the other officers looked up at this remark in surprise. Tamerlane meanwhile felt himself growing angry. Another part of him, however, began to wonder if the woman in red was correct. Should he blast Iapetus out of space while the opportunity was there? Did he dare? Could he live with himself afterward if he did such a thing? After giving his permission for the man to come aboard?

Tamerlane turned and strode toward his office off to the right; it was a room that had until recently belonged to General Nakamura. The thought of it made him extremely sad.

He looked back at Dequoi. "Please inform me when Iapetus comes aboard," he said. And with that he went into the office and closed the door.

3

The Kings of Oblivion marched along through the fog, servos in their combat armor whining softly as they moved, soft soil yielding beneath their heavy, booted feet. At the front of their portion of the larger procession, General Agrippa kept one eye on the monotonous landscape ahead and one eye on the sensor readouts arrayed inside his helmet and scrolling across its transparent ceramic/steel faceplate. He and all the others were alert for any movement, any sign of attack as they continued on toward the location the Dyonari promised was just ahead.

The movement, when it did come, was so faint as to go unnoticed by anyone for the first two seconds. By the third second, it had registered in Major Torgon's vision and he was opening his mouth to call a warning. By the fourth second, before Torgon had actually uttered a word, Agrippa had seen it, as well. He was already in motion by the time the major cried, "Contact!"

Agrippa had his short, broad gladius unsheathed and ready in his right hand as he brought his quad-rifle around with the other. He and the others around him waited, tense, weapons at the ready, as the seconds ticked by.

Agrippa scowled. He could see nothing.

"What is happening?" called the Dyonari commander— Ralin—from up ahead.

Squinting, Agrippa attempted to make out what the movement had been, even as another part of his mind noted the fact that his armor's electronic scanning devices were not registering a thing.

"What is it?" called Commander Ralin again. "Why have you stopped?"

Agrippa kept his eyes focused tightly on the area as he answered, "There's something out there." He nodded toward the wall of fog as the commander walked back towards him.

The commander appeared to exchange a few telepathic words with Commander Merrin, then said aloud, "What did you see? Why aren't our sensors detecting anything?"

"I don't know," Agrippa answered. "And I don't know." He nodded at the swirling gray clouds. "But there is definitely something there."

Ralin frowned at Agrippa. He turned and surveyed the fog for several seconds, then made a sound of impatience or annoyance. "Whatever it was, it is no longer there," he said. "Perhaps it became aware of the full strength of our column, and chose to withdraw, or—"

Agrippa issued his own sound of annoyance and impatience with the Dyonari commander. Raising his gladius high, his already-tall stature only enhanced by the bulky armor, he rushed ahead toward the fog. The Dyonari called out to him but he ignored the words. Before anyone could stop him, he plunged into the gray clouds and vanished.

4

Seated in the big, comfortable chair in Nakamura's old office, Tamerlane had actually fallen into a light nap when Captain Dequoi signaled that their distinguished visitor had arrived.

Iapetus and Tamerlane emerged onto the bridge from opposite directions at almost exactly the same moment. The general in black and gold was escorted by two Lords of Fire and two Kings of Oblivion soldiers in medium-weight combat armor, each carrying a superheated-plasma pistol—the standard issue for use within the hull of a starship, where nearly anything else ran the risk of causing explosive decompression. The general in red was alone, wearing his formal officers' coat with its flaring bottom over his standard uniform. The two approached one another and halted about six paces apart at the center of the ship's massive bridge level. Captain Dequoi looked on from his command seat and the goddess Teluria stood off to Tamerlane's right, leaning with her back against the railing, her dark eyes darting from one to the other of the generals.

"Well, Ezekial," Iapetus began. "I must commend your soldiers on their thoroughness. They searched for weapons in places I scarcely even knew I possessed."

Tamerlane didn't laugh. He barely smiled. "You've come to discuss terms of surrender, yes?" he asked, his tone all business.

Iapetus did smile at that. He actually appeared more relaxed, more at ease, than anyone there had ever seen him. He spread his hands wide at waist level. "I hadn't thought of it, but if you *are* prepared to surrender," he said, "I certainly will be glad to hear your terms."

Tamerlane's mouth tightened into a grimace. "Why are you wasting our time?" he asked. "Why shouldn't I simply blow your ship out of the cosmos right now—and put you out an airlock?"

Iapetus gave a tiny shrug. "If you can do those things, perhaps you should," he said. "But, in the meantime, I have a special message—" He turned and faced Teluria directly. "—for you."

The goddess twitched visibly. Her lips curling downward in distaste, she regarded him with equal parts surprise and contempt. "For me? You dare to even *speak* to me, after the events of Ahknaton?"

Iapetus half-smiled. "An unfortunate series of circumstances," he said. "Allow me to apologize formally." He pursed his own lips and added, "I also have a secret for you, if you would care to hear it."

Tamerlane had no idea what to make of this. He watched and waited, his patience growing thin.

Teluria's expression soured further, but she did step away from the railing and move slowly towards him. "I should open a portal here, now, into the Below—and shove you through it," she muttered.

"Oh, I think Hell awaits most of us present here," Iapetus said in a low growl. "Sooner or later." And then he merely waited, calm and patient, as if he had not a care in the world.

After five endless seconds ticked past—five seconds during which nobody moved or spoke—Teluria grudgingly approached him. She stopped as soon as she stood within arm's reach of him. "Well?" she asked.

Iapetus favored her with a full smile, then raised his right arm and pointed his index finger at her. "You can go ahead and open that portal you mentioned," he said, "but not into the Below. No—this one should go right back over to the bridge of the *Atlantia*."

"What?" Teluria and Tamerlane said it simultaneously.

"And you're coming with me," Iapetus added with a laugh. "Now. Or—"

"Or what?" Teluria demanded. "You are unarmed—not that any of your pitiful weapons could harm me, even if that were not so."

"You know of the one weapon that will harm you," Iapetus replied, his previously disconcerting smile now replaced by a much better-fitting predatory leer. "You know I possess a copy of it." He nodded down at his arm. "I have had its components surgically fitted within my own right arm. With but a thought, I can fire the weapon and rip your living spirit from your body."

Teluria gaped at him. She looked at his index finger, pointing directly at her, then back at his face, seeing his hard expression. She slowly shook her head.

"Impossible," Tamerlane exclaimed. "And ridiculous. My men would've found any weapon—"

"It is not a human weapon," Iapetus stated flatly. "It will not appear on any scans."

Tamerlane started forward, his soldiers behind him, their rifles at the ready. Iapetus halted them with a quick look. "Now, now, Ezekial," he said tensely. "Any false moves and she's done for."

Tamerlane considered this. "Why should I care?" he asked. "Why should I allow you to leave—and to take her with you? Again?"

Iapetus shrugged at this. "I honestly have no idea," he replied. "But I do know that you *will*. Because I know *you*." He laughed. "And—because you know *me*—you know I will kill her without a second thought."

Tamerlane glared at him but said nothing.

"Now, my dear," he said to Teluria, "if you would be so kind as to open a way through to the *Atlantia*—?"

Practically steaming in anger and helplessness, the goddess in red raised one hand and began to peel back the outermost layers of reality.

"What good will it do you to go back to your ship?" Tamerlane demanded. "It's dead in the water."

Iapetus flashed him another smile. "If that's so, then why should you object to us going there?"

The portal whooshed open, a slowly-rotating circle just taller than the top of Iapetus's head. Clouds and lights flashed within it.

"After you," the general said to the goddess.

Casting one last miserable look back at Tamerlane, Teluria walked through the portal. Iapetus followed her. A moment later, the spinning circle of light shrank down to a tiny ball floating at waist-height, and then it vanished utterly.

No one aboard the *Ascanius* was the least bit surprised when, a few moments later, the *Atlantia* came to life, its damage feigned or superficial, its engines back on line and purring.

One of the sensor techs turned to Dequoi and Tamerlane. "Sir," she said, "the *Atlantia* is powering up weapons."

"I knew she wasn't as hurt as they were letting on," Dequoi hissed.

Still cursing under his breath, Tamerlane barked orders at Dequoi and the others on the bridge. The captain was way ahead of him; he'd been issuing orders silently, via the Aether, from the moment Iapetus had come aboard. In response, what was left of the *Ascanius*'s deflector shields charged to capacity while its guns, already pointed toward the *Atlantia*, cycled up for maximum power.

This was done just in the nick of time, for an instant later the *Atlantia* opened fire with its two main forward-facing guns. The nearly-blinding twin beams of coherent light stabbed out and struck the *Ascanius* amidships, shredding the remainder of the shields. A fraction of the blasts made it through and hit the ship in its central living quarters area. Meanwhile the *Atlantia* began to rotate so that its longer row of cannons along the side lined up directly facing Tamerlane's ship.

Alarms on the bridge wailed from the first strike. Fire control teams were redirected to deal with the new damage. The *Ascanius*, already grievously wounded during the battle with the Phaedron comets, teetered now on the brink of utter catastrophe.

And then ice began to form on the floor of the bridge. Tamerlane saw it, instantly recognized it for what it was, and wondered if it would possibly save them—or bring about an even greater doom.

"Contact!" cried the sensor officer, just as he had expected. "Comets dropping hyper off our starboard bow!"

As a new wave of comets swept down upon the two ships, the *Atlantia* held off on firing at the *Ascanius* for a second.

This was all Dequoi needed. He didn't wait for Tamerlane to suggest it. He linked directly to the chief engineer and mentally shouted, "Jump! Now!"

The *Ascanius* spun on its axis and leapt into hyperspace.

Seeing the *Atlantia*, now surrounded by comet fragments, shrink down to a tiny dot and then disappear behind them, Tamerlane smashed his fist down onto the railing. His iron control over his powers slipped momentarily. In response, little fires sprang up all along the rail, bringing crewmembers running with extinguishers to put it out. The general scarcely even noticed.

"Maybe the Phaedrons will finish Iapetus off this time," Dequoi suggested, once Tamerlane had calmed down a bit. "Maybe we've seen the last of him."

Tamerlane gave the old captain a look that expressed his feelings on that score very clearly.

Dequoi reluctantly nodded. "You're right," he said. "I'm beginning to think the only way to deal with Iapetus is to drive a stake through his heart."

"I'm open to any and all approaches," Tamerlane replied. "Yours sounds as good as any. And I'd like just one more opportunity to try it."

5

Back in realspace, the *Atlantia* unleashed a massive broadside against the attacking wave of comets, driving the Phaedrons back momentarily. The aliens responded with a psychic barrage of their own, mental hooks lashing out to ensnare the crewmembers of the human ship.

The officers and techs were screaming in agony all around, unable to do their jobs. Even Teluria had dropped to her knees, clutching at her head and screaming. Gritting his teeth and biting his tongue to the point that blood ran down from the corner of his mouth, Iapetus stumbled to the helm control and shoved the writhing officer out of the way. Then, rotating the ship so that its direction matched that of the *Ascanius* some seconds before, he collapsed on top of the jump engine controls. His fingers clawed for the correct touchsquares and levers. At last he could hold back no longer and he screamed—but as he did, the *Atlantia* lurched forward, away from the Phaedron comets, and shot into hyperspace.

The leader of the Sons of Terra had escaped once again. And he had the power of the gods on his side once more.

Almost immediately, General Arnem Agrippa began to wonder if he had acted too impetuously, too rashly. The moment he passed through the wall of clouds, the fog totally engulfed him and visibility dropped to almost nothing. He raised his visor but it didn't help. He froze in place, worried that if he moved about, he might lose his bearings and never find his way back to the rest of the squad. His common sense screamed at him that he was behaving foolishly, impetuously; that he'd been incredibly stupid to dash into this swirling miasma of nothingness all alone. *The movement was purely in your imagination*, that voice insisted. After all, no one's sensor had picked anything up. And yet an even louder, stronger instinct had seized him and compelled him forward. In truth, he'd had no choice in the matter. It was as if he'd been enchanted. For reasons that entirely eluded him now, he'd had to see what lay in this direction.

Even so, after several long moments of shouting into the fog and looking about, he had nearly come to the conclusion that his wits had abandoned him, and he prepared to head back in what he hoped was the direction from which he'd come. He took a single step in that direction and then the movement flickered in the right rear corner of his vision again.

He froze in place. Looking around without lifting either foot, so as not to lose what little sense of direction he still possessed, he shouted, "Who is there?"

For a second nothing happened. Then the clouds of fog parted and a tall, muscular, armored figure strode out. Agrippa frowned as he studied the man for a few moments. Then he gasped.

The man wore white and green Deising-Arry Mark 5 combat armor. The insignia on his chest represented the III Legion—the Kings of Oblivion. The transparent visor of his helmet was down, reflections from its surface obscuring the features of the person inside. As Agrippa watched, somehow knowing what he was about to see, the other figure slid the visor up.

It was like looking in the mirror.

"What—?" Agrippa began, but faltered immediately. He openly stared at the other figure, who was doing much the same to him.

"So it happens," the twin said in a low voice, clearly speaking more to himself than to Agrippa. "It actually happens."

"*What* happens?" Agrippa asked, still wrong-footed and not certain exactly how to proceed or what to say. "Who *are* you?"

"*This* happens," the twin said. "We meet."

"*Who are you?*" Agrippa repeated, more urgently.

"Who do you think I am? Remember—we are in the Above. And you've been tracing a temporal anomaly. You didn't suppose something like this could happen?"

Agrippa took this in and shook his head. "You're saying you're *me*—from the *future*?"

"If I were you from the *past*, you'd remember it, wouldn't you?"

Agrippa felt his anger rising. "Fine. So—assuming that's true, why are you here? What do you want?"

The twin moved closer. Agrippa in response raised his gladius slightly.

"I have only a few seconds," the twin stated in a low but intense tone, ignoring the weapon. "My crowd is in a hurry, and your crowd will be looking for you at any moment." He snorted a laugh. "This conversation doesn't last long."

Agrippa nodded once. "Alright, then. What?"

"I need to tell you whom to trust. And whom not to."

Agrippa didn't miss a beat. "Solonis?"

"You can trust him. Somewhat."

Agrippa absorbed this and nodded.

"But." The twin's voice dropped even lower; now it was a conspiratorial whisper. "Siklar," he said. "Don't trust Siklar. Don't let him inside the tower." He paused. "I know it will be difficult, but you must find a way."

Agrippa's eyebrows furrowed. "What? Who is *Siklar*?"

"And Torgon," the twin added. "You won't see it coming, but—what?" The twin blinked and looked at Agrippa directly. "That's right—I don't—*you* don't—know who he is yet."

"Wait," Agrippa interrupted, frustration filling him. "What did you say about Major Torgon?"

"If you deal with Siklar, you won't have to *worry* about To—"

A shuddering rocked the bleak landscape, causing Agrippa to stagger forward. He reached out, intending to catch himself on his twin's shoulder or arm—but there was nothing there. He continued in an uninterrupted stumble and crashed to the ground with a muffled thud.

"General!" came a shout from the direction his feet were pointing. Slowly he pulled himself up, just in time to see Major Torgon emerging from the fog. Agrippa noticed that he had one end of a thin cable clasped in his left gauntlet; likely it was a guide line back to the others.

Seeing Agrippa struggling to his feet, Torgon hurried forward and helped him up. "General," he said, "are you injured? Was there an attack?"

"The quake," Agrippa said, eyeing Torgon strangely. The words of the phantom twin still lingered in his mind. Something about Torgon doing something to him— something he wouldn't see coming. And that other name— what had it been? *Siklar*? He wasn't certain now. Cursing softly, he looked all around, but the mysterious twin had vanished—and before providing any real answers as to his identity or to why he had come.

"Quake?" Torgon asked. "I didn't feel anything. Did—?"

"Never mind," Agrippa growled. He had already accepted the idea that the quake that had sent him to the ground was as much a phantasm as the twin had been. He began to wonder if any of it had happened. Perhaps the vapors in this fog had hallucinogenic properties.

Torgon reeled the guide line around his arm as he led the general back in the direction of the others. By the time they at last emerged from the fog and rejoined the combined human/Dyonari party, Agrippa was ready to believe that his strange encounter had been merely an illusion, a phantasm; a mental reaction to something in the environment, perhaps.

He did, however, mention it to Solonis as they resumed their march, and the seer-god reacted in a quite unexpected manner.

"Might I speak with you in private for a moment?" Solonis asked, loudly enough for the humans and Dyonari surrounding them in the party all to hear.

Agrippa nodded and together they angled away from the rest of the procession. Once they were out of easy hearing range of the others, the seer-god said in a low tone, "Tell me what you saw. Omit no details."

Agrippa described what he could remember of the conversation. He found even more of it had slipped from his memory, as though it had happened in a dream and now he was awake. He could feel—could almost *taste*—the remnants of the conversation with the twin, but the specifics eluded him.

"A temporal phantom," Solonis said when the general was done. "An echo from the future."

"I didn't imagine it?" Agrippa shot him a sidelong look. "You believe it actually happened, then?"

"Certainly I do," he replied. "I've seen similar phenomena myself, many times across the ages." He chuckled softly. "I do, after all, travel back and forth through time quite often. It's an activity I am very familiar with—and one that can generate quite unusual situations, such as the one you found yourself in."

"So that was *me*, then," Agrippa said. "Me, from some time in the future—trying to *warn* me—?"

"And doing a very poor job of it, from what you've said," Solonis replied.

Agrippa scowled at this but bit back a retort.

Solonis grew more serious now, moving closer to the big, armored man as they continued to march through the fog. "This future-you said nothing you didn't already wonder about, yes? You were already concerned about betrayal. We both suspect the Dyonari have a hidden agenda that may well clash with our own goals."

Agrippa nodded at that. "It's the other part that concerned me more," he rumbled. "My twin alluded to something negative involving Major Torgon." He shook his head. "I cannot imagine a more loyal officer than Torgon. Such talk makes me less inclined to believe any of it."

Solonis remained silent for a few moments, perhaps thinking it all through. Then he looked up at Agrippa and spread his hands. "I understand your sentiments, General," he said. "Still—it will do no harm to at least keep an eye on him. On *all* of them. Just in case."

Agrippa reluctantly nodded. "And on *you*, too," he added. "The other-me seemed to trust *you* implicitly, yet called into question the loyalties of my own men." He leaned in closer to Solonis, meeting his eyes directly. "I am not entirely convinced this was not something *you* engineered."

Solonis's eyes widened. "I assure you, General—"

Agrippa had already turned and was walking back toward the main body of their procession, ending the conversation.

But Solonis wasn't done. "General," he called as he hurried to catch up with the big man's retreating form.

Agrippa glanced back, annoyed. "Yes?"

"Should you at some point in the near future find yourself on the other side of that conversation..." He smiled. "...Do try to be a bit clearer in your warnings, will you?"

7

I t loomed up ahead of them suddenly; in the dense and unending fog of this realm of the lower Above, virtually everything did that. It was a column of gleaming silver and dull gray, with glowing spots of light and lines of luminous yellow and green and red traced down its sides in strange, zigzag patterns. To call it a column, however, was to sell short its size: it was more a building or a tower. Its diameter was at least a hundred meters, and perhaps more. Its base was sunk into the flat, featureless soil, and of its upper reaches no one could see, for it towered high above into the fog such that its top—if top it had—was lost to sight.

The Dyonari halted as they drew within sight of it and Agrippa signaled for his own troops to do likewise. For a few moments they all stood staring up at it, human and alien alike, in unabashed astonishment.

"This is it," Solonis said. "I saw it in a vision, but did not know where precisely to find it."

"This is it?" Agrippa said. He turned to Commander Merrin. "What exactly *is* it?"

The spindly Dyonari looked from the round gray tower to the human and shook his head slowly. "I do not know. Nor does any other of my party."

"Then why are you so interested in it?" Agrippa asked.

The other commander, Ralin, moved quickly toward them and hissed for them to keep their voices down. "They are watching. And listening," he added angrily.

"Who are?" Agrippa started to say. But before he could get the words out, he saw two strange, dark figures moving within the fog at the base of the tower. It took only a moment's glance to recognize they were Skrazzi—the strange, insect-like aliens they had encountered previously.

"I trust you now have a greater understanding of why we are *interested* in this thing, as you put it, General," Merrin said. "In addition to it being the only other solid object we have encountered in this realm besides the Temporal Vault, it appears that our enemies are quite interested in it as well. That alone should seize our attention."

"Like a flashing light," Agrippa said. "Or a siren."

"Indeed."

At some silent, unspoken signal likely transmitted via telepathy, the two alien commanders simultaneously looked up and to their left. Agrippa followed their gaze. There he could see a number of additional figures approaching through the swirling fog. He reached for the grip of his gladius, but Merrin motioned for him to relax. "They are with us," the alien officer said.

Indeed, the new arrivals turned out to be yet another group of Dyonari warriors. They greeted their fellows with quick bows and salutes. Seeing the humans standing alongside them, they regarded Agrippa and his squad with surprise and suspicion.

"You brought them *here*?" demanded one of the newly arrived Dyonari—the one who clearly held the highest rank of any of them, based on his armor and insignia. He said it aloud, clearly intending for the humans to hear him.

"This is the one from the Temporal Vault, High Commander," Ralin said, gesturing toward Solonis the seer-god.

The new Dyonari regarded the loincloth-wearing Solonis with open contempt. "*This* one? This is the one supposedly so critical to the operation?" He made a sound that was almost a laugh.

Solonis simply stared back at him, eyes level.

The Dyonari slowly shifted his attention from Solonis to Agrippa and the other armored humans. "What about them?" he asked. "Why bring them here?"

"They found the Vault before we did, High Commander," Ralin said nervously. "This one—Solonis—had already emerged from it. He was with these humans."

"I see..."

"Their mission is similar to ours, High Commander," Merrin added quickly. "We felt them to be natural allies."

The High Commander shifted his narrow gaze from Merrin to Agrippa and then back. He appeared unconvinced.

"And, had we simply abandoned them back there," Ralin said, "they likely would have followed us here on their own."

Agrippa snorted at that. He smiled. "Very likely," he agreed aloud. "Your people seem to know what they're doing here much more than we do. We'd like to be of assistance. And then, perhaps afterward, we could be provided with a way back home."

"I will provide you a way back to your worlds *now*," the High Commander said quickly.

"No, no," Agrippa waved the suggestion away. "We intend to be a part of this operation. To help you as best we can." His blue eyes locked with those of the tall, slender alien. "We *insist*," he added, his voice lower and harder than he'd made it in a while.

"As do I," Solonis said.

The High Commander looked from Agrippa to Solonis and back again, clearly sizing them both up. He said nothing. After a moment, he nodded once and turned, walking in the direction from which he had come. The other two Dyonari leaders exchanged uncertain glances, then hurried along after him. "Follow us," Merrin called back to Agrippa.

"General," Torgon said quietly, leaning in, as they marched along behind the aliens. "That guy makes me nervous."

"I concur," Agrippa said, his voice barely above a whisper. "Pass the word along to the squad: Treat these Dyonari like allies. Allies of *convenience*. But don't let your guard down for an instant."

"Yes, sir," Torgon said. He drifted back in the formation and began whispering to the next legionary in line.

Agrippa meanwhile returned his gaze to the leader of the alien forces, who was now conversing with the two commanders. *You're up to something*, he told himself, eyes narrowing. *Something even your own officers don't know about. But what?*

Setting the matter aside but keeping it firmly in mind, he set out after the Dyonari. His squad of Kings followed along behind him.

How many kilometers have I marched today already? he wondered. *And how many more before all of this—whatever it is—is done?*

h," said the strange voice in Tamerlane's dream. "I had been hoping to catch you asleep and traveling through hyperspace at the same time. It has proven remarkably difficult to do so."

Tamerlane heard these words and shifted in his bed, his still-sleeping mind wondering if he was actually awake. The voice hadn't sounded like a dream. It had sounded all too real.

"I have an important message for you, General," the voice continued. "So please pay attention."

"Who are you?" Tamerlane asked, his consciousness slowly emerging.

"That's better," the voice said. "I need you to focus."

"On what?"

"On this: General Agrippa is currently working to prevent the destruction of the galaxy, just as the goddess Aurore described to you. And he needs your help."

Now Tamerlane focused. "Agrippa? Where is he?"

"I am sending you the coordinates now."

"Alright, but—who are you? Why are you telling me this?"

"My name is Solonis. You know the name?"

"The seer-god, yes. But how do I know that—"

"The fact that I am able to speak to you inside a dream, from halfway across the quadrant, should fully satisfy you as to my *bona fides*."

Tamerlane thought about this. "You make a good point," he said.

A pause, then, "Your ship is emerging from hyperspace," the voice of Solonis said. "Outside of it, I can no longer reach you telepathically; I require the amplification it provides."

"I understand."

"You have the coordinates. I trust you will hurry."

"Yes, we will—"

The voice, and the presence that had accompanied it, disappeared from Tamerlane's dream. His mind swam in a sort of half-sleep, and part of it began to believe he had imagined the entire conversation—that he had truly dreamed it.

A chime brought him fully awake.

"General," said Harras Dequoi from the bridge, over a commlink connection, "we have dropped hyper in a location I believe to be safe—for now. I await your orders."

Tamerlane sat up, blinked—and the entire conversation came back to him. Now he knew it had been real.

"I'm on my way to the bridge," he said over the link. "And I have the coordinates of our destination."

"Very good, General," Dequoi replied, sounding mildly surprised.

Tamerlane closed the link and sat on the edge of his bed, frowning. It truly had been Solonis, the seer-god, contacting him—in a dream. He was certain of that now.

And that meant the danger to the galaxy was real, too. And that Agrippa was fighting to prevent it—and needed help. And likely every second counted.

Tamerlane pulled on his boots and ran for the bridge.

A short time and a shorter hike later, the Kings and their alien companions arrived at the forward position where the remaining Dyonari troops were hiding. Agrippa made a quick and unofficial head-count and determined that there were approximately thirty of them. There was no question that it was a formidable force, all told, but the numbers were still low. He turned to Merrin. "I'm assuming the goal is to get to or inside that structure," he said, nodding toward the round tower in the near distance. "Do you have an idea as to the number or disposition of enemy forces?"

Merrin's dark eyes moved across the tower and across the strange, exoskeletoned creatures that guarded it. "They seem to have placed a garrison here, to guard it," he replied. Then he motioned to another Dyonari nearby; this one had been there all along. For a couple of seconds neither made a sound as they engaged in telepathic communication. Then Merrin said aloud, likely for Agrippa's benefit, "Have you determined the enemy's strength during my absence?"

The junior officer looked from Merrin to Agrippa, seeming uncomfortable in the close proximity to a human. Getting ahold of himself, he shook his head once. "Not precisely, Commander Merrin. The High Commander estimates perhaps two or three hundred of the Skrazzi. They have continued to circulate about the structure."

"Two or three *hundred*?" Agrippa breathed. "Of those insect-things?" He shook his head and frowned. "What of the others—the telepathic ones?" He thought of those horrific silver faces rising out of the red light of the comet impact craters. His blood froze.

"The Phaedrons," the junior officer said. "No—we have seen nothing of them here."

"Thank the stars." Merrin shuddered.

Agrippa nodded at that. "If more than one or two of them were present," he said, "I would suggest abandoning the operation now. They are...*formidable*."

"Just what *is* the operation—if I may ask?" Major Torgon interjected from one side. "Since we seem to be involved in it now."

Agrippa introduced the major and then said, "It's a valid question. Beyond simply saying, 'There's a big silver tower and nothing else around here, and so we want to capture it.' If our mutual goal here is to prevent a galactic cataclysm, I assume that means you believe the cause of the disaster— and its prevention— can be found inside that thing."

"The former, very possibly, based on the information we possess," Merrin said. "The latter—who can say?"

"It would be helpful to have more information—some small bit of confirmation, at least," Agrippa growled. "Before we risk our lives attacking it."

Merrin spread his spindly fingers wide. "I am sorry, then," he said, "but I have told you all I know."

Agrippa shifted his gaze from Merrin to the unnamed High Commander who stood by himself off to one side. *All* you *know, perhaps*, he thought to himself. *But all* any *of you know? I wonder.*

"This tower is the epicenter of the cosmic shockwave I have traced," Solonis stated. "I have seen it before, somewhere, somehow. But perhaps not in this same setting." He raised his hand to his forehead and closed his eyes, wincing as though in pain. "It is...odd. But it *is* our objective."

Agrippa looked back at Merrin. "Let us set the metaphysical considerations aside," he said, "and focus on purely tactical matters. We need to get past a garrison of hundreds of Skrazzi and into that tower. The importance of doing so is absolute and vital to the survival of the galaxy. Do I understand the situation correctly?"

Before any of the alien leaders could reply, Solonis answered again. "You do," he said.

The Dyonari appeared annoyed at his impertinence but didn't contradict him.

"Very well, then," Agrippa said, taking a knee and beginning to sketch with his armored finger in the soft soil. "If what we're doing is a frontal assault on a fixed position defended by superior numbers, here is what we must do."

As the others, human and alien, looked on with interest, the General drew his plans in the dirt.

10

As it turned out, Agrippa's plans all came to naught, surviving no longer than any other combat plans tend to survive after first contact is made with the enemy. The sneak attack by the aliens, devastating in its effectiveness, caught the Kings of Oblivion by surprise as they were still forming up their thin ranks and discussing the finer points of their assault strategy.

As Agrippa was pulling his enameled white gauntlet on and gripping the pommel of his gladius, a shout off to his right caused him to turn and draw the blade. He was milliseconds too slow; the big, night-black shape that hurtled out of the fog struck him in the chest with overwhelming force and drove him backward and onto the ground. He scarcely had time to recover before a curved stabbing blade struck down at him. He parried it with the gladius, which had somehow remained clutched in his hand. The needle-sharp tip scraped along the side and hip of his Diesing-Arry Combat Suit's ceramic-synthetic steel outer shell, gouging out a thin furrow before it slid off and stuck in the ground.

LEGION III: KINGS OF OBLIVION

The weight of the thing—a Skrazzi, surely—pressed heavily upon him and he couldn't reach up now to strike with the sword. The stabbing limb was free an instant later and rising, preparing to drive down at him, *into* him.

Part of his brain realized and understood that it had been one of his own soldiers he'd heard; one of his own who had uttered the cry that had alerted him to turn in the nick of time. Given even a moment's respite, he surely would have paused to wonder why the Dyonari guards on the perimeter had failed to sound an alert. Having no time for anything other than survival, however, he drew his foot up toward his chest and then planted it on the rock-hard shell of the Skrazzi. He kicked out with all his might. Somehow his strength, augmented by the battle suit he wore like a bulky second skin, was enough to propel the horrific alien creature away from him.

As quick as he was able, he climbed to his feet and brandished the gladius in his left hand even as he unslung his trusty quad-rifle with his right. The Skrazzi he had launched away from him now surged forward, albeit moving more slowly and cautiously this time. Agrippa watched as it aimed its other limb—the organic disintegrator cannon—directly at him. He understood implicitly that a direct hit from that weapon for anything more than a second would be lethal, given their current lack of complex medical assistance. Therefore, he knew, it could not be allowed to strike him.

In much less time than it took to tell, he fired all four barrels of the quad-rifle at the creature.

The operating manual of a standard An-Ro Quad-Rifle clearly specifies that under most operating conditions, it is a very bad idea to fire more than two barrels in tandem, and one should never fire all four barrels at once. Two of the barrels dispense energy beam/particle beam fire, while the other two unleash solid projectiles—high-speed slugs and explosive rounds, respectively. Each pair generates remarkable heat in the weapon; three can cause serious damage. Four...Well, the engineers at An-Ro surely wouldn't have wanted to contemplate such a thing.

Agrippa's weapon, however, was modified. Heavily, *extensively* modified. He fired all four—and to devastating effect.

The Skrazzi made it halfway across the distance separating them before it exploded in a thousand jagged, chitinous, dripping fragments, some of which splashed across Agrippa's boots.

Grimacing at the sight, the big general whirled about and attempted to take stock of the situation.

The sounds of fighting came from all around, though the ever-present fog made it difficult to identify individual combatants and impossible to take in the overall strategic situation. The Kings of Oblivion were each locked in one-on-one battles with Skrazzi attackers. Agrippa could see at least two of his legionaries down already, though the extent of their injuries was not readily apparent. Only a few meters from him, Torgon was parrying the lightning-fast strikes of a Skrazzi's blade-arm; the major didn't seem to notice the creature's other arm swinging up, leveling its disintegrator cannon.

Agrippa leapt forward, his quad-rifle swinging around toward his back on its heavy strap as he shifted his gladius to his right hand and brought it out and down, striking with all his strength.

The short, wide blade sliced cleanly through the alien's arm just below the elbow and above the organic weapon. The black cylinder dropped to the ground, grotesque dark blood spraying out in its wake.

Torgon had no time to thank the general for coming to his rescue. More Skrazzi, now apparently all fully aware of their presence there, came roaring out of the fog. Agrippa no longer felt certain whether they were even dealing with the members of the garrison they had been watching or with some new crowd erupting out of nowhere. As he brought his quad-rifle back around and opened fire on more of the invaders, hosing the hard-light beams into the charging insectoids, he spared a quick glance over at the Dyonari contingent. He had expected to see them equally engaged in life-or-death struggles with the creatures, but that was not the case. The Skrazzi had yet to attack the Dyonari, and for their part the Dyonari merely stood looking on, seemingly unconcerned.

"What are you waiting for?" Agrippa bellowed to his erstwhile allies. "An invitation? Here it is, then! *Fight them!*"

He recognized the first to move as Commander Merrin. The stoic alien officer unsheathed his long, curved sword and waded in, slashing at the Skrazzi with cold, surgical precision.

"That's more like it!" Agrippa shouted, even as he charged into the next pair of attackers, his own sword slicing into them.

The Dyonari assigned to Merrin's squad hesitated only an instant before following their leader into the fray, and Ralin's warriors did likewise moments later. Within seconds, almost all of the Dyonari soldiers were battling the enemy alongside Agrippa's troops, despite the fact that no general order had been given by their High Commander—a fact Agrippa noted and added to his long list of things to ponder later, *if* he and his legionaries survived.

For quite some time, swords slashed and energy-weapons flashed, and eventually the Kings of Oblivion and their Dyonari allies began to make headway against the wave of attackers. Dead and dismembered Skrazzi bodies lay all around, dark blood pooling underneath them. Finally the surging ranks of enemy combatants reached its end. The creatures never retreated—it was as if they had no notion of the concept—but simply kept charging into the fray until their numbers were exhausted. Agrippa, seeing the combat dying out, unfastened his helmet and pulled it free, taking a knee and gasping for breath. Even one with his near-incomparable physique had an upper limit on endurance, and he had reached his at last.

Within a few seconds, the three Dyonari officers had approached and now stood in a semicircle around Agrippa, with Torgon and two more of the Kings arrayed opposite them. With the Aether not functioning, Obomanu was asking for the other human troops to check in via the audio link.

"Four men dead, General," Obomanu reported flatly. "Two others seriously wounded, but they say they can go on."

Agrippa cursed. "And what of Solonis?"

"I am well," the seer-god stated cheerily, moving forward into view. "Two of your men attempted to protect me during the altercation—something for which I am grateful, despite the fact that their assistance was scarcely required."

Agrippa ignored this and turned to the trio of Dyonari officers. "How did they know we were here?" he demanded. "How did they approach us without your sentries noticing?"

Merrin and Ralin exchanged troubled glances; the High Commander shook his head. "Two of our scouts have not reported in," he said aloud. "I can only assume they were killed by the Skrazzi before the attack, to prevent word of their movements from reaching us."

Agrippa met the High Commander's eyes, considered this, and nodded. "If that's the case, you have my condolences," he said.

The tall alien nodded once back to him. "And you have mine."

Agrippa stood and walked past the others to stand out in the open, directly across from the gray edifice of the tower. In the dim light and fog, it could've been anything from part of a medieval fortress to the landing gear of some unimaginably colossal spacecraft. Idly he wondered what lay inside it that could possibly be worth the deaths of four of his troopers and two of the Dyonari. *If it—whatever it turns out to be—isn't of galaxy-shaking importance*, he vowed to himself, *I will punch Solonis so hard that he will need that tomb—and not for time travel.*

He stood there for several seconds, waiting, looking, assessing. Fastening his helmet back in place, he lowered the visor and accessed the various sensors and lenses at his disposal. Try as he might, he could find no signs of life remaining anywhere around the tower.

Finally he removed his helmet and turned back to face the collection of humans and aliens gathered together. "Very well, then," he boomed. "I believe we have killed them all." He nodded toward the tower. "Time to claim our prize."

And before anyone could stop him—before anyone could so much as call his name— he began to trudge across the open space toward the vast gray cylinder.

11

grippa had anticipated having to search for a way inside. As he ran across the open space between the bulk of the combined forces and the tower, images flickered through his head from ancient literature. He imagined hidden doors; secret passwords; mechanisms that read retina patterns or hand prints or magic words and phrases.

As it turned out, none of that was necessary. The door was standing wide open.

The door, in point of fact, was actually an open space, rectangular-shaped, that stood out quite visibly in the side of the gray metal of the tower. A dim light shone from somewhere inside, flickering slightly. In the dappled, inconstant glow where it reflected off the ground, a narrow trail of blood shone feebly.

Agrippa halted and stood a short distance away, not daring to move any closer just yet, simply studying the opening. It was tall; perhaps six meters in height. About half that wide.

His gaze flicked down to the blood. It definitely did not look to be Skrazzi. Human? ...Perhaps. That much was not clear.

At length Major Torgon, Lt. Obomanu and the others jogged up behind him and hesitated, no one speaking at first. They all gazed at the open doorway and waited to see what the general would do—or what he would order someone else to do. One by one they noticed the blood on the ground, forming a trail leading through the opening, and one by one they frowned and looked to Agrippa. The general was, however, inscrutable. After what seemed like hours but was scarcely more than a couple of minutes, he squatted down and studied the blood more closely.

Those that knew him knew he would never order someone else in his command to venture into a potentially hazardous environment before he did it himself. Even as the Dyonari approached and moved in alongside the Kings, and without even a glance back, Agrippa strode confidently through the doorway.

Nothing happened. No death rays from the walls or ceiling; no blades or arms or trap doors. Agrippa walked through into a dimly lit, plain hallway that curved away to his right. Drops of blood, much smaller now than at the entrance and spaced out, led in that direction. This time he looked back only momentarily; he knew his own troops would follow him in. He only glanced back long enough to see if the Dyonari were coming with them. He was pleased to note that they were, though they did appear somewhat more nervous now than usual.

"General," called one of the alien officers as he entered the tower behind Agrippa. "Perhaps a greater degree of caution is in order—?"

Agrippa shook his head. "Time is of the essence—we don't know how much longer before the..." He searched for a word. "...before the *event*, after we wasted so much time with the battle. And, not incidentally, we have no idea what we're looking for."

"Quite correct," noted Solonis. "On all counts."

Agrippa motioned with his head, indicating the way forward along the corridor. "So we have to *move*."

And so, some more reluctantly than others, the combined human/Dyonari force marched deeper into the strange tower, following the curving corridor and the trail of blood.

12

everal minutes into the march, the hallway opened out into a vast, round chamber, lit by seemingly thousands or millions of tiny lights of every imaginable color, each set into the plain gray metal walls. As Agrippa and the others filed out into the huge room, they became aware that both the ceiling and the floor at the center of the space was open; a shaft several dozen meters in diameter opened in the floor ahead of them, leading down into darkness, while its mirror image gaped over their heads.

"The core of the tower," Agrippa speculated, standing near the edge and gazing down. The small lights ran down into the depths, eventually swallowed by a greater darkness. Moving away from the rim a couple of steps, he inclined his head back and looked up. The same was true, visually, in that direction.

"I believe so," the Dyonari High Commander agreed. He stood next to Agrippa and looked about, then pointed across the opening to the far side of the chamber. "Shall we continue? There is room enough around the edge for all of us to walk."

Agrippa hesitated, then pointed to a spot off to his left. "Wait," he said. "Look there."

The Dyonari followed him as he strode purposefully to the location he had indicated, very close to the opening. A dark patch, larger than the spots they had been following, covered a fair amount of the floor.

"More blood. Ah." The general nodded past the stain to the edge of the shaft. "Whoever came this way, they found a way down, it would appear."

The Dyonari leader leaned out over the abyss and saw what his human counterpart had noted: A stairway, very broad, with steps much farther apart than would be comfortable for the average man or even the average Dyonari, curved down into the darkness.

Every fifth or sixth step had a spot of blood upon it.

The Dyonari commander straightened up and looked to Agrippa. The general smiled flatly and gestured toward the stairs with one gauntleted hand. "Shall we?" he asked.

13

own they went, now some four dozen in number, all combined; the Kings of Oblivion in their white and green bulky armor, Solonis in his loincloth, and the Dyonari in their form-fitting, multi-colored, glass-like suits. As they descended the stairs, the darkness seemed to rise up and surround them, an almost oppressive force unto itself. The Kings switched on bright, narrowly-focused lights that beamed out from the sides of their helmets, while the armor of each Dyonari warrior emitted a glow from every bit of its surface.

For a timeless time they pressed on, the opening where they had entered the shaft no longer visible but lost in the blackness high above them. As they moved, as the strange cylinder consumed them into its bowels, a strange sensation passed over and through them. More than once, Agrippa at the head of the formation felt it necessary to halt and simply stand, his left hand braced against the wall, leaning away from the awful drop to his right. Occasionally he would gaze down into the abyss and idly wonder if something was gazing back into him.

And then, just when it felt as if the stairs would continue on forever like some hellish eternal punishment of mythology, the soldiers spotted the bottom.

Light—brighter than anything they had encountered in a while—reflected up at them as they continued down, and now the floor was in sight. The light, they could tell as they neared the bottom, was coming from an opening on the far side of the shaft.

Agrippa felt an enormous sense of relief as he moved off the final step and onto more of the smooth gray flooring. He shifted to his right to allow the others to file along after him, then pointed toward the opening across the way. As before, it was very tall and wide, as though built to accommodate figures even taller than the Dyonari and broader of shoulder than the legionaries in their heavy armor. "That appears to be the only way out," he told the others. Then, almost as an afterthought, "Weapons ready." Behind him, the alien commander repeated that order to his own troops.

Cautiously, and with the Kings of Oblivion leading the way, the combined force emerged from the shaft and into the light.

The chamber was round, like the shaft through which they had just descended, but it was even larger in diameter. Every surface was of a very light gray verging on dull white. Large banks of equipment that could have been control consoles for a starship larger than anything currently flown by any race stood here and there, like tiny islands in a sea of open space. More consoles faced the broad, curving wall, all the way around. The ceiling of the chamber towered some ten meters above their heads.

Major Torgon turned to Agrippa, eyes wide. "What is all of this?" he asked, mystified. "Who could have built such a facility—and *why*?"

Agrippa removed his helmet and set it on a nearby console, then shook his head slowly. "I don't know, Major," he said, "but it is plain to me that the engineers of this place could have possessed the power, the capability, to threaten the galaxy itself."

"You speak in the past tense," the Dyonari High Commander noted. "My understanding was that we were seeking to prevent a threat in the *present time*."

"That is so," said Solonis, speaking up for the first time in quite a while. "Do not let the lack of inhabitants here dissuade you from the very real danger that is yet posed by this place."

"Meaning what?" Agrippa demanded, his patience clearly worn thin. "It's an automated facility? There is an artificial intelligence at work here? Some sort of malevolent program?"

Solonis frowned but did not reply.

"What of the blood?" asked Torgon, nodding toward the droplets that continued out from the stairway and shaft and into this chamber.

"Follow it," Agrippa ordered.

Torgon nodded, hefted his gladius, and started along the trail, moving slowly and carefully. The Dyonari High Commander and two of his warriors followed along behind him.

Agrippa watched them go, then turned to Solonis. "You know more than you've said thus far," he said in a hushed tone. He gestured at the chamber surrounding them. "Now we are here. Time to share everything."

The dark-skinned seer-god met the general's steely gaze momentarily, pursed his lips and looked away. "I haven't deceived you," he said. He closed his eyes and appeared to be concentrating for a moment. "It hasn't happened yet," he stated. "We are still earlier than the source event—though I feel we are very close now. Whatever is going to happen, it will occur within the next few minutes."

Agrippa nodded. "Yes. But I need more than that," he growled. "Who is responsible? How can I stop it from happening if I don't know—"

"General!"

The call came to Agrippa very loudly and clearly—and it sounded within his head. He whirled about, seeing Torgon and the three Dyonari standing some distance away, partly obscured by one of the many large banks of equipment. "Major," he replied. "You're calling me over the Aether link."

"I—what? Yes—yes, you're right, General," he said. "I did it instinctively."

"It's working now," Agrippa noted. "That's something, anyway." He started toward Torgon. "What do you have, Major?"

"Bodies, sir," Torgon replied. "Dyonari bodies."

Agrippa led a string of Kings and Dyonari in the major's direction. Arriving, the general placed his hands on his hips and gazed down at what his officer had found: Three Dyonari lay on the floor, each of them quite dead. The bodies had been arranged alongside one another in a row, straight out with their arms at their sides.

"Here's another one, sir," Torgon said. He stood next to one of the interface consoles, looking down.

Agrippa walked over and saw a fourth Dyonari warrior reclining limply in a cushioned seat before a broad control panel. The alien soldier was clearly dead, with blood pooled in the seat beneath his body.

"What was he up to?" the general wondered aloud, frustration evident in his voice. He looked from Solonis to the Dyonari High Commander. "What was he trying to do? Why did they all come here?"

The Dyonari leader knelt beside the one in the seat, examining him briefly, then turned his attention to the control panel he had been accessing.

"Do you recognize their markings?" Agrippa asked the leader. "Where could they have come from, to arrive here before us?"

208

The High Commander made a show of studying the insignia on the glass armor. He shook his head.

Solonis had also been inspecting the bodies. He looked up at Agrippa, his expression grave. "Dyonari, here, attempting to bring about a catastrophe," he said. "Just as I foresaw."

"Whatever they were attempting to do, clearly they failed," Agrippa boomed. "Perhaps the chain of events is happening differently this time."

"It doesn't work that way," Solonis replied testily. "This is *not* over."

Agrippa looked around, frowning. "Are there others, then?"

The High Commander raised a hand. "One moment," he began. "Perhaps we should—"

The movement had begun seconds earlier, but it had happened with such silent, unexpected suddenness that it had taken a brief moment for those present to register in their minds exactly what they were seeing. As the Dyonari leader became aware of the gigantic, humanoid shapes moving out into the chamber from hidden recesses in the walls, his words trailed off and he stumbled back a step, then reached for his sword.

Agrippa scowled and drew his gladius. His quad-rifle was already in hand, laid along his right arm, the barrels cycling around with a soft whine. "What is this?" he grumbled, bracing himself for what might happen next.

Four meters tall and very muscular, the strange beings strode from their places of concealment and converged around the humans and Dyonari near the center of the room. They moved almost silently but with clear purpose. Their skin where it was revealed—mainly their bald heads—was light gray and they wore skin-tight metallic uniforms of muted colors; some had blue as the predominant color, while others emphasized red or green. Their dark eyes flicked here and there, surveying the humans and Dyonari caught virtually flat-footed before them.

Agrippa hesitated, then called out to them, "Greetings! We mean no harm—we have come to attempt to prevent—"

The nearest gray giant rushed forward suddenly, silently, gliding across the distance between itself and the human leader in scarcely a second. It was upon Agrippa before he could react. It smashed him with a massive fist, driving him backwards, then pressed its advantage, swinging at him again.

Half a second after that first giant attacked, the others all did likewise. In the blink of an eye, the formerly peaceful environment was transformed into a miniature battlefield.

The Dyonari all had their long, curved swords out and counterattacked, but the giants moved incongruously quickly for such large foes, dodging the slashes and striking with their own multi-bladed weapons they produced seemingly from nowhere. The battle on that side of the room became a sort of halting ballet, with the tall, spindly Dyonari dancing about the almost equally nimble and much taller and bulkier gray figures.

Meanwhile, on the opposite side of the melee, the Kings of Oblivion had instantly and wordlessly reverted to their long-practiced tactics; they backed in toward one another, forming a ring with their guns and swords pointing outward. At the center stood Solonis, protected on all sides by the armored bulk of the human soldiers. Only Agrippa and Torgon were excluded, as they had traveled further across the big room.

"I believe we can safely assume we are on the right track," Agrippa called to Solonis. "These creatures clearly mean us harm."

"Something is not right," Solonis replied, his voice conveying uncertainty.

"Certainly that is so," Agrippa agreed, fending off a gray giant that seemed intent on decapitating him. "We are being attacked, in case you were not aware."

"Not that," the seer-god snapped back, angry. "Something is *wrong* here..."

"Do you mean these...*beings*...are *not* the enemy we seek?" Agrippa dodged a swing and lunged with his sword, missing in turn. "They are not the ones who trigger the event?"

Solonis said nothing for a moment. When he at last began to reply, Agrippa had to shout for him to wait, because a voice had just sounded within the general's head—a voice, strong and clear as it came through the newly-restored Aether link, that he hadn't heard in many hours. A voice he had feared he might not hear again.

"Agrippa," the voice said. "Is that you?"

"General Tamerlane?" Agrippa was so distracted by the voice that he nearly allowed the giant who was sparring with him to crush his face with a massive punch. As the blond general backpedaled, he sent his reply via the Aether: "How are you contacting me? We are somewhere in the Above!"

"Apparently not," the voice of Tamerlane said in his head. "Your beacon lit up a few seconds ago, just after we dropped hyper in-system. You must not be too terribly far away. And in our universe."

Agrippa frowned at this. He had too many questions; it was all too much to think about—particularly at this moment, when he was in a fight for his survival with an alien giant.

"General," he called back over the Aether, "we have much to discuss, and soon. But, for now, if you would excuse me, I have a pressing matter before me."

He could hear it in Tamerlane's voice when the reply came back: Ezekial knew precisely what sort of "pressing matters" Agrippa often found himself involved with. "Very well, Arnem," Tamerlane said. "Stay alive and we will see you soon."

Agrippa broke the connection even as he brought his gladius around in a quick slice, barely missing the giant's waist—the height differential was that great. A second later he raised his quad-rifle and unleashed a particle-beam blast that gouged out a chunk of the humanoid's shoulder. The creature bellowed in pain and staggered back.

"Ah," the general shouted, his eyes burning, "I *can* hurt you!"

As if in response, the giant redoubled its efforts to strike Agrippa with the multi-bladed weapon it gripped in its left hand. Meanwhile the sound of gunfire filled the chamber as the other Kings opened up with their own pistols and rifles. Agrippa found it odd that these gray giants, apparently serving as guardians of this strange facility, didn't seem to possess or carry any distance weapons of their own. Then he saw the one opposite him reach down, and in an instant a rectangular shape had formed in the portion of the uniform at the creature's hip. It extended out, like a box, until the top of it opened and a sort of pistol grip appeared in the opening. The giant grasped the handle and drew what was obviously a gun out, aiming it directly at Agrippa. The general dived to his left, the blinding energy blast only just missing him; a portion of it deflected off the always-reliable Deising-Arry power armor he wore. But, as he rolled and came up onto his feet again, the giant countered with a swing of its other arm, and its gargantuan reach proved more than Agrippa could handle. One of the razor-sharp surfaces of the multi-blade sliced across his cheek, sending a sheet of blood flying.

"General!" Torgon cried, seeing the blade cutting Agrippa's face. He attempted to disengage from his own opponent and come to Agrippa's aid.

The general's blood splashed across the floor and against the side of the nearest equipment console.

One second passed, as Torgon leveled his gun and blasted Agrippa's opponent. The giant spun away and down, roaring in pain.

Two seconds passed, as Agrippa regained both his feet and brought up a hand, touching the raw wound on his face, blood running freely from it.

Three seconds, and a nearly deafening sound filled the room. It was low, deep, resonant; the humans and Dyonari could feel their bones and diaphragms vibrating as much as they could actually hear the sound.

Four seconds, and all the gray giants ceased their fighting and moved smoothly back to their places in the walls. Panels silently slid upward from the floor, sealing them away.

Torgon was shaking his head, trying to recover his senses as the last echoes of the sound faded out. He moved over to assist Agrippa, but the general waved him away. "I'm alright," the human commander told him, even as he swiped a small cylinder across his face. The chemical dispensed from it covered the wound and instantly stopped the bleeding. He looked toward Solonis, standing wide-eyed at the center of the other human troops; between their enemies suddenly disappearing and the bone-shaking sound, most of them appeared extremely disoriented now. "What did you make of that?" the general asked the seer-god, his frustration evident in his tone. "Did that sound herald the event we came here to prevent? Are we too late?"

Solonis raised both hands and closed his eyes for a few seconds, then opened them and shook his head. "No. The shockwaves still travel toward the past. We have not yet arrived at the epicenter of the event." He made his way between two of the Kings and strode toward Agrippa. "But the time grows very short indeed. I can *feel* it."

Agrippa nodded. He turned to the Dyonari officers, who were approaching from the opposite direction.

"Why did the giants flee?" asked the High Commander, clearly puzzled. "Our attacks were taking some slight toll upon them, but not enough to—"

"It wasn't our doing," Agrippa said brusquely. "I'm certain of it." His fingers brushed the slash on his cheek. "The giants were not losing. Something recalled them."

"The sound," the alien commander said, nodding. "Yes. But—*why*?"

Agrippa exhaled slowly, then said to the Dyonari, "Excuse me for a moment." He turned his back on them and walked a short distance away, accessing the Aether as he went. Solonis approached and stood facing him, watching. Agrippa ignored him.

"So—you survived your pressing matters, then?" Tamerlane said when the link was restored. "I never doubted you would."

"Where are you, General?" Agrippa asked. "For that matter—where am *I*?"

"Everything indicates you are on a planet in the SK-9 system."

"A planet. Well." He squeezed his eyes closed for a few seconds, weariness just beginning to sink in after all he'd done since leaving Ahknaton—and all he'd done before that. "So we are no longer in the Above."

"You are not. I'm aboard a shuttle that is at this very moment landing on that planet, and your carrier signal is coming in loud and clear."

Agrippa closed his eyes again, this time thinking. "The shaft," he said. "I felt disoriented somehow as we descended."

"It led out of the Above and into your own universe," Solonis said over the link. "This facility exists simultaneously in multiple dimensions."

Agrippa frowned and looked up at the seer-god. "You are tapped into our Aether frequency," he said. "How?"

"I am a god," Solonis said, shrugging.

Agrippa considered this and accepted it. "General," he said to Tamerlane, "if you are indeed on your way here, your assistance would be appreciated."

"Be there in a few minutes."

Agrippa frowned again. "May I ask—how did you know to come here? How did you know where we would exit the Above?"

"Your friend there contacted us with the coordinates," Tamerlane said.

Agrippa glanced at Solonis again; the seer-god shrugged again. "Just another of my useful tricks," he said. "I thought your associates might prove valuable to us, should we make it this far."

"But how—"

"Time passes more slowly in the Above," Solonis said, "so your General Tamerlane had ample opportunity to gather his forces and meet us here, now."

"I take it not much time has passed for you, Agrippa," Tamerlane interjected. "It's been a few weeks back here in reality."

Agrippa waved a hand dismissively. "The entire tale—from both our perspectives—can be told at a later date. But, for now, understand that we have come here on the same urgent mission we set out to perform when we left you on Ahknaton: to prevent the future shattering of the galaxy." He paused, then added, "And I fear we know as little about its cause now as we did then."

14

They found the external door with little difficulty and it slid soundlessly up into the wall above it, revealing General Ezekial Tamerlane and a cadre of red-clad soldiers and others standing arrayed behind him.

Tamerlane wore his usual dark red uniform of smooth, crisp smartcloth. His short, dark hair was combed to the side and the golden insignia at his collar glinted in the pale light. He moved forward and embraced Agrippa warmly. The blond general smiled in return and clapped Tamerlane on the back.

The Kings moved aside and Tamerlane's party filed in through the giant-proportioned doorway. Beyond, Agrippa could see the shuttle parked in a rocky canyon beneath a pale blue sky; nothing else of the planet they now occupied was visible, but it was definitely nothing like the Above. He felt deeply relieved somehow to be back in his own dimension, and vowed he would not leave it again in this lifetime if he could help it.

"What's our time frame?" Tamerlane asked first. "Hours? Minutes?" He looked around. "Hopefully not seconds."

Agrippa shook his head. "Unknown. My troops are inspecting the equipment now, as is our new friend from the future. Or rather, from the past." He frowned. "It gets somewhat confusing."

"You don't have to tell me that." Tamerlane snorted. He looked toward Solonis. "Can we trust this guy, Arnem?"

"I have it on the highest authority," Agrippa replied. "My own."

Tamerlane gave him a puzzled look in reply, but Agrippa waved it away. "Until we know precisely what we're dealing with here," the blond general explained, "I'm not certain what we should do. Or what we *can* do."

"Take a few quad-rifles or explosives to the place?" Tamerlane asked. "Just trash it all?"

"We don't know if that wouldn't set off the very thing we're trying to avoid setting off," Agrippa pointed out.

Tamerlane scowled. "Yeah, well...That's why I brought these people." He gestured toward the crowd of non-uniformed men and women who had followed him in. "A few specialists I felt might be of use."

"A few?" Agrippa repeated, surveying the more-than-two-dozen individuals now milling about inside the doorway.

Tamerlane shrugged. "I'd rather have them here and not need them, than have them stuck up on the *Ascanius* with the fate of all creation on the line down here." He pulled five figures in particular out of the crowd. He nodded toward the first—a tall, gaunt figure with a hooked nose, wearing a crisp, white uniform. "Brother Regulus of the Ecclesiarchy," he said. In response to Agrippa's surprised reaction, Tamerlane quickly added, "Don't worry—Regulus was on the outs with them, which means he's pretty much the only one of that crowd I trust. He comes with Stanishur's approval." Next he gestured toward a tall, muscular figure to Regulus's right. "This is Major Cassius, one of my best tactical officers." Behind him came an even taller and even more muscular man, who stood beside a lithe, dark-haired woman. Both of them looked extremely dangerous. "These two are Major Titus Elaro and Colonel Niobe Arani. You might remember them from the events on Ahknaton."

Agrippa made a non-committal sound and shook hands with the four. He nodded toward Sister Delain of the Holy Inquisition, clad in her usual black robes and hood. The sister nodded back.

A moment later, Tamerlane approached Solonis and extended a hand. "So—you're the one who has been of such assistance to us."

Solonis gripped the hand almost curiously and held on as Tamerlane shook it.

"He is also the one who sent Aurore to bring us into this affair in the first place," Agrippa noted.

"Ah." Tamerlane looked sidelong at the dark-skinned god. "I trust this was all in a good cause, then," he said. "A *very* good cause."

"The best, General," Solonis said. "We are attempting to save the galaxy."

"From what?"

Solonis hesitated and Agrippa sighed. Tamerlane looked from one to the other, puzzled.

"We are not certain," Agrippa stated, almost embarrassed to say it.

Tamerlane blinked at this. "I understood you don't know what to do to prevent the catastrophe," he said, "but—you still don't even know what—or whom—is responsible?"

"To be fair, General," Solonis said quickly, "I would remind you it has only been a matter of hours for General Agrippa and company."

Tamerlane didn't appear terribly mollified by this. He clasped his hands behind his back and walked a short distance away. Then he noticed the Dyonari for the first time.

"Arnem," he said in a low voice, "we are now working with—?"

Agrippa merely nodded. "Long story," he muttered. "Not worth your time at present."

Now it was Tamerlane's turn to exhale slowly. He brought a hand up and, eyes closed, rubbed at his forehead. "Very well," he said. "I suppose there have been quite a few developments within the Empire while you have all been gone that will surprise you, too." He faced Solonis squarely. "You are supposed to be the one here who has all the answers—or all the answers that are to be had. So—what do we do to, as you put it, save the galaxy?"

The seer-god and Agrippa exchanged uncertain looks. Then Agrippa looked beyond Tamerlane to the crowd he'd brought with him. "You have artificial intelligence experts in your party?" he asked.

Tamerlane nodded. "What do you need?"

Agrippa pointed to the console nearby where the dead Dyonari had been found in the cushioned seat. The body had been removed and placed on the floor alongside the others. "Our only lead so far," he said, and quickly explained how they had tracked the blood drops to this chamber, found three of the aliens dead on the floor, and the fourth having passed away while apparently attempting to do something to the controls.

Tamerlane called for Major Cassius and ordered him to take a couple of experts and see what they could discern from that control panel. Then he turned to Agrippa and Solonis. "If it can be figured out, they'll figure it out," he said.

"Good," Agrippa said, though he didn't sound convinced.

"This is not over, General Tamerlane," Solonis said in a quiet voice.

"What do you mean?"

"My leap into the future granted me no specifics," the dark-skinned god replied, biting his lower lip. "But one thing that stands out as very clear to me is that the Dyonari were..." He hesitated, and when he resumed, he spoke in a very quiet voice. "...If not responsible, certainly *instrumental* in whatever happens."

Tamerlane looked at him. "Dyonari? Well." He gestured toward the crowd of tall, spindly aliens, and his voice was filled with annoyance. "We have plenty of suspects to choose from. Any idea which one of them still finds a way to destroy the galaxy?"

Solonis pursed his lips and appeared to be searching for an answer when Major Cassius shouted to them from the control station. "You need to see this, General." He paused, then, "Generals."

"What is it, Cassius?" Tamerlane asked as the human officers gathered around the console.

"Tell them what you told me," Cassius ordered the two technicians who were now working at the controls.

One of the techs was holding himself awkwardly to one side of the cushioned seat, attempting to avoid the pool of Dyonari blood that still filled it. He nodded toward a set of flashing red lights along the right side of the broad display panel. "An overload is building, sir. A malicious code has been partly introduced into the system. It's a Dyonari code, but I recognize it."

Tamerlane and Agrippa exchanged concerned looks. "Malicious?" Tamerlane asked. "In what way?"

"This is all difficult to read, sir," the tech replied, "but I get the basics of it. It's not all that complicated." He pointed to the red lights. "The malicious code has been slowly opening all the conduits to the various power sources that are coordinated by this facility."

"Power sources?"

"*Vast* power sources," the tech reported.

The second tech shook his head in astonishment. "*Extremely* vast—and that's still putting it mildly."

"It appears to me this place is tied into a sort of network of nearby stars," the first tech continued, "and is able to channel raw stellar energy."

"Good heavens," Tamerlane whispered.

"That's not all," the second tech said. "I heard someone say this place was connected to the Above, and I can definitely believe it. Because there are levels of cosmic power flowing through here that can't be explained even by ripping open entire stars."

"Which, by the way," the first tech added, "I think this facility could do, too."

"Where is it coming from?" Tamerlane asked. "This power?"

The first tech tapped a display to his left; its markings were incomprehensible to the general but he didn't announce that fact. "I'm not entirely sure, sir," he said, "but a rift appears to have opened in spacetime just beyond the orbit of this planet's moon. A stream of raw energy unlike anything I've ever seen before is pouring through it, from...*somewhere* else. And this facility is now channeling that power out into our universe."

Agrippa looked at Tamerlane and simply shook his big, blond head.

"Can you shut it down?" Tamerlane asked. "Or block it somehow?"

"I don't know that anything we possess could block it, General," the first tech answered. "But as to shutting down the system here that's receiving and redirecting the energy back out—that, I believe we may be able to do, sir," the first tech said.

"I've already begun to remove the code," the other technician added. "I assumed it was a safe bet you didn't want it to continue."

Tamerlane laughed. "Yes," he said, "you can safely assume that." He turned to Agrippa. "Well. It's easy to see why this place represented such a threat. That being said—if only all our problems could be solved this easily."

Agrippa bit back a retort with regard to "easily;" Tamerlane clearly had no idea what he and his men had gone through, including no sleep in what seemed like several days now. He gazed around at the chamber and then down at the console with the catastrophically deadly coding that their men were removing now. "I would just as soon permanently seal this place off," he replied. "Or simply destroy it."

"Do we even know what this facility is? What it's for?"

"No," Agrippa said. "Does it matter?"

Tamerlane shrugged. "Who can say?"

Agrippa paused, then looked at Solonis. "Can *you* say?"

The seer-god frowned, formulating a response. He opened his mouth to reply—and another deep, rumbling tone resounded throughout the chamber. Instantly everyone was on guard, weapons raised and ready.

"Here," called one of the Kings off to Agrippa's right.

Agrippa and Tamerlane led the others in the direction of the shout. There they saw a circular passage opening in the floor as a panel slid aside. A second later, one of the gray giants came rising up out of it, slowly and smoothly. The movement halted when the elevator-disc the giant stood upon reached the top and filled in the circular space. The tall, pale-skinned being in its odd, organic/technical gray spacesuit stood impassive, statue-like, towering over the other inhabitants in the room, gazing out at them all. Only its dark eyes moved.

Tamerlane recognized the being instantly. "NM-156," he gasped.

"What?" asked Agrippa.

"The barren world where I was doing clandestine work for the Emperor," he answered. "My team and I entered a

222

cave, of sorts, and several of these beings appeared—in holographic form. They seemed to be trying to communicate with us—to warn us of something, I think—but we couldn't understand them. Then they vanished."

"A number of them attacked us when we first arrived here," Agrippa stated. "I assure you—they were *not* holograms. They were very solid, very real."

Tamerlane looked at him in surprise, then nodded. "Your 'other matters' you were dealing with. Right."

Agrippa returned his gaze to the giant. As it had arisen, he had been looking around for signs of more of them, fearing another attack. This time it seemed things would be different. This time it appeared this was the only one making an appearance. Now, as the human and Dyonari forces formed a broad circle around the strange being, weapons aimed at it, Agrippa barked, "Hold your fire! He's alone!" Tamerlane meanwhile gave the same order to his forces. The Dyonari all waited silently, hands on sword hilts.

The giant turned in a slow circle, staring out at the collection of humans and Dyonari, seeming almost to be studying them. When it had moved in a full circle it stopped, and now its gaze rested upon Agrippa. And then it did something unexpected: It spoke. "*You*," it said, loudly and clearly.

Surprised, the blond general pointed at himself. "Me?"

The giant said nothing for a few seconds, merely staring directly at Agrippa. Then it turned its attention to the two techs at the console. "You are removing the dangerous code. Excellent."

"You speak our language now," Tamerlane said to the giant.

"Yes. It has been downloaded." The giant was silent for another few seconds, the tensions in the room high. Then it turned to face the crowd of spindly, glass-clad warriors. "All Dyonari must leave here at once." It turned to its right and addressed the larger group there. "All humans must remain."

The Dyonari officers blinked at that and glanced at one another. No one moved.

"All Dyonari must vacate the premises immediately," the giant boomed again. "All humans must remain."

"When you say 'remain,'" Tamerlane called to the big figure, "what sort of time frame do you have in mind?"

"For a short time," the giant replied. It turned back to face the aliens. "All Dyonari must vacate the premises immediately!"

Agrippa moved closer to the Dyonari congregation. "You can wait outside if you wish," he called to the three officers. "We will rejoin you as soon as we are able."

Merrin and Ralin looked to the High Commander, awaiting his order to withdraw. The High Commander in turn strode through the crowd of his warriors and over to the console where the two human technicians were removing the last of the malicious code.

The gray giant watched him carefully. Solonis, meanwhile, suddenly frowned and leaned toward Agrippa, about to speak. He did not get the chance.

"Move away," the High Commander said to the two human techs. His voice was low but filled with the cold threat of violence.

The technicians halted in their typing and looked up at the Dyonari commander, puzzled expressions on their faces. "Excuse me?" one of them said.

The High Commander drew his long, curved sword and pointed it at their necks. "Move away from the console or I will kill you both," he said, his voice still hard and even but louder.

The two technicians didn't bother to ask permission from Agrippa or Tamerlane. Not being hardcore fighters but artificial intelligence specialists, instantly they leapt from the two sides of the giant-shaped seat they had been awkwardly sharing and scrambled out of the way.

Agrippa was already moving forward, shocked and angry, when the High Commander dropped into the seat and began to type on the console's controls.

"What do you think you're—" the III Legion general began, but he was interrupted by the other Dyonari warriors moving forward, forming a solid line between their High Commander and the humans.

Agrippa understood that much, at least. The leader had sent out telepathic signals, similar to their own Aether link, ordering his troops to protect him.

"What's your play here, High Commander?" Agrippa called. "We had resolved everything peacefully and were working together."

"I fear you are mistaken, General Agrippa," the leader replied, never taking his eyes off the console or his hands off the controls. He was typing in code, and doing so much faster than the two human techs had been removing it. "We all have our missions to carry out, and I am now carrying out mine."

"Arnem," came Tamerlane's voice from just behind him. "What's happening now? And—should we be taking action? Should *I* be taking action?"

Agrippa understood what the other general meant; he possessed an organic flame power that he had gained during exposure to unexplainable cosmic forces in the Above and the Below, and he was prepared to unleash it. "Not just yet, General Tamerlane," Agrippa replied formally. "I believe we can still work things out peacefully, and avoid launching yet another war between our species and the noble Dyonari." He directed these words toward the High Commander as much as toward Tamerlane. "Isn't that so, Commander?"

"I fear you will be disappointed by the position I must take on this matter, General," the High Commander responded, never hesitating in the slightest as he typed away. "But at least your days of warfare will be over, as will mine. We can, all of us, rest at last." Behind him, the row of Dyonari warriors stood as still and rock-solid as statues carved of glass. "Move one step back, all of you," the Commander ordered, and instantly the alien warriors did just that. A second later, a low hum filled the air.

Frowning, Agrippa moved toward the space the warriors had vacated—but he never reached it. Instead he impacted something unseen. Raising his hands, he felt for it. For a few seconds he resembled a mime as he slid his gauntleted hands across the invisible surface of a wall that now separated the two armies.

"He's sealed them inside a force field," Agrippa announced.

"The overload builds again," the gray giant boomed from the center of the chamber. "The console unit has been locked out. I cannot access it or deactivate it—nor can my master." The giant turned slightly to its left and called out in its resonant voice, "Show me!"

The center of the huge round room filled with the shimmering sparkle of what was easily recognizable to everyone present as a holographic display. It laid out all the stars of the galaxy in a broad, flat swirl of a billion tiny lights.

Agrippa became aware that one of the lights—a star—was pulsing brightly. He moved toward it; it was only a short distance from where he stood.

"I'm not positive," Tamerlane said, coming up behind him and looking at the flashing light, "but I think that's the star this planet orbits."

As they watched, thin, faintly-glowing lines appeared, connecting that star to a dozen around it. Slowly the lines grew thicker, brighter, even as more faint lines spread out from those stars to an even larger number out beyond them. Within moments it appeared as if a spider's web linked the stars. The faint lines radiated out again, now connecting many hundreds of stars. The central one, meanwhile, now pulsed so brightly it was almost impossible to look upon, and the glowing lines that radiated out from it were like laser beams in their intensity.

"No," the giant said, its voice faint at first but then much louder, more forceful, and almost desperate as it repeated, "*NO!*"

15

In high orbit above that unnamed world, the star cruiser *Ascanius* jolted into sudden and unexpectedly frantic action.

Automated alarms had begun blaring in all areas of the ship several seconds earlier, and now Captain Dequoi sprinted out onto the bridge level, perplexed as to what could possibly be so wrong. He had scarcely taken three steps out from the travel tube and onto the bridge before he gained a relatively good idea of why the alarms were sounding. He stopped dead in his tracks and almost stumbled backward in shock.

The entire front half of the circular bridge deck wall was a transparent steel/ceramic window. It currently displayed a spectacular view of the upper portion of the planet, nearly filling the bottom third of the window. Far beyond and in the upper left corner, the planet's star was visible. When last Dequoi had occupied the bridge, just after the ship took up orbit and as General Tamerlane and his entourage were disembarking in the shuttle, that star had appeared perfectly normal; a faint, cool G2 yellow sun, similar to that of Earth.

Now, however, everything had changed. The viewing angle remained as before, but what it revealed was nothing like Dequoi would ever have expected.

The sun that had been a pale yellow dot was now a blazing red inferno. Its circumference had expanded by almost half again. Radiant, blinding prominences and solar flares reached out, threatening to scorch the entire star system to ash.

"Radiation levels are spiking, Captain," one of the sensor officers called out, unnecessarily.

Dequoi blinked and forced himself to move. He strode to the center seat and fell heavily into it, then turned back to speak to the crew. At that moment his executive officer, Commander Ehrens, came racing in, gasping for breath.

"I apologize, Captain," the short, redheaded woman managed between breaths. "I ran here all the way from the—" The rest of the sentence died on her lips. She gawked at the star and unconsciously reached back, catching herself on a railing. "I—what in the name of the Empire is *happening*?"

The captain shook his head. "Don't know, Commander, and can't think of anything we could do to help it," he grumbled. "Our first and only priority now is to get the general and the rest back up here and leave this system as rapidly as possible."

"He's not going to want to hear that, you know," the exec said. She moved around to the front of the bridge and continued to stare at the blazing sun. Fortunately for her, the hyper-dense transparent wall was filtering out much of the glare and all of the radiation, so that neither her eyes nor her general health would not be adversely affected. "I don't suppose anyone knows what's causing this?"

The captain shook his head. "Nor how to stop it." He met her eyes as she looked away for a moment. "If I didn't know better, I'd swear it was going nova."

She looked back at him, surprised. "You mean it's not?"

"It shouldn't," the captain said. "It's too small. And far too early in its stellar lifetime."

"Then why is it doing this?" the exec demanded.

"Shockwave imminent," the sensor officer reported. "Radiation wave continuing to climb."

Dequoi gritted his teeth. "That sun is spewing out a dozen different things, and any one of them is likely enough to take out this ship, all our crew, and the folks down on the planet below us, as soon as it gets bad enough." He shook his head and looked at the exec again. "Like I said, our best and only bet is to evacuate—pronto." He turned to the communications officer. "Get me General Tamerlane. Immediately."

16

In the high Above, in the abandoned Golden City of the gods, six Dyonari warriors sat in the plaza of the great Fountain. And they were bored.

They had waited there for hours, guarding a device that none of them understood. The cube they had assembled, based on memories implanted within their minds by the seers of their Star-City, continued to draw cosmic energy from the Fountain's basin and blast it into the radiant blue sky, through a dimensional tear it had created there, and on—to they knew not where.

And meanwhile they stood guard over it, though no dangers had yet appeared to threaten it or them.

Eventually Co-Commander Mirana stood, stretched, and wandered around the perimeter of the Fountain. "It isn't how I imagined it," she said to no one in particular.

"Imagined what?" asked Madalena.

"A city of gods."

Madalena scoffed. "It hasn't been that in quite some time," she said. "I imagine it has been deserted for centuries, if not longer."

Mirana shrugged. "Even so," she said. "It's where they used to live. I expected..." Her voice trailed off.

"Expected what?"

Mirana shook her head. "I don't know. Something. Something more than just *this*. Just a fountain and deserted buildings and...nothing."

"None of that matters to the mission," Madalena replied curtly.

"Yes, yes—the holy mission," the other said. She shook her head in frustration. "Build a box, and guard it. Such a prize assignment for six of the finest warriors—"

Madalena cut her off. "Mirana, if you have somewhere else you need to be—some place you'd *rather* be, instead of fulfilling the mission given to us by the great seers of our Star-City, then by all means, *go*."

"Go?" Mirana repeated, almost incredulous. "You would have me simply walk away from here?"

"Of course," the co-commander replied. Her mouth twisted upward in a leering grin. "That way I could simply kill you as a deserter, and be done with your constant complaints."

Mirana scowled at this but did not reply. She resumed her stroll around the basin, stopping at the far side to lean over and look closer. Something within the roiling energy-waters had caught her attention. In this portion, the constant churning was at a minimum, the surface here almost placid in comparison to the rest of it. She could see tiny points of light floating within the depths. As she stared at them, she became aware with a start that they were actually stars. Dropping to one knee, she gazed more intently into the abyss. Yes, she realized, they were stars. In fact, she knew with certainty then that she was seeing an arm of the galaxy.

But something, she could also see, was terribly wrong.

With the cry of dismay she leapt to her feet and raced back around the Fountain to the others.

"What troubles you so now?" demanded Madalena.

"Come and see! Come and see!" Mirana's voice was shrill, backed up by a telepathic echo that carried with it terrible dismay. The others all felt it and could sense that it was genuine. They all stood and followed her back around to the other side of the basin.

"Look," she said, pointing down at what at first appeared to be water but was actually raw cosmic energy. "Look at the stars," she said.

The others looked. They saw. They understood, somehow. They realized what they were seeing.

The very stars of their galaxy were being ripped apart.

"This is actually happening," Mirana said. "It is happening *now*. As we watch."

The others all exchanged shocked looks and, if Dyonari could be said to blanch, they did.

"This is *our* doing," Mirana said. "The power to do this is coming from *here*—from the Fountain of the gods."

Again, as soon as she said it, they all knew it was true.

"But—why?" Madalena asked aloud. "Why would our kind wish to blow out the stars? To destroy the galaxy itself?" Her normally level, commanding voice grew as shrill as any of them had ever heard it. "*Why?*"

And then, having asked the question, the answer was provided to them. The final element of hidden memory was triggered. The last failsafe installed by the seers.

They all snapped to attention, moving robotically, and said aloud, "We fulfill our mission. We do our duty."

For several long moments they stood there that way. And then Madalena blinked her eyes, shook her head, and forced herself to move. She lurched away from the other five and staggered forward, lost in a daze. As her senses returned, she looked down and with a start realized she had stumbled to the very lip of the basin. Another step and she would have plunged into the churning energies, and been reduced to her constituent elements in an instant.

VAN ALLEN PLEXICO

Gasping, she drew back and whirled about to look in horror at her five companions. They all stood stock-still, dark eyes glazed over and staring into nothing.

Madalena rushed back to them and grasped Mirana by the shoulders. "Wake up," she cried. "Wake up!"

Her co-commander didn't acknowledge her, didn't speak—didn't even blink. She continued to stare straight ahead, her mouth slightly open. The other four were in precisely the same state.

"This isn't right," Madalena muttered, stalking away from them and looking down, trying to think clearly. "Why is this happening to me? I'm the one who follows orders. I'm not the rebellious one. Not like *her*."

She turned back and glared at the immobile Mirana, then at the others. "*Wake up*," she shouted at them. "Don't you see? We are destroying the galaxy. We six. We are responsible. We have to stop it *now!*"

Still no reactions.

"Fine," she muttered. "I'll do it myself."

She started toward the cube, but then the faintest of sounds behind her caused her to whirl about.

Mirana was rushing directly at her. Her long, curved, transparent sword was unsheathed and raised high. Her expression was impassive. Clearly, her mind was not her own—but her intent was clear.

All of these thoughts went through Madalena's Head in a split second. And then they were cast aside, so that she could concentrate on staying alive.

The sword came down and barely missed her as she leapt to her left. Mirana continued forward, letting the momentum carry her through into the next swing. This attack actually resulted in the tip of the blade scoring a tiny line along Madalena's armor.

Madalena gasped at this near-hit and spun away, at the same time drawing her own sword. For an instant she had thought to draw the small energy pistol that was holstered at

234

her side, but her instincts warned her that if no other technology worked here in the Golden City, it was unlikely the pistol worked. She was grateful for this instinct, because she knew that the time it would've taken to draw the gun—only to have it not function—could well have been all the time her opponent had needed to take her down.

She kept moving, dancing to her left, keeping distance between herself and the robotic Mirana. Anger meanwhile swelled within her breast. The seers—it was all their doing. She had trusted them as the wise and ancient leaders they purported to be, but they had planned all of this from the start. They had planted the instructions for how to build the cube within the minds of the entire team—the cube that was, even now, pouring cosmic energy down into the real universe, and threatening to blow out the stars—but they had also planted overriding mental commands that were clearly on display now, with Mirana. For some reason the programming hadn't fully worked on Madalena, or she had somehow broken it. But all that meant was that she had become the enemy to her erstwhile co-commander.

And Mirana was making that last point exceptionally clear. She charged again, her sword slicing down and then back up and across. She moved with all the precision and grace of any top-flight Dyonari sword-wielder, despite her lack of conscious control. Her blade was getting closer and closer by the moment. Madalena faced a quandary; she didn't want to fully engage her colleague and actually try to injure or kill her, but she also knew if she continued to fight in such a purely defensive manner, sooner or later Mirana would catch up to her and…

No. It was no good. She was already tiring while her robotic-acting opponent showed no signs of fatigue whatsoever. And she knew she couldn't actually bring herself to attack Mirana. She had to try something else—a different approach entirely.

Gritting her teeth, Madalena spun out of the way one last time, backing up several quick steps to gain a little distance, then lowered her sword and called to her comrade in plaintive tones. "Mirana! Snap out of it! If I did it—you can, too!"

The other Dyonari commander stopped and peered back at her, and for a brief moment she appeared to take heed. Her eyes narrowed and she looked to be actively fighting the mental programming planted by the seers. Then the moment passed. Her expression relaxed, returning to the blank stare it had been before. She raised her sword and charged headlong at Madalena.

In the split-second before Mirana reached her, Madalena felt overcome with sadness. Her grip tightened on her sword hilt but she knew she couldn't strike her friend. As Mirana lunged at her, sword descending in what would surely be a fatal blow, Madalena made her peace with the cosmos. Her reflexes, however, had not quite gotten on board. At the last possible moment, keeping her feet planted in place, she shifted her weight to her right and twisted ever so slightly.

Mirana's swing missed by millimeters. Her momentum carried her into her opponent's now-outstretched leg. She tripped. For the first time since the terrible events had begun, she cried out.

Madalena spun about to see what was happening. What she saw caused her to scream as well.

Mirana was perched on the lip of the Fountain's basin, standing on tiptoe, rocking slowly back and forth. One wrong move and she would tumble into the churning energies—energies that could disintegrate even a god.

Madalena didn't hesitate. She lunged for her co-commander, grasping her by the waist, and yanked her back to safety.

Mirana was breathing heavily, out of breath. She looked at Madalena and then past her, over her shoulder. Now it was her turn to scream again.

Madalena looked around and saw what her comrade was seeing. The other four Dyonari warriors had their swords out. They were advancing upon her. Their faces were as blank as Mirana's had been but their intent was clear.

Raising their blades in unison, they charged.

17

No," the gray giant rumbled, staring at the growing web of light within the holographic display of the galaxy. "*No*—this must cease immediately. If it continues, the results will be catastrophic."

Tamerlane had turned away from the others for a moment, receiving a priority message from the captain of the *Ascanius* high in orbit. He sent a reply. Then, "We're on it," he called to the giant. Turning back to Agrippa, he informed him about what the crew of the *Ascanius* was seeing.

"We must act now," Agrippa stated firmly. He had been testing the force field's area—roughly a dome over the entire Dyonari delegation— and its strength, first with his fists and then, very cautiously, with his weapons. The fact that the field deflected any blast back the way it had come caused him to abandon that strategy quickly.

"Yes," Tamerlane agreed, "I think that's very clear. What do you suggest we do?"

Agrippa scowled, turned, and moved still closer to the invisible wall and the line of defenders just on the other side. His eyes moved from one impassive Dyonari face in front of him to the next. At last they rested on the one called Merrin, seemingly the second- or third-ranking officer of the bunch, standing a bit behind the line. He caught the warrior's attention and called to him, "Commander Merrin! You support your High Commander's attempt to destroy the entire galaxy?"

"That's what he's doing?" Tamerlane said, aghast. "Perhaps I should cover their bubble in cosmic fire. Cook them a little inside there!"

Agrippa raised a hand to Tamerlane. "Please, General," he said. "One moment. We don't know that the heat would pass through the field, and we yet have a few moments. I still believe this can all be averted."

"A scant few moments," Solonis interjected. He was reading a set of seemingly incomprehensible figures scrolling by on another display nearby—hardly necessary, given the manner in which the luminous lines were spreading among the holographic stars—and his dark complexion paled. "Whatever we are going to do, we must do it now."

Agrippa moved right up against the force field, glaring through it at the defensive line, almost daring the Dyonari to try to strike him. "You endorse this action, Merrin?" he called again.

"We obey our orders," Merrin said by way of reply. "The High Commander knows what he is doing." He hesitated, glancing over at Ralin, the slightest hint of uncertainty creeping into his high, almost musical voice. "He *must* know what he is doing."

Agrippa could see the cloud of concern and uncertainty pass over Merrin's face. Next to him, the other officer, Ralin, looked similarly sick.

"There is almost no time left, gentlemen," Agrippa called. He gestured toward the lines that continued to flare to life between one star and the next. "You can see what is happening here. Are you on the side of *life* in this galaxy—

or on the side of utter cosmic annihilation? That is the choice put before you now. *Choose!*"

Merrin looked directly at Ralin, the other officer. "What is the High Commander doing?" he demanded.

Ralin shook his head, then turned back to their leader at the console. "High Commander, forgive my impertinence, but I feel you must answer Commander Merrin's question. Please."

One of Tamerlane's I Legion soldiers dashed in from her post outside the tower. "General," she cried. "The sun—it's getting so bright. Like it's about to go nova..."

"I am aware of that, Lieutenant," Tamerlane replied, though hearing it from someone who had just witnessed what was happening firsthand put the situation into even more concrete terms for him. "General Agrippa," he said formally, moving toward the Dyonari defensive line. "I am about to take this matter into my own hands."

"Time is up," Solonis called.

"This must stop now," the gray giant boomed. Slowly it began to move away from the circle on which it stood, stalking slowly in the direction of the Dyonari.

Agrippa saw both Tamerlane and the giant headed toward him. He realized now that there was little chance of avoiding bloodshed. *Massive* bloodshed, on both sides. And even that was assuming they could penetrate the force field. He turned back to the Dyonari warriors arrayed between him and their officers. "Your High Commander," he called to Merrin, while nodding toward the Dyonari who was typing away in the sleek, streamlined white seat. "I'm afraid I never caught his given name."

The two officers glanced nervously at one another, and then Merrin moved forward and leaned between two of the warriors. He whispered, "Siklar. The High Commander's name is Siklar."

Agrippa started to call to the leader again, now using his given name for familiarity's sake, but then his eyes slowly widened. He'd heard that name before.

Siklar. Don't trust Siklar. Don't let him inside the tower.

Agrippa cursed. "Him! *He's* the one my future-ghost tried to warn me about," he growled. "And I escorted him right in here."

"What?" Tamerlane asked as he joined Agrippa at the Dyonari perimeter.

"Never mind." Agrippa pointed at the High Commander. "There is no doubt now. *He* is the danger here. We have to stop him immediately. He wants to destroy the Milky Way." He raised the volume of his booming voice another notch. "Isn't that right, Siklar? You wish to annihilate the entire galaxy!"

"I must," the High Commander replied quickly and openly. "It is the only way to save it."

Both Agrippa and Tamerlane frowned at that.

"How will destroying it save it?" Agrippa asked, his hand on his gladius hilt as he started forward again, now resigned to having to fight the entire crowd of alien warriors.

"The comets," High Commander Siklar said. "They have come to our star-worlds now. They bring the Skrazzi. The Phaedrons. They bring a horrible, lingering death to every being in this galaxy." He stopped typing for a moment and looked back over his shoulder at Agrippa; his expression was one of dedication, not malevolence. "It is inevitable. Our seers have foretold it. The entire galaxy will fall to them—to torture and slavery and then to death." He nodded toward the console upon which he was entering code. "At least this way we will go quickly, painlessly, and take many of their kind with us."

"We'd rather not *go* at all," Agrippa stated firmly. "And I'm betting your own warriors feel the same way." He raised his voice yet another notch; it boomed out as if being channeled through artificial amplification. "They are warriors—fighters trained to give their all against the enemy—not cowards who burn down their own house and the houses of their neighbors at the first sign of trouble." He shifted his gaze now from Siklar to Merrin and Ralin. "Last chance, gentlemen. Will you stand with us—with a fighting chance for survival—or will you choose utter galactic death and obliteration, with the Dyonari going down as perpetrating the greatest act of pan-galactic genocide in all of history?"

Merrin and Ralin were looking at one another now, silently but furtively, and Agrippa fervently hoped they were engaged in a philosophical telepathic conversation, preferably about the merits of rebelling against the command of Siklar. A moment later, that was revealed likely to have been so. Merrin, his expression changing in an instant to one of grim determination, stepped back from his confrontation with Agrippa, turned about and—before any of Siklar's personal guards could move, and practically faster than the eye could see— brought his sword around the other side of the white seat. He held the blade tightly across the High Commander's throat.

Less than the blink of an eye later, the nearest bodyguard drew his sword and lunged for Merrin.

Merrin reacted so quickly that those watching from a distance scarcely saw him move. The entire fight took less that three seconds to play out. The bodyguard drew back from Merrin's defensive move, dropped into a crouch, and swung out with his blade again; Merrin shifted his body just enough that the sword's tip passed a millimeter away from his chest. Then—at just before the three-second mark—he lunged and sliced out and up.

As the third second since the conflict had begun ticked away, the bodyguard's severed head dropped toward the floor of the chamber. Before it had actually hit the gray tiles, Merrin had moved back into his previous position, his sword around the chair, its blade against Siklar's throat.

"Impressive, Commander," Siklar said, out loud. He spoke louder for the benefit of his other bodyguards and for the humans to hear. "I trust no one else will attempt that. I would prefer to have no more Dyonari die at the hands of Dyonari."

"That would be my preference as well, High Commander," Merrin said through gritted teeth, "but know that I will not hesitate to repeat the performance as necessary."

Siklar had paused in his typing. He turned his head slightly to see his junior officer; the task was made more difficult by the incredibly sharp blade at his neck. "Commander Merrin, I call upon you to cease this mutinous behavior at once. If you do, I will forgive it, given the emotional conditions at present."

"You are under arrest, High Commander," Merrin said to him, ignoring the offer. "Please rise and step away from the console."

Siklar barked a sharp order to the remaining warriors: "Arrest Merrin." None of them moved; they merely shifted about uncertainly. Then Merrin issued his own orders: "Stand down." Again no one moved at first. The tension hung in the air for long seconds. Finally, after what seemed an eternity of uncertainty, first one, then another, then all of the Dyonari warriors *en masse* sided with Merrin. Ralin moved over to Merrin's side and said, "I concur with Commander Merrin's directive, High Commander. You are under arrest and relieved of command of this unit."

"Lower the force field," Merrin ordered.

Siklar's personal guards moved in tight around the High Commander, weapons at the ready, but they did not look at all certain of their actions or their loyalties any longer. They were now surrounded by dozens of armed and determined foes, and via the holo display they could see as plainly as anyone else in the chamber the results of what the High Commander was doing.

The leader of the three bodyguards turned his back on the surrounding crowd and spoke directly to Siklar. "Sir," he said, "our position is no longer tenable. We must—"

"Yes, yes." Siklar closed his eyes, inhaled and exhaled slowly, and then deactivated the force field. He rose and moved away as ordered. He glared at Merrin and Ralin. "You are choosing to bring slavery and horrific destruction down upon our people," he warned them.

"No," Merrin said. "*You* were choosing that. *We* choose to fight back."

Siklar shook his head. "There will be no fighting back. The enemy is everywhere. Even now, more of his forces pour into this galaxy. Our own seers have foretold it: his is victory is inevitable and imminent."

Merrin didn't reply to this. He instead shoved Siklar along toward the doorway. Meanwhile the two human techs wasted no time in moving to the console they had been forced to abandon. Quickly they started back to work on deprogramming the overload code.

After only a few seconds of work, the technicians began to argue with one another, and Major Cassius moved between them. Very rapidly he ascertained the problem and then reported it to the two generals.

"The code the Dyonari commander was entering into the system is something they're not familiar with," Cassius stated. "They believed they understood it before, and were getting it removed. This time, though, they aren't making any headway."

The two human generals exchanged troubled glances, but then Commander Merrin stepped forward. "If I might be allowed to take a look at it?" he said.

Tamerlane and Agrippa hesitated only a second before agreeing.

Nodding his thanks, Merrin moved in behind the console as one of the techs scooted out of the way. He studied the display for a few seconds, then raised his hands to the controls and began to type. The two human technicians and Major Cassius all eyed the Dyonari with grave suspicion.

"Gentlemen," Agrippa said from over their shoulders, "I believe we can trust Commander Merrin. We have little choice. And besides—without his actions, we wouldn't have this opportunity to begin with."

The two techs reluctantly nodded, but they remained hovering next to him, watching every movement he made.

After almost a full minute of very rapid typing, Merrin stopped, lowered his hands from the controls, and studied the displays. He nodded to himself, then looked up at Agrippa and Tamerlane. "As I feared," he said. "Siklar introduced the Apocalypse Protocols."

"I don't like the sound of that," Agrippa grumbled; Tamerlane added a, "No."

"It is an older code that my people have used more than once in campaigns against alien forces," Merrin explained. "It overrides power systems on a linked grid and removes safeguards, while simultaneously locking itself out from any other overrides. One can only imagine what it could have done here, given the energy levels available." He stood and stretched. "I could not entirely eradicate it—that would require many hours of work, and with more specialized knowledge than I possess."

Tamerlane frowned. "Then what can we—?"

Merrin continued: "I have, however, deleted the core components." He paused, as though considering his statement, and then qualified it with, "More or less."

"More or less?" Tamerlane repeated, not sounding at all mollified.

Merrin nodded. "From here, your men should be able to complete the job of reducing the power buildup to non-threatening levels, at least."

As the two techs slid back into the broad curved seat and inspected the displays, they began to smile to themselves and to one another. One of them glanced back at Merrin and awkwardly managed, "Um—thank you, Commander."

Merrin bowed his head in response.

Tamerlane and Agrippa thanked him and shook his hand. He bowed to them as well, then returned to the group of Dyonari who were holding Siklar.

"It was you, wasn't it?" Agrippa suddenly said, looking at the captive Siklar. "You sent those Dyonari into the tower ahead of us. The ones whose blood trail we followed here."

"Indeed," the High Commander stated, nodding once. "I had hoped they could complete the operation while my warriors and I kept you occupied outside." His expression was sad; Agrippa could tell that he truly believed he had been doing the right thing. "When they failed to report in, I saw no alternative but to come inside after them, despite the presence of you and your forces accompanying us." He met Agrippa's eyes defiantly. "You know I could have simply ordered the death of all of you when you first arrived in the Above. But I chose to allow you to live."

"We might never know if your warriors could have *succeeded* in carrying out such an order," Agrippa retorted. "But understand—you did order our deaths." He glared back into the alien's dark eyes. "And not just ours—the deaths of everyone in the galaxy." He gave Siklar a sour look and turned away. The High Commander pursed his lips but said nothing in return; a moment later he, too, looked away.

Merrin waited for a quiet moment and then gestured toward the door. "We will, as you suggested, await you outside," he told Agrippa. He and Ralin moved past the humans and toward the opening.

Agrippa nodded and saluted. "You are heroes, gentlemen," he told the two officers. "You did well."

Merrin made a gesture that might have been a shrug. "Perhaps. I hope so. Time will tell."

As two of Ralin's Dyonari led Siklar past the humans, the two bodyguards that stood to either side of the High Commander suddenly drew their swords, unleashed death-screams that had half of those present clutching at their ears, and charged in the direction of the human leaders. Simultaneously with this, as everyone's attention was drawn to the two suicide soldiers, the High Commander reached out. His hand brushed against the face of the nearest soldier to one side: Major Torgon. Torgon stepped back quickly, frowning, fearing a trick of some sort. His hand moved to grasp the handle of his blast pistol. But then Siklar had moved along.

Quad-rifles and blast-pistols fired from almost every human present. The burning plasma bolts, glittering particle-beams and explosive slugs riddled the two Dyonari attackers, actually cracking their transparent but utterly hard armor. One went down at that point, never to rise again. The other staggered back a few steps, shook himself free from those of his own kind who attempted to restrain him, and rushed at the two human leaders again.

Agrippa drew his gladius and prepared to strike, but before he could act, Tamerlane raised his right hand and brought a wave of flame out of thin air to engulf and devour the attacker. Within only a few seconds, the glasslike armor lay charred and almost empty on the floor, the body consumed by the holy fire of the Above.

All the Dyonari gazed in awe at this newly-revealed ability—this manifestation of *the Power*—and at the human who had wielded it. They now appeared to regard him with much greater respect than before.

"I should have tried to burn Siklar through the force field," Tamerlane said to Agrippa, watching them go. "It would've been a lot safer and quicker."

"You don't know that," Agrippa retorted. "It likely wouldn't have worked at all. And even if it did, it could have set off something in the equipment and killed us all—

or perhaps caused the overload effect to accelerate and brought about the end of everything. At the very least, we would now be in a shooting war with those alien soldiers who are presently leaving here peacefully."

"I suppose so," Tamerlane said, making a sour expression. "You did well, obviously." He gave the blond man a wry smile and started to say something else when there came a disturbance near the exit. He and Agrippa turned and moved that way quickly; there they found High Commander Siklar lying prone on the floor, right at the threshold of the doorway. The two guards who had been escorting him were now bending over him, apparently attempting to revive him. His eyes were closed and he did not appear to be breathing.

"What happened?" Tamerlane demanded. "Did anyone see it?"

At first no one spoke, but then Torgon raised his voice. "I witnessed it, General. He simply slumped over."

Tamerlane turned to one of his men—a medic—and asked him to check the High Commander. The man nodded but didn't seem terribly confident in his ability to administer aid to an alien. Quickly he gave way when a Dyonari warrior stepped up and identified himself as, in part, a medical officer.

The alien checked his commander over, touching a few key spots in search of vital signs, and then shook his elongated head to Commanders Merrin and Ralin and the human leaders. "I am sorry," he reported, "but Commander Siklar is dead."

Frowns creased the exotic features of the two Dyonari officers.

"Any signs of injury?" Tamerlane asked the alien medic. "Any signs of—*anything?*"

"Nothing obvious," the Dyonari medic replied, his gaze shifting from the body of Siklar to Tamerlane. "Perhaps he took poison, once he realized his cause was lost."

Tamerlane slowly nodded at this. "Maybe so," he said.

Agrippa motioned toward the remains of the two bodyguards who had attacked moments earlier. "These two certainly chose the suicide option," he noted.

"Death by enemy army," Tamerlane agreed.

"It preserved their honor," Solonis pointed out. "They went down fighting. They didn't surrender. They didn't simply give up and give in. From all that I know of the Dyonari, that is very important."

Agrippa and Tamerlane both nodded at this. They watched as several of the remaining Dyonari lifted the body of the High Commander and carried it through the doorway and out of the tower. As they went, Agrippa couldn't help but stare at Siklar. Something was bothering him about what Solonis had just said, but he couldn't quite but his finger on it. Then he had it: Siklar had given up. Had opted out of the fight, so to speak—assuming he had indeed killed himself. And any other possibility seemed unlikely.

As unlikely as Siklar giving up without a real fight.

And yet there they went, filing out the doorway. There would be no battle between the humans and the Dyonari. At least, not here; not now. Siklar had chosen to surrender and to commit suicide rather than fight to the death. A warrior who was prepared to blow up the entire galaxy—including himself—wasn't willing to fight to the last breath when victory was within his grasp. He had simply given in. It didn't add up.

Watching the last of the Dyonari exiting the big chamber, Agrippa still had a nagging feeling he was missing something—something vitally important.

18

ith the Dyonari gone, and safe passage for them ordered by Tamerlane, Agrippa led most of his III Legion Kings of Oblivion back towards the center of the room. There they blended in with the mostly I Legion Lords of Fire that Tamerlane had brought with him. As they walked that way, Agrippa passed the man and woman the other general had introduced to him earlier. Their faces both appeared flushed and they seemed to be pointedly ignoring one another, even though they were standing very close together. The names came back to Agrippa surprisingly quickly. "Titus Elaro," he said. "Colonel Arani." He nodded to them both and continued on toward the center of the room.

The holographic swirl of the galaxy had vanished. Now only the four-meter-tall gray giant stood there, immobile, gazing out at them.

"Are you in charge here?" Tamerlane asked the strange being. "Because we need to speak to whomever runs this facility. It possesses or has access to an enormous amount of stellar and cosmic energy. The threat it poses, simply by its existence, is unacceptable to—"

"Please pay attention," the giant said by way of reply, interrupting Tamerlane's statement. It raised one meaty hand high. "If you would all focus your attention here..."

The various legionaries and other assorted members of the human group stopped what they were doing and looked up at the gray giant.

FLASH.

19

The tiny gray robot emerged from its usual hiding place in the wall. It moved about quickly but precisely on long, spindly legs and, occasionally, when it dropped down to floor level, on tiny motorized wheels. Its arms—it possessed four of them— extended upward like tree branches from the upper portion of its silver oval shell, and each ended with an array of needles of various sizes. As it moved about the room, it proceeded to jab those selfsame barbs into every living person present.

Solonis watched the robot at work. He'd fallen down when everyone else had, with the flash, but had never entirely lost consciousness and within a matter of moments he was back up again.

"Ugh," he muttered, rubbing at his eyes. "That was unpleasant."

The gray giant strode slowly and ponderously toward Solonis. It stared down at him. "You do not stun easily," it said. It considered him for a few seconds. "You are not human."

"Not entirely, no. But human enough, in this body, to find your stunt with the flashbulb thing extremely annoying."

"My apologies."

"Accepted." Solonis watched as the little robot continued jabbing needles into the Kings of Oblivion. "I know what you're doing," he said a short time later, "and I think it's a good idea."

The little robot finished up with the last three human soldiers. Then it zipped back into its place of concealment, plugging itself into a pair of wall connectors as it did so. An opaque panel slid down in front of it.

"You know?" the giant asked.

"I did come here from the future, after all," Solonis said. He paused, thinking. "Of course, I first went there from the past." He waved a hand. "It gets very confusing. You'll just have to take my word for it. Yes—*I know*. And I approve."

The giant stared down at him impassively, as if looking straight through him. "Your approval is irrelevant," the big being stated.

"Likely so," Solonis agreed, smiling. Then he sobered and turned to stare directly up at the giant's dark eyes. "Do not mistreat them," he said. "They show great potential."

"Certainly more than any of the Dyonari ever have," the giant rumbled, apparently choosing to ignore the implied threat. "Despite their telepathy and their other tricks, the Dyonari are weak of mind. They are arrogant and petulant. They lack the desirable traits these humans possess and they demonstrate considerable vulnerabilities to psychic manipulation and control."

Solonis nodded. "They wouldn't look good in the uniforms, either," he said, before sitting down on the cold floor, cross-legged, to wait.

20

The humans awoke. It seemed to them that only a few moments had passed.

Agrippa groaned and pulled himself up to a sitting position. The Deising-Arry combat armor felt now like a millstone about his neck, dragging him down.

"You're up. Good," came the voice of Tamerlane from behind him.

Agrippa turned, rubbing at his eyes, and allowed the other general to help him to his feet. "What happened?" he asked, looking around quickly to make certain the others were all still alive. "Who or what was responsible for that—and what *was* it?"

"It was a concussion blast," Solonis stated, striding up to them. "Detonated by our friend, the big gray fellow."

They looked to where the giant had stood earlier, but there was no sign of him now.

"How do you know that?" Agrippa asked, frowning at Solonis.

The seer-god shrugged. "It didn't work terribly well on me."

"Why did he do it?" Tamerlane wondered aloud. "If he'd wanted us all dead, or simply thrown out of here, he could have accomplished either or both of those objectives while we were all asleep. Yet here we still are—and alive."

"That is true," Agrippa said. "Did he merely knock us out so that he could slip away while—"

They were interrupted as one of the officers of the I Legion to Tamerlane's left suddenly exclaimed, "Ouch!"

Eyes turned in that soldier's direction, but then another man on the far side of the group also cried out. Within moments, everyone present—including Agrippa and Tamerlane— had come to realize that he or she had been jabbed by something very sharp during their time spent unconscious.

"Set it aside for now," Tamerlane ordered after a couple of minutes of asking around to be sure no one had been debilitated by the pokes they were discovering. It turned out that the jabs had mostly been administered in the legs or hips, and there were no serious complications. "We'll figure this out eventually, but we have other priorities right now."

Tamerlane and Agrippa formed up their two groups of soldiers and technicians and prepared to march out through the doorway and to the shuttle. Tamerlane then checked in with the captain of the *Ascanius*, who reported the local star had settled down a bit, and with the two techs who had resumed typing on the console panel. "Status?" he asked them.

"We just about have it under control, General," one of them reported.

"We haven't been able to entirely remove the base code," the other added, "but we've pretty much got it down to a dormant state."

"You make it sound as if it is alive," Agrippa observed, walking up.

"It very nearly is, General," the first tech said. "But I think we have it isolated and quarantined within the system, at least. As long as it remains trapped where we put it, everything should be fine."

"Very well," Tamerlane declared, nodding. "Then I believe it's time for us to go. After all," he added, "there is a war on."

"Agreed," said Agrippa. "Though I believe we should leave something of a garrison behind, to safeguard this place. Until we can determine a more permanent solution to the threat it poses."

Tamerlane nodded. Together the two started toward the exit—only to realize that the doorway was closed. They stood before it but it did not open. Tamerlane, growing frustrated, turned to the panel of nearly incomprehensible buttons and markings on the wall adjacent to it. Agrippa, meanwhile, sought out Solonis.

"You were awake first, yes?" Agrippa said to the seer-god. "Why is the door closed? Who closed it?"

"The giant did," Solonis replied. "I believe he desired privacy. He wanted to keep our Dyonari friends out."

"Do you know how to open it?" Tamerlane all-but-demanded.

Solonis ignored the tone of the general's question and moved up to the control panel. "Ah, yes," he said. "'I've seen this design before." He reached out and tapped a few colored squares. "That should—"

The door hissed open, revealing the valley and an evening sky beyond.

"—do it. *Oh..!*"

Solonis stepped back, almost tripping over his own feet. Agrippa and Tamerlane brought up their weapons. The rest of the I and III Legion soldiers did likewise as they saw what—and *who*—was revealed standing just beyond the door way: A dark-haired, rugged-faced man clad in a black uniform, a golden stylized eye emblazoned on his chest.

"Gentlemen," said General Ioan Iapetus of the II Legion. Behind him stood dozens of soldiers clad in the jet black of the Sons of Terra. Beside him crouched two of that number, packs of explosives in their hands, seemingly about to plant them. "Thank you for opening the door. You have saved me the trouble of blasting my way in."

21

In high orbit, Captain Harras Dequoi sat in the command chair on the vast, three-floor-high bridge level of the I Legion flagship *Ascanius* and stared out at the green-white planet slowly rotating below. This operation had been, for the most part, dull thus far. Except for the sun almost going nova, he reminded himself with a humorless snort. Yes—except for *that*. But now things appeared to have calmed down remarkably. He had no problem with that. He assumed the generals down below on the planet's surface had things entirely under control, and that the rest of the operation would consist of merely waiting to ferry the troops back aboard.

Alas, he was to prove utterly incorrect in that assumption.

"Contact!" shouted one of the tactical officers at the sensor station, both out loud and over the Aether. "Unidentified vessel dropping hyper—very close by."

Dequoi jerked to full alertness. "Shields!" he barked. "Ready all defenses! Pilots to the fighters!"

As officers and support staff throughout the big bridge area moved into motion, preparing for any eventuality,

Dequoi rose from his seat and moved closer to the main two-dimensional screen just ahead. It was a broad, curving rectangle set into the forward wall that mimicked the transparent steel viewport just below it. The ship was, unfortunately, facing the wrong way for either to be of much use at the moment. "Holographic display," he ordered, and a second later the space between his seat and the viewscreen became filled with three-dimensional images of part of the planet, his ship, and the intruder vessel.

He didn't need sensor or communications officers to confirm it; he knew exactly what the other ship was the moment he laid eyes on it. He'd played cat and mouse with it numerous times over the past few weeks.

"The *Atlantia*," he growled. Flagship of General Iapetus and the II Legion—the traitorous Sons of Terra.

"So," growled Commander Ehrens. "They survived. And they've caught up to us."

Dequoi didn't reply. He saw no need. Both of the commander's statements seemed obvious at face value to him.

"*Atlantia* is launching fighters," the tactical officer reported.

"Launch ours," Dequoi barked.

22

The three generals of the three great Imperial legions stood in a triangle, just inside the tower's vast round control chamber. At Iapetus's back was the open doorway, beyond which stood arrayed a large contingent of his legion, all in black and weapons at the ready. To one side sat some dozen Dyonari, now held prisoner of the Sons of Terra. Another dozen or so lay dead on the ground.

"Why did you kill them?" Agrippa demanded, nodding toward the Dyonari. He was filled with anger and no small amount of grief. "They were our allies."

"They didn't want to let me inside," Iapetus replied sharply. "They got in my way."

"What do you want here, Ioan?" Tamerlane asked, regarding the man with open distaste.

"It's not your position to question me, Ezekial," Iapetus growled. "After all, I am now the supreme military commander of the Empire, duly designated by the young Empress herself."

"You mean the Princess—your hostage," Tamerlane said.

Iapetus shrugged. "Call her what you will—but she is the rightful heir, and she appointed me—"

"At gunpoint," Agrippa barked. "Nobody takes that seriously."

"The Empire takes it seriously," Iapetus said, "and you would do well to do likewise." He turned and spoke softly with an officer just behind him; a moment later, a long, black box was brought forward and one of the Sons took a knee, opening the shining latches that held it closed. As the lid swung open, the glint of gold sparkled out at them. Iapetus, grinning, reached down and lifted the Sword of Baranak in his right hand. "Have you forgotten," he asked the other two generals, "that I also now possess *this*—and that it has become a sort of *de facto* symbol of office, as well?"

"Stolen artifacts and stolen titles," Agrippa spat. "I am not impressed."

Iapetus moved a step closer to the blond general. "I doubt you will be impressed with your next posting, either," he said angrily. "Or your new rank."

Tamerlane started to move between them and attempt to settle things down, but he turned aside as a message arrived within his mind, via the Aether link from the *Ascanius*, high in orbit. He looked away for a moment, hoping the two men didn't kill one another—or, rather, that Iapetus didn't kill Agrippa, at least; he would've welcomed the opposite outcome—while he was taking the call. "Yes?" he sent back. "What is it?"

"General," said Captain Dequoi, his voice tense, "The *Atlantia* has just jumped in from hyperspace, very close to us. They have launched fighters, as have we. Neither side is advancing, however. *Yet.*" His tone was even more anxious now. "What would you have me do, sir?"

Tamerlane glanced back at Iapetus. "My ship has spotted your ship," he said.

Iapetus smiled. "Yes. Stealth is no longer required."

Tamerlane looked away again. "Do nothing, Captain," he sent via the Aether, saying the words aloud for Iapetus's benefit, too. "Hold position. Unless they attempt to start trouble."

Captain Dequoi hesitated, then, "I understand, General. Dequoi out."

The link was severed and Tamerlane turned to his and Agrippa's troopers, who were standing together in a small crowd a short distance behind him, having been about to move out of the tower. He called out, "That goes for all of you, too. No one takes any provocative actions toward the II Legion unless General Agrippa or I give the order." He turned back and regarded Iapetus sidelong. "How did you move all these men down here without my ship spotting you before now?" he asked.

"I had assistance," Iapetus replied with a chuckle. The Sword tip resting on the floor as he leaned upon it like a walking stick with his right hand, he raised his left and snapped his fingers. At the summons, the battalion of Sons parted and Colonel Barbarossa stepped out, leading a woman in dark red robes forward. Barbarossa held an odd little pistol in his right hand and gripped the woman's arm with his left; he wasn't exactly pointing the gun at her, but the threat was very apparent.

"The Lady Teluria was kind enough to open a portal so that I and my soldiers could walk right through to your location," Iapetus explained. "I would have preferred to have come out *inside* this facility, but she claims she was unable to penetrate it while the door was closed."

Teluria was glaring like a caged tiger at Iapetus. The general in turn reached over and took the little pistol from Barbarossa, who handed it over with a slight bow.

"So—you've found us," Tamerlane said, while Agrippa eyed Iapetus with an expression quite similar to Teluria's. "And you've brought your army with you. So—what now?"

Iapetus, the Sword pommel gripped in his right hand and the pistol in his left, made a show of looking around at the inside of the chamber within which they all stood. "I know that this facility can tap into vast power. Almost *unthinkable* levels of power. Certainly that can be of use in our current struggles." He returned his gaze to Tamerlane. "So you will now tell me all about it—and exactly what it is capable of."

"Or?"

"Or I will torture the surviving aliens out there until they tell me everything they know. Then I will work my way through *your* troops. And then I will come back and ask you again."

"About what we have come to expect from you," Agrippa grumbled.

Iapetus allowed a thin smile to form upon his lips. "Actually, I will extract all the information I can get out of the Dyonari regardless of what you do."

"In that case," Agrippa amended, "precisely what I expect from you."

Iapetus's smile broadened. "I'm pleased to have become such a reliable, known quantity to you, Arnem," he said.

"Appointing you the head of II Legion was the worst mistake Nakamura ever made," Tamerlane said bitterly.

Iapetus snorted at that. "Oh, please. It was the only *wise* thing he ever did. With me in charge, the human race has a chance of actually *surviving* all this." He laughed again. "That's more than can be said for your tenure at the helm."

Tamerlane ignored this. "And if you succeed in harnessing the power of this facility," he said, "what then?"

Iapetus gave him a half-shrug. "Then I decide how best to employ it against my enemies."

"You mean humanity's enemies, don't you?" Agrippa asked, still glaring.

Iapetus chuckled. "Is there a difference now?"

"There is only one enemy you should concern yourself with," came a voice from out of nowhere. "Not that it will do you any good."

Everyone turned, following the hollow, echoing words. At first, no one and nothing could be seen out of the ordinary. Then, a short distance away in the direction of the center of the chamber, a swirl of crimson light flooded out of the very air itself. A hole appeared—a hole in nothing but thin air. It expanded outward ever so slowly, colors flaring to life within its depths, until it formed a circle some three meters across. Flames sprang up around its perimeter even as bright lights swam within it.

Behind Iapetus, the Lady Teluria cried out and tried to pull away. The guards that held her gripped her tighter as Iapetus spared a glance and a warning look her way.

"Someone is coming," Tamerlane noted, recognizing the effects of a dimensional portal being opened.

"I know that pattern," said Solonis, from where he stood within the mass of I and III Legion troops, all under the watchful eyes of the Sons of Terra. He had melted into the crowd the moment the door had opened and Iapetus had entered. "I know it, and it is not good."

"Whom do you have there?" Iapetus asked, craning his neck to see who had spoken. "Who among your number considers himself so knowledgeable about the ways of the gods?" He caught sight of the dark-skinned young man in a loincloth and frowned. He shook his head. "I don't know that one, Ezekial. Are you dressing your Lords of Fire like primitives now? Who is he?"

"I'll introduce you later, if you want," Tamerlane said sarcastically. He nodded toward the flaming circle of light. "I think we have bigger concerns now."

The circle grew almost solid, hovering in midair with only the very bottom of its arc touching the floor. Then a ripple appeared in the center, radiating outward. Simultaneously, ice began to form and grow on the floor and walls of the room. From its center, with an effect very much like a splash shown in reverse, a humanoid figure emerged, striding out into the chamber.

Most of the humans present winced and some even cried out. Just to look at the man who had walked through the dimensional portal caused physical and mental distress.

He was tall and slender, clad all in black, with pale skin and dark hair. His facial features were almost a blur; they seemed to shift from moment to moment. Gazing upon him was like looking at an angel—or a devil. He seemed somehow almost too vivid to be real—or rather he made everything else around him seem less real by comparison.

"I...*know*...you," Tamerlane attempted to say, but two things held him back. For some reason, he felt as though his motor functions had slowed in the last few seconds, even as the temperature in the room dropped. For another, despite the fact that a part of his brain was screaming to him that it definitely recognized this guy and knew exactly who he was, another part of his brain seemed to be trying its hardest to override that message with another: a continuing refrain of, "*Just forget him. You never saw him.*" Tamerlane reached up with both hands—it was like trying to swim through oatmeal—and grasped the sides of his head. He groaned— and the sound he made came to his ears as if it had been slowed down by a factor of three or four.

"What...is...*happening?*" Agrippa tried to say, proving only partially successful in doing so.

Iapetus was scowling angrily but he appeared as bothered by the strange affect as anyone else.

"You," Solonis said, stepping forward, ignoring the legionaries and looking directly at the newly arrived figure. "Goraddon. But that's not possible. You *died*."

"You know me?" The man in black turned his head sharply, staring straight at Solonis, watching as the young-looking man in the loincloth continued to move toward him. "How can you resist?" he asked. "Do *I* know *you?*" He wrinkled his nose slightly and appeared to sniff the air. "Ah! Yes. Indeed. Greetings, seer-god," he said, his tone jovial now. He chuckled softly to himself. "You are certainly one to know all about dead gods, being one yourself—yes?"

Solonis nodded. "Oh yes. I have no secrets. I've been dead for quite some time now. I merely linger in this plane until my task is complete."

"Then we have that in common," replied Goraddon, "for I, too, have come here to complete a set of tasks." He smiled. "However, once they have been accomplished, I plan on remaining here in the material universe for some time to come."

"I see," said Solonis. "And what tasks would those be— assuming you don't mind sharing that information."

"Certainly I do not," The man in black said. He gestured toward Tamerlane and Agrippa. "I will admit to entirely selfish goals. First, for their continued effrontery to me, these two must die." He then nodded towards Teluria, where she stood among the black-uniformed Sons of Terra, a look of profound fear upon her face. "And second, this one must make the ultimate sacrifice on my behalf."

"Sacrifice?" Solonis regarded him with curiosity. "That being...?"

Goraddon's smile widened. "She must take my place in the Below."

23

A wave of small, nimble, triangular vehicles dropped away from the spinning cylinder that was the main body of the I Legion flagship *Ascanius*. Their rear engines igniting, the fighters swooped around to join their fellows already arrayed between their home vessel and the enemy flagship. Meanwhile, more of that ship's fighters dropped from it and rocketed their way.

"General Tamerlane ordered us not to engage with them," Commander Ehrens pointed out from her position standing just ahead and to the right of the captain.

"Unless they started some sort of provocative action themselves, first," Dequoi snapped. He jabbed a stubby finger at the display, which showed the II Legion fighters coming their way, rapidly closing the gap between the two sides. "I call *that* provocative."

Ehrens said nothing, merely nodding her head once in acquiescence.

A few moments later, the two squadrons of fighters clashed in the space between the motherships.

"Zoom in," Captain Dequoi shouted as he stood within the holographic tactical display on the bridge. In response, the image moved in tighter on the *Ascanius* and its adversary, the II Legion's *Atlantia*. Dequoi could see the two waves of small and medium fighter craft converging halfway between the two capital ships. The blackness of space was lit by dozens of beams and tracers. Seconds later, explosions were added into the mix.

"Give me the numbers," Dequoi demanded.

In response, the far right portion of the holographic image changed to display the numbers of surviving I Legion ships in red and the surviving II Legion ships in black. The numbers currently read twenty-five for the former and thirty-two for the latter.

Dequoi approached the ship's gunner. "Let's see if we can give our lads some help," he said.

"Aye, sir," the gunner replied. His hands moved over the controls even as he tapped directly into the ship's artificial intelligence via the Aether link. In response, the gun turrets situated along the hull of the *Ascanius* came to life and extended outward, swiveling toward the action. They selected their targets and, one by one, they opened fire. Across the gulf of space, fighters belonging to the Sons of Terra began to explode.

The *Atlantia* wasted no time in duplicating the *Ascanius*'s actions. Its own ship-to-ship guns emerged from their housings and deadly particle beams sliced out, tracking down the fighters piloted by members of the Lords of Fire.

Dequoi kept one eye on the numbers and the other on the intricate maneuvering of the remaining ships. His anxiety increased by the moment. His gunners were having some success, as were the pilots of his legion's fighters. The problem was, the other side was having roughly equal success, and they outnumbered his ships. His forces had reduced the other side to seventeen fighters, but his side now numbered only twelve.

It was then that Dequoi and all the others on the *Ascanius* were very violently reminded just who they faced. This was not a training exercise against other members of I Legion. This was a very serious, very deadly conflict with the Sons of Terra, the most fanatical of the legions—and the most ruthless.

"Captain," one of the tactical officers called from her station. "The *Atlantia* has ignited her engines."

"Decided to turn tail and run, has she?" Commander Ehrens laughed.

But all who were watching the holographic display could very easily tell that running away was definitely not in the plans for the *Atlantia*. Instead, the big II Legion flagship was accelerating—coming directly toward them.

"What are they doing?" Ehrens said now, coming to stand beside Dequoi. "Do they mean to *ram* us?"

The captain watched the *Atlantia* and noted the ship's thruster signatures and drive patterns. "No," he said, shaking his head. "She doesn't mean to ram. She means to board."

"To *board*?" Ehrens was incredulous.

"Their captain doesn't trust the odds in a straight-up, ship-to-ship battle with us, I suspect," he explained. "He'd rather go toe to toe with us in the hallways of the *Ascanius*."

Commander Ehrens appeared stricken. Such a tactic had never entered into her calculations. "What—what do we *do*, Captain?" she asked, ashen.

"We shoot at their ship, and we prepare to evade them, Commander," Dequoi said. "And, failing that—we prepare to fight them, hand to hand."

24

was right, then," Solonis said, peering at the man in black with a mix of curiosity and revulsion. "You *did* die, ages ago."

"Indeed," Goraddon replied with a slight air of annoyance. "But—like you, apparently—I have found ways to work around that inconvenience."

"Might I inquire as to how," Solonis asked, "seeing as that is an area of no small interest to me?"

Goraddon shrugged. "I discovered Vorthan's hidden reserve of crystals. Crystals he had already used to trap the spirits—the essences, and the raw power—of quite a few of our number."

Solonis frowned at this for a moment. Then his expression soured. He regarded the other being with open disgust. "You mean you *fed* upon them—fed upon the *souls* of our lost comrades?"

Goraddon shrugged. "I did what I had to do. I survived." He grinned. "I *thrived*."

"You have become nothing more than a cosmic vampire," Solonis hissed. "Truly the Below is where you belong. It suits you perfectly—to dwell in eternity with the other depraved creatures not fit to walk the higher planes of creation." He shook his head in disgust. "The Goraddon we see now is merely a pathetic ghost; a lost specter, wandering the planes of the multiverse, stirring up trouble here and there."

Goraddon glared at him. "Do not seek to *anger* me, seer-god. Your own pitiful condition might render you unsuitable as a sacrifice to the Powers of the Below, but do not doubt that I can dream up many other ways to torment you in your final hours. Before I slay you in turn."

Solonis shrugged defiantly. "I haven't found death to be as dull as I'd feared. It's almost as good as being alive."

Goraddon nodded. "I will see if I can remedy that situation for you, very soon."

Solonis started to issue a retort, but his words died in his throat as the flaming portal through which Goraddon had passed—a portal that had remained in place since his arrival—now flared to even brighter, blazing life.

"*No,*" hissed Goraddon through clenched teeth, his voice barely audible. "No—leave me *be!* Leave me to handle this on my own!"

Another body began to take shape, to solidify within the blazing portal's depths and move forward into the room. As it emerged, its size and form became readily apparent to all. It was a towering figure, perhaps just under three meters tall—barely able to fit through the opening. It stepped out of the flaming circle but the flames moved outward along with it, clinging to it. It stood there before them, tall and muscular and naked, sexless and bald. Short, curving horns protruded from its head and its deep red skin was on fire. Eyes like hot coals gazed out above a blunt nose and cruel lips. The eyes moved across everyone in the chamber, and as it looked upon them its expression registered a general disregard and contempt. Then its eyes fell upon Goraddon.

"Ah," it said—and its voice was like the sound of a storm; like some massive horn sounding and echoing in the depths; like the voice of a god. Or a devil. "There you are, Goraddon. I feared I had misplaced you."

"I am attending to the matters that remain to be settled between us," the man in black called up to the flaming creature. Everyone present could detect the hint of intimidation—of *fear*—in his voice. "Only a short time more is needed, and all will be resolved."

The cruel mouth turned upward in a smirking smile. "Only a *short* time," the voice that came from the raw matter of the multiverse boomed. "You require only a *short time*."

"Yes," the man in black replied. "Yes, that is so. I assure you—"

"You have always been among my most favored slaves, Goraddon," the voice boomed. "That is why you yet exist—if your present form can truly be called *existence*."

"Ah!" gasped Solonis from within the crowd.

The flaming creature ignored the sound. It reached out with a blazing hand and gently caressed Goraddon's cheek; as the hand moved away, broad black scars formed on the flesh where it had touched him. Goraddon for his part didn't cry out, but he clenched his teeth against the pain.

"I thank you, my lord," the man in black said, his words barely intelligible, "for your favor. Matters are nearly settled."

"Yes," the creature replied. It turned and began to stride back toward the portal. As it reached the threshold it looked back over its shoulder at Goraddon. "Bring your affairs to a close quickly, my slave," it said. "You have five minutes."

And then it stepped through the portal and was gone.

25

The *Atlantia* suffered massive damage as it blasted its way through the last of the *Ascanius*'s fighter screen and then ran headlong into the oncoming fire of the other flagship itself. Nevertheless, it kept coming, its fire kept to a minimum. Clearly its captain meant to capture the *Ascanius* while doing the least possible damage to her in the process.

The *Ascanius*'s gunners were not constrained by such considerations. They threw everything they had at the enemy ship's deflector shields and armored hull. Slowly but surely they chipped away, but in the end they couldn't stop the *Atlantia*'s approach.

"The *Atlantia* will be alongside in thirty seconds," the tactical officer informed them—needlessly, for that information was displayed in the holographic image filling the upper section of the bridge level.

"Do we warp out of here, Captain?" Commander Ehrens asked, her complexion pale white with nerves.

"Run?" Dequoi regarded his second-in-command as if she'd proposed the most ridiculous thing he'd ever heard.

"We cannot abandon General Tamerlane and his party. To say nothing of Agrippa and the other Kings of Oblivion."

Ehrens appeared about ready to panic. "Very well. Then what—?"

By way of reply, Dequoi drew his pistol and nodded toward the exit. "We meet them at the entryway," he told his subordinate. "And provide them a warm welcome."

Followed by a battalion of Lords of Fire marines and crewmembers and anyone else who was aboard and who could point a gun and fire—or, in the case of the cooks, swing a meat cleaver—Captain Dequoi and Commander Ehrens hurried for the main airlock.

26

oraddon whirled about, his back to the portal; it had instantly contracted once the demonic being had passed back through it, shrinking down to barely porthole size. Now it rotated slowly and silently, flames flickering about its rim, Stygian depths barely visible within.

The man in black faced the assembled humans and his expression reflected his humiliation, his urgency, and his fury. One of the most powerful beings in the galaxy—upbraided and embarrassed in front of these poor mortals. It clearly filled him with rage.

During the confrontation with the demonic creature, his iron-willed psychic grip over everyone else present had slipped, and now gasps sounded from the assembled soldiers and technicians. "What in the Above and the Below was *that*?" asked one, incredulous.

"Above and Below? In this case, pretty much just the *Below*," observed Solonis.

Goraddon stalked over to where Tamerlane and Agrippa stood. The two generals moved into combat stances—

cosmic flames danced across Tamerlane's fingertips while Agrippa cycled his quad-rifle—but at a gesture from Goraddon, each of them froze again, along with everyone else present.

"Draw no measure of encouragement from the Demon Lord's words," he barked. "My dealings with him will soon be resolved. Permanently."

Tamerlane and Agrippa both gritted their teeth, straining to make their bodies move despite the overwhelming mental force being exerted almost casually by the man in black. They continued to be entirely unsuccessful.

"I know this place," Goraddon said, looking about, nodding to himself. "It is the one facility in this galaxy with the potential to thwart me. I therefore left a garrison of my warriors here to guard it. I see you managed to get past them." He shrugged. "No matter. I am here now, and I can deal with you all at last, as I should have done all along. "

The two human leaders clearly had retorts they wished to deliver, but the man in black was not allowing them to speak.

"I love my games, and I thought I could play them with you and yours," Goraddon went on. "But the two of you have turned out to be greater thorns in my side than I ever could have imagined." He regarded them with a look of mock sadness. "I am afraid," he said, "that I am not what you would call a graceful loser." He bowed his head ever so slightly. "And so I salute you for your successes, but now your time is at an end."

Before he could take any action against those two, however, Goraddon seemed to notice General Iapetus for the first time, and to recognize who he was. And then to recognize the two weapons he held.

"You," he whispered, turning slowly to face him. He moved closer, regarding the leader of the Sons of Terra with an almost cautious air, as though Iapetus might somehow find a way to break free of Goraddon's mental lockdown.

"You have been the wild card all along. I could never fully take your measure. Even now I am not certain what to make of you." He considered. "That makes you, in my view, even more dangerous. Your sheer unpredictability, and your defiance of any authority beyond your own."

Goraddon reached out and casually took the Sword of Baranak from Iapetus's nerveless fingers. He held it up and seemed to consider it for a moment. "I suppose this might come in handy." Then he noticed the little pistol that Iapetus was straining with all his might to point at him. He frowned. "Oh," he said. "One of those." He snatched it away and gazed at it with distaste. "The sole legacy of dear Lucian. I had hoped these had all been located and destroyed long ago."

Iapetus was clearly struggling to speak. Goraddon regarded him with amusement. He gestured and eased up on the psychic lockdown. "Yes, General? Say your piece before I dispose of you forever."

"Just one word," Iapetus replied.

Goraddon became aware that the General had managed to raise his index finger from his side and was now pointing it at him. Goraddon frowned.

"*Bang*," said Iapetus.

A popping sound as the air pressure changed, and then Goraddon staggered back, the two weapons he'd taken from the general falling from his hands as he clutched at his chest. The god-slayer gun implanted within Iapetus's arm had fired, as soundlessly as those weapons ever did, and point-blank into the man in black.

Its effect, however, was not what anyone present could have wished for.

Those weapons, originally created in part by Vorthan and fully weaponized by Lucian prior to his great rebellion in the Golden City, produced devastating results when fired at one of Those Who Remain. The tiny red crystals that powered the weapons drew the spirit—the *soul*—of a god inside, trapping it there. That very thing had been done to the vast majority of the gods in millennia long gone by. It was the reason why there were so few gods still extant, and why they were known as Those Who Remain. To think that a weapon of that sort could be fired directly into a god, and that entity be only mildly injured, if at all—it was practically inconceivable.

Yet there stood Goraddon, unharmed, unhurt, and with a grim fire burning in his eyes. In a flash he crossed the space between himself and Iapetus, his open hand lashing out in a broad swipe that impacted the general and hurtled him backwards. Iapetus didn't stop tumbling until he struck the far wall. He lay there in a crumpled heap, not moving.

The man in black stood there unharmed, laughing. "That sort of weapon will scarcely harm me, and certainly will not *slay* me," he said, regarding Iapetus with contempt. "Though I will admit that it was ingenious of you to hide it inside your own body. As I told Solonis, I have consumed the raw power of dozens of other gods. Having a fraction of it taken away scarcely bothers me at all."

Goraddon started forward, clearly intent on beginning his campaign of slaughter by finishing off Iapetus. Alas, that was not to be. For as one man in black—the god Goraddon—stepped forward to administer the *coup de grace*, the other man in black—the human general, Iapetus—was snatched away. A panel slid soundlessly open in the featureless gray wall behind the general, revealing at first only darkness. Then a pair of huge gray arms reached out, grasped the nearly unconscious Iapetus, and drew him bodily back into the hidden recess. The panel closed behind him.

Goraddon halted in mid-step and stood there, staring in astonishment. Then he rushed forward and sought a way to open the panel. His frustration only increased with each passing second, because absolutely no signs could be found of the doorway he had just watched open and close.

LEGION III: KINGS OF OBLIVION

At last he whirled and confronted the frozen soldiers of the three legions. And that description was very nearly accurate, because the temperature in the room had dropped precipitously in the past few moments, as the side effects of Goraddon's psychic lockdown increased. Ice now covered all the floors and ran part of the way up the nearest walls.

Goraddon gazed out at the dozens of individuals arrayed before him, most of them clad in the heavy armor of Agrippa's Kings of Oblivion or the deep red and gold of Tamerlane's Lords of Fire. His overwhelming arrogance and confidence had melted away, leaving him exposed to the ridicule of the mortals who stared back at him. Only his absolute control over their motor functions likely kept them all from laughing at him now; laughing at him—at a *god!* It was utterly intolerable.

He strode over to Tamerlane and Agrippa, then looked past them to where Teluria still stood. "Iapetus might have escaped me—for now—but you three remain," he said, "and you are the most important components of my plan." He smiled and gestured to Teluria. "Come here now, my dear."

Being a goddess, she was able to resist somewhat at first. Goraddon frowned at this and redoubled his psychic efforts, as a side effect causing frost to form all across her red robes. In response she began to walk stiffly in his direction, shivering.

Blue lightning flared suddenly from behind Teluria.

Goraddon blinked and raised a hand, stopping the goddess from approaching. As she halted and stood still as a statue again, he moved around her. Now he saw the dark-skinned youth in the loincloth standing there, one hand barely up past waist level, electricity dancing across his fingertips.

"Ah, Solonis," he said. "I had nearly forgotten about you." He laughed. "Perhaps you would serve as a bargaining chip with the Dark Powers, too." He moved closer, pursing his lips. "Then again," he said, reconsidering, "you are but a ghost of a ghost, and entirely too pathetic to bother with."

Solonis managed to gasp out a few words, despite Goraddon's psychic lockdown: "You—are merely—a—*carrion* god," he said. "A corpse—animated—only—by your—*hate*."

Goraddon seemed about to object to that description, but then paused and shrugged. "Perhaps," he said. "But I find existence in any form on this plane vastly superior to being trapped in the Below." He made an idle gesture toward Solonis, freeing his jaw muscles. "If I must hear your ravings, seer-god," he said with a sigh, "by all means let them at least be clear and understandable."

Solonis wasted neither time nor words. "You have managed to pull your corporeal form back together with the help of your demon friends in the Below, Goraddon, but it won't last long. It never does. Already the Below calls to you; it pulls at you, drawing you back down. Only the sacrifice of one of equal power and stature into the Below could grant you a prolonged presence on this plane of existence. And since nobody here is willing to make that sacrifice on your behalf..."

Goraddon laughed at this. "You believed I would be asking for volunteers?" he said with a snort. He raised a hand and behind him the circle of fire blazed to life again and expanded to the size it had been before. Its black depths beckoned.

"You are monstrous," Solonis spat. "I had no idea you had become so—"

"*Enough*," Goraddon said. He gestured again and Solonis froze. Then he nodded toward the still-immobile Teluria. "You," he said, and the mental hooks flew out; the hooks of his awful persuasion, effective against gods as well as mortals. "You, dear lady. You wish to make that sacrifice for me, do you not? You wish to take my place in the Below, that I might remain within this dimension and the Above. I know that you do. Come to me. Come and leap into the Below in my place, and close this breach, that I might press forward with my grand plans for all of existence!"

Teluria stared back at Goraddon, her eyes wide. She slowly shook her head back and forth, then opened and closed her mouth, attempting to speak. Perhaps she meant to object, though no one would ever know. Then her eyes glazed over, all white, and she started forward, gliding toward Goraddon, and toward the awful, spinning maw of the Below.

"No!" cried Solonis, managing by the hardest to break free of the other god's control. He looked about almost frantically, then lunged for and grabbed Teluria by the upper arm. For a couple of long seconds a sort of tug-of-war took place between Solonis and Goraddon, with the goddess Teluria playing the role of the rope. And then, as she began to pull away from him, her arm sliding through his fingers, Solonis cried out. A split-second later, his body slumped to the floor, limp, lifeless.

It was Goraddon who held Teluria by the upper arm now, grinning in triumph. He leered down at Solonis's crumpled body. "And so it ends," he said. "And so my reign begins."

27

The Sons of Terra blasted their way through the main airlock of the *Ascanius* and ran headlong into a murderous crossfire.

The first dozen Sons in their black and gold surged inside, following the detonation of explosives that wrecked the locks on the doorway. As the smoke cleared, Captain Dequoi's position opened up with set pieces and handguns, driving the invaders to their right. No sooner had the Sons been pushed that way than Commander Ehrens, her anxiety now under a sort of control, ordered her own squad to open fire. The first wave of boarders never made it more than five steps inside the I Legion flagship.

The second wave pushed in hard on the heels of the first, and they managed to force their way a bit further inside. These, too, however, Dequoi repelled or cut down.

With this second wave down, the II Legion assault team paused, as if reassessing their plans. The boarding action had turned out to be harder than they had anticipated.

The third push was overwhelming. More of the black-clad soldiers of II Legion came through the entryway this time than in both of the first two assaults combined. Commander Ehrens's position was pushed back first, followed a few seconds later by Dequoi's. As he barked retreat orders, another wave of II Legion fighters pushed in, and the captain began to lose hope of holding them at the airlock area.

"What's the status on the special ops team?" he asked over the Aether link as he organized the withdrawal to the secondary holding position. "Ehrens—do you hear me?"

"Yes, Captain," the second in command replied after a moment. "Sorry—we are in the process of pulling back, and—"

"So are we," the captain barked. "What about the special ops team?"

Another pause, then, "They're on schedule, Captain. At least, that's what I'm told."

Dequoi nodded, suppressing a smile. "Good," he replied. "I'd hate to think we did all this for nothing."

28

grippa and Tamerlane barely noticed Solonis's plight. They were otherwise occupied. As the tug-of-war took place between the two gods, Goraddon's lock on all the others faltered. Straining against their mental bonds the entire time, waiting for any opportunity to move, the two human commanders surged forward, attempting to attack the man in black while he was distracted.

Goraddon saw them moving before they'd gotten close to him. He gestured and both generals froze, becoming statues. Only the tiniest sounds of protest squeaked from their paralyzed throats.

Teluria continued forward in robotic fashion, crossing the space between the generals and Goraddon. She reached him, her mouth still hanging open, her eyes utterly blank. She stood next to him, facing into the mouth of the Below. The fire-rimmed circle continued to rotate counter-clockwise, flames licking upward around the pitch-black circle at the center; the circular opening that marked the start of the tunnel down into the underverse.

LEGION III: KINGS OF OBLIVION

Agrippa could still think, could still feel, but couldn't move or speak. He glared at the man in black, then shifted his gaze to the gateway. He could sense the cold darkness radiating up from its depths. The black opening seemed to call to him. He could almost hear voices crying from down in the depths, alternately pleading for help and pleading for him to come and join them down there, wherever they were. He tried to fight it, to close his eyes, but he could do neither. He suspected—he feared—that if the man in black had not paralyzed him thusly, he might well have already leapt into the pit of his own volition. The compulsion—the awful, horrible compulsion—was that strong.

"Now," Goraddon said, as he reached out and caressed Teluria's cheek. "Now, my dear, you will give your all to ensure my plans finally come to fruition." He turned slightly to glare at Tamerlane and Agrippa where they stood rooted in place, a few paces away. "You two have caused me inconceivable aggravation and delay," he growled. "Twice you have disrupted my carefully-laid plans. I wished your Empire to remain in place a bit longer, with my own demonic allies in control of it—either by possessing the late Emperor or his daughter. But I have discarded those schemes now. I no longer intend to *rule* your Empire and, by extension, your galaxy. Now I mean to see it all laid utterly in *ruin*. My new allies—I believe you are growing familiar with them, yes?—the Phaedrons and the Skrazzi. They will overrun your Empire and the worlds of all the others in this galaxy, slaughtering in the trillions—and beyond." His eyes burned with a luminous fire now, as his voice rose in tenor. "This galaxy will be naught but a charnel house when I am finished with it. *Death!* Glorious death and destruction. A funeral pyre a million light-years across. And as the flames reach up from countless worlds, the power of all that death, all that destruction, will serve to reignite the spirit of my lord Vorthan. And then He will return to us at last, and rule over the charred wasteland that was your galaxy."

Goraddon raised his right hand and turned it slightly. In response, the window-sized circle of fire that hovered near the center of the chamber expanded, growing to more than doorway-size in only a second. With his left hand, he violently shoved Teluria towards it.

The goddess in red stumbled forwards—and then she halted, stopping her forward progress. She turned about and, to Goraddon's astonishment, began to stalk back towards him, her mouth curled into a snarl.

"How are you doing this?" the man in black demanded, his voice filled with anger but also with a hint of fear. He raised both hands and redoubled his efforts at locking the goddess in place. She in turn grimaced but pushed on, now almost arms-length away from him.

"Are you afraid, monster?" Teluria growled—but the voice that came from her mouth was deeper than normal; it belonged to someone else entirely.

"It's *you*," the man in black snapped. "You didn't die after all."

"I died long ago," said the voice of Solonis, speaking from Teluria's mouth. "My ghost is simply too stubborn to know when to quit."

"Get out of my body," the goddess said in her own voice at that junction.

"Can't you see I'm trying to help you?" said the Solonis voice in response—thus causing Teluria to appear for all the world as if she were having an argument with herself. Which, in a way, she was—and in a way she was not.

The red-robed feminine body, currently the object of a mental contest among three separate intellects, each pushing or pulling it a different way, stopped in mid-step. As Teluria's body hesitated, the panicking goddess's own persona frantically and instinctually wrestling for control,

Goraddon took advantage of the opening and rushed forward, his hand coming around to deliver a powerful blow.

It never made contact.

Agrippa, his Deising-Arry heavy-duty armor whining, blocked the god's punch with his left arm. An instant later, he drove his white-gauntleted fist into Goraddon's face, driving him backwards.

Goraddon barely kept on his feet. Halting his momentum backwards, he snarled and rushed forward—only to be knocked aside again by an unseen and unheard blow from his left. Rolling with the impact, he leapt to his feet again and saw Tamerlane standing there, the god-slayer pistol Iapetus had dropped in hand. He fired again, and this time Goraddon went down hard. For all his bluster earlier, the gun did hurt him; he could feel entire reserves of his strength—of the *Power*—being sucked out of him each time he was struck by a shot from it. Tamerlane now filling his vision, he charged forward—

—directly into the swinging golden blur that he recognized only a split-second too late was the Sword of Baranak, now wielded by Agrippa and about to come into very solid contact with him and—

—and down went Goraddon, the blade failing to slice into his animated flesh but delivering a powerful blow nonetheless.

As he rolled over onto his back, the man in black looked up and saw the blond general looming over him, golden sword in his right hand.

"You are too dangerous for me to grant any quarter," Agrippa said, and he drove the golden blade down into Goraddon's torso.

The black-clad god screamed in agony, and again when the human general drew the blade back out—likely to prepare to strike again. Goraddon didn't allow him the chance. He scrambled away, pushing with his hands and his feet across the dull gray floor. A huge wound gaped open in his chest but, instead of blood, raw energy—the *Power* of the Fountain of the Golden City—gurgled out, shimmering like liquid fire.

As Agrippa and Tamerlane advanced, cold murder in their eyes, Goraddon realized he had lost control of the entire assembly. Now all the soldiers—a couple dozen in white and green, and more in red and gold—were advancing on him. His concentration was shot—there was no way he would be able to reestablish the psychic lockdown on so many individuals in his current condition. For the first time in eons, Goraddon the Adversary, the fabled man in black, was *afraid*.

He had good reason to be.

As Agrippa and Tamerlane and Teluria/Solonis and segments of the I and III Legions all closed in on him, and as his very life-force spilled out of the wound Agrippa had dealt him with the ancient sword of the gods, Goraddon backed himself all the way up to the small, still-spinning dimensional portal. Sensing it was behind him, he turned, as if thinking it might represent a means of escape for him.

In a way, it did.

The portal flared to life and expanded to its previous size, resembling a huge round doorway or the entrance to a cave, wreathed in flame and filled with utter blackness. Goraddon pulled himself to his feet and faced the portal fully, hesitating, seemingly contemplating what might await him there and weighing the consequences of leaping through versus remaining here, in this condition.

The decision, as it turned out, had already been made for him.

Before Goraddon could leap through—and before anything else could emerge—Solonis said from Teluria's mouth, to the generals and to the goddess herself, "This body must disappear for a time. There must be no alternatives for..." He/she trailed off.

The others understood. There was full agreement. "Go," barked Tamerlane. "Go now—while you have the chance." Agrippa nodded his agreement.

Teluria's left hand came up from her side and gestured. In response, another portal opened, some distance away from the fiery one. She moved quickly toward it.

"We shall meet again, gentlemen," the goddess said— though later none could say whether it had been Teluria's voice or that of Solonis that had spoken the words.

With a crackle of blue lightning, Teluria disappeared, taking Solonis's spirit-ghost with her.

Goraddon would have struggled mightily to prevent her escape, of course, but something else had his full attention at that moment. The portal wreathed in fire was opening. It was opening, and something entirely repulsive and other-worldly was coming out of it.

The massive body of the Demon Lord emerged from the stygian depths of the portal with a suddenness that shocked everyone present. One moment he was not there; the next, he was erupting out of the circle of fire like some vengeful spirit. The horned monstrosity gazed with disinterest at the humans present for a few seconds, its nostrils flaring and fire boiling from its nose. Then it looked down at the much-reduced figure in black who stood there, cringing.

"So, Goraddon, my slave," the demon said, nodding its head. "Your time is up."

"Yes, my lord, and I—"

"And you have not fulfilled your part of the bargain," the demon replied. "The two human generals yet live. No replacement god has come to me, and I see none present. I therefore invoke the penalty clause of our agreement."

"What?" Goraddon stumbled back, his panic evident now. "No—*no*, that's not *fair*. All is in readiness. Teluria will be a perfectly—" He stopped in mid-sentence as he turned about and realized that the goddess in red was nowhere to be seen. "Wha—where did she *go*?" He stumbled away from the portal and the Demon Lord, now scarcely maintaining his balance. His voice was so panicked as to be shrill. *"Where is she?"* he cried.

And then the Demon Lord's talons closed on him.

The man in black realized what was happening too late to change it. He struggled to get away, his arms flailing madly, hands grasping for any purchase. He caught Tamerlane by the sleeve of his red smartcloth uniform and tried to hold on.

Tamerlane unleashed the cosmic flame upon him.

Releasing the general's uniform as the fire bit into him, he managed to shriek once, twice. Then the demon's claws fully locked onto him and dragged him kicking and screaming back through the portal and into the gaping maw of Hell.

The swirling, fiery doorway snapped closed, a pressure wave nearly knocking everyone over. And then it was done.

Goraddon the Adversary—the man in black—was gone.

At least, for now.

No one in the control chamber celebrated. None of them even spoke. They all simply breathed; breathed, sat down on the floor, and tried to forget that to which they had just borne witness.

Unfortunately for the men and women of the three legions gathered there, the worst was yet to come.

29

The special ops team from the *Ascanius* was, in truth, simply a squad of I Legion marines who were willing to volunteer for what was likely a suicide mission.

Strapped into a tiny capsule, they had been ejected from the far side of the flagship, where—if all had gone according to plan—the *Atlantia* had not noted their departure. They then were to curve around their mothership, hugging close to its hull to avoid detection if at all possible. Finally, because the two ships had now been forcibly joined at the airlocks by the Sons, they were to zip across the now-very-short distance between their ship and the *Atlantia* and attach themselves to its bridge section. From then on, it was anyone's guess what might happen.

They'd made it around the *Ascanius* and were now hurtling across the void between the two ships. Fortunately, that was an extremely short trip, as the two ships were linked—forcibly—at the docking ports. Even so, it felt to the men and women aboard the little pod as if they were out there, exposed to enemy fire, for hours.

At last they reached the *Atlantia* and swept over its hull, moving as rapidly as possible toward its forward section and the bridge.

"Almost there," breathed Major Talin Trekiyak, the marine in charge of the operation. He was leaning over the shoulder of the pilot, Captain Darius Pettway. "You're doing fine so far."

"The fact that you're alive to say that," Pettway grumbled, "supports your theory."

Trekiyak didn't laugh. His eyes were glued to the tiny, two-dimensional screen that was his and Pettway's only means of seeing out of the tiny, barrel-shaped vehicle. In truth, all it was, essentially, was a life support cabin fitted out with maneuvering engines. "Three seconds to contact," he announced to the other seven soldiers crammed inside with them. "Brace!"

The capsule smashed hard into the hull of the *Atlantia* and locked on. Instantly energy lances slashed downward, cutting through layers of steel, ceramics, insulation, wiring, and more, until the way was open directly into the bridge level of the enemy flagship.

"*Go!*" Trekiyak shouted. "*Go!*"

The nine marines leaped down through the hole and into the command level of the *Atlantia*. The officers of that ship were taken completely by surprise and were utterly unprepared. The maneuver was nothing they ever would have expected from the Lords of Fire, a legion that carried itself with such feigned—in their eyes—dignity and honor.

In truth, that was precisely why Captain Dequoi had first dreamed up the idea of preparing to do it. He knew it was a maneuver the Sons of Terra might well attempt, but no one else. The sheer notion of turning the tables in such a way appealed to a perverse streak in Dequoi, and he'd ordered his marines to practice it over and over until they could execute it at a moment's notice.

That preparation was paying off now.

LEGION III: KINGS OF OBLIVION

The I Legion marines fanned out across the bridge level, their guns blazing as they shot the officers and techs that presented them with no alternatives.

As Trekiyak himself leapt over a railing and advanced on the captain's center seat, the *Atlantia's* surviving officers formed up a defensive line, surrounding and protecting their captain. Those officers opened fire and a hail of plasma blobs shot in Trekiyak's direction. He dove behind the navigational console, the troops that had followed him in doing likewise before rising up to return fire.

Like the marines of I Legion, the Sons of Terra officers had opted for plasma guns in order to reduce the risk of penetrating the hull and venting the atmosphere into space. The superheated spheres that fired from the weapons generally wouldn't harm the ship's structure but would leave a pretty severe hole in a human body; even one covered in smartcloth.

Trekiyak's Lords of Fire marines, on the other hand, hadn't taken the time to break out the plasma guns. They'd simply snatched up their normal assault weapons, energy blasters and quad rifles. The sound those weapons made within the enclosed space of the *Atlantia's* bridge was deafening, and the danger they represented to the integrity of the vessel was real and extreme. Part of the rationale of utilizing such dangerous weapons aboard a ship was the psychological effect; the enemy might be more willing to surrender if the alternative was suffocating in the vacuum of space.

The Sons of Terra didn't appear troubled by such concerns. They kept up the fight, battling to the last soldier standing. At last Trekiyak had to resort to hurling a pair of stun grenades across the bridge. He understood that doing so might well damage the ship beyond repair—perhaps even send it careening out of orbit and down toward the planet's surface, with him and his troops still aboard. At this point, however, he was willing to take that chance. The alternatives were seeing either the *Atlantia's* officers defeat his boarding party, or the *Atlantia's* own assault parties succeed in taking the key stations aboard the *Ascanius*.

The shock grenades, fortunately, did their job and nothing more. They knocked the remaining Sons of Terra soldiers on the bridge down flat, keeping them there just long enough for the marines to move in and take them all prisoner.

Seizing control of the ship's functions, Trekiayak immediately disconnected the *Atlantia's* airlock section from the *Ascanius*, hurling quite a few very startled Sons of Terra out into the void. He then began locking down other decks and sections, sealing the remaining Sons in their cabins and work areas. Within four minutes, the *Atlantia* was completely under his control.

"Captain Dequoi," Trekiayak sent via the Aether to his commanding officer on the other ship, an immense feeling of satisfaction sweeping over him at a job well done. "Code gold. Repeat, code gold. All is well here. The *Atlantia* is ours."

30

Four more shuttles that had descended from the *Ascanius* landed in a broad circle near the tower. No sooner had their landing gear touched down than their hatches slid open and dozens of I Legion troopers emerged, clad in everything from crimson smartcloth to their own variations of the Deising-Arry heavy armor, weapons at the ready. The horde of soldiers rapidly fanned out, moving against the outnumbered and utterly surprised Sons of Terra and surrounding them.

Word had reached the Lords of Fire and Kings of Oblivion on the planet's surface just ahead of the shuttles themselves: The II Legion flagship, *Atlantia*, had been captured by Tamerlane's soldiers in orbit. The Sons of Terra still aboard it were now all prisoners of the Lords of Fire, at least for now. There would be no relief, no reinforcements, coming to assist the party on the ground. Considering that so many starships belonging to all three legions had already been lost over the past few months in combat with the many attacking powers, from the Rao to the Riyahadi, none of the legions had much left to throw at the others. Being only a single legion, the Sons of Terra found themselves at the most severe disadvantage against the I and III. For all intents and purposes, the civil war among the legions was now over, and Tamerlane and Agrippa were the winners.

Colonel Barbarossa, now the de facto leader of the II Legion, was many things: he was a good soldier, a canny political operative, and arguably even a successful double-agent, having posed as essentially a defector from the ranks of Iapetus's armies before switching his loyalties back over to the Sons of Terra at a critical moment weeks earlier.

One thing Barbarossa was not, however, was a fool.

"General Tamerlane," he said, loudly and clearly and mostly for the benefit of his own army. He saluted. "General Agrippa." He saluted again. "I acknowledge your tactical advantage in orbit and in the field, as well as the disappearance of our own general. Therefore, as acting commander of II Legion, I submit myself and my forces to your overall command." He bowed his head and waited to see what would happen next.

Tamerlane exchanged quick glances with Agrippa and then stepped forward. He spoke as loudly and clearly as Barbarossa had. "Colonel, I acknowledge your wise action and I thank you." He gazed out at the dozens of troops clad in black—troops that until this moment had been ordered to capture or kill him—and he added, "I welcome the good men and women of the Sons of Terra back into the fold, and into the good graces of the Empire." Then he leaned forward, very close to Barbarossa, and whispered, "If I didn't need you to keep this lot of murderers and cutthroats in line, I'd kill you myself, right now."

Barbarossa appeared to accept this statement in good humor. "Understood, General," he said with a half-smile.

Tamerlane only bristled at this. He started to turn away, then paused. "Colonel," he said, "aren't you the least bit curious as to what has become of General Iapetus?"

Barbarossa appeared to consider this for a moment, then stuck out his lower lip and shrugged. "Not particularly, no, General," he replied. "Just as long as he isn't coming back."

Tamerlane blinked at this. Then he laughed. He couldn't help but do so. "Very well, Colonel," he said. "To be honest, I believe that might mark the starting point of a decent working relationship between us."

31

I will be sending you back shortly," said the voice that echoed down from the ceiling, "once your programming has been slightly adjusted."

"Programming?" General Ioan Iapetus nearly shouted the word. "Programming? I'm not a robot! Not a computer!" He wrestled against the metal bands that held him firmly down in the gray metal chair. "You can't just *reprogram* me!"

"Indeed I can," the cold, mechanical voice stated. "And clearly such adjustments are needed. You demonstrate that fact even now."

Iapetus fought to hold his panic down. The big gray alien that had grabbed him and pulled him through the hidden door had disappeared into some other portion of the facility; from what little he had seen thus far, the place was a labyrinthine maze of cold gray walls and dim lighting. Before it had shuffled away, however, it had shoved him into this chair and held him there long enough for the bands to emerge and clasp him in place. A few moments later, the ceiling had begun talking to him. And it was infuriating.

"I am General Ioan Iapetus, regent and *Taiko* of the Imperium," he stated, keeping his tone even and under tight control. "If you—whoever you are—wish to engage in productive and mutually beneficial diplomatic relations with my government, you can start by letting me *go!*"

"I have observed you since your arrival on this world," the voice said by way of response. "I have studied your words, your attitudes, your posture, your manner— everything about you."

Iapetus scowled at that. "Why?"

"Because I find you of potential use," the voice said.

"Use? To you?" He scoffed. "Do you mean as a hostage? As a slave? What?"

"The Dyonari have a term for it. I am not certain what it would be in your language." A pause, then, "Their term, in your language, literally translates as, 'A physical extension of the true self.'"

This meant nothing to Iapetus. He reddened. "What I will extend will be an invasion fleet, onto this planet, once I'm out of here," Iapetus growled.

"That would be inadvisable."

"Why is that?"

"Because my forces outnumber yours at the present time by a ratio of roughly twenty to one. And that number only increases by the moment."

This brought Iapetus up short. He blinked, absorbing what the voice had just said. Then, "Your forces? What forces?"

The mechanical voice seemed perfectly pleased to discuss this topic. It held virtually nothing back, cataloguing numbers and types of capital ships, carriers, fighters, dreadnoughts, troop transports, and so on. It listed types and numbers of personal firearms, ammunition, flight-packs, shields, armor, and more. After five minutes of this Iapetus felt he had a very firm understanding of the arsenal possessed by this strange entity. "Alright—enough," he said, and the voice halted in mid-sentence. "So—assuming all of this is true—"

"It is true," the voice said. "I have no reason to fabricate this information."

"Where is it?"

"These vehicles and munitions are stored in various secure locations throughout the galaxy." Mist wafted down from the ceiling and a holographic display formed within it, showing rows of the very starships and tanks and transports the voice had just described. They sat within vast hangars— each of them utterly empty. Not a living soul was visible in any of the pictures.

"And where is your army, to actually *employ* all of these things?" Iapetus asked, frowning as he watched. "Where are the soldiers and drivers and pilots and medics and—?"

"A new army is being...*created*...even now," the voice replied after a few seconds of silence.

Created? Iapetus started to ask what it meant by that, but the voice started up again.

"I have been dormant for some time." A touch of sadness seemed to form within its otherwise flat, emotionless tone. "During my hibernation, those who once served me have mostly died out. Only a scant few remain—and they will not endure very much longer."

"The big gray aliens," Iapetus guessed.

"Yes."

"How long has it been? Since you were last awake?"

A pause. "Twenty-one thousand of your years," it said at last.

Iapetus could scarcely process that. One thing about it struck him immediately, however: it was before humans first came to the stars. Whatever this entity was, with its giant fleet of ships and arsenal of weaponry, it had not reached out into the galaxy to enforce its will in all the time since the human race was still stuck on Holy Terra, barely able to fly to the Earth's own moon. The thought of it staggered him. And then the wheels in his mind began to turn.

"Are you one of the gods of the Golden City?" he asked.

"No. I have become aware of the beings to which you refer only in the time since I reawakened, but I know nothing of them."

"Oh." Iapetus found that little bit of information interesting. The gods hadn't been active, or even known, twenty-one thousand years earlier? He filed that away for possible later use.

For a few seconds neither of them spoke. Then Iapetus decided to throw the dice—to attempt the gambit he had been forming within his mind. Alas, he didn't get the chance.

"It appears you are needed," the voice said to him before he could get a word out.

"Needed? For what?"

"There is an overload in the system. Rogue programming has been introduced, and a very potent source of energy is being channeled into my systems. It could prove catastrophic."

"Catastrophic as in—?"

"As in the complete destruction of every star in the galaxy."

Iapetus struggled to comprehend this. "Yes," he said at length. "Yes, I do believe that requires addressing."

"Therefore," the voice continued, "I must move my timetable forward. Your reprogramming—"

That word again. "That's not necessary, I assure you," Iapetus said quickly. A mechanical arm had emerged from a recessed panel next to his chair and a long needle in turn emerged from it. He eyed the arm and the needle nervously as it slowly extended toward him and added, "Simply watch me. Judge me based on what you see in the next little while."

The arm and the needle continued relentlessly in his direction.

Iapetus swallowed. He had no real idea what "reprogramming" might entail, but he was certain he wanted no part of it.

"Wouldn't you rather have me...*undiluted*?" he asked. "The real me? Pure? *Effective*?"

The arm continued in his direction for another second, and another...and it halted. It remained there, unmoving, less than a centimeter from his arm, as a bead of sweat formed on his brow and slowly wound its way down his cheek. Then the arm reversed its course and retracted back inside the recess.

Iapetus slowly exhaled. He realized he'd been holding his breath.

"Very well," the voice said. "You will have another opportunity to demonstrate your worth."

"That is a wise decision," Iapetus began. "I—"

A flash, nearly blinding him, followed by a low hum. Iapetus reeled, his muscles seizing up. When the hum ceased, he slumped forward, almost unconscious.

"What—what *was* that?" he demanded when he could speak again. Spots were dancing before his eyes.

"I have downloaded a unit of information directly into your cerebral cortex," the voice replied. "You now possess the basic knowledge necessary to operate the control console and possibly—*possibly*—overcome the hostile programming that has been placed within it."

Iapetus closed his eyes and thought about what the voice had just said. He almost gasped as he saw within his mind the control station, the touchsquares and levers and displays—and found that he knew precisely what each did, and how to operate the entire system.

"Alright," he said, impressed. "I understand." He chuckled to himself. "I *literally* understand."

The metal bands holding him down snapped loose and retracted. Unsteadily at first, he stood.

"Don your new uniform, if you are to enter my service," the voice said.

Iapetus looked down and saw an odd, metallic, multi-colored outfit lying on the flat surface of a console nearby. He started to object, then shrugged and began to undress.

A minute later a door slid open across the room. Now suitably attired, he walked toward it, then paused and looked back into the room. "No threats?" he asked, half-mockingly. "No, 'Do it or else?'"

"If you fail, the galaxy dies," the voice said. "I assumed that was all the motivation you required."

Iapetus considered this and nodded. "Excellent point," he said. He continued to the doorway but then stopped again and turned back. "You never told me who you are," he said. "Or *what* you are. Or where you come from."

"I have had many names—been called many things—down through the ages," the voice replied. "But the answer is simple. I am merely a machine." It paused, then, "The machine that operates this facility. This one—and many, *many* more like it throughout the galaxy."

"Well, machine," Iapetus said, "it has been a pleasure to make your acquaintance." Then he did something he almost never did. He smiled. And with that, he passed through the doorway and it slid closed behind him.

The expression on his face was placid as he re-entered the control room of the tower, but his mind was racing. He understood that the entity with which he had been conversing would be watching, and likely judging, his every move, his every word. He resolved to make as positive an impression as possible.

Being...*nice*...to Tamerlane and his band of criminals would be difficult. But the potential rewards... He visualized that vast fleet of ships, those rows of tanks, and—if the voice were to be believed—soon enough the armies manning them, all waiting for someone with the wherewithal to step forward and lead them.

Yes, he decided. Yes, he could most definitely be nice to Tamerlane and Agrippa, if need be.

At least for a little while. At least long enough to try to prevent the destruction of the galaxy.

After all—if it was destroyed, how could he conquer it for himself?

32

ome moments earlier:

Titus Elaro had been sweating profusely from his intense effort to break the mental control over his muscles being exercised by the man in black. Now that the strange being was gone—apparently dragged away by a creature straight out of the Inferno—Elaro found that he had control of his body back. He wiped at his forehead with the sleeve of his red uniform and turned to say something to Arani, only to see that she had already hurried over to speak with General Tamerlane. Meanwhile, General Agrippa was ordering everyone to begin exiting the tower.

Frowning, Elaro turned the other way and accidentally stepped into the path of a soldier in the heavy white and green armor of III Legion—one of Agrippa's men, moving very quickly. The two collided and each of them staggered back, though Elaro got the worst of it and barely managed to avoid falling down.

"Sorry," Elaro said, recovering his balance and blinking. "I didn't see you." He awaited the inevitable retort of a legion soldier, which likely would consist of either an admonishment to watch where he was going, or an apology similar to his own, depending upon the rank and disposition of the trooper in question.

Instead, the big armored figure merely stared at him for a second through the one-way visor of his helmet. His blast rifle was gripped in his right hand and for an instant, inexplicably, Elaro felt sure the soldier was going to aim it at him. As it happened, the man did not. Instead he turned back and continued on his way, moving deeper into the room while everyone else was moving out.

Elaro watched him go for a minute. He had noticed the name on the left breast of his armor—"Torgon"—but it wasn't one he was familiar with. After another second he shrugged, turned, and hurried along on Colonel Arani's trail.

33

ne of Tamerlane's officers saluted and reported that all members of the Lords of Fire were present and had vacated the premises of the tower. Tamerlane thanked the man before turning to Colonel Arani. They stood outside the strange tower facility, a short distance beyond the exit, the others of their legion in their red and gold gathered nearby. Off to their left, General Agrippa was assembling his Bravo Squad in their now-somewhat-dulled Deising-Arry Mark V armor.

"Are we ready to board?" Tamerlane called to Agrippa.

The big blond man raised a hand—"A moment, General,"—and turned to one of his officers, speaking in somewhat urgent tones.

"What is it?" Tamerlane asked, strolling over. "My shuttles are all set to carry us up."

"We seem to be missing someone," Agrippa said, looking annoyed.

"Iapetus, yes," Tamerlane said. "But I have no idea what happened to—"

"No," Agrippa interrupted. "Not just him."

Colonel Arani followed the general over, Titus Elaro trailing behind.

"Then who?" Tamerlane asked.

Agrippa appeared very troubled. "Major Torgon," he said. "He's a tank and colossus driver normally, but he has been serving as my second during this operation."

"He's not on the Aether link?"

"No. His icon doesn't even light up in it."

Tamerlane frowned, puzzled. He nodded toward the door in the side of the tower through which they had all just exited. "Do you suppose he's still inside there? Maybe something is blocking his signal."

"Why would he be?" Agrippa replied. "I issued the order to evacuate, and—"

"He *is* still in there," said Titus Elaro.

The two generals turned and looked at him. "He's what?"

"I passed a Torgon on the way out. He was headed back inside."

The two generals exchanged puzzled looks before both hurried towards the tower. Arani and Elaro followed behind them. Tamerlane ordered the others to continue boarding but to not lift off yet—just in case.

The four entered the tower chamber again and at first it appeared as if they were alone. There was no sign of Torgon or of Iapetus—a thorough search earlier had failed to turn up any trace of the general—or even of the big, gray being. Agrippa called out but there was no response.

The four stood there a moment, each of them uncertain. "Could he have slipped back out while no one was looking?" asked Arani.

"He'd show up in the Aether link," Agrippa said, looking off to one side, clearly growing frustrated.

Tamerlane, Agrippa and Arani each received hails via the Aether link at roughly the same instant, and each turned away, communicating mentally with the person calling them. Titus Elaro, meanwhile, not being a high-ranking officer in one of the two legions represented, didn't receive a hail. He stood there for a few seconds, then strolled further into the chamber, circling around and past various banks of equipment and control consoles. There was one in particular he was headed toward, and hearing the sudden outcries from behind him made him all the more certain he had guessed correctly.

Rounding the last corner, Elaro saw exactly what he had by that point expected to see: Major Darius Torgon, late of the III Legion "Kings of Oblivion," ensconced in the off-white curved seat of the control station everyone had been so focused upon earlier. Torgon's Deising-Arry armor was off and lay in sections on the dull gray floor. He had also removed the underlying exoskeleton and it now sat off to one side, leaning against another console, looking for all the world like some emaciated being that had given up on life and lain down to die. He wore only the dark gray body glove with its myriad of small, round contact points that transmitted muscle-signals to the exoskeleton and armor.

"Torgon?" Elaro called, moving toward the man, fully expecting to encounter the invisible force field that he did indeed run into a second later. "Major—what are you doing?"

The major's hands were engaged in the one activity Elaro had feared they would be: they were moving across the controls of the console that could create an overload in the stellar power system.

Elaro turned as Agrippa arrived beside him, followed a moment later by Tamerlane and Arani.

"The *Ascanius* is reporting the local sun is flaring again," Tamerlane was saying. Then he realized what he was seeing in front of him and he fell silent.

"Torgon!" Agrippa shouted. He beat his massive, armored fists on the clear surface of the force field that separated the major from the rest of them. "Torgon—you're causing a chain reaction! You're going to blow out half the stars in the galaxy—at least—if you don't stop!" His lips curled back in fury. "Torgon!"

"Major Torgon isn't here," said a voice that came from the mouth of the major but was not his. "My apologies—but I have had to appropriate his body." A pause, then, "He did, of course, give his life in a good cause: the completion of my sacred mission."

"Who—?" began Tamerlane, but Agrippa interrupted. "Siklar!"

Torgon's hands hesitated in their typing and Torgon's head turned to look out through the force field bubble at the four of them. "Yes, indeed. I am now Commander Siklar of the Star-City of Dalen-Shala. And I will not be deterred from completing what I was sent here to do."

"You didn't just die," Agrippa growled, understanding now. "You did some kind of alien trick—you jumped from your head into Torgon's."

Torgon's head nodded. "That is essentially it, General," said Siklar's voice. "The seer showed me how, before he died."

"The who?"

"Never mind." Torgon's hand motioned in a dismissive manner; the movement appeared stiff somehow, as if he had expected his fingers to be much longer. "Now, if the four of you will excuse me for a few more moments, I will conclude my business. And then we can talk." He smiled. "We will have plenty of time then—all the time left in existence." He touched a control and the holographic image of the Milky Way reappeared. The local stars were already flaring brighter, and the spider's web of energy connecting them was growing vividly bright. Moment by moment, the overload spread.

"Stand back," barked Agrippa. He leveled his An-Ro quad-rifle in the direction of Torgon/Siklar and pulled all four triggers. In response all four barrels erupted. Energy beams, particle beams, and explosive projectiles all struck the barrier simultaneously. The interaction of the firepower and the shield nearly blinded everyone present, but when Agrippa ceased fire, nothing had changed.

Agrippa cursed and pounded on the force field again with exoskeleton-enhanced muscles even as Tamerlane moved to the other side and conjured up a blast of cosmic flame. The waves of fire washed over the invisible bubble that surrounded Torgon/Siklar but when they parted and receded the field still stood.

Torgon's face smiled at them, only a few beads of sweat running down its side. "You waste your time, Generals. The last moments of existence would better be spent in quiet contemplation or prayer to whatever gods you serve." He turned back and touched another series of controls.

"Siklar—don't do this," Tamerlane called. "We defeated the enemy! Goraddon is gone!"

"His hordes remain," said the alien voice coming out of Major Torgon's mouth. "Whether he directs them or not, they have already been led here, to our galaxy. They have already descended upon us. Our fate remains the same, and the enemy's victory remains inevitable—unless I take their victory from them."

Elaro was watching the display screens as Tamerlane argued and Agrippa pounded. "We are approaching the point of no return, sirs," he observed. "If there's anything that can be done...!"

Tamerlane looked at him, then at Arani and Agrippa. He shook his head.

"What if you order the *Ascanius* to nuke this location right now?" Agrippa asked, breathing heavily and wiping sweat from his forehead from his futile labors.

Arani and Elaro reacted to this with surprise, but both quickly found their resolve and nodded.

Tamerlane hesitated, then nodded as well. "I don't know what else to do, and we are all dead otherwise," he said. He activated the Aether link to his flagship and prepared to give the order.

"Captain Dequoi," he said when the commander of the *Ascanius* came on the line, "load nuclear warheads into the forward tubes and—"

"Belay that order, Captain," came another voice over the mental link.

"Sir?" replied Dequoi.

Tamerlane was puzzled. "Who is that?" he sent over the link, "Who countermanded my order?"

"Look behind you," the voice said—and Tamerlane realized he was hearing it both in his head and out loud. He turned, as did the other three a moment later.

Arani gasped. Agrippa raised his gun.

Tamerlane's mouth dropped open. "You," he said.

General Ioan Iapetus was strolling almost leisurely towards them.

"Me," Iapetus agreed.

At first none of them had recognized him. His old, black III Legion uniform was gone. In its place he wore a tight, metallic, very high-tech-looking outfit which still featured black as its main color, but with some red, green, and blue mixed in, forming a sort of stylized feather motif down his arms and legs. His expression, however, remained as grim as ever—there was no mistaking that face.

Agrippa stepped forward, blocking his path. "Your legion is back under Imperial control, Iapetus," he growled, "and you are under arrest."

Iapetus merely waved a dismissive hand at Agrippa's remark. "We have much more important business to tend to at the moment," he said. "Haven't you noticed what's happening?"

"We are well aware. But you need to explain what's going on," Tamerlane ordered. "What's happened to your uniform?"

"No time for that right now, Ezekial," Iapetus said. He nodded toward the possessed body of Torgon at the controls. "Don't you understand? We have very little time left in which to save the galaxy!"

34

ou are too late," the voice of High Commander Siklar said to them from within the force field bubble. "We are moments away from the point of no return." He busily typed away at the controls. "Soon all the sentient beings in our galaxy will be out of the reach of the evil ones forever."

Off to one side, General Iapetus—now in his strange new uniform—sat on the floor, working feverishly. He had removed a panel from one of the consoles and was attacking the futuristic-looking equipment inside as if he had trained all his life to do it. Tamerlane was extremely curious as to how he had gained all this new knowledge about the technology in this control center, but Iapetus wasn't answering any questions at the moment. Tamerlane decided to let him be for now; he had nothing else to lose and no other ideas.

Just when Tamerlane was frustrated enough to say something to him again, Iapetus pre-empted him: "I believe I have it," he called. "Be ready. We will have little time."

A faint, almost subliminal humming sound that had filled the area all this time suddenly vanished. Simultaneously, Agrippa stumbled forward; he had been pressing against the invisible force field with all his might when it, too, went away.

It took the others only half a second to realize that their obstruction was gone. Instantly Titus Elaro and Arani leaped to the attack, seizing Torgon from either side. The possessed human soldier didn't resist; he raised his hands and stood up from the seat, a look of triumph etched on his borrowed face.

"I surrender," he said, bowing his head to them. "I freely hand myself over to your custody now."

At this, Tamerlane's own expression darkened. "It's too late, isn't it?" he said, a sick feeling creeping over him. "We are too late."

Iapetus moved into the control seat before anyone could stop him. He took one thorough look at the state of the systems, then let out a sound of disgust. "He may be right. It very well may be too late."

"And how would you know this?" Tamerlane demanded. "How did you suddenly become such an expert on this technology?"

"Training," Iapetus replied, not looking up.

"Training?" Tamerlane gazed down at the other general with an incredulous expression. "How could you have had time for any training?"

"He had it pumped into me along with all the other lessons," Iapetus said. "It only took a few seconds." He smiled up at Tamerlane. "But I am a new man now."

Tamerlane regarded him with a look of extreme skepticism but did not reply.

"Who did that?" Agrippa asked. "Who are you talking about? The gray giant?"

"Him? Oh, no," Iapetus replied. He continued to type. "His kind were simply the previous operatives here. But their time has ended." He laughed. "I was referring to the entity to whom this facility belongs."

"And that would be—?" Tamerlane asked impatiently.

"Hold on," Iapetus barked, cutting him off. "We have arrived at the critical moment." Both of his hands were flying about the controls now, touching various surfaces and lighting them up different colors one after the other. He resembled a virtuoso pianist at work at the keyboard.

Everyone crowded about, watching, struggling to accept the fact that the fate of the entire galaxy seemed to rest literally in the hands of General Ioan Iapetus.

"Yes," he whispered, "yes, I think I see..." He manipulated the controls again. "If the power levels in this junction can be lowered just a bit..." Sweat was pouring down the size of his face now. "Yes—*yes*—!"

Alarms began to sound throughout the chamber. The lights switched over to red.

"No," Iapetus breathed, his eyes flicking from one display board to the next. "*No!* No, I *had* it—"

"What is it?" Tamerlane demanded. "What's happening?"

Everyone squeezed in tighter now, trying to see, as if they could understand what the arcane alien displays might tell them.

"The overload has breached the last of the containment walls I had set up," Iapetus explained quickly, even as he frantically continued to hammer away on the board. "It is entirely out of control now. There's not a thing in the universe that can stop it." His hands came to a rest and he looked up at Tamerlane and Agrippa. He appeared devastated. He shook his head. "It's all over, I'm afraid. It's *over*."

"No," Tamerlane said. "No, there has to be *something*..."

The voice of Captain Dequoi came to Tamerlane over the Aether link. "General, this sun is about to go nova. Again. We have to get out of here *now*."

"It's far from the only one, captain," Tamerlane replied, his mental voice filled with defeat. "There's nowhere else to go."

"If only we could fit the whole galaxy into Solonis's time vault," Agrippa muttered. "Perhaps we could—"

"Time?" Iapetus looked up from where he had been hunched over, brooding. "That—that just might be the solution!"

Tamerlane and Agrippa looked at one another, puzzled. "What? You can't just move the entire galaxy through time," Agrippa said.

"No," Iapetus replied, beginning to type again, "but I can divert the axis somewhat—from horizontal to vertical, so to speak. I can move this overload in time." He hesitated, looked up at them, and added, "Perhaps."

"What are you talking about?" Agrippa asked.

Iapetus didn't reply. He was working more frantically than ever now.

"How much longer do we have?" Colonel Arani asked, leaning in and watching Iapetus working with renewed enthusiasm.

"The zero-moment will arrive in approximately fifteen seconds," Iapetus said. "And—as you might suppose—we will know immediately afterward if I have been successful with what I am attempting."

The final seconds ticked by. Tamerlane and Agrippa glanced at one another and shrugged. "Here's hoping he knows what he's doing," Tamerlane said.

"And may the gods help us all," Agrippa added.

"You don't need the gods right now," Iapetus stated as he furiously typed at the controls. "You need something much better. You need *me*."

Titus Elaro looked at Arani and held out his hand. Arani hesitated, then took it.

The zero-moment arrived.

35

And the galaxy did not shatter.

At least, not at that moment.

Iapetus raised his hands from the controls and exhaled slowly and deeply. He looked like a concert pianist completing a particularly long and grueling piece.

"You did it, then?" Tamerlane asked, not quite believing it.

"We're still here," Arani said, looking around. Then she looked down at Elaro's hand holding hers and abruptly pulled free.

"What did you do?" Agrippa asked.

"I did precisely what I said I would do," Iapetus replied. "I sent the blast through time, along two already-existing faults in spacetime. Um. Among other things."

"You did what?" Tamerlane said, shaking his head in confusion. "You sent it *where*?"

"You mean, 'When,'" Iapetus corrected him.

Tamerlane grunted. "Fine, then—*when*? The past or the future?"

"Both."

Agrippa suddenly looked up, his eyes wide. "Oh," he said. "*Oh!* I believe I understand now." He frowned. "At least, somewhat," he added.

Tamerlane, surprised, turned to him. "*You* do? Then would you care to explain it to *me*?"

"This was the moment Solonis was searching for," Agrippa said. "The splash in the pond."

"The what?"

"That central moment, from which the waves of destruction radiated out into the past and into the future simultaneously."

Tamerlane shook his head. "I have no idea what you're talking about."

Agrippa shrugged. "It's...well...complicated," he said. "Solonis could explain it better."

"Too complicated for me," Tamerlane said. "But, in any case, we are still here and the galaxy didn't blow up. That's good enough." He tapped into the Aether link. "Captain, how does it look from up there?"

"Everything has settled back down, General," Dequoi replied. "And thank the stars for it."

"Again—not the stars, not the gods," Iapetus growled. "Just *me*."

Tamerlane ignored him and passed the good news on to the others. "Now," he said to Iapetus, "I have a great many questions for you."

"I expect that you do," Iapetus said, "but I have little time. I will answer what I can."

Tamerlane frowned at this. "Little time? You have all the time in the world. You no longer command II Legion."

"Indeed I do not," the other man replied. "I resign my commission outright."

"I'd already stripped it," Tamerlane said.

Iapetus shrugged. "Either way."

Tamerlane was taken aback by this. "Colonel Barbarossa commands the Sons now."

"Of course he does. And he will do a fine job." Iapetus hesitated. He stood from the control seat and leaned in close to Tamerlane. "But I wouldn't trust him too terribly far," he said in a lower tone. "You should keep an eye on him, Ezekial. As often as you can."

Tamerlane blinked. He wasn't sure whom he was speaking with anymore. Had Iapetus been possessed, in the manner of Solonis's human body, or Torgon? He asked Iapetus this outright.

The former general only laughed. "No, no," he said. "I am still myself, I assure you." He pursed his lips and looked up toward the ceiling for a moment. "Let us say I have merely had my consciousness expanded. Tremendously."

"You and the gray guy were doing drugs?" Tamerlane asked, almost laughing.

"Actually, we *were*—in a manner of speaking. He had some very powerful ones. I don't recommend them, though, if you plan on going back to your old way of thinking and living."

Tamerlane brought his hands up to his eyes and rubbed at them distractedly. "I don't know what to make of this," he said at length. "Agrippa is explaining cosmic metaphysics and Iapetus is happily resigning from his own legion. Maybe the galaxy did get blown up, and I've been hurled into the backwards-universe or something."

Iapetus chuckled at this while Agrippa dropped heavily into the control seat that Iapetus had vacated.

"My time grows extremely short, General," Iapetus said. "You had other questions?"

"Where are you going?" Tamerlane asked, staring openly at the new uniform the other man now wore. "For whom are you working?"

"I now serve the master of this facility."

"Aliens?"

"No. Not precisely. No."

"But you have a new 'master' you will be working for."

"Yes." Iapetus chuckled again. "As do both of you."

"We do?"

"In a manner of speaking. You'll see."

Tamerlane waved this away. "Enough with the riddles. You said you sent the power overload into both the future and the past. If you sent it into the past, why are we still alive, here and now? Why does the galaxy still exist around us?"

Iapetus nodded at this. "It is a puzzle, I'll admit." He stroked his chin, thinking. "My best guess is that I was successful at funneling it into either the Above or the Below as it traveled back in time."

Tamerlane's eyes widened. "You mean you just blew up the Above?"

"Or the Below. But not necessarily. Physics work differently there, in each of those realms. And whatever happened back then, it always happened."

"What?" Tamerlane frowned.

"The explosion, or overload, or whatever ended up manifesting itself back then—it has always happened that way. As we were born and grew up and lived our lives up until this moment, it was always that way."

Tamerlane struggled to comprehend this. "So—so you're saying whatever happened in the past, you didn't really change it. You just caused it to happen back then, as it always did."

"Precisely." He chuckled. "You're catching on, Ezekial." He sobered. "So that means, for example, that we didn't just wipe out the Golden City."

"That's a relief," Tamerlane said. He paused. "I think. Maybe."

Iapetus was staring off into the distance. "In fact," he said, "it could very well be that the blast I sent backwards in time could have gone into the Above, thousands of years ago, and ripped open the very fundament of..."

Tamerlane stared back at him as his voice trailed off. "Oh. Oh, no," he said, shaking his head. "No—you can't mean you think that you blasted open the hole in the Above that became the Fountain...?"

Iapetus shrugged. "How could we know for certain? But it is one possibility."

Tamerlane gaped at this idea. He could have just been complicit in the actual creation of the Fountain in the Golden City—the power source of the gods. "But—but that would mean that the gods themselves are not really divine, but merely—"

Agrippa interrupted them. "Gentlemen," he said, "it's all well and good to consider what the blast that went backwards in time caused. But—given that it clearly did not destroy us—I am far more concerned about the blast that Iapetus sent into the future—because that one still looms ahead of us." He explained to them quickly what Solonis had said—what the seer-god's time-traveling spirit form had seen in the distant future. "All of this—everything my legion and I have done since coming here—has been to avoid that very fate. Are you telling me it's *still* going to happen?"

Iapetus darkened. He looked down at the control panel and the readouts. "I can't be certain," he replied after a few moments. "Perhaps such things are simply unavoidable. Unalterable. Written into the fabric of reality." He shook his head. "Even with an expanded consciousness, I still don't understand the universe."

"It does seem as if, in attempting to avoid the shattering of the galaxy in the future, we have inadvertently made certain that very thing will happen," Agrippa grumbled.

Tamerlane exhaled and shook his head. "The future can tend to the future. We saved the present, and that's my main area of concern. That's enough, for now."

Agrippa didn't argue the point but he didn't look terribly convinced.

"And now," Iapetus said, "if you gentlemen will excuse me, I have work to do."

"Here?" Tamerlane said, still reeling at the thought of Iapetus simply walking away from his old life and his old ways. "You're staying here?"

"For now," the other man replied. "There's work to be done here, and then at other facilities across the galaxy."

"There are more places like this?"

Iapetus laughed. "Oh, many more, Ezekial."

Tamerlane frowned. "Should that concern me as much as I think it should?"

"No. Quite the opposite."

Tamerlane started to argue, then bit back his reply and shook his head again. "Alright, fine." He nodded to Agrippa, who slowly pulled himself up from the big seat. "We have pressing matters ourselves, don't we?"

"Indeed," the big man replied. "We were in the middle of losing a war, last I checked."

Iapetus grinned at that. "Oh, I wouldn't give up just yet," he said.

"And why is that?" Agrippa asked as he and the others moved toward the tower's exit. Ahead of them, Titus Elaro and Colonel Arani led the captive Torgon/Siklar toward a shuttle.

Iapetus shrugged theatrically as Tamerlane followed Agrippa out, the last of them to go. "You never know," he said. "There's always hope." He turned then and watched as the big, blond general paused and stared off into the distance. Iapetus called, "Agrippa."

The big general turned and looked back.

"Your warning never makes any difference. There's no point in going wandering off in the fog, trying to find yourself. Just let it go."

Agrippa appeared extremely puzzled for a moment, and then realization came to him. He started to say something back, then seemed to think better of it. He merely turned and walked toward the shuttle.

Iapetus only laughed at this. He saluted Tamerlane in Legion fashion one last time, then stepped back inside, and the door to the tower slid closed for good.

Tamerlane stared at that door for a good ten seconds, but he had no idea what to think or to say—and now no one to say it to, if he had. Shaking his head, he turned and jogged the rest of the way to the last of the shuttles.

"Arnem," Tamerlane said quietly as he climbed inside and seated himself a short distance away from the other general, "Did we just score a great victory—or suffer a tremendous defeat?"

But, for once, Agrippa had nothing to say. He was staring down at the floor of the craft, his expression grim. At Tamerlane's prodding he merely shook his head. "I failed on every level today, Ezekial," he said. "The Shattering still happens. I lost Torgon. And we're still losing the Empire."

Tamerlane took this in and unexpectedly he found Iapetus's final words to be something of a comfort—more than he would have expected. "There's always hope," he repeated. And, "It's not over yet." He considered for a second before adding, "Alien invasion; the fall of the Empire; the destruction of the galaxy... At least it can't get any worse."

BOOK TWELVE
EMPIRE IN ASHES

1

Two weeks later, it had gotten far, far worse.

Tamerlane stood at the center of the strategium aboard the *Ascanius*. Against the curving wall ahead of him were Agrippa—finally out of his heavy armor and clad in a much more comfortable standard smartcloth uniform of white and green—and Niobe Arani, along with Titus Elaro, Sister Delain, and the Lady Teluria, plus certain other officers and technicians. They watched in grim silence as Tamerlane controlled the huge holographic display with motions of his hands.

"They are moving past the Inner Worlds without overrunning and conquering each of them completely," Agrippa observed, his voice a low rumble. "Their numbers are so great, they are slipping past our pickets and defensive positions and converging—"

"On the Earth," Tamerlane finished for him. He zoomed the three-dimensional galactic map in tighter on the Inner Worlds—the dozen Imperial planets closest to the Earth. Some were further in or out along the plane of the galaxy; others were above or below Earth, relative to their current view. The enemy fleets—waves of comets, now joined in recent days by actual spacecraft—were each represented by a tiny red dot.

The display was filled with tiny red dots. They appeared like a gigantic swarm, surrounding and penetrating the Empire in a great, fuzzy sphere that was steadily constricting toward the center. Toward Sacred Terra.

"Their leaders in the field—the Phaedrons—are psychic creatures," Agrippa noted. "Their primary weapon is fear— the fear they create in their opponents." He stepped into the holographic cloud image and strode across to stop next to Tamerlane. Before the two of them floated a tiny representation of Earth. He reached out a big hand and cupped it with a delicate touch. "Perhaps they understand that threatening the sacred homeworld directly is a very effective strategy for generating fear. And fear in turn might aid in the final collapse of all organized resistance."

"Not just the homeworld," Titus Elaro added, his expression grim. "The palace."

The others looked at him.

"I know the Empire hasn't used the Old Palace as its capitol in centuries," Elaro explained, "and the Rahkmanovs never did. But the princess is there now. And the symbolic value…"

Agrippa nodded slowly. He looked up at Tamerlane. "He could be right. Capturing the ancestral homeworld and seizing the Old Palace—or destroying it—could shatter whatever morale remains among our troops and our people."

Tamerlane considered this and shrugged. "Whatever their rationale, the end result is the same. If Earth falls, this is all over. We're finished."

"Finished?" Colonel Arani sounded incredulous.

"For the most part, yes," Elaro said. "Think of it. The human race would have been swept from all its worlds, including its birth world. We would be a vagabond people, wandering about the periphery of the graveyard of our old domain, likely pursued by the victorious aliens and their forces."

Arani simply looked at him for a moment, then shook her head and turned back to the generals. Her face was flushed. "That can't be allowed to happen," she said with firmness. "It cannot."

"Colonel," Tamerlane said to her, not unkindly, "trust me—I fully agree, and I intend to do everything possible to avoid it."

Arani blinked and then nodded. "I know, sir," she said. "I just—"

Tamerlane gave her a reassuring smile and raised a hand. "I know, Colonel," he said. "This is all very hard to hear, I'm sure."

"It is infuriating," Agrippa growled. "I can't help but think that things could have turned out differently if Iapetus and the Sons hadn't held back so very long."

"Well, they're not holding back now," Tamerlane said. He pointed to several small rows of blue dots arrayed just beyond Earth. As sparse as they were, they represented the largest single set of units representing human forces visible within the display. "They're manning the front lines." He chuckled. "Barbarossa has proven remarkably...adaptable to his new circumstances."

"You mean he's obeying your orders," Agrippa said with a snort.

Tamerlane laughed once and nodded. "That's one way to put it."

"What of the princess?" Arani asked.

Tamerlane shrugged. "She's fine. Had no idea what was going on. She's young. She simply did what the adults told her to do. And of course Iapetus and his crowd treated her well."

"They wanted her full support," Agrippa noted.

"There's that, anyway," Arani said. She paused, then, "I heard Barbarossa even gave back the Sword of Baranak."

"That's correct," Tamerlane replied.

She looked from Tamerlane to Agrippa, not seeing it. "So, what's become of it?" she asked.

Tamerlane gave a half-grin and turned to Agrippa. The blond general in turn smiled.

"I gave it to someone who will get the best use out of it," Tamerlane answered.

"Indeed I shall," Agrippa said. "It's safely stored for now, but I will bring it out before the end. Never fear."

Titus Elaro moved forward and appeared to be studying the waves of red dots more closely. Their hollow sphere—hollow at the center, around the unconquered Earth and its environs—now encompassed the entirety of the rest of the human realms. The Anatolian Empire was nearly gone, and the Riyahadi Caliphate and the Chung worlds were naught but red smears. The chaotic panoply of DACS worlds was a mixed bag, with the enemy having passed many of them by entirely in order to head straight for the heart of human space. Beyond, the vague area where the Dyonari Star-Worlds were known to frequent was half-overrun, with occasional and generally very garbled reports coming out of that sector that spoke of tragedies and atrocities. Of the Rao sphere of influence, only a few worlds remained clear of the red–dot invader.

"If you see something the rest of us have missed, Major," Tamerlane called to Elaro, "by all means, share it."

Elaro shook his head. "I wish, General. But I honestly don't see a way out of this one."

Teluria stepped up then. Her hands were clasped about her back and her red robes flared around her. "Perhaps it is time to consider another option," she said. Her eyes flicked to each of their faces as they looked up at her.

"What option is that?" Arani began to ask.

Tamerlane cut her off. "No," he said.

"But—"

"No."

"May we at least hear her suggestion, General?" Arani asked, annoyed.

"I know full well what her suggestion will be," Tamerlane said, "and I do not intend to entertain it. Not for a second."

Arani continued to frown until Elaro leaned over and whispered something in her ear. Arani's eyes widened and for an instant it looked as if she would speak, but then she frowned and shook her head.

"You refuse the Exodus Option outright?" Teluria asked, her eyes moving over them one by one. "You would rather remain here and die—"

"Than have you lead a paltry few of us into the Above?" Tamerlane nodded. "Yes. Yes, I would rather die defending my home than run away and leave all the still-surviving billions to their grim fate."

"I have had more than enough of the Above to do me for one lifetime," Agrippa added with a humorless laugh.

"I agree," Arani said after a few moments' reflection. She sounded as if she were surprising herself. "It's hard to say that. The thought of turning down a chance to escape the apocalypse..." She trailed off, then shrugged. "But General Tamerlane is right. We owe it to the human race to fight for it until the end."

Teluria seemed astonished by this but, after a few seconds, she appeared to accept it as their final decision. She faded back to her position against the wall.

For several seconds no one spoke at all. They all simply stared at the halo of red that threatened to engulf the human worlds, and the galaxy in its entirety.

"So that's it, then," Tamerlane said. "We fight. To the bitter end, if need be."

The others nodded.

"How soon until the enemy forces reach the Earth?" asked a feminine voice from back along the wall.

They all looked. It had been Sister Delain who had spoken. This was surprising to nearly everyone present, given that she rarely ever spoke.

"Three days," Agrippa said. He gestured with his right hand at a particularly large clump of red dots that were concentrated within a portion of the Inner Worlds sector that didn't actually contain an inhabited planet. "I suspect that this is their final invasion force. It appeared very suddenly here in the past twenty hours, and there's nothing of value between it and the Earth."

"By the gods," Colonel Arani whispered. "It's huge."

Sister Delain looked at Agrippa and then at Tamerlane. Neither spoke. She stepped out into the light and frowned at them. "Then what," she asked, "are we doing *here?*"

The others all reacted with surprise at this, but Tamerlane merely nodded. "She's right," he said. He looked up at the domed ceiling high above and accessed the Aether link. "Captain Dequoi," he called. "Set course for Earth. Best speed." He started to say something to Agrippa, then caught himself and reactivated the link. "Captain," he said. "Forget best speed. Forget all safety margins. I want to be there *immediately.*"

"I'll set an all-time speed record, General," Dequoi replied. "Have no worries about that."

Less than a minute later, the *Ascanius* leapt into hyperspace.

2

"E verything?" the supply officer repeated, surprised. He squinted back at Tamerlane, the glare from the landing zone's perimeter lights bright in his eyes. "You want me to unload *everything?*"

"Everything," Tamerlane nodded. He moved a step back as a hovering cargo-carrier floated by with a roar, its bed filled with munitions, supplies, and not a few soldiers crowded on top or hanging onto the sides. It was but one of many units that had already been ferried down from the *Ascanius* and all the other surviving Imperial ships that had made it back to Earth thus far. After the vehicle had passed, the general moved in closer to the officer again. "All the hovertanks, all the troops, all the—" He frowned. "Do we have any remaining Colossus walkers?"

The officer considered this. "Five of the larger ones on this ship," he replied. "General Agrippa's the one who liked to keep a large collection of—"

Tamerlane was nodding. "I'm well aware of the general's predilections for heavy ordnance," he said. "Unfortunately, those units are all lost behind enemy lines now. All we have is what we have."

The supply officer frowned deeply at this. "That being the case," he said, "if you were to press me on it, I could probably get another two or three of the units that are down for maintenance back up and running pretty quickly. Maybe a week."

"The invasion force reaches Earth in less than two days," Tamerlane said.

The officer didn't miss a beat. "I'll have those eight walkers ready for you later today, sir," he said without a hint of humor.

Tamerlane almost—*almost*—laughed. Instead he saluted and strode away, feeling only marginally better about the utterly lost cause into which he was about to lead the last of the human race's armies.

"I keep a few here," came a deep, resonant voice from behind him.

Tamerlane turned. Agrippa was striding up, resplendent in his newly cleaned and polished white Deising-Arry power armor. The golden Sword of Baranak hung from his waist.

Tamerlane regarded him and smiled. "The enemy will surely reconsider their actions when they get a look at you," he said.

"Doubtful," Agrippa replied with a snort. "But perhaps after I decapitate a few dozen of them..."

Tamerlane nodded. "That's the spirit." He hesitated, then lowered his voice. "Speaking of spirits—what's the morale like among your troops?"

Agrippa shook his head. "It could be better, Ezekial, there's no doubt. They know the odds they're facing—what we're going up against. But...I believe they also understand what's on the line. What this is really all about."

"And that is?"

Agrippa pursed his lips. "Honor," he said. "It's about honor. It's about how we conduct ourselves as we go to meet our fate—whatever that fate may be."

Tamerlane considered this and finally nodded. "I'd like to believe we have some kind of chance, though."

Agrippa shrugged. "Perhaps. I would never rule it out entirely. Still…"

"Yeah," Tamerlane said. "I know." He nodded back in the direction Agrippa had come—the direction of the III Legion landing fields. "Now—you said something about having a few Colossus walkers hidden away here?"

Now Agrippa grinned. "A dozen," he said. "I kept them secret because I didn't want Iapetus and the Sons getting their hands on them."

"I'm very happy to hear that," Tamerlane said. "Where are they?"

"I hid them in the one place I guessed Iapetus would never think to look." Agrippa consulted the chronometer linked via the Aether. "They should be along any moment, actually," he replied.

A few moments later, massive horn blasts sounded from behind them. The two generals—and everyone else in the vicinity—turned and looked. What they saw took their breath away.

The landing fields currently being used by the three legions to ferry down troops and equipment partially surrounded the vast Old Palace complex that occupied the center of the European continent. Ages ago, thousands of square kilometers of landscape had been leveled and rebuilt as curving rows of massive arcologies—buildings the size of cities, each towering over a kilometer into the sky and holding millions of citizens. The arcologies swept in a semicircle around a central point—the location of the Old Palace, residency of the emperors of old and the bureaucracy that ran the Empire, the Terran Alliance before it, and whatever existed before that, since lost to history.

The Old Palace itself covered more than a dozen square kilometers, with vast domes and spires just visible beyond its towering ramparts. A pair of dull metal gates some five hundred meters in height provided the only visible point of access to the palace, and those gates had been firmly shut from the time Tamerlane's and Agrippa's shuttles had begun to land some hours earlier.

But now as the horns sounded again, the two gates parted and began to swing slowly open. In astonishment those thousands of soldiers and support crewmembers working in the front courtyard gazed up and attempted to come to grips with what they were seeing.

Through the now-open gateway strode a Colossus walker—huge, man-shaped, and so tall it nearly scraped the top of the gateway with its head. Its body was painted mostly white and green, indicating it belonged to the III Legion. Plasma cannons, missile launchers, beam projectors and many other oversized weapons covered its arms and shoulders. It was awe-inspiring to behold. But what truly shook the minds of the onlookers was what came behind it: another Colossus walker...and another...and another...

The procession took some six minutes to pass through the gateway. In all, twelve of the gargantuan war machines strode out onto the landing zone and lined up in formation, like a small group of soldiers, but moving in what seemed like slow motion and all out of rational scale.

Tamerlane took this spectacle in without comment, but when it was done at last he turned to Agrippa, grasped him by the shoulder, and smiled. "Thank you," he said.

"What do you mean?"

Tamerlane laughed. "Whether we have any sort of chance or not, none of our troops could possibly look at this display and not feel we are throwing everything imaginable at the enemy." He clapped Agrippa on the back. "This, my friend, is honor. This is going out with a bang, not with a whimper.

This is punching the enemy hard in the face even as they drag us down."

"Oh, have no doubts about that," Agrippa replied, smiling back now as he gazed up at his walkers. "These will most assuredly punch them. And punch them *hard*."

3

In towards the Earth streaked thousands of elongated, organic-looking, mottled black starships. Dim red lights shone from their viewports and tendrils of energy trailed from their guns. Skrazzi warships and troop transports, they had emerged from hyperspace just beyond the outer fringes of the solar system, accompanied by a scattering of a few dozen of the blood-red comets that contained their masters—the hideous, telepathic creatures called the Phaedrons.

The Sons of Terra had prepared to resist as best as they could, though the aliens didn't know and didn't care about the identity of those opposing them. For them, all humans were the same: a nuisance; a bother; a weed to be ripped out of the garden. Their nihilist garden of death.

The II Legion defenses just beyond Mars tore into the Skrazzi fleet with the savage ferocity to be expected of troops that had been trained by Ioan Iapetus. At last free to vent their ferocity and fanaticism unchecked, they hurled nuclear warheads, particle beams, solid projectiles, hard light, and every other variety of advanced and not so advanced weaponry available at the enemy. The toll the Sons wrought upon the aliens was vast and fearsome indeed.

It scarcely slowed them down.

The Skrazzi blasted their way through and past the Mars Line the Sons had established with little trouble and continued inward, again not even slowing as waves of Imperial battleships—anything that could be lifted into orbit and fitted with a gun—flung themselves against the oncoming tide of darkness.

Again the enemy swept through and onward, losses mounting to a level that would've been considered catastrophic to any rational army or navy but barely noticed by the Skrazzi.

At last the invaders reached far Earth orbit and encountered the last—and the toughest—of the defenses. While still in command, General Iapetus had positioned his largest lasers, railguns and beam projectors on massive platforms above the Earth, as well as on the planet's moon. Together these batteries opened up a sustained fire that proved to be overwhelming and devastating.

The aliens stuck back, first directing extreme-velocity projectiles and disintegrator beams from their organic ships—disintegrators almost identical in effect to the weapons engineered into their own bizarre physiology, though many times larger and more powerful—at the platforms. When this stratagem yielded limited results, and results that were not fast enough to satisfy their masters who lurked behind the front waves of the fleet, they resorted to kamikaze, suicide attacks against the orbital defenses. While costly, these proved more effective and eventually resulted in the destruction of nearly all the platforms. The way to Earth now lay open and undefended.

With over half their fleet shredded or vaporized but their goal in sight at last, the Skrazzi began to release their landing pods for the planetary invasion. Their ultimate target, because of its psychological value as well as its strategic importance, was the Old Palace that occupied a sizable portion of continental Europe. The Imperial Princess dwelt there now, as well as the top military officers of the Empire. It had to fall, and fall soon, to yield maximum value for the attackers. They dared not bombard it from orbit, for they wished above all else to seize it intact. That meant a troop landing would be next.

And so the first few Skrazzi scout forces began to land, their foul insectoid claws stepping out of their descent craft and touching the soil of Sacred Terra. Meanwhile, still in orbit, their ever-cautious Phaedron masters turned their powerful psychic minds outward for the first time in days, reaching for the ambient signal of their own master, to commune with him and share the news of their impending and total victory.

To their astonishment, they found that his signal was no longer there. It had vanished. It might as well be that he himself had vanished.

And that was when the Phaedrons, those creatures so adept at creating and sustaining a deep and irrational fear in their enemies and intended victims, began to taste some small measure of fear themselves, for the first time.

Summoning up their resolve, they put the issue aside and pressed on. The order was given. The invasion of Earth began in earnest.

4

olonel Niobe Arani watched from atop the Old Palace's walls as the great conflict unfolded.

Some in the ranks were already calling it the Nightfall War, the Last Stand, or simply the Apocalypse. They thought of it as the greatest tragedy mankind had ever faced. She understood that, of course. But for her, personally, it was different. For her—and she never would have admitted it to anyone else—it was almost clarifying.

Staring certain death in the face had a way of doing that, she supposed.

She had wrestled with her feelings for Titus Elaro for weeks now, ever since meeting him, coming to care for him, and then discovering him to be a spy put into place by Iapetus and the Sons of Terra. For a time she had walled him out completely. But he had switched his allegiance to Tamerlane's I Legion, pledged his loyalty, and been nothing but sincere and helpful ever since. For days she had wrestled with this—with whether or not to warm up to him again. Then had come word of this invasion, and suddenly such things scarcely mattered any longer. Friendships, relationships, love—what did any of that matter, in the face of such implacable, overwhelming hate?

In fact, as she thought about it, the entire mission to defeat Rameses and liberate Ahknaton now, in hindsight, took on the air of a pointless enterprise. At the time nothing had seemed more important. Of course, at the time, bringing Rameses back into the fold seemed a key component in helping to present a more united front against the dark enemy. But now, with nearly all of the Empire crushed under the merciless heels of the invaders, their partially-successful mission on Ahknaton had become a mere footnote.

The grim blackness that hung about her was obvious to the men and women under her command, and so they mostly left her alone. So she stood there atop the walls, in the position Tamerlane had assigned her, watching as the enemy comets and landing craft descended and the Colossus walkers, hovertanks and infantry moved out to meet them in the field.

She had thought briefly to complain—to protest this assignment. Clearly Tamerlane had placed her here, within the walls of the Old Palace, in an effort to keep her safe. She'd started to request—to *demand*—to be allowed to lead the last of her old Nizam Legion and any other troops that could be given to her out into the fray with the first wave. But then she'd reconsidered and simply accepted the orders. Her reasoning was simple: Everyone here was going to die today—*everyone*—and it scarcely mattered whether she stood in the field or on the walls when it finally happened.

The glare of the blood-red comets streaking down from the sky caused her to squint. Their numbers had increased tremendously in the past few moments. That likely meant the legion ships in orbit above the Earth that had been shooting many of them down as they dropped from hyperspace were now being overwhelmed or destroyed entirely. If the planetary defenses and the fleets in orbit were gone or nearly gone, she expected the numbers of enemy forces on the ground to rise accordingly. The only thing that surprised her so far was that the enemy had not simply resorted to orbital bombardment. But then, she knew they wanted to claim the Old Palace intact. Additionally, they hadn't used that strategy in any of their campaigns prior to attacking the Earth. They seemed to prefer to take out the space-borne defenses and then land boots—or hideous alien feet—on the ground, so that they could do their dirty work in the flesh. Or in the insectoid exoskeleton.

And so now as she gazed out across the broad landing fields where, hours earlier, Tamerlane and Agrippa had overseen the final unloading of all the defensive equipment they could get their hands on, she saw the lines of human legionaries preparing to face the onslaught of many thousands of Skrazzi, the primary foot soldier of the enemy.

The enemy. Therein lay the biggest irony of all. She had witnessed the man—the god, the being—who had engineered all of this being dragged down into the Below by a demon prince. But despite Goraddon's absence, the forces he had set in motion continued to press onward, their goal crystal clear: the utter annihilation of the human race, and of all native sentient life in the galaxy. What the worlds of Man would look like after it was all over, Arani didn't wish to contemplate. In any case, neither she nor anyone she knew would likely be alive to see it.

More comets fell to earth. More hordes of Skrazzi emerged, their black carapaces shining in the afternoon sun. They advanced by the thousands; by the tens of thousands. They slashed with their blade-arms and they blasted with their disintegrator arms and they exploded in showers of gore when one of the soldiers of the legions managed to hit them with a weapon that could cause them sufficient harm. And still they came, more comets landing, more strange dark spacecraft settling to the ground around them, more

Skrazzi leaping out to join in the attack. And more, and more.

The Colossus walkers were doing a remarkable job. They blasted away at the newly-landed comets and spaceships with their massive plasma-cannon arms, melting dozens of them on the spot, before anyone or anything could emerge. They fired rockets and missiles into the densest portions of the Skrazzi lines, blasting them to pieces. And the simply walked over the ranks of enemy forces, squishing a dozen or more to paste with each step.

Alas, such success couldn't last forever. The enemy began to land larger vehicles from their swarm beyond Earth orbit, some of which survived long enough to split open and disgorge massive land craft of their own. Some had tracks like old-fashioned tanks; some hovered above the ground; some had legs and walked in the manner of the Colossus machines, or like gigantic insects. Within minutes the numbers of enemy walkers and floaters exceeded the number of human walkers. Then they began to exchange fire.

The gods of the Golden City were impressive, certainly. But no one who was there that day, on the battlefield before the Old Palace of Terra, could ever again be impressed by a mere human-sized god. For those at the final battle of the Nightfall War witnessed machine-gods half a kilometer high trading plasma blasts and missile barrages across a dozen kilometers of distance, then rushing into grips with one another, wrestling physically, and crushing the infantry of both armies like ants beneath their feet all the while. It was stunning. It was awe-inspiring. It was terrible.

It went on that way for nearly an hour. Arani would not have predicted beforehand that the legions could have held out even that long. Individual acts of courage and sacrifice abounded, however. The human race had its back to the wall—to the abyss. Every soldier fighting there that day fully expected to die. Not a one of them expected to live to see another sunrise. And so they gave everything they had, and more. Eventually they found some small measure of success, as the first wave of enemy walkers was beaten back or destroyed.

There was no time for celebrations. Agrippa's white walkers stalked relentlessly forward, driving toward the heart of the enemy landing zone, seeking to blast away the ships and comets before their passengers could disembark. For a time they were successful at this, and the human forces rallied. Lords of Fire and Kings of Oblivion and even Sons of Terra joined together and charged across no man's land, firing their weapons at any dark shape that dared expose itself. The concrete landing fields and formerly lush gardens that surrounded the Old Palace had quickly been churned to mud—mud littered with the flattened, burned and dismembered bodies of both sides of the conflict. Through that mud the soldiers slogged, slowly gaining ground, slowly pushing the invaders back, slowly closing in on their central hub of ships and grounded comets.

Then a second wave of enemy walkers and hover-vehicles emerged from landers just over the horizon. And then a third wave. They crashed into the III Legion machines with overwhelming force; the sound was like thunder, deafening and disheartening all at once. For another half-hour the two small armies of machine-gods smashed away at one another as the infantries of both sides had no choice but to withdraw out of the way and await the outcome.

Agrippa's walkers accounted themselves well. Unfortunately, the enemy's numbers were far greater, and continuously replenished by more vehicles landing.

Arani watched this play out from her vantage point atop the walls and understood the outcome that was increasingly obvious. She nodded her head, accepting what she had long known was inevitable. The Imperial legions were going to fight gallantly and to the bitter end—that she'd known all along. They were also going to run out of soldiers and equipment long before the enemy did.

She took a certain satisfaction in gazing down at the seeming ocean of dead aliens and their wrecked war machines. The Earth might well be theirs in only another few hours at most, but they would be gravely depleted from this battle. Whatever number of them remained to plant their flag atop the Old Palace would be a much diminished force from what had first entered Terran airspace.

The battle entered its second hour—this fact alone surprised her—and then began to go badly for the legions. This fact did not surprise her at all. The last few Colossus walkers were surrounded and beaten down by the enemy's largest machines. Soon all twelve of them were naught but smoking debris covering a vast swath of the muddy battlefield. The human forces lost heart then and began to retreat, back toward the walls of the palace. This, Arani knew, was pointless. If they were somehow all able to withdraw inside the walls and keep the force field in place overhead, they might hold out another hour or two. But then, given no other options, the enemy would likely resort to full-scale bombardment and sooner or later would penetrate the shield and reduce the ancient edifice to dust.

But something unexpected happened. Before the leading edge of the retreating legions could reach the gates, a blast of horns sounded from within the walls. The gates, still open, now disgorged another procession of walkers. Eight of them—the eight that had been in the shop, all now fully repaired, or at least repaired enough to go into battle, when the fate of the world and its people was at stake.

Sadly, the rally was short-lived. The eight Colossus machines proved to have been cobbled back together just enough to get them into motion, but compared to Agrippa's elite walkers that had been secretly stored within the Palace, these were walking death traps. Their guns were faulty, their engines undependable, their armor cracked or thin. The enemy, seeking to avoid another encirclement like the one they'd just overcome, lit into these new walkers, scarcely allowing them to get far beyond the gates. Ten minutes after they had strode out to attack, the repaired Colossus machines lay in flaming ruins.

Now nothing stood between the invaders and the walls of the Old Palace.

The retreat signal went out over the Aether and the surviving soldiers in red, blue, black and green all abandoned their posts and began to trudge through the wrecked fields toward the gates. Hot on their heels came the enemy horde.

Arani watched this happen and inhaled deeply; the air was a seething morass of smoke and death, but she ignored this. She nodded to herself. So—as expected. She would be in the heart of the battle, because the battle was coming to her.

Grasping her energy rifle, she motioned to the others under her command who stood alongside her on the wall to follow her. Then she ran for the stairs.

5

As the retreating soldiers raced through the half-open gates, they passed within the gateway two figures that stood like rocks amid an onrushing stream. Ezekial Tamerlane and Arnem Agrippa waited there, staring out at the oncoming foe, preparing to make one last stand. Flames danced about Tamerlane's arms and Agrippa held the massive Sword of Baranak in his outstretched hand. Seeing them, the survivors took heart; many of them actually stopped and turned, inspired to join their two leaders. Soon enough the two had become the nucleus of an island of resistance, a knot of heavily armed soldiers waiting there before the gates. Waiting for the enemy. Waiting for death.

The Skrazzi did not disappoint. They came on like a tidal wave and smashed into the last lines of legionaries, not faltering until they at last broke upon the rock that was the generals' position.

Agrippa swung the sword; it was a scythe, slicing through rows of alien attackers with each motion. Tamerlane unleashed his cosmic flame, burning the Skrazzi where they stood. The two were not gods, but the death and destruction they dealt upon the enemy at that moment of the battle was awe-inspiring and almost divine.

The attackers quickly grasped that these two figures posed the gravest threat to their campaign. They concentrated their efforts against the two generals, pouring more and more of their forces into a direct, frontal assault against the little island of defenders led by the man in the red uniform and the man in white armor. As the Skrazzi, climbing over one another in their fervor to reach the two, closed in on Tamerlane's side of the formation, Agrippa took notice. He shifted a quarter-turn to his right and struck, beheading a trio of the vile creatures with the golden blade. As he did so, the Skrazzi on his side of the crowd struck. They couldn't use their disintegrator weapons in such close proximity to one another—and, as the humans had observed from the start, in the heat of combat they tended to apparently forget they even possessed those weapons. Instead they preferred to rely upon their wickedly curved blade-arms as first, middle and last option—and this was what they employed now, diving en masse at Agrippa, overpowering the soldiers around him and nearly overwhelming him with their sheer mass.

And some of their stabbing blows made it through. Through the soldiers who sought to shield him; through his rugged Deising-Arry power armor, and through his tough hide. The blond general cried out despite himself as two of the needle-sharp blade-arms penetrated his flesh in almost the same point, nearly skewering him.

The surviving legionaries around him leapt to his defense and drove the attackers away, and then Tamerlane burned them to cinders. But the damage had been done; Agrippa had dropped to one knee and blood ran heavily from the twin wounds. It looked as though he'd been bitten by a gigantic snake.

The attack ebbed for a moment at that point, and Agrippa seized the opportunity. He gritted his teeth and pulled away the white ceramic/metallic armor component from that quadrant of his chest to expose the bloody wound. Then he looked up at a shocked Tamerlane.

"Do it," he growled.

Tamerlane blinked, then understood. He didn't hesitate. There was simply no time. He reached down, pressed his hand to Agrippa's chest, and summoned the flame.

Despite all his toughness, the big man screamed.

Tamerlane, filled with rage now, pulled his hand away. The bleeding had been successfully stopped. He met Agrippa's eyes. "Can you stand?"

The other general didn't answer. He merely stood. He grasped the hilt of the Sword of Baranak and raised it high. "Let them come again," he said, his voice ragged and filled with pain but still booming. "Let them come and *see* if I yet live."

Tamerlane smiled fiercely at his friend and comrade. Then he turned back as the men and women around him shouted—for the enemy was doing precisely what Agrippa had dared them to do.

Rescue came this time from a different direction. As the forces around Tamerlane and Agrippa began to give way once more to the attacking horde, Colonel Arani struck from the side. She and her troops had descended from the heights of the walls in record time and they moved in without hesitation, driving a wedge into the Skrazzi formation. Titus Elaro battled at her side, and for once she didn't seem to mind that. The two of them barked orders and their forces responded, protecting the two generals and allowing them to continue their devastating counter-attack.

A moment later, Sister Delain—now surrounded by a dozen heavily-armed brothers of the Inquisition—fought her way to the rear of the island of resistance, where she contributed to the cause by using her own powers to distort and partially hide the human soldiers from the enemy. As she worked, she saw Tamerlane glance back quickly at her and smile. This filled her with an unexpected sense of happiness, and she lamented that soon they would all be dead.

"Close the gates," Tamerlane shouted over the deafening din. Simultaneously he sent that command via the Aether link.

Hearing him, Arani was glad she had decided to come down from the walls and join him. With the gates closed, there would be nowhere left for the human forces to retreat. They would have no choice but to make this their final stand. She did not wish to die inside the Old Palace, run to ground by an already-victorious horde of aliens. She much preferred the idea of dying here, in combat, and next to the generals. And next to Titus Elaro.

The gates clanged shut, the sound like the death knell of the galaxy. Briefly Arani wondered if they had made the right decision after all, before, at the Tower Between the Worlds. Should they have allowed the Dyonari to simply destroy the galaxy, thus saving it from genocide or enslavement at the hands of the enemy? For a moment her resolve on this point faltered; perhaps they should have embraced oblivion when they were given the chance. Perhaps it was nothing but foolish hubris for them to have believed they could somehow fight against this force—fight and win.

But no, she decided at length, even as the overwhelming wave of Skrazzi closed in. No, this was better. Either way they would all be dead, but at least this way, they were going down fighting. The human race was going down defiant to the very end. Let the Skrazzi and the Phaedrons have what remained of the galaxy now. It was no longer her concern—no longer humanity's concern. All that mattered now was making peace with the situation, preparing for death—and taking as many of them along with her as she possibly could.

Arani gritted her teeth, swapped out power cells in her blast rifle, and readied herself for the final onslaught.

And then something wholly unexpected happened.

In the days that followed, the survivors would tell many different tales of what they saw, there on the battlefield in the midst of so much death and destruction. Only a few things remained constant among all the various stories, but they were generally the things that mattered most.

There on the plains of ancient Terra, before the Old Palace of the grand emperors of antiquity, General Tamerlane and General Agrippa and the final remaining soldiers at their command had resolved to make their last stand. The enemy had closed in around them—an enemy so confident of inevitable victory that the strange reluctance of the Phaedrons to involve themselves directly in the battle went scarcely noticed by the Skrazzi leaders. As did their subsequent silent withdrawal from the battlefield and up into orbit, and then back into hyperspace.

Let those strange creatures who seek to command us do what they will and go where they want, the Skrazzi commanders crowed to one another in their harsh clicking and chittering dialect. *They are not needed here! Their debilitating psychic fear-mongering will be wholly unnecessary. There is no hope for the Earth under any circumstances.*

And so the hammer was poised, awaiting the final blow, and with it the decimation of the last of humanity's defenders.

At that moment, as that little island of human resistance had become surrounded before the gates of the palace and grim fate closed relentlessly in, a sudden sound had caught everyone's attention and caused them all—human and alien—to turn and look up at the sky. What they beheld there was unthinkable; it was impossible. The starfleets of the Imperium and its neighbors had all been eradicated in the previous days and weeks. There simply could not be anything left to send against the enemy.

And yet, there in the skies above old Earth, a vast flotilla of starships was descending from the heavens, their guns blazing as they blasted into the waves of stunned and suddenly panic-stricken Skrazzi.

The humans of the three legions before the palace walls could do nothing but watch—and watch in awe; in stunned silence—as the newcomers methodically blasted, bombarded, and otherwise shredded the enemy. It took some time to eliminate them all, but the assault was as relentless and methodical as it had been unexpected, and eventually every single Skrazzi crawling about the surface of the Earth had been slaughtered.

Then the wave of ships circled around and began to land.

7

From the moment they began to touch down on the surface of Sacred Terra, the Phaedrons could sense—could *feel*—that something, somehow, had gone very wrong. Even before the strange and unexpected fleet of starships dropped out of hyperspace and began to annihilate their comets and the Skrazzi armada in high orbit with a blinding barrage of weapons fire, they knew that—inexplicably, impossibly—they had drawn a losing hand.

What had seemed an easy and utterly inevitable victory had begun to go sour in what passed for their mouths the moment they failed to contact Goraddon the Adversary—or even sense his presence in the universe at all. Following that, their invasion force had suffered casualties far beyond what had been projected by its leaders as it struck at the Earth. Goraddon had assured them that his stratagems would result in the utter collapse of morale on the part of the humans. Clearly he had been wrong about that; they had somehow rallied and, despite their paltry numbers at this stage in their many wars, they had mounted a strong and spirited defense of their ancient homeworld.

When the Phaedrons reached out once more, desiring to advise Goraddon as to the status of the campaign and seeking his advice and assistance with regard to the newly-arriving wave of unknown ships, they again found no traces of him whatsoever. It was as if he had fallen down a hole in the universe.

Or—as if something had *dragged* him down a hole in the universe.

Now their earlier nervousness gave way to outright fear. Those who had always dealt in that sensation now felt it themselves—and felt it in full force. Without the steadying presence of Goraddon and his remarkable ability to calm the Phaedrons and direct them to a singular purpose, their more natural instincts—if anything about the Phaedrons could be termed "natural"—took over. One after another, they turned their blood-red ice-comets about and began to retreat back into the long dark between the galaxies where they dwelt.

They had found something that frightened them at last, and they were leaving our galaxy behind.

For now.

Tamerlane and Agrippa led the surviving legionaries out to meet this new, vast, and astonishingly effective force. Arani and Elaro hurried along beside them, a few hundred soldiers of all three legions trailing along in their wake. They were likewise followed by Sister Delain and other remaining members of the Inquisition. Curiosity filled each of them— curiosity and no small amount of fear. For if this force could dispatch the Skrazzi so capably, and then effect a landing on Holy Terra, what *more* might they be capable of?

More to the point—who exactly *were* they?

The Imperial soldiers arrived at the edge of the zone where the new ships had landed and Tamerlane held up a hand to stop them from advancing further. They stood there, watching, waiting, not daring to guess what form of alien creature might dwell within.

The hatch on the nearest ship—a large, apparently heavily-armed shuttle—unlocked and slid slowly open.

Tamerlane stepped forward, flames at the ready. Agrippa waited a half-pace behind him, the Sword of Baranak in hand. The others readied their weapons and watched, most of them holding their breath.

A second later, figures began to emerge. They wore brightly-colored uniforms of metallic reds and blues and greens and other colors. They appeared entirely humanoid. And they looked very, very familiar.

Tamerlane nearly stumbled backwards in shock. Behind him, even mighty Agrippa gasped. So, too, did the others as they saw what the generals had seen.

Before them across the narrow divide stood four figures, all clearly human. A blond man, an Asian woman, a bald man, and a dark-haired man.

Tamerlane studied them closer, not believing what he was seeing. But there was no denying it. He was looking at Agrippa and Arani and Elaro. And himself. Bigger, more muscular, more *chiseled* somehow—but unequivocally *them*.

"Who—who are you?" he began, but his voice faltered. No one in his party could quite speak yet, either.

The big blond man who looked exactly like Agrippa ignored the obvious awkwardness and smiled warmly, and it was a smile to inspire armies and fortify worlds. "Greetings," he said. "My name is Eagle." He gestured toward the others on either side of him. "This is Raven, Falcon and Hawk. We are the Hands of the Machine." His smile widened. "And we have come to save you all."

EPILOGUE:

1

The last thing Teluria expected to see as she walked out into the plaza at the heart of the Golden City was a small group of aliens sitting around the basin of the Fountain, obviously deeply engaged in an argument.

Moments earlier, as she had passed through the gateway of the city of the gods and had moved along the main boulevard, she had as usual been cursing the fact that no god could open a portal within the walls of the City, thus relegating her to walking in from beyond the borders of the realm. She had also been thinking about her recently-completed parting from Solonis. That procedure had not been pleasant, but it absolutely had been necessary. His presence within her mind had been driving her nearly mad.

She had been able to endure his consciousness residing within her head for barely a day after the incidents in the Tower. At that point, she had decided it was time for him to go. And so she had traveled to a dead world far out in the fringes of the human empires, and there forcibly separated herself from him. As his ghost-spirit had emerged from within her body, she thought she'd sensed him being snapped forward in time again, as if he somehow had formed an unbreakable connection to that far-future period where the galaxy had been shattered. She gave but a few moments of her concern to him and his plight, however. She was distracted with a dozen different things, truth be told. Yet in an instant all of those worries evaporated from her mind as she emerged into the plaza and confronted the five Dyonari sitting there—six, if one counted the dead body lying nearby.

She opened her mouth to speak—to react in some way—but found she had no idea what to say. Certainly nothing she could think of wouldn't sound comical if she uttered it aloud. It was simply inconceivable that a little band of mortals—albeit aliens—had managed to penetrate all the way into the heart of the great City.

Questions sprang to mind instantly: How had they passed through the gates? How had they gotten to this level of reality at all? The Dyonari were well-known to possess the ability—either through super-advanced technology or psychic powers or some combination thereof—to travel into the lowest reaches of the Above. But none of them had ever made it *here*. Never.

As she stood there, sputtering, the aliens took notice of her at last. Their squabbling trailed off and they merely gawked at her, apparently as uncertain of how to react to her presence as she was of theirs. They tensed, but no one reached for a weapon. Yet.

Teluria summoned up her dignity, pulled her red robes tightly about herself, and strode forward. She raised a hand in greeting. "Welcome to the Golden City," she called to them as she approached. "Might I ask—how do you come to be here?"

The four males stared back at her, dumbstruck. The female, who quickly made it clear that she was the leader, stood straighter and nodded her head respectfully. "I am Co-Commander Mirana. We apologize for trespassing," she said. "We—we may have been misled."

"About a great many things," one of the warriors behind the leader added, anger apparent in his tone.

"I...see," Teluria replied. She glanced over at the body of the sixth Dyonari, another female, lying on her back off to one side. "Is she—?"

"Dead," the leader said. "Yes." Her expression was bitter. "She was Madalena. She was my friend. My comrade. My co-commander of this mission."

Teluria nodded. She looked about, growing concerned. Was some sort of wild predator loose—here in the city of dreams? "What killed her?" she asked them.

"We did," one of the male warriors answered. His voice was as bitter as the look on his leader's face. "We *all* did."

Teluria couldn't help backing up a step at that. She considered her next words carefully. She started to ask why they had killed the other woman, but decided it wasn't the main thing she needed to know at the moment. Instead, she asked, "Why are you here?"

The five aliens glanced at one another nervously. Then the leader said, "We were ordered to come. It was our mission."

"More than that," the male warrior who had spoken up before said. He stepped forward aggressively, but toward the leader, not toward Teluria. "It was programming—put into our heads, as if we were robots," he all-but-shouted. "Tools to be used and discarded." His lips curled into a scowl. "And to what end? To destroy our own galaxy!"

"Vinizan!" The leader whirled at him admonishingly, but it was too late. The truth was out.

Teluria gasped. "Ah! Yes—of course. This had to be where the energy was coming from. The Fountain. It *had* to be."

As the male warrior—Vinizan—had moved forward, something behind him had become visible; something the others had been standing in front of, blocking Teluria's view. Now she rushed forward and saw it: a cube, constructed of some transparent material, with a parabolic dish at its top, aimed at the sky. A cable of some sort trailed from it over the edge of the basin, down into the cosmic "waters." Everything clicked into place for Teluria now and she moved backwards, getting away from them quickly, her expression one of near-horror.

"No—wait," the leader cried, her voice pleading. "We didn't know—didn't understand what we were doing. The seers—the seers controlled us. Forced us to do things completely against our will."

"The Dyonari seers?"

"Yes!"

Teluria nodded. That made perfect sense to her. "Which Star-City?"

Mirana hesitated, now appearing truly frightened for the first time.

Teluria stepped forward and raised her hands high. Lightning flared around her. "Tell me!" she commanded. "Or I swear none of you will leave this city alive."

"Dalen-Shala," the one called Vinizan blurted.

The leader whirled on him, angry. "Why would you tell her the name of our home?"

He merely shrugged. "The seers brought all of this about. They deserve whatever fate befalls them. Besides," he added, "aren't they both dead now?"

Mirana started to offer stern reproach, but then appeared to lose heart. She deflated and simply lowered herself to the ground, sitting there glumly, her chin in her hands. "I wash my hands of all of this," she muttered. "Had I truly understood what we were doing, I never would have obeyed the orders to come." She hesitated, then added bitterly, "That is, if I'd been given a choice to begin with."

Teluria gazed down at her, weighing her words. She started to reply but never got the chance, for at that moment a loud, powerful, booming voice echoed across the plaza. It was one Teluria had not heard in many, many years, yet she recognized it instantly. It held intensity and force yet was at the same time feminine and attractive. She turned and saw precisely what she expected to see: a vision in silver and black, advancing across the plaza like a juggernaut.

"Teluria," the newcomer boomed. "Tell me what is happening here. Now."

Teluria bowed her head quickly. "My lady Karilyne," she said to the vision in gleaming armor. "I am pleased to see you once again."

"Now," Karilyne repeated. Her voice had shattered armies and sent stout warriors cowering at their mothers' aprons. Her sword and her axe were swift and powerful and renowned throughout the cosmos. Her only superior in combat—and also her former lover—Baranak, god of battle, was long dead. Now no one challenged her—particularly when she was aroused with wrath and fury.

The Dyonari all took a knee and bowed their heads. The reputation of the ice queen reached even to the star-cities of the path-walkers.

"We came here under duress, great Karilyne," Mirana said quickly. "But we accept responsibility for our actions."

Karilyne frowned and looked to Teluria. "Explain," she said.

Teluria did, and quickly.

At the end of the story, Karilyne pursed her lips as her gaze shifted from the Dyonari to Teluria and back. She shook her head slowly. "A sordid tale," she muttered, "and one of great hubris—and great transgression."

The Dyonari kept their heads bowed and none of them responded to that.

Karilyne thought for another moment, then strode across to the cube the aliens had constructed. She raised her axe and swept it across in a single broad, powerful stroke. The cube shattered into a million fragments. Teluria had to leap back as shrapnel from it flew in every direction.

The ice goddess turned back to the Dyonari. The males were practically cringing now, but the leader, Mirana, dared raise her head and stare back up at her.

"I will not flinch from your gaze, great Karilyne," Mirana said in a strong, clear voice. "I know full well the nature and the depth of my transgressions, whether performed willingly or not. I accept whatever punishment you see fit to mete out." She exhaled slowly. "I deserve far worse than you could ever do to me."

Karilyne stared back into those dark, alien eyes for a moment, as Teluria held her breath. The goddess in red expected the axe to come around again at any moment.

It did not.

"You four," Karilyne barked at the males. "Go. Go now."

They looked up at her hesitantly. "Go?" one of them asked, his voice tremulous. "Go where?"

"What care I where?" Karilyne snapped back, her eyes burning with fury. "Find your own way home. If you can."

The Dyonari hesitated for only half a heartbeat after that. Then they leapt to their feet and ran for the gates. Karilyne didn't bother to watch them go.

Mirana did. She watched them as they fled, then looked back at the goddess in silver and black. "What of me?" she asked in a voice thin and weary with regret and pain.

Karilyne regarded her for another few seconds in silence. Then, "Get up," she ordered—but this time her voice had softened somewhat. "Come with me."

Hesitantly the Dyonari woman rose and stood next to Karilyne. "What would you have of me, my lady?"

"You have been torn down to your depths. Your will has been broken." She smiled grimly. "You have become raw material that may be shaped into something colder, harder. Better." She glanced at Teluria, who wisely looked away. "And I am an excellent sculptor," she added.

With that, Karilyne turned and strode back toward the gates. She didn't look to see if Mirana was following her. She knew it—and indeed she was.

Before they passed out of the plaza, Karilyne turned back and looked at Teluria. "Oh—and what of you?" she asked, her voice casual now. "Will you remain here, and reign over a kingdom comprised entirely of yourself?"

Teluria laughed at that. "I am not the god of evil," she said. "But I do have a purpose now, at least for the moment."

Karilyne continued to stare back at her, waiting.

"The Dalen-Shala Star-City," she said. "It seems I have business there." She offered the other goddess a wry half-smile. "Feigning death is an old trick among the Dyonari elders. We shall see what the truth is."

Karilyne absorbed this and considered it for a moment. Then, as she understood, she smiled—and her smile was a fearsome thing indeed. "I approve," she said. "Let justice be done."

With that, Karilyne and Mirana exited the plaza and the Golden City itself, bound for wherever the ice queen abided in these latter days.

Teluria waited a few minutes and then followed along the same path that led out of the city. As soon as she was far enough away, she opened a portal and stepped through.

The bridge of the *Ascanius* greeted her.

2

Reality tore itself asunder and out stepped a woman clad in black. An army followed behind her. She raised her hands and both she and the army vanished.

The seers of Dalen-Shala, seated there in their smoky chamber deep within that vast Star-City, did not react to this strange development at all at first. Perhaps each of the two believed they had only imagined such a bizarre, unprecedented thing happening. But when they each glanced at one another, frowning, the message was clear: "You saw something."

The First Seer sent a frantic mental signal to the warriors who perpetually guarded the doors leading into their chambers. He managed only a few unintelligible syllables, however, before invisible hands grasped him and dragged him to his feet. A moment later he saw the same thing happening to his counterpart.

The guards, alerted by the aborted call for help, opened the door and started in. Instantly energy weapons fire and projectiles erupted out of nowhere, smashing into the guards and driving them back.

Both of the seers, meanwhile, were pulled bodily across the chamber. Each started to object, to cry out with actual voices, but it was too late. Strong, powerful, and entirely unseen arms lifted them both and threw them through the portal. They tumbled through darkness streaked with light, landed hard, and rolled to a stop against one another in a heap.

"What—*who*—?"

Behind them the portal vanished, closed, and at least a dozen human soldiers in red uniforms appeared as if from nowhere.

"Welcome to the *Ascanius*, gentlemen," came a human voice from in front of them. "I would ask that you not attempt any mental tricks for the next few moments, as you are being closely monitored and any such efforts will be detected and punished."

Slowly managing to right themselves and sit up, their aged bodies protesting all the while, they stared up into the face of a black-haired man clad in a dark red uniform. Beside him was the woman in black—the one they had seen only briefly before she had somehow caused herself and the soldiers with her to vanish.

The man in red raised both hands, palms facing upward, and fire sprang from them. The flames danced there as he stared down at them. "My name is General Ezekial Tamerlane," he told them. "This is Sister Delain of the Holy Inquisition." His eyes moved from one of them to the other. "You have been brought here to answer for your crimes."

"Our...*crimes*?" the First Seer croaked, relying on his spoken voice. "*What* crimes?"

"Galactic genocide," came a female voice from off to one side.

They turned as one and beheld a goddess. It was Teluria of the Golden City. They knew her instantly. They bowed their heads.

"You are accused of the attempted murder of the sentient population of the galaxy," General Tamerlane continued.

"Only 'attempted' at this moment in time," said Sister Delain. "Remember, General—for all we know, they yet succeeded, at some point in the future."

Tamerlane nodded.

"I also hold you directly responsible for the death of a certain Dyonari," Teluria added.

The two seers both frowned at this. "What?" asked the first.

"She was Co-Commander Madalena. I trust that you remember her. After all, she acted in your service, and your orders led to her death."

The seers glanced at one another. Their increasing uneasiness was apparent.

"Now, gentlemen," Tamerlane picked back up, "we could have a trial, public and open. But that could lead to all sorts of difficulties between our people and yours. And, the stars know, the last thing the human race needs at this juncture is another war." He raised his right hand higher, and the flames that wreathed it flared brighter. "Or we could simply declare your guilt as manifest and obvious—after all, it *is*, yes?—and I could proceed with a summary execution."

The seers gasped and drew back, now openly fearful.

"That, too, could lead to complications," Tamerlane added. "And so..." He turned to the woman in red.

"And so," Teluria said, moving to the forefront, "the general has asked me to resolve the situation. And resolve it I shall." She smiled, and her smile froze the blood of the two aliens. "For all anyone on your side of things knows, a god or goddess opened a portal into your room and dragged you away." She smiled. "And that perception is perfectly fine with me. I simply wished to give the good general and his people a firsthand look at the two of you, before…" Her voice trailed off and she smiled at them again.

"We very much appreciate that," Tamerlane was saying even as Teluria gestured to open a new portal.

She nodded to him, then grasped the collar of the first seer and hurled him through. A moment later she did the same with the second. Then she turned back to Tamerlane one last time. "I bid you farewell, General," she said. She hesitated then, reaching out and stroking his cheek. She appeared wistful—something highly unusual for her. "I apologize for my behavior when we first met. I could make excuses—Goraddon was controlling me, and so on—but it wouldn't be fair. I knew what I was doing. And I was wrong. I'm glad you've allowed me the opportunity to make a few amends."

Tamerlane bowed to her. "Your assistance has been invaluable, Lady, and I will always be grateful. As will the Empire." He looked back up at her and smiled. "I believe, whatever your faults may have been in the past, you've gone a very long way toward redeeming yourself in these last few weeks."

She gave him a dubious expression by way of reply, then laughed. "You will excuse me. Those two must be seen after before they attempt to escape."

"You intend to punish them," Tamerlane said, the words in the form of a statement rather than a question.

"Oh, most assuredly I do," the goddess replied. "In ways they can scarcely imagine." Then, "Goodbye, Ezekial," she said. "I very much doubt you will see me again."

With that, Teluria swept through the portal, her robes flying behind her, and vanished.

Tamerlane watched the portal close, considered for a moment, then turned to Sister Delain. "Upon reflection, I fear those two might have preferred to choose the summary execution option over what she has in store for them," he said.

"Then I'm glad you didn't offer them a choice," Delain replied bitterly.

He continued to stare at the spot where the portal had closed for a few seconds longer. Then Delain reached out, took his hand, and pulled. "You've grown too tense again," she said. "You need to relax."

Tamerlane looked down at her, smiled, and allowed her to lead him away. The hatch at the rear of the bridge closed as they passed through it.

Titus Elaro watched them go, grinning. Then he turned to Colonel Arani.

She took one look at his expression and snorted. "Don't even think about it," she growled.

Dejected, Elaro crossed his arms and leaned back against the railing, staring out at the stars.

For a few seconds no one said anything, and only the low hums and beeps of the ship's systems and the low murmur of the bridge officers working at their stations filled the air. Then Arani leaned in close, her voice a whisper so low even he barely heard it, and said, "You're not telling me you're giving up that easily, are you?"

It took him a couple of seconds to process this. When he finally did, he turned—just in time to see her stepping through the rear hatch. She looked back at him and smiled—a smile as radiant as a new dawn.

Elaro's breath caught in his throat. He felt the weight of the world—of the *galaxy*—lifting off his shoulders for the first time in days.

He was off the bridge and through the hatch less than two seconds later.

3

The sun had just begun to drop below the edge of the high walls surrounding the Old Palace on Sacred Terra, washing the ramparts in a bronze glow and paradoxically granting the entire tableau a sense of both ancient permanence and transient ephemeralness. The smells that wafted up from the vast ruin of a battlefield that was the palace's exterior grounds remained severe and all-pervasive, even these many days after the last body had been removed. The very earth around the ancient complex had been traumatized by the events of the Nightfall War, to say nothing of the hearts and minds of the people who lived there, and who had—somehow—lived through it.

On a broad balcony that extended out from the throneroom and across much of the width of the central sanctum itself sat two men, their legs up on ottomans and their heads leaned back against cushions. They were not soft men, indulging in endless recreation or laziness. These two were hard men; men who had led the resistance against the invading hordes. These were men who had not won the war on their own, but who—by simply managing to stay alive and to keep a substantial portion of the rest of the human race alive until unexpected help arrived—had won a substantial, almost incalculable victory all the same. No, these were not slothful men engaged in idleness. These were warriors of the first rank, able at this late date at last to enjoy perhaps a brief moment's rest; to catch their breath before plunging onward into the next fray.

As the sun vanished below the wall's edge and the lighting shifted, casting them into deep shadow, the taller and more muscular of the two spoke up. "The Earth is nearly secure," he rumbled. "Only two continents remain to be cleansed." He shifted in his seat, his wounds troubling him. "It is taking this long only because—"

"I know full well why it's taking this long," the dark-haired man in red replied. "Because I have severely limited the number of troops they can send down. But I have no intention of allowing that army of clones to gain a foothold on this planet. Not if I can help it, anyway." He shook his head for emphasis. "We will do this ourselves."

"Honestly, Ezekial," the big man said after a moment, "do you truly believe we could deny them and their army the Earth right now, if they chose to take it? The only reason their numbers here are limited is because they have *chosen* to honor your limits. Their forces vastly outnumber ours. Their technology is superior. And—unlike us—they haven't just spent the past few months being beaten down across a hundred theaters of action on half a hundred worlds." He inhaled deeply and winced as the pain stabbed at him again. "To the contrary, everything I've seen of theirs so far appears brand new. Sparkling clean. As if it has just rolled off the assembly lines." He snorted a laugh. "Including their soldiers—which is likely true."

"I doubt we could deny them anything they set their sights on," Tamerlane replied dryly. "But that isn't the point. If I'm able to put my foot down and set certain areas of the

Empire as off limits to them, and they will respect my wishes on that, I intend to do so. I would be remiss *not* to." He gazed off into the distance for a moment, then continued, "Especially with Iapetus now on the inside, working with them."

"Certainly," Agrippa agreed, nodding. He turned his head stiffly—his healing was coming along slowly but surely, the doctors all agreed—and met the other man's eyes. "Just as long as you cling to no illusions."

"Illusions?"

"Illusions as to exactly whom it is that decides where these people go and where they don't. It's not *your* orders that are keeping them off the Earth now. It's *their* decision not to land in force."

Tamerlane took this in but didn't reply. In his heart he knew that—he knew it very well. But that didn't mean he had to like it, or even wanted to think about it. At least, not more than he had to.

"What do you think of them?" Agrippa asked after a brief silence, broken only by the sound of a palace servant bringing them fresh drinks and leaving them on the small table between their chairs.

"The Hands? Isn't that what they called themselves?"

"Hands of the Machine," Agrippa said. "Whatever that is."

Tamerlane spread his hands before him. "They're *us*, aren't they? Clones? Genetic duplicates, force-grown in a remarkably short time."

"An astonishingly short time," Agrippa agreed. "The technology behind them—the technology that allows them to exist at all—is far superior to our own. Yet another reason to be wary of them, and to remember that, for all intents and purposes, *they* are in charge now—not *us*."

"I wouldn't go that far," Tamerlane shot back. "The Empire is still in our hands."

"Is it?" Agrippa regarded him dubiously. "Is it truly?"

Tamerlane frowned but said nothing.

"What do you suppose Iapetus is up to right now?" Agrippa asked, changing the subject as he sensed Tamerlane growing agitated. "Is he still the happy servant of his new mechanical master and its clone army? Or has the old Iapetus begun to resurface yet?" Agrippa considered his own words and laughed. "Of course the man is happy. We thought he was making some sort of selfless sacrifice by staying behind—but of course what he actually did was to ally himself with what is now the most powerful—and independent—military force remaining in the galaxy." Agrippa shook his head in wonder. "He must be thrilled."

Now Tamerlane laughed. "I hope he's still happy. For his master's sake as much as for his own. Because—let's be honest—no matter how blissful and content Ioan Iapetus might appear to be, under the surface I'm confident the same cold, hard man is still present. When the day comes that our old Son of Terra reawakens, well—" He winked at Agrippa. "May the gods help that Machine."

4

Machine? Do you hear me?" called Ioan Iapetus impatiently. He had been shouting at the ceiling for some time now, but receiving no reply. It had begun to grate on him.

"Do not think you can only converse with me according to *your* timetable," he said. "I gave up everything I had and agreed to help you—to work with you—because the very fate of the galaxy lay in the balance." He spread his hands. "As far as I can see, the galaxy yet exists. The crisis has been averted—at least, for the present. And so I would speak with you about the next stages of our plans." He waited, and still no reply. "Do you hear me?" he demanded, his voice now louder still. "I said I would converse about the next stages of—"

"Of *our* plan?" came a cold, almost mechanical voice from nowhere, echoing throughout the control room.

"Yes," Iapetus replied. "Precisely. We can—"

"You think of yourself as an *equal* to me?" the voice asked.

"An equal? Well, now—that's not the issue, or the point," he said. "I merely wish to draw up our—that is to say, *the*—plans for the next stages of our—of *the*—operation."

"What operation would that be?" the voice asked.

Iapetus frowned. "The orderly policing of the galaxy, of course. The restoration of stability and security following the events of the past few weeks."

The voice was silent for a few moments, and Iapetus grew agitated again, suspecting it had abandoned him once more. But then it returned, asking, "You believe I should devote my resources to that end? To becoming actively involved in this galaxy again? To seeking to impose my will upon it?"

Iapetus shrugged, though he had no real idea if the intelligence with which he was conversing could see that gesture—or understand it. "You possess the resources. An entire vast army, plus ships to carry them about, weapons and armor and—"

"I have possessed that starfleet and all the weapons in my arsenals for ages," the voice stated evenly. "And now, with the DNA of your kind—a rising people, with so much potential—serving as the basis for a new army, I find myself fully prepared for any possible challenges that might arise. One has been defeated now. Should I not simply return to my dormant state until the next comes along?"

"You must be *proactive*," Iapetus replied, "so that such a circumstance cannot arise again."

"Perhaps. There is merit in your words. But still I wonder. Having the *means* to enforce the peace—to conquer—does not necessitate *doing* so. Nor does it have to naturally follow."

"I believe it does," Iapetus countered. "Possessing the capability, you therefore inherit the responsibility."

"Do I?" The voice seemed to ask this as a genuine question, with none of the cynical tone that had marked much of its statements up till now. "You believe that my simply having soldiers and weapons at my disposal means I must use them to enforce a particular set of standards upon the galaxy?"

Iapetus nodded. "I do." He paused, his eyes narrowing. "Or," he continued a moment later, "you could leave that all to me. Grant me command over your forces. I will be happy to lead them—to direct them in a campaign to stabilize and secure the realms of mankind and beyond." He smiled up at the ceiling, imaging somehow that that was where the entity lived. "You need not lift a finger—or whatever appendages you possess. You can leave the galaxy safely in my care."

The voice remained silent as seconds ticked by, then minutes. Iapetus waited. He clasped his hands behind his back to mask his nervous movements. He had thrown the dice. Everything hung on the entity's reaction and response to his proposal. He had placed himself in this position deliberately, the moment he'd come to understand that his own legion was broken. Broken and handed over by that weakling Barbarossa to Tamerlane and Agrippa without his permission! From that moment forward, this new, seemingly mechanical entity and its clone warriors and ships had appeared to him to represent the truly dominant rising force in the cosmos—and he intended to rise along with it.

After a few more seconds the voice returned, delivering its verdict. Iapetus listened carefully and with great anticipation for what it said—for what might lie ahead.

"I have calculated ten million different possible options and outcomes," the voice told him. "And I have decided to follow your advice."

Relief and excitement washed over Iapetus. "I am very pleased to hear that," he said.

"I will order my new army forward, to move about the galaxy, dispensing justice and countering all threats to the peace and security of the sentient beings who inhabit it."

"Excellent," Iapetus said. "Now—I have a few ideas as to the disposition of forces along—"

"But," the voice interrupted, "I have no intentions whatsoever of allowing *you* to lead it."

Iapetus stopped short and frowned. He looked up at the ceiling again. "What—what do you mean? Surely your army needs a *general*—a sound strategic mind—to guide it in the field? That is what I offer—what I can provide."

"What you offer is of value, I will admit," the voice said. "But it is valuable within certain parameters and in certain circumstances only."

"I disagree," Iapetus began. "I strongly object to—"

"Even so," the voice said, "your selfless act of leaving behind your people and your own army to come and assist me is noted and appreciated, and I vow to make the most of that sacrifice on your part."

Iapetus was growing extremely agitated now. "*What? What does that mean?*"

Silence.

"*Speak to me! Do you hear me, machine? What does that mean? Answer me!*"

Iapetus was so angry, and so busy looking up at the ceiling and yelling at it, that he failed to notice the tiny robot that scooted out from its concealed compartment in the wall nearby and rolled up next to him. An arm extended from it, a long needle at its end. A liquid dripped from the tip. The robot jabbed Iapetus with the needle, causing the former general to cry out, more in dismay than in pain. A second later, he had fallen to the floor, unconscious. A moment after that a second, much larger robot moving on triangular treads rolled out, extended its thick, telescoping arms, grasped Iapetus firmly, and began to drag him away.

When next the former general awoke, he found himself being loaded by that large robot into a sort of transparent, vertical box—a *casket*, the thought came to him, as he tried to shake the sleep from his brain.

"What are you doing?" he cried, attempting to wrestle himself free. It was too late. The robot shoved him back into the recesses of the box and a clear front panel slid down, sealing itself tight, trapping him inside.

"As I told you before," the voice said then, the sound now coming from a small speaker set into the inside of his box, "your willingness to contribute—your sacrifices in doing so—are noted and appreciated. In order to make the most of your contributions, I have decided to keep you in suspended animation until such time as you—and your ruthless style and manner—are needed."

"What?" Iapetus shouted his objections even as he smashed his fists into the transparent panel in front of him. He beat at the glasslike substance relentlessly, until his fists bled, all to no avail.

"You!" he cried. "Machine! *Listen* to me! *Hear* me! This is a *mistake*—this is *not* what I—"

A gas flooded the box.

"No! *No!*"

A second later, Iapetus slumped into a deep sleep. A moment after that, the box retracted into a niche in the wall and a gray panel slid down over it. He was gone; it was as if he had never been there.

General Ioan Iapetus had effectively vanished from the galaxy, and from history.

For now.

eneral Marcus Ezekial Tamerlane strode into the small conference room of a remote space station in a remote corner of the human-occupied portion of the galaxy. He chose a chair, pulled it out, and sat down. Then he waited.

It had been several months since the end of the Nightfall War. Agrippa had fully recovered and was back out among the troops, helping to clear away the last stragglers from the invasion and to rebuild the shattered worlds of Man. He and Tamerlane had settled into a formula for governance that seemed to be working, at least for now: Tamerlane tended to most of the political decisions, while Agrippa dealt more directly with the surviving elements of the legions and with the infrastructure repairs now desperately needed throughout the Empire. They both knew that, sooner or later, the young Princess Marens would come of age and possibly take the Empire in a different direction. For now, however, they served as co-regents, and they were both determined to do all the good they could do in the time they were allowed.

That was what had brought Tamerlane here, to Alsatia, just beyond the borders of the Imperium. Alsatia had been a member of DACS—the Dominion of Allied Core States—for many years, but had always retained its independence even within that loose arrangement. Its brutal, absolute dictator had kept it that way—but in recent weeks he was rumored to have died, and been replaced by a new and mysterious leader who, the stories went, might have also played some role in the dictator's defeat and death.

It was this new man Tamerlane had decided to come all the way out here to meet in person, to invite to participate directly in the negotiations that might bring Alsatia and some of the other DACS-affiliated worlds into the Empire. The gods knew the Empire needed all the new blood and resources it could get now, as it struggled to recover from the devastation of the war. Alsatia promised just that—if its mysterious new liberator and ruler could be persuaded to throw his and his people's lot in with them.

As Tamerlane sat ruminating over all this, the weight of the metaphorical crown weighing heavily upon his brow, the door opposite him slid soundlessly open and a tall, dark-haired man in a blue semi-military uniform strode in. He stood gazing down at Tamerlane for a second, whereupon the general pulled himself to his feet and extended his hand.

The two shook while looking one another up and down.

Tamerlane was struck by one thing in particular. While this other man possessed long, lank hair that nearly reached his shoulders, his overall complexion and features bore no small resemblance to...*him. Could this be one of my distant relatives?* he wondered. Immediately he dismissed the notion as ridiculous—but still, the similarities were profound.

"General Tamerlane," the man said. "It's a pleasure to meet you at last."

Tamerlane nodded respectfully. "Likewise, sir," he said. And then, striving to be diplomatic, "Ah—I wasn't briefed on your preferred form of address. Is it Mr. President? Lord? Your Majesty? Or—?"

The other man smiled at this. He gestured for the general in red to take a seat before doing the same himself.

"I typically use no form of honorific," the man in blue said after a moment's reflection. "Most often I am simply known as Markos. Markos the Liberator."

Tamerlane blinked at this. Something about the name sounded a chord within his memory. Something old; something from ancient history. He frowned, thinking hard—and then he had it. "Markos," he exclaimed. "Yes. The legendary ruler of Mysentia of the Outer Worlds." Then he frowned deeper. "But—that name was later revealed to have been a false identity, used by—"

"By me," the man in blue replied with another smile.

Tamerlane was by now extremely confused. What was this man saying—what was he attempting to put over on him?

"By *you?*" Tamerlane laughed uncomfortably. "That's amusing, sir, but—"

The other man was not laughing. He was no longer even smiling. Instead he stood. He waited while a very puzzled Tamerlane did the same. Then he gestured with his left hand, and a swirl of light appeared in midair. Quickly it expanded into something Tamerlane had become intimately familiar with in recent times: a trans-dimensional portal.

Tamerlane gawked openly at it. This was something he had not expected. "You—" he began, but the other man cut him off.

"Better to simply show you," he said. He laughed. "That way you won't have to decide if you should take my word for it or not." He paused, then looked Tamerlane up and down once again. He seemed somehow pleased. "I had come to believe all of my line was dead and gone," he said. "It has been quite a shock—and a relief—for me to learn, these past few days, that an orphan boy from the Empire— its new ruler, in fact—is Dorion's great-great-great-great grandson."

"Dorion?" The name was familiar, somehow, but Tamerlane couldn't quite place it. He stared back at the other man, not sure exactly what to say.

"And Agrippa," the man in blue said. "He is well now? There were rumors that he was grievously wounded in your final battle."

Tamerlane was still attempting to come to grips with the man's previous statements, and was taken aback by this question. He nodded absently. "Yes—Arnem is himself again." He pictured the big general in his mind and chuckled. "As if nothing had happened to him."

The other man smiled at that. "Good. That is hardly surprising. He has done well for himself. My old enemy—" He paused, seemed to think about his words, and resumed, "My old *friend* would be proud of him."

"Your friend?"

The man didn't elaborate. He motioned again and the portal surged with power, little traces of lightning racing along its interior. "This way," he said, gesturing for Tamerlane to go first. "After you."

Tamerlane stared into the depths of the inter-dimensional gateway the other man had somehow opened. "Where does it lead?" he asked.

Markos the Liberator—or, rather, the god that had, for thousands of years, used that alias on occasion—laughed again, harder. "To the Golden City, of course," he said. "To visit your birthright."

Tamerlane swallowed hard. Somehow he'd known all along that's what the man was going to say. It explained so much. Even still, it was hard—almost impossible—to accept, and lingering doubts and skepticism remained. Nevertheless he found himself nodding.

"Don't worry," the other man added. "I'll have you back before dinner. After all—you have an empire to rebuild."

Tamerlane smiled at that, and together they stepped through the portal. It vanished in the air behind them.

5

The ghost of a god stood on a dead world and screamed his frustration at the shattered stars.

It had happened. Despite all his hopes, all his efforts, all his travels and his labors, it had *happened*. The galaxy had been torn asunder—broken to pieces by cosmic forces too vast and powerful to contemplate.

He gazed out at the ruins of the old empires and the wreckage of starships beyond counting—to say nothing of the dead, in their incomprehensible numbers. He could feel the vibration in the very fabric of reality; he could sense the shockwave that had traveled here and now, from the dim past, to wreak this disaster.

Futility. All of his feelings as he confronted this cataclysm could be summed up in that single word: *Futility*.

It could have been different. But for a tiny happenstance here and there, it *would* have been different. It all would have been avoided, and the galaxy would have continued on as it had before—as it *deserved* to.

But no. For all his knowledge and experience and power, he had been unable to shift the course of galactic history by even the tiniest bit.

Time now to give up, then? Time to declare his labors a failure? Time to accept the course of history as it seemed, irrevocably, to be written? In a galaxy where so many untold trillions had died—where even the gods themselves could die—was it time at last for him, too, to acknowledge what had long been the truth? Was it time for him to lie down and die?

The temptation was great. His energy was ebbing; his corporeal form could not long endure now. So easy to just give up, to let it all go. To let himself, and the galaxy, die.

But no. No, he could not accept that. Not so long as life and energy remained to him. Not so long as some measure of the *Power* yet resonated throughout the cosmos.

No, he would try again. He would pick himself up and go back again and this time—*this time*—he would succeed. This time he would correct all those little things that had caused his failure. This time he would get it all right.

He moved then, a ghost drifting over a graveyard—but a ghost with purpose. Perhaps the most ironic purpose of all, for a ghost: the purpose of *preserving* life.

He would need a way to get back—back to the critical moment. Back to the great cosmic splash whose ripples had led him this far into the future, and to their ultimate result—a shattered galaxy. He would need a conveyance that could carry him back through time. A Temporal Vault.

He could build such a device. He knew he could; somehow he knew he had done so before.

But first, he would need a new body...

THE END
OF
LEGION III: KINGS OF OBLIVION
AND OF
THE SHATTERING TRILOGY

THE SAGA OF THE SHATTERED GALAXY
BEGINS IN
HAWK: HAND OF THE MACHINE

THE STORY OF THE MURDER OF THE GODS
AND LUCIAN'S QUEST FOR THE KILLER
IS TOLD IN
LUCIAN: DARK GOD'S HOMECOMING

o the trilogy is complete, and quite a few questions I've left hanging for years now have been answered at last (though not all of them!). I thank you for taking the journey with me.

I don't rule out the possibility of more "Legions" in the future, but this book completes the particular story I set out to tell when I started, more than two years ago— the story of how the galaxy came to have been "shattered" during the time of Hawk, and where he and his fellow Hands came from. Obviously, a few other mysteries remain, but the clues to answering more than one of them can be found in the pages of the three books you've just read. (For example, here's a freebie you may have missed: Certain names of important and seemingly different characters are duplicated in my books. This is not laziness on my part. It is most definitely intentional.)

If you haven't read *Lucian: Dark God's Homecoming* or *Hawk: Hand of the Machine* yet, you might want to go there next. The events of Lucian take place much earlier than this trilogy, and the events of Hawk are set much later, so that "The Shattering" acts as a sort of bridge between them. Other books are coming, if all goes according to plan, as well: I've had sequels to each of those novels on the drawing board for some time now.

One last time, I have to extend my thanks to Wayne Reinagel for spending a long lunch with me one afternoon, hashing through what I wanted to accomplish with this trilogy and what the characters and legions would be like. I also have to thank my wife, Ami, for all that she does and has done to help me make these books the best they could be.

Many, many thanks to Mark Williams for the incredible cover art he produced for the new editions of these books. And a thanks to Alexander Maisey for introducing us. You can find more of Mark's artwork online at http://marrilliams.deviantart.com and you can contact him at Markwilliams3979@gmail.com.

A huge shout out to the great writers, artists, editors and publishers of the Pulp Factory for nominating Legion I: Lords of Fire for Novel of the Year, and for making it a short-listed finalist. My appreciation knows no bounds.

My thanks to the writers over the years who have produced material that inspired and drove me onward in the creation of this series. Those are phenomenally talented people such as Jim Starlin, Dan Abnett, Jack Kirby, Graham McNeill, Roger Zelazny, Christopher Moeller, Peter F. Hamilton, Vernor Vinge, and Larry Niven. I also found John Julius Norwich's comprehensive three-volume history of Byzantium to be of enormous inspirational use, as well as J. M. Roberts' *New History of the World*.

Lastly but certainly not least(ly), I must thank each of **you**. These books would have been written whether anyone out there was reading them or not—that's what a writer does— but it is enormously more satisfying to know that others are appreciating the hard work being put in, and (if all goes well) the story that has resulted. Here's to you, faithful readers. You have my undying thanks.

One way or another, we have not seen the last of Tamerlane, Iapetus and Agrippa!

About the Author

Van Allen Plexico writes and edits New Pulp, science fiction, fantasy, and nonfiction analysis and commentary for a variety of print and online publishers. He's been nominated for numerous writing awards and won the 2012 PulpArk Award for "Best New Pulp Character." The first volume in this series, *Legion I: Lords of Fire*, was a finalist for Novel of the Year in the 2013 Pulp Factory Awards and the New Pulp Awards. His best-known works include *Lucian*, *Hawk*, the *Assembled!* books, and the groundbreaking and #1 New Pulp Best-Selling *Sentinels* series— the first ongoing, multi-volume cosmic superhero saga in prose form. In his spare time he serves as a professor of political science and history. He has lived in Atlanta, Singapore, Alabama, and Washington, DC, and now resides in the St. Louis area along with his wife, two daughters and assorted river otters.

Van Allen Plexico's Sentinels
Super-hero action illustrated by Chris Kohler
   The Grand Design Trilogy
   Alternate Visions (Anthology)
   The Rivals Trilogy
   The Order Above All Trilogy

Also by Van Allen Plexico
   Lucian: Dark God's Homecoming
   Hawk: Hand of the Machine

Other Great Novels and Anthologies
   Gideon Cain: Demon Hunter
   Blackthorn: Thunder on Mars
   Blackthorn: Dynasty of Mars
    By Ian Watson

Nonfiction:
   Assembled! Five Decades of Earth's Mightiest
   Assembled! 2
   Super-Comics Trivia
   Season of Our Dreams &
   Decades of Dominance (Van Allen Plexico and John Ringer)

All are available wherever books are sold, or visit
WWW.WHITEROCKETBOOKS.COM